A Journey of a Thousand Miles

Written By: Kimberley Hall

Dedication

To all the soulmates out there who yearn for a love that transcends the ordinary:

May this book be a beacon of hope, a reminder that true love can conquer even the most daunting obstacles. May our story be the catalyst that awakens your soul, ignites your passion, and forever changes the landscape of your heart. May it be the gentle breeze that soothes your soul, the raging fire that burns away your fears. May it inspire you to hold on to your dreams, to believe in the impossible, and to never give up on the love that you know in your heart is meant to be. May you find strength in the darkness, courage in the face of adversity, and joy in the little moments that truly make life worth living. May your love be the guiding force that illuminates your path, fills your heart with joy, and inspires your soul.

To all the lovers who have been separated by distance, circumstance, fear, or fate,

May our story be a testament to the unbreakable bond that true love creates. May it inspire you to hold on to your love with every fibre of your being, to fight for it with every breath in your body, and to never let go to the person who makes your soul come alive. May your love be the revolution that overthrows the doubts, the fears, and the obstacles that stand in your way. May it be the fire that burns bright enough to illuminate the darkness, the storm that rages strong enough to shake the foundations of heaven, and the love that endures long enough to last a lifetime. May our story be a reminder that true love can overcome even the most insurmountable odds.

To all the soulmates who are still searching for each other:

May our love inspire you to keep searching, to keep believing, and to never settle for anything less than you deserve. May you find your person, your partner, your best friend, and your soulmate, and may your love be the stuff of legends, the kind that is spoken of in whispers, and the kind that is remembered for generations to come,

This book is dedicated to you, dear soulmates, may our love story be a battle cry, a call to arms, and a reminder that true love is always worth fighting for. As you read this story, may you be transported to a world where love knows no bounds, where hearts beat as one, and where souls are forever entwined. May you be inspired to love without limits, to dream without fear, and to believe in the impossible.

A Journey of a Thousand Miles – A Reflections Saga

Chapter One

We, each and every last one of us have a singular journey of winding roads and narrow passages that lead to the here and now. Mine is but one journey to be told, as it relates to raising my consciousness. Where to begin isn't as simple as the beginning, or my nightly visits to the stars. No, it's been a journey of mazes that have found me at the highest peaks and the lowest depths.

So I begin in the middle. All my life, I've been told that the things I experienced as a child were not possible. Then it was that I was crazy. A witch. It's been repeated so often, that I actually believed for a time that I was completely out of my mind. I'd been medicated...forced to see the world through a haze. A fog of disillusionment. Yes, here is where I'll start. Now, this is a ride and sometimes it will take us back in order to get to the point. But I suppose those elements were always leading me somewhere.

Rewind to my childhood, filled with countless imaginary friends and the things that go bump in the night. Basically anything from Casper the friendly ghost, to the things only nightmares should be made of. A very fearful time in my life. I was always seeing something, but I had no idea I was seeing things no one else could. I remember being at a birthday party one day and playing in the corner by myself with my dolls. A little girl came up to me and tapped me on the shoulder. She was wearing a powder blue dress and the top of it resembled the straps of overalls. Her hair was blonde and curly. She looked to be around my age at the time...four or five years old. She told me her name was Emily, and she asked if she could play with me. I wasn't like most children, as I didn't seem to fit in with anyone. No one ever wanted to play with me, I was the weird one. I often played alone. This time however, I was happy to have someone actually want to play with me, without them having to be forced into it. We started to play and she was asking me a hundred questions, as little girls that age tend to do. I didn't think anything was unusual. She was fun! That was of course until I heard the whispers between my mother, father and my aunt off in the other corner of the room.

They had been watching me intently and my mother appeared shaken by what she was seeing. I overheard part of their conversation,

"Tommy, I'm really worried about her! Who is she talking to?! There's no one there! I'm scared...I think she needs help!!" my mother exclaimed.

My father looked at me and then back at her again.

A Journey of a Thousand Miles – A Reflections Saga

"She's fine Victoria! She's just gifted...she's special...Look at her! She's obviously playing with someone. Kids have imaginations sure, but hers is beyond anything I've ever seen. She's just different that's all. She's FINE!"

He appeared to be getting frustrated with her accusations of his baby girl being a total nutcase. He wasn't trying to hear such things. He knew I was different, and I'm sure he knew there would be plenty more interesting adventures in raising me, but he loved me unconditionally.

My aunt also knew I was different. From the day I was born she had told them I was incredibly gifted, and that I needed to be nurtured more than the average child. She told them I was a sensitive, much like herself and that this was just the beginning. She tried to explain to the both of them what to expect, but my mother wouldn't hear a word of it. She was off in her own little magical fantasy land of having perfect children I suppose. I remember that conversation like it was yesterday. It was to be the first of many.

You see as time went on, I started to see and hear a lot more than any young child should ever have to witness. There were what seemed like constant arguments between my parents about my special little *"gift"*. That's what they called it—it was beginning to feel more like a curse. I just wanted to be *"normal"* more than anything, but the reality was—I was far from it. I remember hearing them screaming and yelling at each other and the impact it had on my very soul. I remember my brother and sisters pulling me into another room to get me away from all of the negativity, but it didn't matter. I could feel the energies from the negativity clawing at my flesh. It stung worse than a bee sting...like my skin was on fire. I couldn't understand any of what I was feeling and it frightened me.

Soon the night terrors began, and I would wake up screaming that someone was trying to pull me out of my bed. They would wait for the lights to go out and then, they would come. My nightly visitors. The horror they would bring me still haunts me to this day. They loved nothing more than to scare me and they succeeded every time. After months of repetitive nights with no one sleeping, my parents finally decided it was time for me to share a room with two of my sisters, in the hopes that whatever I was going through would cease. It worked like a charm and I couldn't have been happier. Maybe I really was just a scaredy cat as my sisters so often referred to me. Maybe it really was just *all in my head.* They told me I was such a baby for being afraid of the dark. You're damn right I was! You would be too if you had to endure the trauma I suffered. In any case I was happy to not be alone. For the first time in a long time, I felt safe again. The night terrors stopped completely. I would still see the visitors, but this time it was only in my dreams. It was such a relief. Maybe they were right. Maybe I was just crazy!

A Journey of a Thousand Miles – A Reflections Saga

Nearly a year went by without any incident. I was left alone to play with my *"imaginary friends"* and I was seemingly normal to the public eye. I had learned it wasn't such a good idea to tell the lady in the grocery store that her mother who had passed away recently, was standing right behind her. These were not *normal* childhood behaviours and I wanted to be, or at least appear to be just like everyone else. So I would spend a lot of time just playing with my friends in the backyard. Talking to the grass, the trees, insects and the birds that always seemed to flock around me. I had many friends. They just weren't the human kind.

On one particular day I remember, I was playing outside in the dirt like usual, and I heard a sound above my head. I looked up in the trees and saw a baby bird come tumbling out of it's nest. I caught him just in time that I saved him, but he was still injured. It broke my heart. I felt his pain and I knew I needed to help him. Without a second thought I wrapped him in my sundress and ran into the house. My mother nearly lost her mind when she saw what I was holding.

"Where... where did you get that? Don't bring that in here!! It's dirty and full of disease. Go put it outside and wash your hands. Why are you playing with dead animals?" she asked.

Her tone was more of shock and fell somewhere between inquisitive and demanding.

"I found him mommy..he fell out of the tree. He's just a baby and he's hurt! We have to help him or he'll die!" I cried.

My father overheard the commotion and came to investigate.

He smiled at me with deep love in his eyes "You're so beautiful Ava...do you know that?! You have such a big heart. We will help him! Let daddy go find you a box." He was beaming with pride.

I think he must've figured out that I was an animal empath at this point. Although at the time, I'm not sure he even knew what that was. He just knew I needed to help this poor baby bird, and he was pleased at how kind and selfless I was. He went to retrieve the box and we set a towel inside for it to be wrapped in. Then we brought it into the dining room and set the box down on the table.

"We will need to go find something to feed this little guy." he said.

He led the way toward the back door and we headed outside to dig for earthworms. I was completely appalled when I discovered what we were going to be doing with these earthworms. I often played with them too. I was well aware that everything was alive, and these little earthworms were no exception. I loved the Earth and all of her creatures, but he explained to me that this was how nature operated, and somehow I found comfort in that thought. I knew it meant that the bird would die if it didn't eat and so, I wiped back the tears with my dirty hands and continued pulling them out of the ground.

A Journey of a Thousand Miles – A Reflections Saga

That night we carried the box up to my room, as I wasn't leaving him alone with my mother. She would surely put him back outside once I fell asleep. I demanded he sleep with me. For weeks I slept with that little bird and I cared for him every day. I even took him outside to play with me. Then one day he was healed and ready to be set free. It was both one of the saddest and happiest moments of my childhood, but I knew he couldn't stay with us forever. I had loved and cared for him, and now it was time for him to go back to his own family.

"I bet his mommy will be happy to see him again!" I told my father as he was crouching down to place the box.

"I bet she will...You did such a great thing for him Ava. I'm very proud of you. Okay now, it's time to lift the lid. You can do it on the count of three okay?" he asked. "One—Two—Three!!"

I lifted the lid as he reached three and the bird flew up into the very same tree he fell out of. I was amazed. "How did he remember where he lives daddy?" I asked.

He was just about to give me the answer, when we heard a lot of chirping from above. His family was greeting him. They sounded happy to see him.

I waved up at the trees and shouted, "Goodbye little bird! I hope you'll still come visit!"

We turned to go back into the house. As we were nearing the porch a bird flew up onto it and started tweeting at us. It was the same bird I had rescued. I think he was coming to say thank you. Of course he was! Any six year old would know that. He would be the first of many rescues I would come by in my lifetime. It became very clear to my parents that I was definitely a healer of some kind. We would go for walks and I'd always find something to bring home to care for. Anything ranging from injured ladybugs to tadpoles to stray cats and kittens. Our house became a zoo! At one time we had fourteen cats total including two litters of kittens, a turtle, a hamster, a rabbit, some fish and a dog. I became the animal whisperer, and every time I went to play outside, a bird would always fly down from that same tree and land on the fence. My mother told me it could've been any bird, as they all look the same, but I knew in my heart it was him.

A few months went by and my parents started arguing again. The negativity got so strong in the house, that it wasn't long before my "monsters" returned. It no longer mattered if I was in a room with other people. They would come in and I would immediately hide under the covers or shield my eyes from them any way I could. This only made them scare me more, and they would begin to shake my covers at night and pull on my ankles. I had nowhere to hide. I knew the only way to make them go away was to shut my eyes tight and scream as loud as I could. My father was always the first up the stairs. He always thought someone was hurting his baby girl. I sure screamed convincingly enough.

A Journey of a Thousand Miles – A Reflections Saga

There was no denying that something was going on, but they assumed it was a result of all the fighting they had been doing, as the events always seemed to escalate during these high negativity evenings. I remember my mother being at her wits end with me. I was keeping everyone awake and she was growing more irritated by it all with each passing nightmare I would have. I remember after about five nights of screaming, my father decided to sleep next to my bed. It helped me a lot. The night terrors improved drastically. Was it really just me? Was I really losing my fragile little mind? I wasn't so sure. I know what I saw and felt and it definitely wasn't a dream!

Soon the nightly visitors weren't the only thing I was dealing with. I began to feel everyone around me. Their thoughts, emotions and even their pain. It brought whole new meaning to the term, growing pains. Why was I feeling everything all of a sudden? I had felt things before, but nothing to this degree. I remember the nights my father would take turns rubbing the Charley horses out of my sister's legs, and then coming to rub mine. She was going through a growth spurt, and the leg cramps were unbearable for us both. I overheard my parents say that I was far too young to be feeling them. Maybe I was just far more sensitive then they realized, but I knew one thing for sure, it hurt like hell.

There came a point where I couldn't stand it anymore and so I went to rub her legs myself. Usually she would cry for hours on end while she suffered through the pain, but this time was different. This time she was fast asleep within minutes. Had I healed her? I didn't know, but I was grateful that neither one of us had to feel that pain anymore. As soon as her pain subsided, so did my own. It seemed I had discovered something new about myself. Something I didn't even know was possible. From that point on, anytime she got a muscle spasm, headache or so much as a fever, I laid my hands on her and willed the pain away.

"I want to be a doctor and heal the sick." I thought.

This was a very good start.

After I learned about my newfound ability, I seemed to be drawn to people in pain or suffering in some kind of way. I would read their energies and go up and grab the hands of strangers, just so I could send them healing through my touch. They always seemed to smile at me, but then they would get the look on their faces of confusion. Like they were caught off-guard by the feelings I gave them, and they didn't understand why they felt that way. I was just happy to be able to help them. Every day became a new adventure for me to seek out those in need. I felt it was my mission in life. I even told everyone I encountered, that I was here to change the world. I started talking about going home, and my mother would always explain to me that I was home. I gently but firmly corrected her every time. I told her I was just here to help others, and that once my mission was complete I would leave this place. She seemed to listen, but was she really hearing me?

I wasn't so sure.

Chapter Two

It seemed with each passing day, I was growing into who I was, and the stories I told were incredible. I started talking about reincarnation, death and the afterlife. I told my parents that the little girl I was always playing with had told me that she was actually my spirit guide. That she didn't actually look the way I was seeing her, but that she appeared to me this way because most children are more comfortable playing and speaking with other children, and that soon the day would come when I would see her in her true form. My imagination was 'extensive' according to my mother. She told me I should start writing stories. I don't think she ever believed a word of what I was saying, but she listened nonetheless.

As time went on I was introduced to more *imaginary friends* as Emily would bring along new guests with her. We all played together nearly every day. She would tell me stories about the astral realm, and how people who were in limbo were stuck there until they crossed over into the light. She also told me about how they lived their lives completely oblivious that they had actually passed on. I was told that I had been assisting them for years. This made sense to me. It explained my scary nightmares. They just didn't know how to get to where they needed to go.

I remember a dream once where I saw a little girl, and she was huddled over in a corner crying hysterically. When I approached her, she turned to look at me and wipe the tears from her face.

I remember asking her, "What's wrong? Are u okay?"

"I—I can't find my mommy! We were driving to school and there was a big truck and my mommy she... she tried to miss it and then she was gone and I was *HERE*!! I wanna go home!" she whimpered.

I told her not to cry and reassured her that I would help her find her mommy. I held out my hand and we started to walk down the road together. We walked for what seemed like hours, and there were monsters trying to scare us at every turn, but my fear wasn't present in this moment. I knew I had to help her. Every time we saw something scary she would nuzzle her face against me to hide her eyes.

"It's okay...Don't be afraid. They can't hurt us. Let's just find your mommy okay?!" I told her reassuringly.

She was definitely younger than me. She didn't look any older than four years old. She seemed to trust me, and to believe every word I said. We eventually came to an alleyway, and we heard someone call out,

"Jesse?! Jesse where are you? Jesse!!!"

A Journey of a Thousand Miles – A Reflections Saga

The little girl got excited and looked up at me with light beaming in her eyes.

"That... that's my mommy!! You found her, you found her!!!" she exclaimed.

We followed the voice and there stood a woman in a red silk button down blouse, and black dress pants with black pointy shoes. When she saw us she started running full force in our direction.

"Jesse?! Oh my God you're alright!! the woman shouted.

"Oh mommy, I was so worried. Where did you go?! Why did you leave me mommy?" the little girl cried.

Then the happiness and relief seemed to drain from the mother's face as she looked around in horror.

"Oh my god, what... what is this place?!" she asked.

I told her that I wasn't quite sure, but we appeared to be somewhere else. I called out to Emily and she came skipping up the sidewalk behind us. She seemed to read the woman's mind as she approached

"Welcome to the astral." she said. "Some people call it the fourth dimension or limbo. In any case this is where all spirits go to cross over. It is the bridge between your world and the place you call, Heaven."

"Are, are you telling me we're dead?!" the mother interrupted. "Is that what you're telling me right now? That Jesse and I died?!!" she fell to her knees and began to weep into her hands. "I'm so sorry Jesse!..It's all mommy's fault!"

Jesse approached her mother and knelt down beside her. "It's okay mommy. Don't cry. You didn't mean to. We can be together here...it's okay." she told her.

"It can be hard to accept being in this place, but I can show you where you are going" Emily revealed. "Follow me!"

She led the three of us out of the alleyway, and back onto the road.

There were a few turns and then we saw it. The brightest white light I had ever seen. It looked like the sun had come down to Earth. It was even brighter than the sun. I had to shield my eyes, but Jesse and her mother seemed to be drawn to it. They started walking toward it, and I followed behind shielding my eyes.

"You can't go any further Ava." Emily warned me. "This place they are going to isn't for you to go right now. This is the afterlife...it is Heaven, paradise or whichever you wish to call it." she continued.

I nodded to let her know that I understood, and took a few steps back. Jesse and her mother turned around to face me. Her mother walked up and took my hand gently in hers

"Thank you for bringing my daughter back." she whispered. Then she turned and walked back to her daughter.

"Goodbye! Thank you!" they both shouted, and then they continued walking into the light.

It seemed to get brighter as they got closer to it. Soon I could only see their silhouettes and then...they were gone. I was so happy to help them and eager to get back and tell everyone about what I had just seen. I ran

A Journey of a Thousand Miles – A Reflections Saga

back to where I had first appeared in this place...only everything seemed to have changed. Nothing looked the same anymore. The buildings, the roads; everything had changed. I was on what looked like a battlefield.

There were strange men dressed in camouflage and they were carrying rifles. I could hear the sound of bombs going off in the distance..There was smoke and fire everywhere!

"Get out of here little girl! You're gonna get yourself killed! What are you doing here?! Leave! NOW!" one of them shouted at me.

"Bu' but I don't know where I am!!" I cried. "How do I get back if I don't know where I am?!"

Just then the man looked at me with concern in his eyes, and walked over to me. He seemed to be deeply concerned for me, as he lowered his weapon and turned his back on the gunfire going on all around us.

"Where's your mum an' dad? This isn't a place for children...run along now. They're probably worried sick about ya." he said.

Just then I heard a thundering BANG come from behind us, and the man fell forward onto my feet. A bloody wound had seeped straight through his back and into his chest.

"Oh my god!" I screamed. "I...I think you've been shot!"

He rolled over and looked at me. I could see the fear and pain in his eyes, and my heart broke for him. The pain was so real for me to watch him suffer, that it was as if I had just witnessed my own father laying there dying. Tears streamed down my cheeks and I fell to my knees crying hysterically.

"I...I'm so sorry!! I shouldn't have distracted you. You would still be alive if it weren't for me!"

I began to sob even harder, as I cradled his head in my lap, watching his breathing become more shallow and laboured. I knew he was about to die, and my fragile little six year old heart was breaking as each painstaking second passed.

Then I heard that fateful sound...You know the one...The one they call, the "death rattle", as he took his very last breath. I sat there with him and apologized over and over again. He was right! I never should've come here, and now I didn't even know if I was ever going to make it back home. I began to cry so loud that the sound of my own wailing seemed to drown out the sounds of men dying, and bombs going off all around me. I could no longer hear the blood curdling screams of death. Just then I felt someone tap me on the shoulder. I was afraid to look at first, but the touch felt gentle and peaceful.

I turned to see Emily standing there. She had the look of sorrow in her eyes and that look seemed to amplify when she saw the dead man lying in my lap, as she stared at the remnants of my tears which were now staining my face.

"Oh Ava...I'm so sorry I left you. I needed to make sure they got there okay." she explained.

"He's dead!" I cried out "And it's all my fault."

I began to sob again at the mere thought I had just cost someone their own life.

"He was always dead Ava. That's why he's in this place. This is the astral. It's where everyone comes when they die. He was a military man. He died years ago and he's refused to go into the light. He doesn't believe there is a place for him after death. He doesn't think he deserves to go there, because of all the lives he's taken while being in the war." she explained.

"B- but if he's already dead, why did he just die again?! How can you die if you already did?!" I asked confused.

She grabbed onto my shoulders and motioned for me to stand up. I refused. I wasn't leaving this poor man by himself. He died alone, and I was deeply saddened by it all. He didn't deserve to die alone. No one deserves to die alone. It was as if in that moment, lost in my thoughts that Emily read my mind.

"He didn't die alone Ava...You were with him. At least this time you were. He's going to wake up again soon and it's all going to start again." she explained.

"W- What's going to start again?!" I interrupted.

"The war!" she said "He keeps living out the day he died over and over again. Until he goes into the light, this is what he's faced with. He created this place for himself. This was all he knew. Let's wait a little while for him to wake up, and I'll show you what I mean." she said.

Hearing her words seemed to both comfort me, and sadden me at the same time. This seemed to be his own personal hell. Why would anyone do that to themselves? I gently lifted the man off of my lap and laid him on the ground. I stood up beside her and watched intently, as it suddenly looked like someone hit rewind on the scene. She was right.

It was starting all over again!

Chapter Three

Suddenly the man appeared in front of us. He was in the same position I had seen him in before. Everything was the same. It was like I was experiencing some sort of deja-vu. He turned to me, and then he repeated the exact same words he had used before.

"Get out of here little girl! You're gonna get yourself killed! What are you doing here?! Leave! NOW!" he shouted.

I wasn't sticking around for round two, that's when I turned to Emily and asked

"Do you know how to get us out of here?"

"Of course! Follow me....this way....hurry up now." she replied.

A Journey of a Thousand Miles – A Reflections Saga

She didn't have to tell me twice. I was going to do whatever she told me to do. I just wanted to go home. We turned and ran off the battlefield, and headed out towards the road. Then we slowed to a walk again.

"Okay!" she said. "You're safe now."

We continued to walk for a few minutes, until we had reached a bridge.

She pointed to the bridge and said "That's the way home...follow the bridge until you reach the end and it will bring you back."

"Thank you!" I shouted back at her as I ran up ahead.

I ran as fast as I could across that bridge, and then I saw a light. It looked like the other light I had watched Jesse and her mother walk into, only this one was smaller and not quite as bright. I didn't need to shield my eyes this time. I ran straight into it. Suddenly I felt my body begin to vibrate and I felt like I was falling. It felt like I had walked right into a rabbit hole that was bottomless.

I was frightened by this free fall, and I screamed out for help. Just then I felt someone touch my arm and begin to shake me

"Ava? Wake up sweetie...it's just a dream. It's okay. Daddy's here!" he said reassuringly. "Just wake up honey."

I opened my eyes to see the concerned look on my father's face. I was never so happy to see him as in that very moment. I sat up and hugged him tightly.

"Thank you daddy! That was a scary place." I told him "I...I don't ever wanna go back there." I said almost pleading with him.

He smiled at me then and hugged me tighter than ever, "It's okay...it was just a scary dream. You're home and you're safe. Let's go make some pancakes."

He always could cheer me up, and today of all days I was going to need it.

Over breakfast, we chatted about making plans for our next fishing adventure. My father had been taking me fishing ever since I was about two years old. Although I could only remember from about the age of three on. I remember when he used to take me down to the riverfront, to a place that had a large cement slap with a fence surrounding it's perimeter. He used to slather what seemed like an entire bottle of sunscreen on me, and set out chairs for the two of us. Then he would get our fishing lines set up, always keeping a watchful eye on me. He had once even used a rope to tie around my waist and then tied it to the fence. I guess he was always afraid that because I was so tiny, the fish were going to pull me in one day. That protective measure always makes me giggle when I look back on that memory. Fishing was just for the two of us. It was our bonding moment and I loved every minute of it.

A Journey of a Thousand Miles – A Reflections Saga

On Saturdays he would take me to this restaurant in the mall, to play Pac-Man and have lunch, which was always followed by mint chocolate chip ice cream. It was our favourite flavour. Little did I know that our bonding moments would soon be cut short.

It was early summer the following year, and I was about to turn seven. My father and I were talking about my upcoming birthday party plans, and the fishing adventures we had yet to have. I was so excited. We had even planned a trip to Disneyland, and a family camping trip too. I was told the family had taken these kinds of trips before, but I guess I was far too young to remember at the time.

Things seemed to be going great...and then the unthinkable happened. My mother and father began to argue again. More than ever before. My father was becoming depressed about not being able to work since his injury, and that depression led him to drink almost every night. They would fight about everything it seemed, and one day it got so bad that my mother told him to leave. I was absolutely heartbroken.

My father was the only one in our house who seemed to understand me, and accept me for all of the craziness I was. Now who would I talk to? I remember them calling all of us to the table, and sitting us down to tell us of their plan. My father was going to be moving out, and he would be leaving immediately after the talk was over. My mother looked at me with sadness. She could probably hear the audible sound of my little heart breaking.

"Ava please don't be upset, you guys hear us fighting all the time. It's not good for any of us. We just don't love each other anymore." she explained.

I knew she was trying to break it to me gently, but I was furious with her.

"Maybe if you left him alone and didn't always scream at him, there would be no yelling!" I shouted.

I couldn't help myself. I felt the fire burning inside of me, as if it were about to seep from my pores at any given second.

"This is your fault!" I continued. "You just don't want anyone to love me do you?!" I had lost it. "You know what mom?!....I...I HATE YOU!!" And with that I stood up and stormed my way up to my room. Stomping as loud as I could all the way. The fire was taking over me now, and I grabbed my door, put all of my weight behind it, and slammed it as hard as I could. Then I fell down onto my bed and sobbed uncontrollably into my pillow. As far as I was concerned, life as I knew it, was over!

It didn't take long for a gentle knock on the door.

"Go away!" I demanded. "I never wanna see you or speak to you again mom!"

A Journey of a Thousand Miles – A Reflections Saga

The knock came again, and still I ignored it, as I continued to scream and yell into my pillow. Just then, I heard the door open, followed by the sound of footsteps approaching my bed. Then the feeling of someone sitting down gently beside me. A warm and gentle caress on my back. One I knew all too well. It was the touch of my father. He had come to comfort me, and say his goodbyes and I love you's. His touch was always such a deep sense of comfort for me. I pulled my face out of my pillow and hugged him tight, sobbing into his chest

"It's not fair! Why do you have to leave? Why can't she go instead?" I asked.

He pulled me away, gently from his chest, and warmly, yet sorrowfully looked me in the eyes.

"Do you know how much I love you?!" he asked. "Do you know that I will never leave you and I'll never stop loving you...not EVER! Daddy and mommy fight way too much honey, and it's not good for any of you guys to have to live like that. I'm not leaving forever. I just need to go away for awhile so your mommy and I can calm down and talk about this, instead of yelling all the time. Your mother can't leave because she is your mother and you need her." he explained." I know you're upset right now, and you don't think she loves you, but she really does sweetheart, and I need you to do something for me okay? I need you to forgive her. I need you to forgive both of us. Can you do that for me?" he asked.

I nodded in agreement. Still, "But... but none of this is your fault daddy! Don't you see...she's evil! She doesn't ever want me to be happy does she?" I asked.

My father looked down at me and chuckled, "Oh my dear sweet girl! You are so sensitive to everything. Your mother isn't evil. She loves you deeply. I know she doesn't understand you right now, but I promise in time she will. Just give her a chance okay?" he insisted. "I love you baby girl..daddy will see you soon. I have to go now. Be a good girl for mommy okay?"

I kissed and hugged him goodbye, fighting back tears again, as I told him I loved him too. I could feel the tears starting to well up in my eyes now, as I knew his departure was imminent. I sat there watching him as he made his way toward the door. I sprang up from my bed as he reached for the doorknob and ran up to him

"Daddy wait! Please don't leave me...take me with you. Please daddy! I wanna go with you. I can't live without you!" I pleaded with him.

I grabbed my suitcase from my closest and began to pack frantically. I was so consumed with what I was doing, that I didn't notice the tears begin to well up in his own eyes, as he watched his baby girl frantically packing in desperation.

"Almost done daddy. I—I'm almost ready!" I told him.

"I'm sorry honey...you can't come. I will be back for you I promise. This is not goodbye forever. It's just for a little while. I love you." he said with a deep sadness in his tone.

When I finally finished packing I had turned around to see that he was gone! I ran out of my room and practically flew down the stairs after him.

A Journey of a Thousand Miles – A Reflections Saga

"Wait daddy!! I'm ready now! Please daddy take me with you!" I pleaded again.

When I got downstairs he was nowhere in sight. I ran to the door just in time to see him pulling out of the driveway. He saw me and waved before driving off. I fell to my knees and cried at the front door, as I watched the only person who ever truly understood me, drive out of my life. There I sat in a puddle of tears. Heartbroken and alone. I cried in the doorway for what seemed like forever, and then I heard footsteps behind me. It was my mother. She grabbed me and lifted me up trying to console me as she did so.

"It's okay sweetie. He's coming back. I promise you that you will see him again. Don't cry." she said. "Come in the kitchen and help me make supper."

I hated her in that moment. She did this to me. She was to blame. It was all her fault as far as I was concerned, but just as I was about to scream at her again, my father's last words to me began to replay in my mind

"Be a good girl for mommy. Can you do that for me?"

I spoke the words out loud as if I were saying them directly to him, "Yes daddy..I'll do that for you."

I wiped the sweat and tears from my face, and pulled the mess that was my hair back into place. It was then that I realized this would be the first of many struggles I was going to face, and I refused to be defeated by it.

That following Friday my father returned for me, just like he had promised. I was ecstatic when my mother had told me earlier that day, that I would be going to spend the weekend with him. No sooner had the words left her mouth, that I ran upstairs to pack. I grabbed the suitcase that I had packed in desperation last week, and dumped the contents onto my bed. I grabbed my Kid Sister doll, and stuffed her into the bottom. I then grabbed some clothing, and two changes of PJ'S and stuffed them on top. The suitcase was overflowing, and I had to sit on it to get it to zip, but I was ready.

I looked over at the clock, and noted the time, only 12:00 noon. My mother had told me he was coming to get me at 2pm, and I was definitely anticipating his arrival. Time seemed to be going by so slowly though, and I decided to keep myself busy until he arrived. I grabbed my colouring book and crayons from the bottom drawer to my dresser, brought them over to my bed and sprawled myself across the mattress. I wanted to make my father a nice picture. He always loved whenever I had made him stuff. My father seemed to be the only one who ever truly appreciated it. As I lay there, lost in my own little world, just colouring away, I thought about all of the wonderful things we would do that weekend. I was deep in concentration, focusing on not colouring outside the lines even a little bit. I wanted it to be absolutely perfect for him.

A Journey of a Thousand Miles – A Reflections Saga

Just then I felt a familiar energy surround me. It was Emily...only this time I could only feel her and not see her. I didn't know why that was.

I called out to her "Emily...Emily is that you? Why can't I see you anymore?!" I asked.

There was no reply. I thought this was very strange, because whenever I felt her energy and acknowledged her, she always appeared. This time was different though, and I didn't understand why. I felt like she was playing games with me, and I didn't think it was very funny at all. I had wanted to tell her how excited I was, because I was going to stay with my father for the weekend, and I missed him so much. I wanted to ask her why she hadn't been coming around lately, especially after that traumatic event I had just endured. She was supposed to be my friend. She was supposed to help me, and talk to me when I needed her the most. As my friend, I thought she was supposed to at least try to comfort me by offering words of reassurance. I became angry with her.

"Why is she being so rude?" I wondered.

I suddenly started to grow very tired. It was like something suddenly came over me, and I couldn't keep my eyes open. I looked at the clock once more to see what time it was, 12:15pm. I decided to take a nap. I'm not sure how long I was out for, but I went on to dream that I was in a beautiful meadow. The birds were singing, flowers were blooming all around, there were deer grazing up ahead, and butterflies...lots of butterflies. It was a breathtaking place. The sun was shining and it felt so warm and comforting against my skin. I started to walk toward the deer, when something caught my attention out of the corner of my eye. I turned and glanced in that direction and that's when I saw her. It was Emily. She was skipping along the trail and singing a song...although I couldn't make out the words. I called after her.

"Emily!! Emily over here!" I shouted.

She turned around and smiled at me. "I was wondering when you would get here! This was the only way you were going to see me, and the only way I could talk to you. Took you long enough." she laughed.

"That...that was you? You made me tired?! Why?" I asked.

"Because," she said "I was screaming out to you as loud as I could...waving my hands at you even, but for some reason, you couldn't see or hear me. This was the only way I could reach you. I didn't want you to think I had left you or something." she replied.

I stood there confused. Trying to process her words carefully. Why was I not able to see her or hear her if she was making it obvious she was right there?

"I don't understand." I said in my confusion. "Why can't I see or hear you anymore?"

"Because, you shut me out...you shut everyone out. The thought of losing your father caused you to shut down completely. I never left you. I've been with you through it all. You just closed your heart off to me." she told me.

Kimberley Hall   17

A Journey of a Thousand Miles – A Reflections Saga

She began to walk toward me and I that's when I noticed there was a big difference about her. She was much taller now, and she appeared to be older than the last time I had seen her.

"What happened to you?" I asked. "Why do you look like you got older all of a sudden?"

"This is what I've always looked like." she explained "Well actually... I'm even older than this, but this is all that you're ready for at the moment. I'm growing with you. Isn't that cool?!!"

Emily was just about to lead me down the passage way, when I heard my mother's voice calling for me off in the distance

"Ava...your father is here."

The excitement was enough to pull me from my dream state, I jumped up to grab my suitcase, and hurried down the stairs. As I reached the landing, I saw my father standing there at the front door, and I rushed over to greet him with hugs and kisses. He scooped me up into his arms, just as quickly as I'd reached them.

"There's my girl! How have you been? Are you being good for your mommy?" he asked, kissing my cheek about a hundred times.

"Of course daddy!" I laughed. "Can we go now?!!" I asked impatiently.

"Yes" he said. "Let's go!"

He carried me out to the car, and reached across to put my seat belt on for me. There was that protective father I was so used to. I welcomed every little bit of love and protection he offered. I heard my mother shout from the porch

"What time will you be bringing her back?" she asked.

"I'll call you!" he shouted back.

Then he walked around to the other side of the car, put my suitcase in the back seat, closed the back passenger door, and got into the driver's side.

"You want to hear some music?" he asked.

I nodded and soon I could hear the start of our song.

"I've got sunshine...on a cloudy day. When it's cold outside, I've got the month of May. Well I guess you say..." the voice from the radio belted out.

My father turned to face my direction, and started singing the rest of the tune to me. I loved it when he sang to me, and I especially enjoyed it when he danced with me. Sitting there, listening to the song play on the radio, I was suddenly brought back to those moments when I was about two or three years of age, and my mother would be in the kitchen doing the dishes or fixing dinner. My father would always walk right up to her, grab her around her waist and start dancing with her as he proceeded to serenade her. It was always a tender moment between them and always made me smile so big. Then he would look over, see me watching the two of

A Journey of a Thousand Miles – A Reflections Saga

them in adoration and he would walk over to me, scoop me up in his arms and the three of us would dance together. Those were some of my happiest memories of the two of them. I was deeply inspired by the love they shared, and I knew that someday I wanted to find a man who would do the very same things with me. It was the most beautiful display of love and affection I'd ever witnessed. I loved seeing the two of them happy and in love.

Suddenly, I was snatched out of my flashback, when my father announced that we had finally arrived. I looked up to see the same restaurant he had always taken me to. Although now, I still can't seem to recall the name of it. The two of us played in the arcade for hours. It was so nice to finally spend time with my father again. A week had seemed like an eternity, and I wasn't looking forward to Sunday, when he'd have to bring me back to my mother. If I could've stopped time and stayed with him there forever...I would have. I knew it wasn't possible though, so for now I was going to enjoy every single moment. That day, my father had even introduced me to a good friend of his that he had met through work. His name was Allan. He seemed like a nice guy, and the two of them had made plans for him to accompany us to the park and our next fishing trip the following day. They seemed to be great friends. I was happy to meet anyone that my dad was friends with. Allan had just met me and he gave me two rolls of quarters so I could try and beat the highest score in Pac-Man. I was one determined little girl, and he didn't have any kids of his own, so he figured he would give me some money to enjoy myself. After dinner, while the three of us were headed out the doorway, my father turned back and said,

"Hmm I think we are forgetting something. Do you know what that is sweet girl?" he asked.

"Ice cream!" I shouted excitedly.

When we had pulled into the parking lot to his apartment building, he turned to me and said,

"I know what you're thinking. It's only temporary though."

We walked inside, and I was immediately drawn to his fish tank. He had a huge aquarium set up in the dining area and it was full of Piranhas. They were so beautiful, and yet they were vicious things too. I remember my father sticking his hand in the tank several times when we were all living together. They didn't even bite him, but if we stuck a net in there, they would always go crazy and attack it. Literally chew a hole right through the netting at lightning speed. He also used to put the change from his pocket in the bottom of the tank, and then go back and retrieve it later, bare handed and when no one else was around to see him do it. I think he only did that to make it seem like he wasn't completely crazy.

Time flew by and Sunday came quicker than either of us wanted it to. My father dropped me off and kissed me goodbye, promising he would come back for me next weekend, and every weekend after that. It was what my parents had agreed on, and I was more than happy with that arrangement. It gave me something to look forward to.

As soon as I got inside, I headed up to my room to tell Emily all about my visit. I sat down on my bed, and called out to her. There was no reply. I called out to her again and still nothing. Why did I shut her out? How was I going to fix this? I needed my friend back. I was determined to figure it out, but for now it was bedtime. I got into my PJ'S and laid down in bed.

I don't even remember closing my eyes for five whole minutes, before a rustling sound came from my closet, and the door slowly creaked open. I could hear footsteps approaching my bed, as well as the sound of someone breathing heavily. It was the sound of laboured breathing. I felt the fear and panic building up in my entire body. Just then, someone grabbed my ankles hard, and I let out a blood curdling scream. My visitors were back, and this time my father wasn't here to save me. I must've screamed out about seven times before my mother finally came up to see what was going on. She became frustrated with me as always,

"I've told you a hundred times Ava..Monsters aren't real! Now go to sleep!" she demanded.

She slammed my door behind her as she headed back into the hallway. My sisters, Jane and Anne, who I normally share a room with, were gone to their father's house for the entire summer. How was I going to get through this? I didn't know, but I knew I would have to find a way. I pulled my blankets over my head, and shut my eyes as tightly as I could.

-Please don't bother me anymore tonight. I just want to get some sleep. I thought to myself.

I don't recall sleeping at all that night. Someone kept grabbing at my ankles, and trying to scare me. It was working, but there was nothing that I could do. I laid there and kicked my legs out every time something grabbed hold of them, and shouted,

"Leave me alone!"

After what felt like forever, the attacks just stopped and it was quiet. Were they gone?!

Chapter Four

My visitors seemed to be coming like clockwork now. Every night around the same time, I would hear my closet creak open, the same laboured breathing, and footsteps creaking across the floor toward me. On this

A Journey of a Thousand Miles – A Reflections Saga

particular night, I had decided I'd had enough. As fearful as I was, my mother had told me I'd have to face my fears someday if I were ever to conquer them. It was easy for her to say. She wasn't the one being tortured by demonic entities or whatever you want to call them. I'm quite sure she would've been scared out of her wits if she had ever experienced even half of what I did. As the footsteps got closer I ripped the covers off of my head, and peered into the darkness in the direction I had heard them. When I saw the figure there in front of me, I couldn't speak. I couldn't move and it became difficult to breathe. My heart sank into my stomach, and all I could do was gasp in utter shock. There lumbering toward me, was the man from the battlefield. The man I had watched die in front of my very eyes in that awful place. He was standing at the side of my bed.

"Help'...help me! Where am I? How did I get here?" he asked.

This time I felt no fear at all.

"You're dead!" I told him. "You died a long time ago. You're supposed to go into that light. It's the only way you can be at peace." I explained.

Here I was...a nearly seven year old girl...sitting up in bed talking to a ghost. Was this what I could expect for the rest of my life? I sure hoped not. I began to explain to him that I knew he was a good person. That he only hurt people because it was a part of his job. I knew he felt remorseful for all he had done. I could feel the sadness in his energy.

"I...I ca- can't go ba- back to that place" he replied.

He sounded like someone who was trying to talk while shivering. I spent what seemed like hours talking to him. He told me of his family back home. That he had a wife and two sons he had left behind. I began to feel for this man...for this ghost or whatever you want to call him. After awhile of me trying to convince him he was a good man with a kind heart, he seemed to change. The wound in his chest healed up, and he began to talk normally again. He told me he missed his wife and sons dearly, and that just once he wished he could see them. He told me how he had returned to their home together, but it became obvious to him that they'd all moved away and that he had scared the living daylights out of the new family that resided there.

"I took too long to come back." he suggested "and they moved on without me."

Just as he finished speaking those words, something came to me. I began to see a vision of a dark haired woman in a yellow and white sundress, walking with two little boys in what appeared to be the astral. She was wearing one of those fancy white sunhats women often wore to the beach, or expensive dinners.

"Sarah?" I asked "Is her name Sarah? And the little boys Johnny and Michael?"

"Yes!" he shouted. "Do ya see them? Oh tell them I said hello won't ya please?!" he pleaded.

I told him they were all in the astral. That they had all passed on. Although I wasn't sure how. They appeared in my vision, to be searching for him. This news seemed to please him, and he thanked me over and over again before he went rushing toward the closest. And then he was just gone.

A Journey of a Thousand Miles – A Reflections Saga

My seventh birthday, had come so fast and was over just as quick as it had arrived. It was nice because this time, I had everyone at my party. Even my father had stopped by to bring me a gift, along with lots of hugs and kisses. He had also promised to take me somewhere special to celebrate during our next weekend together. I was looking forward to it for sure. Allan had come by with him that day too, and he brought me a huge surprise....a puppy!

"Oh my God, Allan! Thank you!" I shouted excitedly.

I was definitely not expecting a puppy. I had been begging both of my parents for one for over a year!

"You are most welcome Ava." Allan said, smiling.

It truly was the best party ever! One I was not going to forget any time soon. That was for sure.

The weekend I was to spend with my father came a few days later, and this time, he came to pick me up in the morning. He stood in the doorway, and as he watched me come down the stairs with my suitcase he began to laugh. My suitcase was humongous in comparison to my tiny little frame. It made me almost fall over carrying it.

"I think you're going to need a bigger suitcase than that pumpkin." he said. "I guess your mother didn't tell you, but you're coming to stay for three weeks!" he exclaimed

"Yes!! Oh my God...thank you mom!!" I shouted.

And then I went rushing over to kiss and hug her in gratitude.

"You're the best mom EVER!"

She nodded and smiled in appreciation for my display of affection, as I went flying past her, and back up the stairs to pack more clothes. Just what does an excited seven year old girl pack? you might ask. Well, If memory serves me correctly, I had just pulled all of my drawers out of my dresser, and started dumping them into a second suitcase.

"Hope this is enough!" I exclaimed, returning downstairs.

"Um...Yeah...I think you have your whole dresser in there...should be enough!" my father laughed.

I had no time for humour this time. I was one excited little girl and I was on a mission. I dropped the suitcases on the floor and bolted for the front door. My father of course stopped me in my tracks, and reminded me to say goodbye to my mother. It was going to be awhile before I saw her again. I obliged him and then rushed past him and out the front door. I let myself into his car and fastened my own seat belt.

"Let's go...Let's go!" I cried out excitedly.

I leaned over and opened the passenger door behind me, trying to make it easier for him to load my suitcases into the back seat. He could tell I was very excited, and he wasted no time trying to talk to me about it.

A Journey of a Thousand Miles – A Reflections Saga

We waved goodbye to my mother, and off we went. I had no idea where we were headed yet, but I knew it had to be a ways out, because we had been driving for longer than I remembered the usual ride to his place being.

I was surprised when I saw the sign for Chatham. I knew exactly where we were going now. It was my favourite place of all. Wheels Inn was the name of it, and it had everything for kids there. It was a family oriented place, but it was really just a huge indoor play area for kids. They had games you could play to win tickets for prizes, a huge playground with a slide that brought you into a massive ball pit, a ton of rides and even a swimming pool. It was owned by my uncle Jack. We used to always go there as a family, but this time it was just my father and I. I played so hard that day and swam my little legs off so much, that I fell asleep on the drive home. I was sleeping so soundly, off in dreamland, when suddenly I felt someone had picked me up and was now carrying me. I smelled the familiar scent of my father's Old Spice cologne, and was comforted by it. I snuggled into him and let him carry me. I missed that feeling. The feeling you get when you're a kid and you fall asleep watching television, or even while on a car ride, then someone carries you to your bed and tucks you in. My father always did this for me. His embrace was so gentle and loving. I missed those tender moments most of all.

Our weeks of adventure together went by in no time. There were trips to the movie theatre to see the latest Disney movie, walks to play at the park, fishing almost daily, going out to eat, and of course ice cream...LOTS of ice cream. Soon my father crushed my little heart by announcing that our weeks of adventure had come to a close, but he did share some good news too, that he and my mother had settled their differences, and that they were talking about him moving back home soon.

I was so excited for that. I simply couldn't wait. That night, he took me out for dinner and ice cream one final time, and then he brought me home. When he stopped the car in the driveway, he told me that he wouldn't be picking me up the next weekend because he had to go out of town, but that he would be picking me up the following weekend for another two weeks to make up for it. I was upset, but I understood, and was looking forward to the next time. I was just happy to be able to spend any time at all with him.

Once we had gotten out of the car, he carried my suitcases into the house, and I ran to tell my mother all about the fun we had together. Then I ran up to kiss and hug him goodbye. He picked me up in his arms and whispered to me,

"I love you my sweet angel. I'll see you soon. Be good for your mom okay?"

I nodded and he set me back down on my feet, then turned and walked out the door to head back to the car. I ran outside and waved goodbye to him from the sidewalk.

"I'll see you soon daddy! I love you" I shouted.

A Journey of a Thousand Miles – A Reflections Saga

I went inside and helped my mother clean up in the kitchen. I told her my father had told me the good news, that they were thinking of getting back together. My mother smiled at me and said,

"Yes, we've talked about it, but we don't know exactly when that will be just yet. Your father needs to stay there until at least the end of the month because of his contract with the landlord." she explained "But that's going to go by very quickly... just you watch and see!"

I smiled and continued tidying up in the kitchen, before making my way upstairs to my room.

I was excited to tell Emily the great news. My father was finally coming back home! To say I was excited, would've been the understatement of the century. As I reached the top of the landing and opened the door to my bedroom I was in shock. All of my things were gone. My dresser, my bed and even my toy box. They were all just gone.

"Mom?....Mom!" I shouted down the stairwell. "Where's all of my stuff?" I asked.

My mother approached the bottom of the stairway, and told me that she had moved all of my things back into my old room. She said I was a big girl now, and she thought I should have my own room again. I was actually pretty excited about it. I had this whole ghost thing under control now. She was right. I had learned to face my fears, and I had managed to conquer them. I was no longer afraid anymore, because I understood why they were coming to me. They weren't intentionally trying to scare me. They just wanted my help. At least that was what the majority of them wanted anyway. I was a big girl now, and I was about to prove it to everyone.

I opened my door and gasped when I saw who was standing there. It was Emily!

"Oh my gosh!" I exclaimed "H'…how am I able to see you again?" I asked. "Is it because I'm so happy my parents are getting back together...that I opened my heart to you again?"

"I'm afraid there's more to it then just that... I think you should probably sit down." she suggested.

After the talk with Emily, I sat there in sheer disbelief. The things she had told me shook me down to the very core of my being. Was it all true? Was this all really going to happen? I shuddered at the thought, but I knew she had come for a very good reason, and I also knew it was to warn me. It was the only thing that could explain why I was suddenly able to see her again. It made perfect sense. She told me there was going to be a man who would hurt me deeply. She told me it was going to scar me for a very long time. She came to warn me to be on the lookout for this man. I didn't even know such a man. Definitely not one that would ever do the unspeakable things she had mentioned this man was going to do. I thanked her for coming to warn me. We hugged and then we said goodbye until next time. I changed into my PJ'S and got into bed. What she just told me was going to be something that just might haunt me forever.

Chapter Five

It didn't take me long to fall asleep. Must've been all that fresh air I had. I was back in the astral by the looks of it. It was a desolate place. The streets were empty, and there was no sound to be heard for miles.

"*Why would I come here?*" I thought to myself.

I decided to explore a bit. Maybe I would figure it out soon. As I walked, I could hear the sound of what sounded like panting behind me. I turned to see a golden retriever heading in my direction. He looked happy to see me. I knelt down to pet him, he started licking my hand and wagging his tail excitedly.

"Where did you come from big guy?" I asked. "You had to have come here with someone. Where's your owner boy?" I said, glancing all around us.

After a few moments I stood up, and started walking again. Suddenly the dog started jumping at me to get my attention. He started to run up a bit further ahead, and then he began to bark at me.

"*I think he wants me to follow him*" I thought to myself.

I had to run just to catch up to him. It felt like we were running for miles, and I had to slow down to catch my breath, yet the dog continued to bark at me to keep going. And then he led me to a house at the very end of the street. It appeared to be very old, and uninhabited for quite some time. The green shutters were hanging off of the window ledges and the front porch appeared to be falling apart. The wood was rotted and chipping away throughout most of it. I stared at the house for a few moments, before the dog ran up the stairs to the porch. The staircase collapsed under his weight, and he jumped the rest of the way, as he used his head to motion for me to come with him. I climbed onto the porch and peered at the door which appeared to be already half open.

As soon as I got inside, I was hit with a wave of the most foul odour I'd ever encountered in my life. I had to use my hand to cover my mouth, to stop myself from breathing in whatever was emitting that awful, putrid smell.

As I walked through the kitchen, the scene was laid out before me, like something out of a horror movie. I saw dirty dishes scattered across the counter and kitchen table. There were also remnants of rotting food covering them. Flies buzzed all around me, and there we maggots in the sink. I quickly covered my mouth and began to gag uncontrollably. I nearly vomited, but luckily I was able to keep that at bay. I was so disgusted by it all, and I couldn't wait to get out of there. As I continued to follow the dog, I soon found out what it was that he had been trying to show me. He led the way through the dining room, and down a long, dark hallway, to a door that was shut tight. I could hear a strange sound on the other side of it. I couldn't quite make out the sound, but it sounded like a loud buzzing noise...like a room full of even more flies. I grabbed my t-shirt and held it over my nose, as I reached for the knob of the door. The dog began barking continuously at me, and I knew that whatever he wanted me to see, it was going to be just on the other side of this door. I opened the door slowly, and let out a loud shriek, as I gazed upon the story that unfolded before my eyes.

There was blood, and brain matter covering the far wall. There were flies everywhere. It was the most gruesome thing I had ever seen in all seven years of my young life, and I wanted to run out of there as fast as my little legs could carry me. As I turned back toward the doorway, contemplating going back out the way I had come in, I heard another sound

"Hell...Hello?! Who...who dere?" the voice asked.

I turned and walked toward the bed and followed the voice.

"Wer...Wer ma dawg? Ya took 'em didn' ya?" the voice asked accusingly.

I stopped in horror as I had finally managed to locate the source of the voice. There on the floor in front of me was a young boy. He looked to be about twelve or thirteen years of age. He had on beige trousers with a blue and black flannel button down shirt. He was lying face down on the floor, and had a huge hole in the back of his head. A shotgun in his hand. The hole was gaping so wide that I could see directly through it, and into the carpet beneath him. I didn't want to see what his face looked like. I wasn't prepared for that. Maybe I should've just asked him to stay that way, because no sooner had I imagined what the horror of his face might look like, that he began to try and pull himself up. I closed my eyes as I saw him get up to his hands and knees. I felt his energy right in front of me now, and I knew whenever I got the courage to open my eyes again, that he was going to be right there in my face. I took a deep breath and prepared myself.

"Whah?...Whah wrong?" he asked "Why ya got yer eyes closed like dat?"

I opened my eyes and tears filled them instantly. I began to back away from him. It was more horrific then I ever could've imagined. It was so much worse. The stuff your nightmares are made of. Half of his face had been blown off, the other half was mangled and barely holding together. The skeletal structure of what was left of his lower jaw was exposed, there was blood and brain matter in his hair. His only remaining eye was barely in its socket. I was terrified to look at him. I shielded my eyes with my arm. "What happened to you? What were you doing with that shotgun?" I asked.

He looked down at the floor, at the shotgun and then he raised his head again

"I was cleanin' it." he replied "Why whah wrong? Did sumthin happen? Did I shoot mah dawg er sumthin?" he asked inquisitively.

"N...No...Not exactly." I replied.

A Journey of a Thousand Miles – A Reflections Saga

"Well den whah is it?" he asked, confused and panicked.

I looked at him with sadness in my eyes. I knew then that he really didn't know.

"You didn't shoot your dog. He's right here, but I think you may wanna see for yourself." I told him.

With that, he stumbled across the hallway into the bathroom, and I waited for the sound of what was sure to follow upon his discovery

"OH MAH GOD!!!WHAH HAVE I DONE?!" he screamed, and then he began to sob uncontrollably.

"Mah po' mutha! Oh mah God...ma Pa...Dey must be so mad with meh. Dey told meh a hunderd times not ta touch 'is gun. I didn' listen. I was jus' tryin ta do sumthin special fer 'em. Clean it up real nice an' all. We was goin' deer huntin nex' week, and I just wanted ta surprise 'em!" he cried.

Suddenly the fear of his appearance left me, and my heart ached for him. How sad and alone he must've felt in this place. What it must feel like to be all alone here, to not even know how you got to this place, or to not even realize that you're dead. I walked over to him and placed my hand gently on his shoulder. He was no longer a horrific monster to me. Now he was just a scared little boy, and I needed to help him. I was going to do whatever it took to help him find some peace.

"There is a light. I can help you find it. If you go into that light, you won't have to be in this place anymore." I explained.

The boy turned to look at me. His face appeared to be healing now as the realization began to set in.

"Y'...Ya would do dat fer meh? Wer is it? Can ya take meh the-?" he asked.

"Yes I will take you there, but I'm not really sure how to get there from here. I'll have to call my guide for help!" I interrupted

"Okay...I'm ready ta go now." he said.

"Emily...We need your help please." I called out. Just then she appeared in the open doorway of the house. The flies started to disappear and the boy's face was back to normal.

"I'm here." she replied. "Are you ready?" she asked.

I nodded and the boy nodded.

"Okay then...let's get out of here!" she said.

We followed her outside and the dog ran up alongside of us. It wasn't nearly as far of a walk this time. Seemed like only a short distance and we were there.

"That's it...That's where you need to go!" she told him as she pointed toward a big oak tree.

I was confused.

"But there's no light there...It's just a tree." I told her emphatically.

"There's a light there...just wait and see! Go ahead." she said to the boy. "Walk towards that big tree there and you will see the light." she explained.

A Journey of a Thousand Miles – A Reflections Saga

The boy began to walk toward the tall oak tree, and then he stopped and turned around

"Wait..can ya guys come too?" he asked. "I'm kinda scared ya know." he said sheepishly.

"I will come with you just to make sure you get through okay?" Emily told him reassuringly.

The boy stopped and turned around again

"Wait" he said "I wanna say bye."

He walked over to me and hugged me tightly.

"Thank ya fer bein' ere fer me." he said.

Then he began to walk toward the tree again. I stood there watching, wondering how this tree was going to become the light I had seen before. Suddenly I felt a warm tongue on my hand. I looked down to see the retriever seemingly smiling at me.

"Wait...What about his dog?!" I called after them.

"He's already crossed over." Emily called back "He just came to help the boy do the sa-" she continued, her voice beginning to trail off.

I looked down at the dog again, but he was gone. I stood in awe as the big oak tree appeared to be opening up. And then that huge, bright shining light appeared again. Soon the entire tree had become this light. I watched the boy walk in front of it, and then turn and wave before disappearing inside.

Just then I saw Emily come skipping up the road. The light had vanished and the big oak tree was there once more. As if there had never even been a light.

"I'm confused." I told her "Why was there no light there all along? How are people supposed to get through it if they can't SEE it?!" I asked confused

"It only appears when they're ready." she said. "Could you imagine wandering around this place with a big bright light in your face? Not knowing where you are or how you got here?" she asked. "You helped him to be ready. If it weren't for you he might still be stuck here." she said "Come on...let's get you back home!"she suggested, as she skipped along the road and motioned for me to follow.

Within a few minutes we were back at the bridge. I remembered my last trip back, and I wasn't looking forward to this one.

"I'm scared." I told her. "I don't like the way it feels...it's so scary."

"Just close your eyes and focus on counting to three. Before you get to three, you will be back." she explained.

I thanked her again for her help, and then waved goodbye.

A Journey of a Thousand Miles – A Reflections Saga

I walked slowly over the bridge. I was still afraid and shaking, but I knew this was the only way I was going to get home again. I knew I definitely didn't want to get stuck in that place. It was bad enough that I was pulled there every night. I closed my eyes as I approached the light, held my breath and without a second thought I jumped right into it. I could feel that terrifying feeling again, and then I remembered what Emily had told me to do. I began to count out loud

"One....two..thr-" I no longer felt the feeling.

She was right. I would be sure to do this every time now. It made the transition so much easier.

I rolled over in bed, and wiped the sleep from my eyes. I glanced at my window to see it was still dark out, and then I glanced at the clock. It was only 3:00 AM. I decided that maybe I should go back to sleep. I closed my eyes and wondered what awaited me in my dreams next. Nothing could prepare me for this one, and to this day I often still wonder if I could've changed anything.

Back in the astral, I felt a cool summer breeze on my skin. As I glanced around, I happened to notice that I was standing just a few feet from my father's apartment building. I thought this was a bit strange, as I usually end up somewhere I don't often recognize. I felt, since I'm here, this would be the perfect opportunity to go and visit my father. I knew he would be asleep, and wouldn't be able to see me, even if he suddenly woke up, but I still wanted to see him and kiss him on his cheek. I walked up the sidewalk leading to the doorway of his apartment building. It was a white high rise, with one of those secured entry systems where you had to buzz to get inside. As I stood there in front of the building now, I suddenly realized I had forgotten this fact. I studied the buzzer panel trying to figure out how to gain access. Surely I couldn't just buzz someone to just let me in. I guess I was going to have to wait to see him until he picked me up in three days. I became frustrated and a bit annoyed by it all.

"*Why am I here then?*" I asked myself.

 I didn't know why. It made no sense to me. Suddenly a thought came to me...my inner voice

-*This is the astral* it said. -*Why don't you just try walking through the door?* it suggested.

I didn't even know if it would be possible, but I decided to try it anyway. What could it hurt right? I approached the door once more, and braced myself for the impact I was about to feel as a result of running into a door. I took a few steps back and ran toward it with my eyes shut tight. I was waiting to feel the pain from the blow, but it never came. I opened my eyes and was astonished. I was inside! I decided to make a mental note to remember this little secret for later visits. I walked to the elevator, and walked right through the door. Once inside I glanced at the numbers on the control panel on the wall. I was trying to remember what floor he lived on.

"*Was it five or six?*" I asked myself.

A Journey of a Thousand Miles – A Reflections Saga

I couldn't seem to remember. Great! How was I going to see my father if I couldn't even remember what floor he lived on? I decided to try something that came to me all of a sudden. Much like what had happened earlier, when I didn't know how I would get through the front door. I closed my eyes and pictured the interior of my father's apartment.

"Take me to dad's apartment." I ordered.

I opened my eyes and saw that it had worked. I was now standing in his dining room.

Everything was dark, but my eyes began adjusting to the light almost immediately. I walked through the dining room and through the kitchen toward his bedroom. When I got into his bedroom, I noticed his unpacked suitcase leaned up against the far wall.

"*He must've just gotten back*" I thought to myself.

I glanced over at the bed, and saw him laying there. He was fast asleep. I watched his chest rise and fall with each soft breath he took. He looked so peaceful. I walked quietly over to the side of the bed, and sat down carefully beside him. He didn't stir in the least. I watched him for a few moments, before leaning over to kiss him softly on his cheek. I didn't want to wake him. I wasn't sure if he really would be able to see me or not if he did in fact wake up. I mean...can you even imagine how that might all play out? I definitely didn't want to scare him. I just wanted to be in this moment with him forever. This was the happiest moment of my life as far as I was concerned, other than when I got a puppy of course! I had hoped I'd have more astral visits like this one. I told myself I would find a way to do this every night if I could. I sat there with him until to my horror, he began to stir. I was pretty certain that he was starting to wake up, and I wanted just one last moment. I leaned over in his ear and whispered softly

"I love you daddy...so...so...much. I'll see you soon."

I think he may have heard me. No, I'm fairly certain he did. He rolled over in bed, and began to sit up, wiping the sleep from his eyes.

"Ava?!....Ava is that you?" he called out into the darkness.

I got up from the bed before he could turn around to face me, and ran out of the bedroom as fast as I could. I could hear the sound of his footsteps advancing toward the door. I needed to get out of there, but he was already directly behind me. He walked toward me in a hurried pace, and then he walked straight through me. I realized then that he couldn't see me, but he most definitely could hear me. I stood there watching him, frantically search for me in every room of the apartment. He looked puzzled.

"Must've been a dream." he said, as he walked back toward the bedroom and closed the door.

I listened for him to get back into bed, and then I whispered

"No daddy....It wasn't just a dream. I'm here. I love you."

I made my way back through the kitchen and into the dining room and waited for a few moments, trying to collect my thoughts on what had just taken place, before walking towards the door to the apartment. Once outside in the hallway I walked back toward the elevator, and stopped in my tracks when I saw her standing there.

"Emily?!...What are you doing here?" I asked. "Oh my God Emily...You will never believe what just happened! It was so awesome!" I exclaimed. "Why can't I come here all the time?" I asked. "This is so cool!....I saw my father asleep and I got to kiss him and talk to him. He heard me Emily...He heard me!! Can you believe tha..."

I stopped speaking abruptly when I noticed the look on Emily's face. There was the look of pure, deep sadness in her eyes.

"What's wrong" I asked. "Is everything okay?!"

"No Ava...I'm afraid it's not! I have something very important to tell you." she announced. "You might want to sit down...This isn't going to be easy for you." she said.

In that moment my heart dropped into my stomach again. "What now?!" I asked.

Chapter Six

Suddenly I awoke screaming at the top of my lungs, my eyes remaining closed.

"No....No....It can't be...Oh my God...Nooooo" I screamed. "Please don't leave me! I can't live without you. I need you!" I pleaded.

I felt my mother trying to shake me awake. I just couldn't seem to stop screaming the same thing over and over again. I was inconsolable. Completely devastated at what Emily had just told me. Most of all I was terrified of what was coming, and there was absolutely NOTHING I could do to stop it. My mother kept trying to get me to look at her.

"What?....What's wrong Ava?.....Calm down and tell mom what's the matter." she told me, a wave of concern just below the surface of her tone.

I was crying so hard, and I couldn't seem to catch my breath. I could barely make it through a word

"N...N...No" I stuttered through my crying. "He...He can...can't...le..leave."

"Who Ava? Who can't leave?" she asked.

"Da...Da...Daddy!" I continued in hysterics.

I struggled even harder to catch my breath after uttering those words, and I knew she was going to ask me what I was talking about.

A Journey of a Thousand Miles – A Reflections Saga

"What are you talking about? Daddy can't leave? What do you mean?" she asked.

I slowed my breathing as I prepared to tell her what I myself had just learned. I managed to get it all out in just one syllable this time.

"Daddy!" I said. "He's going to leave." I shouted.

I could feel the tears getting stronger now.

"What do you mean he's going to leave?" she asked concerned. "Daddy's not leaving anywhere...he's coming back. He even told you that he's moving back in soon." she explained.

"N...No he..he's not!" I shouted. "I just saw Emily in my dream...and she...she told me....she told me that daddy is going to DIE!!" I yelled out, and then the tears returned, and this time it was like someone had opened up the floodgates to my very soul, and the tears just started pouring out of me this time.

"Your father is not going to die! It was all a bad dream. Everything will be fine." she announced. "Now go back to sleep. It's only 6:00 AM!" she leaned over and kissed me goodnight, and then got up and started toward the door.

I lay there in my bed, wide awake. There was no way I was going back to sleep. I was afraid of what else I would be told. I was furious with Emily's news, and there was no way I wanted to hear anymore of what she had to say. Not for a very long time. I had decided that Emily and I shouldn't be friends anymore. All she seemed to give me lately was bad news. I had enough of her, and I was preparing myself to shut her out forever. Why would she tell me such horrible things? Was she really my friend, or did she just want to hurt me like everyone else? First the news about the man, and now this. Yup I'd had just about enough bad news to last a lifetime. If I got rid of her, then maybe none of it would even come true. Maybe she was the evil one. I felt so emotionally exhausted from all of the crying I had done, that I suddenly grew very tired again. But the thoughts kept circling my mind, and made me cry even harder than before. I lay there crying and rocking myself back and forth. Until the exhaustion took over and I drifted off to sleep again.

I awoke the next day with the thoughts of what Emily had told me, still running rampant through my mind, but I needed to let all of that go. I had convinced myself that Emily was a liar, and she was just trying to hurt me. Why else would she tell me such horrible things? She was supposed to be my guide. She was supposed to help me. Wasn't she? Did she really think telling me all of this would help? I wasn't going to listen to her anymore. When she came to me the next time, I was going to send her away.

"I would rather have no friends, than have a friend like her!" I thought to myself.

I grabbed out my colouring book and crayons, and began searching for the page that she and I had coloured together. When I found it, I took out my black crayon and began to scribble over it angrily. I wanted no part of her. No reminders...EVER!. I had finally released the emotions I was feeling, when I suddenly heard my

A Journey of a Thousand Miles – A Reflections Saga

mother calling me down for breakfast. I threw the colouring book into my toy box, and the crayons on the table next to my bed, then I proceeded to get dressed for the day before making my way down to have breakfast.

When I got downstairs, my mother had made me Eggo's and bacon. One of my favourites. I was appreciative of the gesture, but not very hungry. I ate the bacon and left the rest on the plate. I knew she was trying to cheer me up, and I was grateful for that. As I was finishing up with eating, the phone rang. It was my older sister Kim, calling to see if she could pick me up for lunch, shopping, a movie and a sleep over. It was pretty clear to me my mother had called her, and though I didn't feel like having a pity party, I was always happy to see my big sister.

Kim often took me places and we did your usual sisterly types of things. I sometimes had sleep overs with her too. She and my two other sisters Marie and Grace, have the same father as me, and they were all living with their mother at the time, but I always enjoyed every opportunity I had to see them. Are you ready for some confusion now? I am the youngest in the family. I have five older sisters and one brother. Let me try and explain the dynamics of how all of this works. Okay, so here we go. Kim, Grace and Marie all share the same parents, but I only have the same father as they do. Then we have Jane, Anne and Timothy, who also share the same parents, however I only have the same mother as they do. Confused yet?

Imagine being me and trying to explain that fuckery to other people. Apparently, since I don't share the same maternal and paternal parents as they do, that would make us only half siblings. Either way, to me, they were all my siblings, none of this half blood garbage acknowledged here. Since I'm the baby sister of the family, they were always very protective over me. Now I know you are probably thinking that's great and all, but trust me it's not all it's cracked up to be. Being protective also meant that they were all up in my business 24/7. Doesn't sound so fun now does it? On top of that, some of my siblings loved to tease and poke fun at me. I guess that was just the typical behaviour between the older siblings and younger ones. Kim, Grace and Marie, never did any of that though. They were more about making sure I had everything I needed, and ensuring that I would grow up to be a kind and decent human being. They didn't have time to care about much else beyond that.

I finished up my phone conversation with Kim, and then handed my mother the phone so she could speak to her too. She told me she would be picking me up at noon. It was already 10:00 AM, so I rushed upstairs to get ready. I grabbed out a fresh pair of PJ'S and some clothes for the next day, and carefully laid them out on the bed.

"I'll leave them there until I can pack my toothbrush too." I thought to myself.

A Journey of a Thousand Miles – A Reflections Saga

This way, I wouldn't forget anything. I was so excited to have a sleepover with my big sister. We always had a great time together, and I knew this time wasn't going to be any exception. This would definitely help take my mind off of all of the bad thoughts I had been having. That dream had really messed me up.

I walked over to my dresser, picked out a sundress and grabbed my white dress sandals from the floor. I gathered them up and headed downstairs to bathe and get ready. I knew I was going to be in the tub for at least an hour. I was always a fish when it came to the water, although at this time I couldn't swim. Whenever I would go into a pool, I stuck to the shallow end only. I didn't know where that fear of water had come from, but I was born with it. I was a bit of an odd child. I may not have been able to swim, but I still loved being in the water. It was always so calming and peaceful for me. I guess my fear wasn't really of water after all, it was more like a fear of deep water.

After my bath, I changed into my sundress and sandals, both of which Kim had bought for me on our last shopping spree. I brushed through my naturally curly hair and yelled for my mother.

"Mom? Can you come and help me?" I asked.

I asked her if she wouldn't mind putting my hair in cute little pig tails. I always hated when she did my hair. Not because she was rough or anything, okay maybe she was a little bit, but because my hair was so curly, it would often knot on itself, and putting a brush through it was sometimes the equivalent of hell for me. It felt like someone had taken a rake to my scalp, the hard pulling that often followed, was enough to give anyone a headache. After the torture of getting my hair done was over, I reached down and grabbed two small yellow ribbons from the basket beneath the sink, then I proceeded to tie them into pretty bows. Now I was ready.

"You look adorable!" my mother told me.

I had always hated that word. That was a word that people often used to describe babies, and I was no longer a baby. I was a big girl! I was always told I had an

"*old soul*", like I was seven going on forty-seven.

People often forgot the fact that I really was just a child. Despite the cringe that went through me as she uttered the word, I thanked her anyway. I didn't want to be rude. After we had gotten my hair just the way I wanted it, I proceeded to brush my teeth. As I glanced up at the mirror, I took notice of just how puffy my eyes looked in that moment. It was obvious that I had been crying for hours on end. There was nothing I could do to hide my sadness now. It was written all over my face. Hopefully, with any luck, Kim wouldn't notice.

A Journey of a Thousand Miles – A Reflections Saga

Chapter Seven

I ran to the living room to check the time, hoping I didn't have much longer. 11:30 AM, almost time. I wanted to leave this place before Emily tried to come back and talk to me again. I had left her rather abruptly after our conversation, and this time I didn't even need to cross the bridge to get home. I was so overcome with grief and anger, that I closed my eyes and all I had to do was simply think about leaving there, and just like that, I was taken straight back to my bed. The crying I had experienced in the astral, was so powerful that it followed me back home. I shook those thoughts about what had transpired in that place out of my mind as quickly as they began to intrude. I refused to let any of it get me down. I was going to enjoy every moment, in the moment from now on.

As I made my way back down the hallway, I stopped in the bathroom to retrieve my toothbrush from the cup, then headed upstairs to wait for Kim. I grabbed my clothing from the bed, and packed it neatly into my suitcase, stuffing my Kid Sister doll on top. For as long as I can remember, I had both of the Buddy and Kid Sister dolls, but Buddy reminded me of the *Chucky* doll from those *Child's Play movies*, so he always had to sleep in the closet. Kid Sister on the other hand, slept in bed with me every night. She was my best friend. If you ever had the chance to see photographs of me, she would always be right there too.

I had finally finished packing my suitcase, and headed downstairs with it to wait. I turned on the television and watched a few short programs to help pass the time. Before I knew it, it was time to go. I heard her honk to let me know she had arrived, and I ran to my mother to kiss her goodbye...before bolting out of the door with my suitcase in hand. I dropped the suitcase, and ran up to hug my big sister.

"Well it looks like someone's ready to go!" she laughed. "Are you ready then?" she asked.

"Yes! Let's go!" I shouted excitedly.

She began the list of sister type questions...

"Do you have your toothbrush? Your PJ'S? Did you remember to pack enough clothes? Socks?" she asked.

"Yes! I remembered all of that. Can we go now....pleaseee?" I pleaded.

"Yes...We can go now" she said, as she started up the engine.

I quickly leaned over to buckle my seat belt, before she put the car in reverse. As we got further down the road, she looked over at me with a smile on her face.

"Remember what I've taught you?" she asked.

A Journey of a Thousand Miles – A Reflections Saga

Of course I had remembered. She had been letting go of the steering wheel and letting me steer the car as we drove, but only down the quiet streets. I was thankful for the driving lessons. I had always had a curiosity about what it would be like. Ever since I was about the age of three. As I reached for the steering wheel, suddenly I had a flashback to the time we were all over at my grandmother's house, and my father was taking me to the store for my daily Kit-Kat bar. It was our little tradition. That day, he had just buckled me into the front passenger seat, started up the engine, and then remembered he had forgotten his wallet inside the house…leaving me and the keys in the car while he went inside to grab it. I was a very curious child, and I had watched him so many times before. I wanted to try out what I had observed him doing.

I quickly unfastened my seat belt. and climbed into the driver's seat. I mimicked the actions I had seen him do countless times before. I pulled the gear stick back and placed my little foot on the accelerator. I was tiny, so I had to stand up and hold my foot there on the pedal. Even though I was standing up, I could barely just see over the top of the steering wheel. All at once and to my amazement, the car started to roll backwards. I pushed my little foot down as hard as I could, and then all of a sudden the car flew backwards. It was pretty scary then, and I didn't know how to stop it. Thankfully the car came to a grinding halt, when it crashed into the front porch of the neighbour who lived across the street.

My mother and father both came rushing across the street to see if I was alright. I remember the sound the tires made as they continued to spin in the dirt, as my little foot remained pressed on the pedal, but the car refused to go any further. My father opened the door, saw that I was alright, and did something I wasn't expecting him to do. He started laughing hysterically. He couldn't even help himself. He couldn't possibly be mad at me. I was just a toddler, and it was his fault for leaving a curious three year old in a running car alone. He reached in and gently scooped me up from behind the steering wheel and held me tight. He kept checking me for signs of injury, but there were none. I was completely unscathed. He never did leave me alone in the car again though. Not even for just a few seconds.

"Are you ready to try again?" my sister asked, snapping me out of the flashback.

"Yes, Will you keep your hands close though in case I mess up?" I asked concerned.

"Of course! Okay are you ready? Put your hands here like this." she instructed, as she lifted my hand up and onto the steering wheel, and then she let go.

I was always nervous when it came to this point. I think it had a lot to do with the experience I had when I was three. It seemed to stick with me. Reversing a car at a fairly high speed, when you're too small to see over the steering wheel, and don't know how to stop it, coupled with the jolt one experiences when you hit something at that kind of speed. Yeah, that'll stick with you. It's enough to shake anyone up. I remained focused as we

A Journey of a Thousand Miles – A Reflections Saga

rounded the bend to get to her street. She then told me it was time to turn, and she guided me to help make the turn into the driveway. Then we put the car and park and Kim proceeded to turn off the engine.

"You did it!" she yelled excitedly. "Good job!"

I was very proud of myself. As proud as I'm sure any seven year old little girl might be.

Kim proceeded to carry my suitcase toward the house for me, as I ran up the front porch ahead of her and held the door open. I was always trying to be as helpful as I could be. We carried the suitcase upstairs and then tried to decide what to do next. We decided on The Olive Garden for lunch, as I was famished from not eating very much at breakfast.

After lunch, the two of us headed to the mall. We wanted to look for a few more cute dresses for me. My sister always bought me the most beautiful dresses and shoes. She liked making me all fancy. Something I would come to grow out of quickly. I could never manage to stay clean like cute little girls were expected to do either. I always managed to get myself "*filthy*" as my mother would often put it. You could put me in a cute frilly dress, send me outside for no more than ten minutes, and I would return looking like I went rolling through mud. My mother absolutely hated that. Hey, what else do you expect out of a tom boy? Hell, I was actually supposed to be a boy, but I surprised everyone that day. Boy did I ever. I was even born on Friday the thirteenth and on the eve of a full moon. I guess you could say that my parents figured out rather quickly that I was going to be one hell of a force. After hours of checking out a variety of stores, making various purchases, we began to make our way back to the car.

"What do you think about renting a movie tonight?" Kim suggested. "We can get a whole bunch of junk food and just lay in my bed and watch movies."

"Sure! That sounds like fun." I replied.

We drove off from the mall parking lot, and headed in the direction of her place. Making sure that along the way we stopped off at the video store.

"Okay...Pick whatever you want." she said.

I bolted for the kid's section. There was a movie I was dying to see, and I was really hoping they had it there. I looked at all of the covers on display in the kids section, and then I spotted it. I reached up and pulled the case off the shelf.

"The Little Mermaid?" she asked "That looks interesting. Is this your choice then?"

I nodded and smiled.

"Alright..sounds good to me...Let's go!" she shouted excitedly.

A Journey of a Thousand Miles – A Reflections Saga

I couldn't wait to watch it. I was beyond excited. I remembered seeing the previews for it on one of my other Disney movies, and was looking forward to seeing it someday. Now I would have the chance!

On the way back to her place, we stopped to grab some Whopper combos at Burger King, and then we made a pit stop at the store around the corner for junk food. When we finally got back to her place, we headed upstairs with all of the treasures we had bought earlier that day. We had a goldmine of purchases. We tossed the bags in the corner of the room, and sat down on the bed to eat our food. Kim leaned over and grabbed the remote control to turn on the television. America's Funniest videos was on. One of my favourites. I had always loved that show. It often made me laugh, and I was definitely the girl who loved to laugh.

"We will watch our movie after you have a bath and we get in our PJ'S okay?" Kim said.

"Okay sure." I replied.

After my bath, Kim dried, combed and braided my hair into a french braid. Then we settled into bed with our bag of goodies and pressed play on the movie. I only got up to the point where Ursula changes Ariel into a woman...in exchange for her voice. Somehow, I managed to fall asleep.

I was a bit disappointed when I woke up the following morning, and realized I had fallen asleep and missed the rest of the movie, but Kim assured me that she would rent it again the next time we had a sleepover. I was looking forward to that next time. She was the best big sister anyone could ever ask for.

After lunch she drove me home and helped me to carry my things inside. She had bought me so many things during the seven years of my life, but these were by far some of my favourites. There was even a 14k Gold ring. It had a square on the top and even had my initials on it. A. D was engraved into the square, and it had a little diamond in the corner of it. I was going to be sure to cherish it always. My mother wasn't surprised when we walked into the house that day Kim brought me back, bags in hand. I always seemed to come back with more than I had originally left with. We showed my mother the clothing, hair accessories, new shoes and of course my new ring. Then Kim kissed me goodbye, and told me she loved me. I told her I loved her too and thanked her for taking me and buying me all of this great stuff.

"It was my pleasure!" she said, as she headed out of the door, making her way onto the front porch.

I stood in the doorway and watched her pull away, waving goodbye to me one final time. I was so grateful for her. She was my big sister and I needed her. At that time I had no idea how much, but something told me I was going to find out sooner than I could've imagined.

A Journey of a Thousand Miles – A Reflections Saga

Finally, the next day was Friday, and I would be seeing my father again. I couldn't wait. I had missed him so much. I knew that seeing him would make me feel better about my bad dream. I couldn't wait to tell him all about my adventures with Kim. I knew he was just going to love my new ring too. The only other piece of jewellery I owned was a gift from my godparents. A 24K Gold cross that I had received at my baptism. Although I didn't start wearing it until I was around two or three. I never took it off. Not even to take a bath. You see, I was raised Roman Catholic and was taught all about God, his son Jesus and of course the angels. I loved them all and was told as long as I was wearing it, that they would always protect me. I believed with all my heart that this was true. Yet I still didn't understand why they let me be tortured like that every night by the monsters. That part made no sense to me. I was taught never to question God though, and so I never did. Maybe it showed that I was in fact protected, because I was never harmed in any way by these monsters in my room. Maybe that's what my parents and godparents really meant. In any case, I was still afraid of what might have happened to me if I ever took the necklace off. What is the term? God fearing. Yep, that was me!

I carried my suitcase upstairs and began to unpack my things. I transferred my clean clothes back into their proper places in my drawers, and changed into my PJ'S. Kim was so good like that. Any time she took me, I never came back with dirty clothes. She always washed them for me whenever I was with her. She was always trying to make things easier for everyone. It was just her way. She reminded me so much of my father. She even shared his looks and loving, gentle personality. She was practically his twin.

After I had finished unpacking, I walked downstairs to grab a snack from the kitchen and then proceeded to sit down in front of the television. My brother Timothy was home, and he was seated on the opposite end of the couch from me. He appeared to be watching The Simpsons. It was his favourite show. He watched it so much in fact, that he often knew which episode was coming on, simply by the intro it had. Sometimes I hated watching movies and TV shows with him though, because if he had seen something before, he would always tell you exactly what was going to happen next. And if he hadn't...well then he would still guess what was going to happen. It was enough to drive anyone crazy. I just wanted to watch and find out for myself, but as time went on I too began to notice how predictable they all were. I was glad to see him home. I had missed them all so much, but I wondered why it was just him there.

"Where are Jane and Anne?" I asked.

"They're still at my dad's." he replied. "I wanted to come home...didn't want to be there anymore." he said.

I accepted that response. I didn't pry or ask any more details as to why that had been. He often got upset if anyone asked too many questions about his life. He wasn't the type to express himself a whole lot either, unless he became angry and couldn't hold it in anymore. Those were the outbursts you hoped you weren't present for. Still, despite his anger issues, I understood him and loved him regardless.

A new episode of The Simpsons was starting.

"Oh this is a good one!" he told me.

I smiled and went back to eating my snack as we both continued watching in silence. Soon my mother appeared around the corner,

"Did you eat your supper?" she asked.

"No mom." I responded. "I wasn't very hungry. This is good enough for me." I told her, holding up my snack.

"Okay then, just make sure you don't stay up too late...and Tim...don't watch nothing scary with her. I don't need her having nightmares." she scolded as she walked back into her bedroom and closed the door.

I rarely even saw my mother these days, unless it was for her to make something to eat or to use the bathroom. She had made herself scarce, a prisoner in her own bedroom. I spent most of my time upstairs by myself anyway, unless my siblings were home. Sometimes though, I found myself just wanting to spend time with her. Then there were other times where I just really wanted time to myself and to be left alone. It was just the way things were. I could honestly take it or leave it.

I'm not sure how many episodes of the Simpsons Tim and I watched that night, but it seemed like a marathon of them. By the time I glanced at the clock again it was midnight.

"I need to go to bed Tim." I told him "My dad is coming to get me tomorrow...goodnight....love you." I said.

I don't think he heard a word I said. I also don't remember him telling me he loved me much, if at all actually. It was just the way things had been between us my whole life. I knew he loved me. He just showed it differently. In his own way. Still, I wanted to hear him say it back every now and then. I chalked this time up to maybe he just didn't hear...yeah that had to be it. He was too engrossed in his show. I got up and headed to the bathroom to brush my teeth and wash my face before bed. As I neared the doorway I heard him call out

"You going to bed? Okay goodnight!"

"Goodnight!" I shouted back.

I turned on the water and wet my toothbrush...then stopped and turned it off to listen closer. I could hear the sound of footsteps creaking across the floorboards directly above my head. As in, my bedroom! I listened intently and heard it again. No, this was not my imagination. Someone was up there, but who? It couldn't be either one of my sisters. They were still at their father's house as my brother had mentioned earlier. I didn't know when they would be back either. I called out to my brother

"Tim....Do you hear that too?" I asked, my voice beginning to tremble.

"Hear what?" he asked.

"Never mind...It's nothing." I answered.

Oh but it wasn't nothing. It was definitely something. I heard it again. I didn't have the slightest clue who or what it was, but I was getting very close to finding out.

As I walked up the stairwell, my heart began to pound in my chest. My ears started to ring, and I suddenly lost the ability to hear audible sound. My palms started sweating, as I gripped the railing to steady myself. I suddenly felt dizzy and hot. You might just say I was scared shitless. I stopped halfway up the stairs and tried to calm myself. Then I heard a

"*THUD*"

Something had fallen on the floor, it sounded like it was rolling across it and toward my bedroom door.

"Tim?!" I called again. "Can you come here for a sec?" I asked, sounding a bit more terrified now.

A few seconds later, I heard my brother's footsteps walking through the hallway toward the staircase. Then I saw him peek his head around the corner

"What's up?" he asked. "Everything okay?"

He must've seen how pale I was. I know in that moment I probably had no colour in my face...I felt it.

"Can you come tuck me in please?" I asked with a smile.

He began to walk up the stairs behind me, I let him walk past me before I followed after him. I didn't know what or who was in my room, but one thing I did know for sure...I wasn't going to be the first to go in there and find out. Wasn't this what big brothers were supposed to be for? To scare away the monsters that were under your bed right? I held my breath and tried to steady my racing heart as my brother's hand reached for the doorknob to my bedroom door. Just then I began to hear my inner thoughts.

-Should I warn him that I heard something in there? Would he even believe me, or would he call me a baby too?

I decided not to say anything. I just let him turn the knob and push the door open. Moment of truth. I wasn't ready, but I was going to have to be. The door swung open into the darkened room. It was so dark that neither one of us could see a thing. Tim walked into the room ahead of me, and switched on the light. I took a step back, holding my breath again. Waiting for the big reveal. But there was no big reveal. There was just...nothing. I was shocked. What had I heard then? It couldn't have been my imagination, but just when I thought I might actually be losing it, I looked down at the floor and laying there next to my bed, was the flashlight I had kept on the table next to it.

Did it just fall off by itself? I wondered.

I didn't think so. Tim walked over to my bed and pulled back the covers.

"Did you brush your teeth?" he asked.

"Yes." I replied.

"Alright then...get into bed and I'll tuck you in." he said.

I walked slowly over to the bed, still trying to figure out what I had heard.

"*I know I heard something*" I told myself as I climbed into bed and laid down on my pillow.

My brother started to pull the covers up over me, and then proceeded to tuck them underneath the sides of my body.

"Snug as a bug in a rug. Have a good sleep." he told me. "What time is your dad coming tomorrow?" he asked.

"Mom said around noon." I responded.

"Alright then, you had better get some sleep." he suggested. "Goodnight." he whispered and then he switched off the light and left the room, closing the door behind him.

He was right. I really should get some sleep. After the door had closed, I rolled over to face the wall, trying to get comfortable. I was just about to drift off to sleep, when I heard a scratching noise coming from behind me on the floor next to my bed. My eyes shot open as I listened closely. There it was again. Then something jumped on the bed and I let out a loud scream. Whatever it was it started attacking my feet. I could feel sharp claws and teeth through the blanket covering my toes. The claws pierced my skin and it stung. I screamed again. This time I could hear my brother running up the stairs and approaching the bedroom door. I shut my eyes tight as I prepared for him to open it. He was about to witness the monster attacking me. If he didn't believe me before...he was about to now. The door opened and I waited for the

"Oh my God what is that?!" to escape his lips.

He switched on the light and began to laugh hysterically.

"Is this what you were screaming about?" he asked mid laughter.

Chapter Eight

I sat up in my bed and looked down at my feet. There looking up at me, was one of my fat cats I had rescued as a stray, He was big and black. I named him Midnight. I had found him, his brothers and sister caught between two wooden fences in the alleyway on my way to school one day. They were only a couple of days old

A Journey of a Thousand Miles – A Reflections Saga

at the most. There was an entire litter there, all alone with no mamma. It was winter time when I had found them too. They would've frozen to death if I had just left them there, and I knew it. After I happened upon them that morning, I quickly took off my winter coat and wrapped them up in it. I then carried them back home, and pulled out one of the big drawers to my dresser. Stuffing a flannel blanket inside to keep them warm, I placed each one of them on the blanket and wrapped it around them. They were still very young, which is how I knew something had to have happened to their mother.

There is no way she would leave them alone while they were still so little, and in the wild? No way would that happen, unless maybe she thought they would be safe there. They were newborns, so young their eyes weren't even open yet. I had to feed them milk from an eye dropper. I remember when my mother had first found them in my room. She had heard them mewing one day while I had been away at school, and went upstairs to investigate. When I returned home from school that day, she was sitting at the table looking upset with me. She told me that we absolutely could not keep them, but that we would take care of them until they were old enough to give away. I agreed. That's not what happened at all though. As time went on she bonded with them all, and when the time came for them to leave... she couldn't bring herself to give any of them away. They had become family.

Now, as I sat there staring at the sweet and innocent face of my cat Midnight, I couldn't help but start laughing too.

"I should've known it was you!"

Midnight just looked at me as if to say,

"What did I do?" then he came and curled up beside me and looked at me with a look that said, *"pet me please."*

I happily obliged him. After Tim had finally managed to compose himself again, he said goodnight a second time and headed back downstairs. Midnight just laid there with me. I lay there petting him for a few minutes. Stroking his silky black fur. Feeling his body vibrate as he began to purr with contentment. Soon the sound of it provided me with a sense of warmth and comfort and it managed to lull me right to sleep.

I felt the all too familiar feeling of floating off of my bed, but I was so ready to get to tomorrow that I welcomed the transition. I arrived in the astral once again. The area was desolate and had very muted tones to it. It was a small town from what I could gather, and I could hear the sound of leaves rustling along the ground behind me. The sky was growing very dark and the air was chilling to the bone. I walked along the dirt path searching for answers. This was much like the other places I had visited, but there was something different about it this time, although I wasn't really sure what that difference was just yet. I continued walking and suddenly stopped in my tracks as the sound of hurried footsteps could be heard from behind me. Was someone following me? I turned around to see that there was no one in sight. I knew that I heard something, but maybe it was just my mind playing tricks on me. I could feel the energy creeping up on me. It was an unmistakable feeling that was all too familiar to me in my young life. Someone or something was definitely there. I called out to the silence

"Hello? Is someone there?" I asked.

No reply.

I decided to ignore the feeling, and turned back around to continue down the path.

I came to what looked like an old shopping centre. It appeared to be dishevelled, and had most definitely been abandoned for years. I started to turn the corner and continue on down the street, when I heard the sounds behind me again. Someone was definitely following me. Suddenly a fear crept over me, and before I could give it a second thought, I was running toward the abandoned shopping centre. I ran up to the door and straight through it, just like I had before when I visited my father in the dream I had a few nights back. I was beginning to become a pro at this astral business. I was definitely feeling proud of my accomplishments. That feeling of pride quickly turned to disappointment as I suddenly realized no one could ever understand any of this. They would think I was absolutely bat-shit crazy, and so it would be something that I'd have to keep to myself forever. It was to become one of my many secrets. Profound experiences I could not share. I was saddened by that thought, but I quickly snapped out of it when I began to hear the sound of voices that now seemed to be surrounding me.

"Who is she?" a voice whispered.

"I haven't the foggiest idea" said another.

"Well then why don't ya ask er ya twits?! Oh that's right the two of ya are useless...FINE... I'LL ASK ER MYSELF!!" boomed a loud voice.

The voice frightened me. The others were whispering to each other and they seemed very curious, but this voice was more demanding. He didn't want to know...he demanded to know who I was, and why I had broken into the store.

"Who the hell are ya? And why have ya intruded ere?! Are ya trying to steal from me?" he asked accusingly.

"No...n..no sir! I just got here and someone was chasing me so I ran in here to hide" I explained.

"Awww the poor thing! She looks scared Joseph...why don't ya go easier on er?!" a female voice suggested.

A Journey of a Thousand Miles – A Reflections Saga

The voice had an accent..maybe Southern? I could feel her energy nearby, but I couldn't see a thing. It was so dark in there that I couldn't even see my hand in front of my face.

"Don't ya tell me what to do Sydney!" he yelled

"She's a thief! She broke in ere to steal from us and ere ya are doting over er. Yer pathetic...the both of ya!" he exclaimed "Now, Show me this thing that chased ya."

I didn't hesitate. At his request I started walking toward the door and slowly pushed it open. Then I turned to see him appear in the doorway behind me. He was a tall, lanky looking man. His hair was oily and stringy. His face was mangled, and his skin was barely clinging to his bones. He was wearing a cowboy hat, a stained white tee shirt and blue jeans with holes in the knees, and there were what appeared to be three fresh knife wounds, right there in the center of his chest. He also had a bullet hole in the side of his head. I took a step back from him and glanced in the direction I had first come from.

"I came from this way." I said as I pointed.

He looked confused. He took off his hat and scratched his head. His hair was so thin that it looked like someone had glued pieces sporadically to his scalp

"There's nothing that way dummy! I've been ere and it's a dead end...How could ya come from a dead end?!" he asked inquisitively.

I could tell that he was nearing the point of disbelief, his tone changing. It was then that he paused for a minute or so before he finally spoke again,

"Yer nuttin but a liar!" he said accusingly.

Just then I felt even more fearful as I looked down at his waist to see that he had a gun holstered to his belt.

"If ya don't start talkin...I'm gonna shoot yer face off!" He shouted at me.

I watched as he reached for the gun and extracted it from its holster. He stared at me with a rage I had never seen before, and frankly hoped to never see in my life again. He pointed the gun in my direction and prepared to fire it. I dropped to my knees begging and pleading with him not to shoot me... and I waited to die. I waited for the moment when my life would cease to exist. When my seven year old life would be cut short by this crazed lunatic who had no qualms about shooting an innocent child in cold blood. I wondered how that would play out in the real world, but that moment never came. Just as I braced myself for the agonizing pain I was about to endure, I heard two voices shout out

"STOP!!! Are ya crazy?!" they both asked in unison.

That's when I looked up to see a short pudgy woman step into the light. She was wearing a flowered sundress and a white apron. Her hair was pulled back into a bun, although it was badly needing a redo. Half of it was hanging down on her neck. Her arms and legs were covered in what appeared to be deep knife wounds, and her chest still had the knife sticking out of it. It was a horrific sight for anyone to behold, let alone a seven year old girl. I glanced at her in horror.

"*How can they not know they're dead?*" I wondered.

"Good Christ Joseph...ya look like hell!" she said.

"Ya should go look at yerself ya cow" he shouted back at her.

This of course started an argument between the two of them. The energy they were giving off was so intense, that I began to feel light headed and I needed to sit down. They continued bickering back and forth between each other, and then things got really intense. Joseph raised the gun and pointed it at her chest.

"**BANG!!**"

the sound of the gunshot was so loud that it caused my ears to ring. I watched as the realization of what had just ensued hit Joseph hard. He dropped to his knees and cradled her head in his lap. He began to sob uncontrollably and looked at me as if to plead for my help. Then he began to shout at me.

"This is all yer fault!" he said. "If it weren't for you she'd still be alive...get the hell outta ere!"

I watched in horror as he stood up and pointed the gun in my direction again. It was then that I saw a familiar face standing behind him. It was Emily! She rushed toward me at almost super speed

"Time to go!" she said hastily. "He's going to kill you! We need to leave right now."

No sooner had she uttered the words, that there was a quick flash and everything around us appeared to be going in slow motion. Everything was moving so slow it almost appeared as if time had been frozen. The only two people who weren't frozen were her and I. She quickly grabbed me and we were quickly transported to safety. I'm not sure where we were exactly, but I do know that in that moment I felt safe. Once everything returned to normal I asked her why she was so concerned.

"We're in the Astral aren't we?" I asked and Emily nodded.

"So why were you so concerned? I can't die here can I?!" I asked.

"Yes!! Ava you seem to think this is some kind of fantasy you are in right now. Like none of this is real. I assure you this is VERY real!" she explained. "When you are in the astral your soul leaves your physical body, but is still attached to it in a way. If your brain were to ever catch onto this, you would surely die. If you are killed in the astral you will most certainly die in real life...Er...You know what I mean. Outside of this place! Your body doesn't know the difference. Death is death...this is not a dream. Do you understand what I'm telling you?" she asked.

I nodded and then shook my head even more confused.

"No not really! If it's so dangerous for people to come here, then what am I doing here in the first place?!" I asked in frustration.

A Journey of a Thousand Miles – A Reflections Saga

"You are very special Ava. In each lifetime you were born into, you made the conscious choice to return here often and assist those who may become trapped." she explained. "Although I'm not really sure what you are doing here now. You need to get back. There's so much about to happen and it's important that you are there for everything. Come on...I'll take you back home!" she suggested.

I woke up the same way I always do...as if nothing ever happened.

"What was she talking about?" I wondered.

I glanced at the clock and saw that it was one in the afternoon. My father was supposed to pick me up an hour ago! I jumped out of bed and hurried to get dressed.

"Why is he late? He's never late! Did I miss him?" I asked myself aloud.

I rushed downstairs to my mother's room, and burst in

"Where is my daddy?!" I asked "Have you heard from him? Why isn't he here?"

She looked at me for a second, but she didn't answer right away. She just sat there, staring at the floor for a few moments before looking up again to speak.

"We don't know! He should've been here to pick you up. He was supposed to call me last night to let me know if there was going to be any change in the plan, but I haven't heard from him in almost three days now." she explained. "He's probably just busy. I'm sure he will call soon. Why don't you go and pack your things so you are ready to go when he comes?" she suggested.

I knew she was trying to comfort me, but it wasn't working. I felt it deep in my soul. I felt the disconnect between my father and I. Something was very wrong. I could feel it.

I went upstairs to pack my things, trying to ignore the ominous feelings that seeped through my veins as if they were made of ice water. Maybe I was just playing into my fears. That dream hadn't helped any that's for sure. No matter what I did, I couldn't seem to shake this dreadful feeling. I called out to Emily. I needed her reassurance.

"Emily can you please come here for a minute? I need to talk to you." I shouted, but there was no response.

"What a friend she is" I thought to myself. *"Why is it that when I need her the most she isn't there for me?"*

I tried calling out to her again but there was nothing. It was just dead silence.

Chapter Nine

I decided to play with my dolls for awhile to pass the time.

"Maybe he just ran out of gas. Yeah that must be it." I told myself.

I could hear the sound of the phone ringing downstairs, followed by the sound of my mother's voice as she answered the call. From what my little ears were able to discern, she was on the phone with my uncle Larry. He was my father's twin brother. The two of them were close. She must've called him to see if he had heard from my father. By the sounds of the conversation he hadn't either, but he and his wife were planning to go over to his apartment to check on him.

"Okay, let me know if you hear anything will you? Thank you Larry." my mother said, and then I heard her hang up the phone.

I got bored with my dolls rather quickly, or maybe it's just that my mind was more focused on seeing my father and learning of his whereabouts. I'm not really sure. But I did know that now, I was worried. I decided to take my mind off of it for awhile. I wanted to colour a picture for my father. He had always loved whenever I made him things. He would often tell me that the gifts made from the heart were better than any store bought ones. They were priceless and should be cherished as such. So there I was busy colouring away, and admiring my work, when suddenly I felt a presence in my room. It was a calm and gentle presence, and I got the impression that it was almost saddened by the sight of me. At first I ignored it and continued working on my masterpiece, but then I felt it coming closer and closer to me.

"Go away!" I shouted. "I can't help you right now...I'm worried about my daddy. Please just go away and come back later."

"Oh my dear sweet Ava." the voice said in a saddened tone.

It was in that moment that I froze...with fear...with disbelief..maybe even utter shock. In any case I began to pray out loud.

"No God!!! Please no. It can't be." I cried out, as my eyes instantly welled up with more tears than I think my little seven year old body was prepared for.

They were raining down on the page now. I was crying faster than I could manage to wipe them. It was a never ending stream. I begged and pleaded with myself and with God

"Please....Please don't let it be true...why?!" I shouted.

"Ava please sweetheart....please look at me." the voice pleaded.

A Journey of a Thousand Miles – A Reflections Saga

That was when I prepared myself to face my worst fears head on, and that was the moment I looked up to see my father standing there next to my bed. He was dressed all in white and he appeared to be radiating light from within his body. It was a light like I had never seen before. Warm, bright and it had a peaceful feel to it. He appeared to be very sad as he continued to talk.

"I'm so sorry my angel girl. Daddy is so sorry. I came to say goodbye honey. Please be a good girl and take care of your mommy...she's going to need you. I need you to be strong my angel. My dear sweet baby girl...I love you so. You will always be my baby girl. I have to go now baby." he explained.

"No daddy please....please don't leave me. I need you daddy! Puhleaseee." I pleaded, in between the tears that were still streaming down my face uncontrollably.

"I'm sorry baby but I have to. Daddy never wanted to leave you...not ever! But this was always what was supposed to happen I guess. I know it's not fair, it's just the way it is sweetie. I promise you will all be okay." he told me.

He leaned over and kissed my forehead.

"Goodbye my angel...be a good girl....daddy loves you." he whispered, and then... he was gone!

I put my head down on my pillow, and began to cry harder than I think I had ever cried in all seven years of my life. I even felt physical pain. My soul had been crushed and I felt it in every way imaginable. Crying so hard had actually made me feel sick. I thought I might throw up any minute. I fell over onto my bed and curled up into the fetal position, wrapping my arms around my knees, which were now pulled up tightly to my chest. I cried so hard that I fell asleep. I wished in that moment, that my father had taken me with him. All I wanted right then was to die.

As my physical body slept, I tried desperately to find Emily in the astral. It took, what seemed like forever, but I finally managed to find her. She was sitting on a park bench just staring off into space. As she became aware of my presence, she turned toward me, her facial expression solemn.

"I'm sorry Ava." she began "I'm so sorry that I couldn't be there for you for all of that, but your father asked me not to." she explained.

"And just what do you know about MY father?!" I yelled.

"I was the one who told him how he could reach you guys! You see...he was a bit shocked when he first learned that he was no longer alive. Ava, he was absolutely devastated. I found him wandering around here in the astral, screaming for help. It was really quite sad...the pain and desperation in his eyes. I didn't have the heart to tell him at first, but then I sort of felt like maybe it was my responsibility...so I explained to him what happened and assured him that he was entitled to one last goodbye if he wanted it." she explained.

A Journey of a Thousand Miles – A Reflections Saga

"Oh gee Emily...thanks for that! You're such a great friend. I needed you and you weren't even there! You know what?! I've had just about enough of you. I never wanna see or speak to you again!! I HATE YOU!!" I screamed. "I'm going home and you had better not follow me either."

I closed my eyes, letting my anger, frustration and pain take over, and before I knew it I was back in my room.

I had been asleep for hours and yet, it felt like it had only been just a few minutes. I awakened to the sound of my mother's voice yelling at my brother, and whoever else was home at the time.

"Tell me where he is! Don't play games with me Timothy...I know he's here...I just saw him in my room. You know what?! You're grounded for lying to me. Tommy..Tommy stop fuckin around. C'mon let's go! I know you're here...you can stop hiding now. This isn't funny at all!" she yelled.

I don't think I ever ran down the stairs so fast in my life as I did when I heard my father's name being called. Was he really in the house? How had her and I seen him and no one else could? How had he come through the door without anyone noticing? The questions were endless, but then they came to a halt as I remembered my astral visit where I had gone to see him. And then it hit me... all at once. The reason no one else could see him was because he was a spirit. He had died. My loving father, the man whom I adored, the man I loved with every fibre of my being, was gone forever.

I turned on my heels quickly, and ran back upstairs to my room, throwing myself onto my bed. All I could do was sob uncontrollably, as I realized that now my life would be forever changed. The one person who loved me despite my scary gifts, the one who understood me, or at least tried to was gone, and now I truly was all alone in this world. I continued to cry and let my overwhelming emotion take me into a deep sleep. I had given up on my guides, on God and I had even given up on any chance of happiness ever again. I had just given up... on everything!

A Journey of a Thousand Miles – A Reflections Saga

Chapter Ten

I awoke to the sound of my mother's voice calling to me from downstairs.

"Ava, could you come down here for a minute? Your uncle Larry and Aunt Krissy are here. We'd all like to talk to you please." my mother shouted up the stairwell.

I could tell by her voice that it wasn't going to be a good talk. She was trying to disguise the sadness and pain in her voice, but she wasn't fooling me. I got up from my bed and prepared myself for the news. Was I prepared to hear those fateful words come out of their mouths? I wasn't sure. Walking to my bedroom door, wiping my tear stained face as best as I could, that was when I realized that I wasn't ready at all. I wasn't ready to hear anything they had to say. Maybe if the words were never spoken, this would cease to be my reality.

I know how silly that must sound, but that's just the way my desperate little mind processed things. I felt the loss, pain and sadness flow through me, like an endless river, an unforgiving one at that. I felt like I had been caught in the rapids and like I had been thrown overboard, desperately flailing about in the water and gasping for air. I was drowning in the weight of what this all would mean for me. I knew in my heart what had happened, I didn't know how it happened, but I knew my father had died, and I didn't care to hear anyone's condolences. Nothing they had to say could offer me any sort of comfort right now. There was nothing that would bring my father back. And that was all that I wanted.

I rushed down the stairs and hurried past everyone in the dining room, before bolting out of the front door. I had made up my mind, right then and there. I was going to run away. As far and fast as my little legs would carry me. But there was nowhere to run. I knew the dangers of being alone in the world as a child, and I didn't want everyone to have to deal with the worry of me turning up missing too, I was seven, but I wasn't stupid. The backyard would have to suffice. I ran into the yard and climbed the big crab apple tree. This place was my solace. This was where I always went when things got tough for me. This tree was like my second home. I may have only been seven years old, but I had already dealt with more stuff than most people deal with in a lifetime. I always felt better in this tree. It allowed me a place of solitude, and the freedom to be invisible whenever I needed to contemplate life's harsh realities. My mother had called out my name several times and tried to convince me to come inside.

"Leave me alone!" I shouted, "I don't want to talk! I'm FINE!" I yelled again.

She obliged me, and I was so thankful for that. It must've been hours that I stayed up in that tree. Reliving all seven years of my life that I could recall. Reliving the happy memories I had once shared with my father. All of those happy memories that we would never get to create again. I cried as I thought about what the future would hold. My father would never get the opportunity to watch me grow up and have children of my own. He'd never be able to walk me down the aisle when I finally met that special someone. He was going to miss out on EVERYTHING and this angered me so much. Why me? Why did I have to be the one to suffer? Why did it have to be me that was going to have to grow up without a father? What did I ever do to deserve this? Why not punish the bad kids? Had I not prayed enough to God? Did I commit a sin that I wasn't even aware of? It was in this moment of all of the questions, that I began to scream at God.

"Some god you are!" I yelled out. "Thanks for nothing! Is this how you show love and compassion for your children?! You love us so much that you like to watch us suffer? You're pathetic and I hate you. This will be the last time I ever speak to you. I'm turning my back on you now! Do you hear me up there God?" I shouted, reaching down to my neck for the crucifix necklace adorning it, and then I began to pull as hard as I could.

I pulled with all of my little might until the chain snapped with a **"CRACK!"** Yes, this was the moment I had truly given up on God. He had let me down for the last time, and now it had gotten very personal between us. I whipped the necklace out of the tree, flinging it toward the ground.

"You're a joke!!!" I screamed.

As I was climbing down from the tree, I could hear the sound of the neighbour kids playing outside in the front yard, and that's when I decided that I no longer wanted to be alone. I just wanted to be with other children. Children who didn't know my father was dead, and who wouldn't ask me a million questions about how I was doing and everything else. I was ready to be distracted by anything and everything I could be. Now I just wanted to remember that I was still a kid and do what kids did best...play!! I wanted to forget for one minute that I was now and would forever be... fatherless. I wanted to forget that I was now going to be alone in this world. Sure I was surrounded by many people, but not one of them understood me or my gifts. Everyone always viewed me as the weird child. Maybe there was a way for me to be *"normal"* now.

Maybe it had to happen this way. Maybe I wasn't meant to keep my gifts. I sure didn't have any use for them. I had always viewed them more as a negative attribute of mine than a positive one anyway. Some people called it a blessing, but it felt more like a curse to me. My mother sure wasn't convinced it was a blessing at all. It was devil's work in a lot of people eyes. Especially in our religion. I remember the term *"witchcraft"* very often being used to describe my abilities. I couldn't understand how people could be so cruel and judgmental of anyone..let alone a seven year old child. It wasn't like I ever asked for these so called *"gifts"*. I was born with them, and I really had no idea why. I sure didn't ask for any of it. But still, I had them.

Not much I could do about it now. All I knew was that my father played a vital role in my continuing to develop them. He believed I was given them for a reason. He believed that I was special, and that God blessed me this way so that I could use them to help others. Now what would be the point? There would be no one else in this world that would convince me to continue with their development. How was I going to help anyone, when I couldn't even save my own father? I didn't care about them anymore. I wanted them gone. Maybe my mother was right...maybe it was *"devil's work"*, and I was now being punished for using them. Surely that would explain why my father was taken from me. It must've been to teach me a very important lesson. God was punishing me for all of my sins.

I played there in the front yard for about thirty minutes or so with the other children. It was almost as if I wasn't even in my body. My movements became almost robotic and I was deeply lost in thoughts. Those thoughts were quickly interrupted, when I noticed the truck pulling up in our driveway. It was the truck that belonged to the father of my two sisters and brother. It meant that my sisters were returning home.

"Oh just great!" I thought to myself. So much for escaping reality for even ten minutes. They were both going to take one look at my face, and then they were going to know for sure that something was wrong.

"Well here goes nothing." I told myself, as I prepared for the fateful question to be asked.

Within seconds, Anne noticed,

"What's wrong Ava?" she asked.

"You look upset...like you have been crying a lot. Is everything okay?" asked Jane.

I took a deep breath and braced myself, trying to find the right words to use without breaking down into a puddle of tears again. The two of them looked at me with deep concern, anticipating my response.

"N...No." I mumbled trying to hold back the tears.

"Well then tell us what's wrong!" Jane insisted, probing for further details.

"My...my da....dad.. daddy...he's..he's DEAD!" I shouted and that was when my eyes betrayed me again as they let the tears flow once more.

"WHAT?!!!" my sisters both cried out together in disbelief. "What are you talking about? What do you mean he's dead?!"

"You heard me!" I cried "HE'S DEAD!!"

They didn't say anything. They just stood there in the sheer shock of it all. I couldn't even believe the words as they were coming out of my own mouth. I didn't want it to be true either, but sadly it was. It felt like a nightmare, and I was more than ready to wake up from it all now.

"Oh...Oh my God!!" my sister Anne cried out. "I....I don't even know what to say! Oh my God...I can't believe this. Ava I'm so sorry! What happened?!" she demanded.

"I don't know! Mom, Uncle Larry and Aunt Krissy are all in the house talking about it right now. Uncle Larry went to my father's apartment and they....they found him dead." I stammered.

How did I even know what they had found? I refused to speak to anyone at all, so I had never even gotten a single word of the story, but somehow I knew everything I was saying was indeed factual. I don't know how I knew...I just did.

"Well then how do you know he's dead? You could be totally wrong." they both offered.

"Maybe you just had a bad dream." Jane suggested.

"No!" I yelled "I know he's dead because I saw HIM...He came to me in my room! Mom saw him too. We BOTH saw him!!" I explained, in between frustration and the tears. The tears that had failed me and crept up on me once more.

"Let's go in the house." they suggested. "We don't know what's really going on until they tell us right? We know this is hard for you, but we will be with you okay?!" they offered in a comforting tone.

Then they both bent down, and each grabbed a hand to help me to my feet. My legs were wobbly under me, but I managed to regain my balance. Yet that moment was fleeting. I was so overcome with grief that it was difficult for me to stand, and it was obvious as I soon as I started to take a few steps. I nearly fell down the stairs to the front porch. That was when my sister Jane told me she was going to give me a piggy back ride. I loved piggy back rides from her, but at this moment I was left unaffected. I was far too worried about the conversation that was going to take place once we entered that house. Nothing in this world could prepare me for the nightmare of reality I was about to collide head on with. A conversation I will remember for the rest of my life. As we got up onto the porch and my sister Anne reached for the door, I begged her for a moment. Just one moment for me to pull myself together.

Chapter Eleven

That brief moment I was afforded, seemed to pass by very quickly. It was a moment I wanted to last forever. Just a moment....a forever kind of moment. That was all I needed. Please just let me stand in this one moment on the porch forever. A moment that allowed for me to still have my father, but of course I knew that was never going to happen. It was time to find out what had happened to him, once and for all.

My sister Anne reached for the door again. Jane placed me back onto the ground and was now ushering me inside. I think she stood there more or less to stop me from turning and bolting for the door. She knew me too well when it came to difficult or stressful situations. I felt everyone all at once, It was a lot of energy to take on and running seemed like the best way to get away from it all, but this time I couldn't run. I had to face it all. As we walked inside I could hear the sounds of my mother wailing in the living room. She was on the floor next to my aunt Krissy. Aunt Krissy was consoling her now, running her fingers through her hair. It was as if the shock of it all had finally worn off, and my mother was brought to her knees in the overwhelming emotional pain I was certain she was feeling in this moment. Her energy was radiating toward me. I felt like I had just gotten slammed into by a truck. A truck that was carrying every possible emotion that comes with grieving the loss of a loved one. It hit me all at once. I wasn't just feeling her grief and sadness. I was feeling the sadness of everyone around me. My uncle was saddened too, but he seemed more collected than everyone else. My mother hadn't even noticed us enter the house, and when she finally looked up, she stifled her wailing to a sob...trying to catch her breath, she motioned for me to come to her. I rushed to her side and as soon as she touched me we both began to cry uncontrollably.

"I'm so sorry Ava....I'm so sorry." she cried as she pulled me close to her and began to cry hysterically.

"What's going on? What happened to Tommy?" my sister Jane demanded.

No one said a word at first. My aunt motioned for my sisters to come sit down beside her on the loveseat. As they did she began to tell the story. I guess maybe she forgot that I was there, or maybe she thought I was mature enough to hear it. Did I even want to hear this?! I didn't have much of a choice because just as I was thinking that I didn't want to know, she began to tell us what she and my uncle had found.

"As you know....we couldn't reach him for the last few days....Nobody had seen or heard from him and so your mother asked us to go check on him to make sure everything was alright...B...But when we got there his door was unlocked and his apartment was trashed. The aquarium had been smashed and there was water everywhere!" she explained. "The bathroom door was open a crack and I could see that the light was on in there." she continued. "So we opened the door and we could see that he was lying there naked on the floor. It looked like he had just stepped out of the bathtub because the tub was still full of water and it was ice cold. I think he must've slipped and fell by the way he was laid out. He was all bruised up from falling. He was face down and his hands were out in front of him. It appeared to us based on his position, that maybe he had slipped or something and tried to break his fall. We had to really push the door to get into the bathroom because his body was blocking it." she continued as she began to cry. "I'm so sorry Ava." she apologized with tears streaming down her cheeks now.

You could tell she was having flashbacks of what she had just witnessed, because she had a blank stare in her eyes.

"Victoria, we need you to come with us...we have to go to his apartment to clean up. Don't worry his body is gone." she explained. "We called the police and they called in the medical examiner to come and get him. He's going to have an autopsy performed over the next day or so, to determine his cause of death." she explained. "They're expecting us. Come on, let Larry and I help you to the car." she said.

"Okay, but I need to call the girls an... and everyone and tell them wha..what's going on." my mother stammered.

A Journey of a Thousand Miles – A Reflections Saga

"We've already called everyone. Vic. It's all taken care of." my aunt assured her. "Let's go and do what we have to do and get this over with." she suggested.

Both she and my uncle helped my mother up to her feet. It took a bit of effort as my mother was in such a state of shock, that her legs seemed to buckle from under her as she wobbled to stand. I watched with tear stained eyes as they ushered her toward the door. She appeared as I would imagine someone on death row might appear as they were being led to their death. She definitely was dreading every second of that walk. My mind started going about a thousand miles a minute. The only person who ever truly understood and accepted my *"gifts"* had now been ripped away from existence. What was I going to do now?! Why was God punishing me? What had I done to deserve such cruelty?

"Screw God!" I thought. "There's no way this loving, caring and compassionate God I was taught about would ever allow such horrible things to happen to me!"

I was screaming so loud in my head that I thought at some point the sound would break free. I scrambled to my feet and ran as fast as I could upstairs. My room seemed very cold and distant from my current reality. It seemed that all four walls were closing in on me. My whole world was closing in on me, and it didn't seem to be letting up. I threw myself down onto my bed and began wailing uncontrollably into my pillow.

"This is it!" I thought to myself.

"This is the last day your life will ever matter."

I don't even remember closing my eyes, but I must've at some point because I was awakened by the sound of someone in the hallway. I slowly sat up, rubbing my eyes while trying to adjust them to the now pitch black curtain that surrounded me. It seemed that the day had quickly turned to night. I heard my bedroom door creak open slowly and I rushed to shield my eyes from the blinding light that filtered in from the hallway.

"Ava? Are you okay?!" my sister Jane asked concerned.

"Okay?! Okayyyy?!" I shouted "Would you be okay if your father was taken from you? Yeah I didn't think so! Just leave me ALONE!!" I yelled "I'm FINE!!"

Apparently she wasn't going to honour my wishes, because just as I had finished screaming those final words, she crept across the room in a gentle yet cautious manner. She sat down on the bed beside me and pulled me into her chest.

"I know it hurts." she said "But I promise everything is going to be okay. You'll see. You know he will always be here. Even if you can't see him he will always be watching over you. You will always be his little girl."

She stated those words as if she knew them to be factual. I didn't know exactly what it was in those words, but they seemed to give me and odd sense of comfort. I sobbed into her chest until I cried every tear I could possibly shed. Then I laid down on the bed once more, and asked if she would lay beside me for awhile. She obliged without hesitation and I drifted off again.

It seemed like I'd only been out for a few minutes, but realistically it had been hours. I awoke to the sunlight beaming in through my window, and tried to muster the physical and emotional strength it was going to take me just to get out of bed. I was completely exhausted from all that I had endured the day before. It's amazing how much grief can take out of someone. It's downright crippling. I glanced over at the clock to see the numbers 12:00 pm, and suddenly shot up out of bed like a jack in the box. I had slept for fourteen straight hours, and yet I still felt like I hadn't slept a wink. I rushed over to my dresser and started rummaging through my drawers, tossing clothes about the room, frantically searching for my necklace that I had ripped off my neck the previous day. Where had I put it?! I sat down on my bed and tried to trace back to that moment after I had flung it out of the tree in my backyard.

"Did I pick it up?" I wondered. I really wasn't sure at this point, but I knew if my mother saw that it was missing from my neck, she wasn't going to be too pleased with me. I had to find it! I dressed quickly, rushed down the stairs and headed straight for the back door. I could hear my mother calling out to me from the kitchen

"Ava....where are you going?" she asked.

"Just outside to play mom." I shouted behind me. "I just need some air."

With that I bolted out through the back door and hurried down the steps. I ran over to the crab apple tree and began pushing the grass aside with my feet. It was a 24K gold chain. Surely it wouldn't be too difficult to locate against the green palette that lay surrounding me. I must've been out there for more than an hour trying to find that damn thing. I was getting ready to give up, when I finally saw the gold shimmer of the chain, just a few feet away from where I had been standing. I walked over to it and picked it up with caution, as if the metal was going to burn into my flesh. As I held it, I began to have flashbacks of the last time I had held it in my hand. The things I had said in sheer anger and disgust with God, for allowing such an unspeakable tragedy to enter my life. I wondered if he was even listening in that moment. Frankly I didn't care either way. I meant every word. I had given up on God....On faith....On everything! This was it for me. Anger took over me again in that moment and I began to lash out at God once more. Only this time it was done completely under my breath.

"I hope you're happy!" I thought to myself.

"I don't know what you are punishing me for and I don't care anymore. If you wanna strike me dead then so be it! At least I know I'll see my daddy again! I truly hate you with every part of my being. I don't even know why I'm bothering to talk to you. It's not like you are listening or even exist. You're a joke!"

I could feel my face growing hotter and hotter with every thought. I flopped down into the grass and stared at the cross that seemed to glare back at me from my palm. It was as if I was being mocked by it. I couldn't stand holding onto it any longer. I stood up and shoved it into my sock. I managed to do it just in time too, because just then I heard the screen door open behind me.

"Ava what are you doing out here?" my mother asked.

"Nothing mom. I told you I just wanted some air. I'm coming in now." I assured her.

"Good!" she muttered. "Lunch is ready."

I walked back to the porch and climbed the stairs to go inside. As I opened the door, the smell of grilled cheese and french fries filled my nostrils. I didn't have much of an appetite, but I wasn't up for listening to the lecture that was sure to follow had I rejected the meal. I entered the bathroom to clean up for lunch and turned on the faucet. I leaned down over the sink to rinse my face with water, hoping to cool the fire I could feel still seeping through my pores. When I looked up at the mirror I was startled by a familiar face behind me. I was completely caught off-guard, which caused me to jump back and let out a quick scream.

"What's going on in there? Is everything okay?" my mother called after me.

"Yes mom! Everything is fine. I just....uh....I saw a spider." I responded hastily.

"Well hurry up and wash up." she urged. "Lunch is getting cold."

"Coming!" I announced. "I'll be there in a minute" I quickly closed the door and looked back at the mirror, but all I saw was my own reflection staring back at me.

"Huh, I wonder where she went." I thought to myself.

Just then I felt a quick tap on my shoulder. It was a gentle tap, but still startling enough to make anyone want to jump out of their skin. I spun around to see her standing there.

"What do you want Emily?!" I snapped. "I thought I told you to leave me alone."

For a minute or so Emily didn't say a whole lot of anything. She just looked at me with deep concern and sadness in her eyes.

"I'm really sorry Ava. I wanted to tell you a long time ago, I wanted to warn you that it was coming very soon, like sooner than you thought, but would you have even believed me?" she asked with sadness in her voice.

"I don't care! You were supposed to be my friend." I shouted.

Just then I overheard my mother's voice again.

"Who are you talking to?!" she called from the kitchen.

"No one mom. I didn't say anything."

I glared at Emily one last time before turning to bolt through the doorway.

Lunch took much longer than it should've, as I found myself struggling to get each bite down. Even after all of the time it had taken me, I had only managed to eat half of the sandwich. My mother sat across the table from me and scribbled something down on a notepad in front of her. I watched her curiously and determined that she was making a list of food items she needed to purchase for my father's funeral the next day. The mere thought of that made me shiver. As if a sudden gust of wind had blown into the room. I felt my hair move ever so slightly against whatever had caused the breeze. It was then that I glanced up to see the image of my father standing directly behind my mother. I was frozen in that moment as I stared at him in awe. I felt the tears begin to well up in my eyes, as he waved to me from behind her shoulder. I knew in that moment that she must've felt his energy, because she suddenly shifted in her chair and turned to look behind her.

"Who are you looking at?!" she asked inquisitively.

"No one!" I replied "I was just daydreaming again. I'm not really hungry mom." I stated. "Can I eat this later?"

She nodded her approval and I got up from my chair to walk toward the kitchen, directly where my father was still standing. I walked toward him carefully. I wasn't sure what it was going to feel like to walk through him. As I moved toward him, he held out his arms as if he was motioning for a hug. Only when I got close enough he vanished. I felt my heart sink deep into the pit of my stomach, as I continued toward the kitchen, placing the barely touched remnants of my lunch into the microwave and headed for the stairway leading to the upstairs.

Once in my room I bent down to retrieve the necklace from my sock and placed it on my nightstand. I walked over to my dresser and removed some of my craft items from one of the bottom drawers and sat down scattering them on the floor in front of me. I knew the day I was dreading was drawing nearer and I wanted to make sure I would be prepared for it. I pulled a sheet of construction paper from its pad and a few sheets of blank paper from the packaging. I always enjoyed making crafts, and there was always something that could spark my creativity. It didn't take much these days. I lay on the floor and began to draw a picture of my father and I. I drew a bright sunny day with the two of us down by our usual spot at the river, fishing. It was one of my fondest memories and I was sure it was one of his as well. I proceeded to glue the drawing to the inside of the folded sheet of construction paper. I then took another sheet of blank paper and proceeded to write him a letter to take with him to heaven.

The letter read: *"Daddy I love you so much. I'm so sad that God took you away from me. My heart is broken and I don't know if it will ever be whole again without you. How am I supposed to live now? Why did you have to go? You're going to miss everything now! Why couldn't you just say NO??? God is a jerk and I will never forgive him for this. Please don't forget me daddy! Please come see me whenever you can. I love you.*

Love your baby girl Ava xoxo."

Tears began to stream down my face, as the harsh reality began to set in. The reality that I was now and from this point forward, fatherless. The tears fell softly on the page, smearing the ink where they landed.

"Goddamn it!" I shouted "Now I have to start all over again."

A Journey of a Thousand Miles – A Reflections Saga

I was beyond frustrated. I had put my heart into every word and printed as neatly as I could. I had been so careful not to smudge the ink with the side of my hand. A struggle we lefties deal with everyday. I had taken so much care in getting every letter just right. I had even changed up the colours of each letter. Red, blue and then purple. Now as the ink ran along the paper it looked sloppy. I ran downstairs to grab a tissue to blot the tears, hoping my doing so wouldn't make it worse. When I returned, I noticed that the tears had created almost a perfect heart shape directly in the middle of the page. I decided to blot it very carefully so as not to disturb the image my broken heart had created. I decided to leave it that way to dry. The words were a bit smeared but still legible. I wondered if he would think it was a nice touch. My father had always cherished my personal touches on my artwork, so I was fairly certain this would be no different. I remember he would always tell me that they were always his favourite to receive, and he had kept many of my creations in a box we had made special together, just to hold them. I remember the fun we had creating it that day too. It was an old shoe box that we had painted blue with a golden shimmer. We even glued a picture of him and I on the very top. On the very front he had written

"From my heart to yours" with one of those silver metallic pens.

He had put so much care and thought into creating it, that I knew how much he would treasure its contents. I decided I would go down into the basement to look for it later. First though I needed to finish my project. I set the letter aside to dry and pulled one of my colouring books and box of crayons from beneath my bed. I searched carefully through the book for the perfect picture. I decided on a picture of a landscape that depicted flowers, butterflies and a rainbow on a bright sunny day. I sprawled across the floor on my stomach and proceeded to colour the page. When I was finished I examined my masterpiece and grabbed a pencil to sign my name in the bottom right corner. My father had always told me how important it was for an artist to sign their work. Was that what he thought of me? An artist? After writing my name in what looked like a fancy style of printing, I reached for my glue and began to trace over the letters. After I had finished, I took some of my silver glitter, sprinkled it over the glue and shook the excess off into the garbage. I held it back once again and admired my creation. It was perfect! Just then I heard my mother calling me from the bottom of the stairs

"Ava...are you up there?" she asked.

 "Yes mom." I responded.

"What have you been doing up there all this time?" she inquired.

"I'm just making a goodbye card for daddy." I responded.

 "Oh okay. I'm going out to the store with aunt Krissy...I'll be back soon. Your sisters are here if you need anything." she told me.

 "Okay mom. Love you!" I called out.

A Journey of a Thousand Miles – A Reflections Saga

I reached for the letter and examined it to make sure it had dried thoroughly. I then took my scissors and began to cut around the outer edges, making a fancy border as I went along. I glued it down to the inside of the card on the opposite side of the drawing, and folded the construction paper closed again. Now I needed to draw an image on the front. I decided to draw a golden cross and two doves on either side at the top. Then I wrote the words *"I'll miss you daddy"* along the bottom of the page. My card was now complete. I had even taken the time to make an envelope for it to keep its contents private, and then when I was finished, I tucked the coloured page inside the card before placing it in the envelope and taping it shut. I didn't want anyone to see or read it. This was a private goodbye from me to him. It was for his eyes only. I went over to my dresser again, but this time it was to get my clothes out for the following day, and to gather my PJ's to take downstairs for my bath later on that evening. I heard clattering noises coming from the kitchen and then the sound of my older sister Jane calling up the stairs.

"Supper is almost ready. Why don't you come down and wash up?" she suggested.

"Okay." I called back "I'm coming!"

I made my way down to the dining room and sat in my usual spot at the table. By now I was starving and ready to eat. Jane placed a saucer in front of me with two hot dogs cut up with ketchup on the side. The only way I liked to eat them. Then she placed a small bowl of Kraft Dinner directly beside it. She had drawn a smiley face with ketchup on top of the noodles. She proceeded to pour me a glass of cherry Kool-Aid and handed it to me.

"I hope you're hungry!" she announced. "Because I made lots!"

Anne came and joined us at the table. We sat there, the three of us and ate our food in silence. My mother had yet to return, and my sister Anne kept glancing at the clock, as they had expected her back hours ago. She didn't let it show on her face, but I could tell she was starting to grow concerned. The phone suddenly rang, as if it were reading her mind. It was my mother calling to let us know she and my aunt were on their way back, and that she would be needing our help to bring in all the bags when they arrived. We quickly finished up our meal and headed outside to meet her.

We must've carried twenty shopping bags inside. It appeared she had bought a bunch of snacks, side dishes and food trays for the wake we would be having after the funeral. Seeing all of it made it really sink in. This was going to be the second worst day of my life, and I was dreading every minute of it. This would be the end for me. The last time I would ever see my father again. I tried to hold back the tears long enough for me to be alone, but they seemed to come all on their own. I had absolutely no control over them, and I kept wiping my eyes with the sleeve of my shirt every opportunity I had to do so. No one seemed to notice. They were all too busy rushing to put everything away. My mother grabbed the folded up list she had written earlier that day, and began to mentally check off the items one by one. I watched as she mouthed the words before stopping suddenly.

"Shit!" she yelled out. "I forgot the damn eggs. How am I going to make devilled eggs without the Goddamn eggs?!" she asked frustrated.

Only it wasn't really a question proposed to any of us. More like talking out loud to herself.

"We can ask Aunt Krissy to go back." my sisters suggested in sync with one another.

"No.....yeah...yeah okay then. That's what we're gonna have to do." my mother announced.

With that she picked up the phone and dialed my aunt's number. Luckily my aunt hadn't gotten too settled in just yet, and suggested she stop at the store near our house to buy some.

"Thank you Krissy. I'm sorry. I've just got so much on my mind right now." my mother apologized. "Okay, I appreciate it. See you soon."

After hanging up the phone she glanced at the clock and then in my direction.

"I think it's about time you go and take your bath young lady." she said "It's getting late and tomorrow is going to be a long day."

Boy was she right! Nothing could have prepared me for what was in store for all of us that day. We arrived at the funeral home about an hour ahead of the scheduled start time. It was customary that the family arrived earlier than everyone else. Something about giving us privacy to mourn the loss of our loved one in peace. When we walked into the funeral parlour my aunts, uncles, cousins and sisters were there to meet us. My aunt Krissy was the first to rush over to us and greet us with warm hugs and kisses. I never understood the need for this, especially when she had just seen us yesterday. What changed from then to now? In any case I was happy to see her. I knew with me being the youngest in attendance, she would be sure to keep me close by her side. I watched as some of my relatives walked out of the adjoining room with pure sadness and tears streaming down their faces. They took one look at me, and immediately rushed over to me to shower me with kisses and condolences. The energy that filled the room at that moment was overwhelming for me. I was already trying to compose myself for what I knew I was about to see in that next room, and the energy I was picking up now was almost suffocating to say the least. I think my mother sensed it, because it wasn't too long after, that she pulled me from the crowd that had gathered around me. Taking me off to the side, she knelt down in front of me and asked

"Are you ready to go see him now sweetie?"

That question stung more than any pain I thought I had ever experienced up to that point.

"Ready?! I'm never going to be READY!" I thought to myself, but I knew I had to go in sooner or later.

I looked at her and swallowed hard as I nodded in agreement. She turned to look at my aunt who seemed to read her mind, as she walked over to us and they each took me by the hand and led me toward the entrance of that dreadful room. I walked slowly as I could hear the sounds of wailing coming from just around the corner. I stopped and tried to gather the courage to take even one more step, as I felt my knees growing weaker by the second. I felt as though I was about to vomit and stopped again, taking a few slow and deep breaths. My legs had turned to jello. My aunt must have been reading my mind because suddenly, she bent down and picked me up to carry me. I put my head down and nuzzled my face into her shoulder, shielding my eyes from everyone. I felt her walk about twenty steps, and then she stopped. I knew that we were there, and I knew that once I lifted my head I was going to see my father lying in that coffin. Well his body anyway. I knew that whenever someone died that it was just their body that remained. There was no life force there any more. It was just an empty shell. That person that once inhabited in that body, was long gone. I was always afraid of the dead. Funerals freaked me out and I never wanted to go anywhere near the coffins. Now I knew I had no choice. This time it was different. This wasn't just anyone lying there. This was my father! I took a few deep breaths and lifted my head, keeping my eyes closed tightly.

"It's okay Ava. Don't be afraid. It's going to be okay." my aunt spoke softly. You don't have to open your eyes right away. Take your time sweetie." she suggested.

I would've taken a lifetime if I could've, but I knew I didn't have that long. I couldn't let them take my daddy away and put him in the ground without me being able to say at least one final goodbye to him. I opened my eyes slowly and then shut them tight again. We were standing almost directly in front of the coffin. I avoided looking at it at all costs, and instead looked down to my left. Someone was kneeling in front of it with his hands folded in prayer. A rosary dangling around them. He was the spitting image of my father. At that time I was in such a state of disbelief by what was happening, that I almost mistook him for my father.

"Daddy's not dead! It was just a joke! A bad dream." I said, trying to convince myself.

My wishful thinking was interrupted, when the man who looked like my father turned to me and said

"Come here sweetheart. Come and see Uncle Larry."

He turned just enough to give me a direct view into the coffin. That was the moment I felt my whole world come crashing down around me. Suddenly all the sounds around us faded out, and the walls began to close in on me. It wasn't a joke or a bad dream. This **WAS** my reality! Tears filled my eyes as my uncle reached for me and scooped me up into his arms. I felt him hug me tightly as he kissed me on my forehead, and started swaying back and forth with me. Much like someone would to soothe a crying infant. He knelt down again with me in his arms, and leaned me closer to the coffin so I could touch my father's hand. If it had been anyone else in that coffin, I never would've touched that body, but this was my father and I knew this would be my last opportunity to ever see or touch him again. I remember it like it was yesterday. His hand was cold and his body felt as stiff as a board. It almost didn't feel real, and yet reality was right there staring me in the face. It was time to face the music. I looked at my mother and asked her to pull the envelope from her purse. I lifted my father's hands which were wrapped with a rosary and tucked it beneath them. I leaned over to kiss him on his forehead, and then I whispered

"Goodbye daddy. I'll miss you. I love you so much! I'll be okay now daddy, just please come and see me soon."

Just then I heard some commotion coming from behind us, I turned to see my three sisters Grace, Marie and Kim. They rushed up to me, paying no attention to the coffin at first, and then began to smother me with hugs and kisses. We all shared a moment and cried, and then my uncle Larry set me down on the ground and backed away to give all of us some time alone with our father. It wasn't long after he stepped away, that my sister Grace began to freak out. She became very upset and began to shout

"This is not my dad! He doesn't even look like him...what did you people do to him?!" she demanded. "Look at his hair! This isn't how he combs his hair. This is all wrong!" she suggested "Don't worry dad. We will make you look the way you always do." she said.

That was when she motioned for someone to give her a comb, and she proceeded to comb my father's hair. Parting it off to the left in the exact way he always did. She stepped back to look at him and seemed satisfied that now he looked like himself again. She leaned over the coffin and kissed him on the cheek. It was an emotional moment for everyone that was there to witness the four of us crying, refusing to let our father go. I vaguely remember one of my sisters trying to jump on the coffin as it was closed and being prepared to be carried out to the hearse. Although I can't quite remember who it was now. I just remember one of them jumping up on it and saying

"No you can't take him! I'm not ready for him to leave us."

Just then, her boyfriend stepped up. He had to grab her and pull her away.

Chapter Twelve

The ride to the cemetery seemed like the longest ride of my life. The four of us were there in the car directly behind the hearse. It was always quite strange to me how it rained that day as we were on our way there, and then stopped almost as soon as we arrived. It was almost as if our pain was made manifest through the sky. The funeral procession was extremely long. I remember we turned off onto the highway and I glanced behind us, noticing that the line of cars that followed went as far as my little eyes could see. It was a beautiful service. We buried him in Heavenly Rest Cemetery near Highway 3. As the service was coming to a close, I sensed him nearby. I looked up and off a ways into the distance. That's when I caught a glimpse of him standing there among the trees, once again dressed all in white. He looked like an angel. To this day I'll never forget that moment for as long as I live. Little did I know it wouldn't be long before I would find myself back there again. Much sooner than I could imagine.

After the funeral we went to the wake. I remember carrying food trays inside the hall where it was being held. I had never seen so many people gathered in one place before, but I was touched by how many had come to say their final goodbyes to my father and to celebrate his life.

When we returned home that evening, I was completely exhausted. I'm not even sure how I managed to get inside. All I know is that someone must've carried me, because I awoke the next morning in my bed. I was still wearing my dress from the funeral, and my cross was still hanging around my neck. Luckily for me, my mother hadn't noticed I had broken it. I managed to hold it together by wrapping the clasp with some scotch tape. I knew I had to wear it that day, because someone would surely have noticed. Thank God they didn't.

I sat up in bed and pulled it from my neck again. That was the very last time it would ever be worn by me. I tucked it into the drawer of my nightstand, and crept downstairs for something to drink and snack on. I hadn't eaten much the day before, as one might imagine. I had no interest in food. Now however, I was absolutely famished. I set my snack on the counter, then headed into the bathroom to wash the remnants of my tears off of my cheeks. I could feel the stickiness of them there. Some of my hair had matted against one side of my cheek. I had half expected to see Emily behind me in the bathroom mirror when I looked up again, but she never appeared. I was somewhat grateful for that. I never wanted to see or speak to her again. But still, a part of me was wishing she would show up to at least comfort me.

I grabbed my snack from the kitchen and headed back upstairs to my room. I just wanted to be left alone. The isolation from everyone was oddly comforting. I wasn't sure how many more condolences I could be offered before I lost my young and fragile mind. How many reminders can one little girl handle? I stayed up in my room the entire day that day, only coming out when absolutely necessary. My sisters had brought plates of food up for me and left them outside my door. I was grateful that no one tried to force me out of my sanctuary, and I wasn't sure how long it would be before I was going to feel ready to come out again. I planned to stay there forever or at least until my bladder left me with no other choice.

A few more days passed before I had finally mustered up enough courage to creep out of my room and downstairs among the living again. I had spent the majority of my time shut in there colouring, watching some of my favourite movies and listening to music. I also spent a great deal of time reminiscing. I was dealing with the grief of losing my father in my own way. But now, it was time to face the world once more. After all, as much as I may have wanted to, I couldn't stay in there forever. I slowly crept toward my bedroom door and pressed my ear up against it to listen for anyone who might be downstairs. I may have been ready to come out of hiding, but I still wasn't quite ready to talk to anyone. I could hear the sound of the television on in the living room and wondered if I was quiet enough, whether or not I could manage to sneak downstairs to the basement without anyone ever noticing. I wanted to find that box my father and I had made together to store all of the gifts I had created for him over the years. I wanted that box to be mine now. It held a lot of memories and many pieces of my heart. I guess in a weird way, I thought that if I could collect enough of the pieces of it that maybe, just maybe I could find a way to make it whole again. I was willing to try anything to take even a single ounce of this pain away. The weight of it all felt like it might crush my young soul at any given moment. Who was I kidding? As far as I was concerned my soul was buried that day with my father, and I would never be the same again. Now, I just wanted to get downstairs without being seen. That was all that I cared about. I reached for the door and slowly pulled it open, being careful not to let it squeak. I stood quietly in the hallway and listened intently again. The television was still on, and I could hear the sound of the channels being flipped through. I decided to wait a few more minutes for whoever was watching it to locate a channel of interest. A few minutes passed and I listened once more. I could hear the theme song for The Simpson's just beginning to play. I knew just by that sound alone that it had to be my brother Tim. It was one of our favourite shows to watch together. I really missed sitting and watching it with him. It had been quite awhile since we last shared a brother and sister moment. I decided that once I located the box, I might venture into the living room to sit with him for awhile.

Tim was never one for prying too much. He understood that sometimes people had a strong desire to just be left alone, and I was sure this would definitely be a moment we could just sit in silence together and share a few laughs.

"Lord knows I could use quite a few of those right about now!" I thought to myself, as I slowly tiptoed my way down the steps, but it didn't matter how quiet I tried to be, the house we lived in was old and of course had to have wooden staircases. They would always creak beneath your feet. Not very forgiving for someone trying to move around in silence. Still, I tried to walk even lighter to avoid being noticed. As I reached the landing, I peered around the corner to see that it was indeed my brother who had been watching television. He had been alerted to my presence as soon as I had stepped down too, because of course my big fat cat had to be laying right at the foot of the stairs. He let out a loud screech when I stepped down onto his back paw, startling Tim. I quickly bent down to examine his injury.

"Oh Midnight I'm so sorry buddy! I didn't see you there." I told him.

He looked at me with the look of minor annoyance and then proceeded to lick his paw.

A Journey of a Thousand Miles – A Reflections Saga

"Hey! How ya feeling?" Tim asked.

"I'm okay. I just need to get something from the basement." I announced.

"Okay. Why don't you come up after that and watch some TV with me?" he suggested.

"Yeah okay. That sounds good. I'll be right back then." I answered, making my way toward the basement stairs.

I slowly opened the door and peered down the steep stairwell into the pitch blackness. I absolutely dreaded going down there. The things I had encountered in that basement had terrified me so much, that I usually had to ask someone to wait at the top of the stairs so I could run down and grab whatever I needed to and then race back up as fast as I could. My brother and sisters had teased me about it every single time

"Oh no...the Boogeyman is gonna get you...watch out!" they taunted in my head.

It was cruel, and yet they truly had no idea what I had seen in the basement to put that kind of fear in my heart. I still remember what happened that had scared me out of my wits too. The images are forever burned into my memory. My mother had been doing laundry that day. I was typically the one who would help her with the household duties whenever I had the opportunity. I loved helping everyone as much as I possibly could. Dishes, laundry, making beds, folding clothes, setting the table etc. Any help I could offer, made me one very happy girl. As I was saying, on this one particular day my mother and I had been doing quite a bit of cleaning. We had just finished washing all of mine and my sisters' bedding. We were upstairs in my mother and father's bedroom, and I was helping her make the bed. Suddenly, we heard the sound of the dryer buzzer going off to let us know that the load had finished the cycle. My mother was in the process of putting the pillow cases on the pillows, and asked me to go down and switch out the loads. I had never had an issue before, so I of course agreed. I grabbed the basket we had just carried all of the bedding upstairs in, and headed downstairs. At first nothing seemed out of the ordinary except for the prickles that crept up on my arms and neck while I made my way toward the washing machine. I could hear the sound of my mother humming from the room directly above me. The sound was travelling through the vent that was situated directly above my head. I'm not quite sure why, but that sound always seemed to comfort me. It was always my favourite thing when she would lay my head in her lap and run her fingers through my hair while humming a tune. I could fall asleep that way every time. I was smiling and listening to her carry on while I began grabbing the clothes from the dryer and placing them into the basket beside me. When I had finished emptying the dryer, it was time to retrieve the clothes from the washing machine and transfer them over to the dryer. As I was leaning over into the machine, I could swear that I heard footsteps behind me. I assumed that it was just the sound of my mother walking on the floor above me, so I continued grabbing the wet clothing out and tossing them into the dryer. I was about halfway through the task, when I heard the sound of footsteps again. This time I determined that they definitely couldn't be my mother's because they were coming from directly behind me!! As they grew louder, I began to feel panicked. My heart started racing, my palms became sweaty and I began to tremble. I recognized this feeling immediately. It was a feeling I knew all too well. There I was alone in the basement with whatever was now just a few feet behind me. I started frantically pulling the clothes out from the washer and throwing them as fast as I could into the dryer. That's when I heard a sound I will never forget. It was an eerie hissing sound. It almost sounded like someone with emphysema. The breathing was very laboured and it was now right up against my ear. I could feel the air brush across my skin, causing every hair on my body to stand on end. I tried to move but I couldn't. I was frozen in fear. Then it spoke to me through shallow breaths.

"Ava..Ayvaaaa. Help...help me...I can't breatheeee." it pleaded.

I tried to scream but no sound came out. That's when it grabbed my shoulder and spun me around. There standing face to face with me was a young woman. She was clearly dead, as her eyes were sunken into her head. Her flesh was grey and shrivelled. It appeared to be rotting from the inside out. The stench of her was enough to make me gag. She looked at me and reached for her neck. That's when I noticed she had a rope tied around it. Just then I could hear a blood curdling scream pierce the air and it was then that I realized it was my own. I no longer cared about the task I was sent to perform. All I cared about was getting the hell out of there! I think I must've magically flew to the stairs, because I don't to this day remember how I made it to there so fast. I darted up the stairs so quickly I was skipping steps as I ran. My mother was already halfway down them after hearing the scream I had just let out. I nearly ran right into her. I think I might have even been able to run straight through her that day. If given the opportunity. I had never moved that fast in all of my life. She looked at me with deep concern.

"What the hell happened?! Why were you screaming like that for?" she asked frantically.

I couldn't speak at all. I just rushed my head into her chest, squeezed her as tight as I could and began to wail so much that I was struggling to catch my breath. What I was feeling in that moment was sheer terror, and I knew this wasn't going to be the last time either. My mother held me tight and told me everything was going to be okay. Was it? Somehow I highly doubted that. She was my mother and she was supposed to protect me, but how would she ever be able to protect me from things like this? The mere thought of her helplessness made me cry even harder. After I had calmed down and finally managed to catch my breath, she asked me to tell her what had happened in the basement. How was I supposed to tell her? What exactly could I say? Everyone already thought I was crazy enough as it was. I knew she would never believe me. Would you? After her trying to finally pry it out of me for a good hour, I finally gave in and told her everything. I'm pretty sure she didn't believe me at that point because her face said it all. She gave me one of those blank stares. Much like people do when they slip off into their own little world. Or maybe it was the look of being utterly shocked. Maybe it was a combination of both. In any case she never made me go anywhere in that house alone again. If I had to go upstairs for

A Journey of a Thousand Miles – A Reflections Saga

something, someone had to be waiting at the landing. If I had to go into the basement for anything, someone had to come halfway down the steps and watch me. It became my everyday routine from that point on.

Now here I stood at the top of the basement steps. Peering down into the darkness. Trying to determine if anyone was waiting for me down there. I stepped slowly onto the first step and switched on the light. The faint sound of buzzing emanated from the fixture as it struggled to come to life once again. I wasn't sure why that was exactly. My father had replaced it twice since we had moved in. He had even put brand new bulbs in it, and yet it always remained dimly lit despite his best efforts. I gently stepped down onto the second step. Suddenly an eerie sensation came over me. It was very similar to the one I had felt that day I had encountered the woman with the rope around her neck. I wasn't sure why I was feeling it again. Was it because she would be waiting for me down there? Was it just my fear taking over because of the traumatic experience I had the last time I went down there alone? I wasn't sure, but I definitely wasn't willing to find out either way. I darted back up the two steps and slammed the basement door shut behind me. My brother looked at me oddly just then, but he didn't say a word. I think he always knew I had been telling the truth the whole time. I walked into the kitchen to grab myself a snack.

"Did you want anything Tim?" I asked.

"No thanks." he called back.

I leaned over to peek into the refrigerator, and grabbed a kiwi fruit from the bottom drawer. I grabbed a knife and spoon from the silverware drawer and sliced the Kiwi in half. I reached into the cabinet and pulled a bowl down from the middle shelf and placed the fruit inside. Then I poured myself a glass of juice and headed into the living room and sat down next to him. He looked over at me briefly, and then glanced back at the television again. I decided I would ask my mother for the box whenever she returned from wherever she had gone. I sat back on the couch and dug the spoon into the center of the fruit.

"What are we watching?" I inquired.

"Pet Semetary!" he announced.

I always enjoyed watching horror movies, but this one I had yet to see. My mother didn't care for them at all and she also didn't like me watching them either. She felt they had something to do with all the *"nightmares"* I would have. Little did she know that horror movies or not, I was living a nightmare out every day. The movie actually wasn't scary at all. That was of course until it got to the part where her sister is shown twisted up in the bed, and she has that creepy voice. It reminded me of the way the woman in the basement sounded. That was more than enough to freak me out. My sisters had come in just a few minutes before that part, and they were laughing hysterically at me. They could clearly see that I was covering my eyes. I didn't want to see what she looked like, but they insisted I had to watch and that I shouldn't be such a *"chicken."* I was tired of them picking on me all time. Especially now, after all I had just gone through. You would think they would cut me a break. I guess that's just what older siblings are good at. Tormenting the younger ones. They seemed to get quite a rise out of torturing me these days.

My mother came home just as the credits were rolling. It was a good thing for all of them that she didn't come home while it was still on. She would've never tolerated them picking on me like that, and they would've been scolded for letting me watch it.

She stood there, bags in hand and just glanced at the screen and then at all of us.

"What are you kids up to?" she asked.

I never could determine if she was about to lecture us or if she was just simply inquiring. Her tone was always seemed to be somewhat on the harsher side.

"We're just watching TV." my brother told her.

"Well I can see that!" she said. "Girls, come and help set the table please. Dinner is on its way." she announced.

We did as we were told to do. No one ever complained or questioned her when we were told to do something. We just did it. About a half hour later the doorbell rang. My mother had ordered one of our favourite take-out meals. Fried chicken, Cole-slaw, macaroni salad, french fries and gravy. We didn't eat out very often so it was always a treat when we did. To be honest, I don't think she ordered takeout that night to treat us. It was most likely due to her being physically and mentally drained, and not having any desire to cook. It was written all over her face just how tired she was. There were dark shadows beginning to encircle her eyes and they were quite puffy from all the crying she had done over the past week. She looked like she hadn't slept all week either. I wondered how long it was going to take before she finally succumbed to it. The exhaustion I mean. You see, I wasn't the only one who had barricaded myself inside my room. She had done the very same thing since the day of the funeral. I was thankful for my older siblings though, because they had to take over all of the housekeeping duties as well as the cooking. She just didn't have it in her to do much of anything anymore. It seemed that she too had lost a part of herself when my father passed. Would we ever be the same without him? Only time would tell.

Dinner was eaten in complete silence. Afterwards I helped my sisters clear the table, and my mother headed back to her room without so much as a word to any of us. I was beginning to feel as if I had lost both parents simultaneously, and I guess in a sense I had. I didn't like seeing her that way. All the colour had drained from her. The life that once graced her face was gone. The sparkle in her eyes had faded. She was just empty inside now. I felt her pain. I felt my own too. I wondered which one I was feeling in this particular moment. How could I even distinguish between the two? I slipped into a deep moment of reflection while I was drying the dishes and passing them to my sister to be put away. That's when I heard him.

A Journey of a Thousand Miles – A Reflections Saga

"Ava, please go to her and make sure she's alright. Will you?"

I nearly jumped out of my skin. The voice had startled me. It completely caught me off guard. I turned to look at both of my sisters. I was certain they had both heard him too. The voice was loud enough that I was sure everyone had heard it. Gauging their non reaction, I finally concluded that they hadn't. Was I hearing things? Maybe it was just my own wishful thinking. I wanted so desperately to speak with him. To hear his voice one last time. I must've created it in my own mind. I handed over the last of the dishes to my sister Jane, and headed toward my mother's bedroom to do as I was asked. I knocked lightly on the door. I didn't want to startle her. This was quite easy to do. My mother was edgy by nature. It didn't matter how gently you spoke or touched her to wake her, she would always react startled. I waited a few minutes for an answer, but was met with dead silence. I slowly opened the door and peaked my head inside. There standing at the side of the bed was the unmistakable image of my loving father. My mother was fast asleep and he had his hand on the side of her head, gently caressing her hair. She didn't stir in the least. She was fast asleep. He motioned for me to come to his side. I closed the door as quickly as I could. My siblings were sure to freak out if any one of them had witnessed such a thing. It was such a tender moment between the two of them. I could see the sadness in my father's eyes, and could feel the overwhelming love he was projecting to her through his touch. He always had the warmest hands. The most gentle touch. I was going to miss that feeling. I stood beside him, and watched her sleep soundly before turning to him and speaking through a whisper.

"Daddy, was that you I heard in the kitchen?" I asked.

He didn't respond. Instead he just turned to me and smiled. I glanced down at his hand to see that he had stopped caressing my mother's head. Almost immediately, she turned over to face away from us. I wondered if she was still fast asleep or if was she beginning to wake. Almost as if reading my mind, my father spoke to me but it wasn't aloud. The communication seemed to be telepathic now. Maybe he knew she wasn't in a very deep sleep anymore. Despite the fact that we were not speaking audibly, he still spoke with the softness one would use when trying not to wake a sleeping baby.

"I'm very worried about her. She's so saddened with loss that she's forgetting she still has all of you to care for. She's falling into a deep depression. Please keep an eye on her for me." he said with deep concern.

"I will daddy, I promise I will!" I said reassuringly.

He reached his hand around the back of my head and pulled me toward him. I closed my eyes and felt a soft breeze caress my forehead and somehow I knew that it was a gentle kiss. He had always kissed me on my forehead, and I always felt the love he exuded in the simplicity of his touch. It was always pure and was a fiercely protective kind of love.

"Daddy loves you. I'll be watching over you always. I have to go now. You will always be my little girl." he announced.

A Journey of a Thousand Miles – A Reflections Saga

I wanted to stay in this moment forever, but I was quickly slapped in the face with the reality of things when the sensation of his touch faded and so did he. I stood there for a few minutes. Tears began to well up in my eyes as I called out to him in my mind

"Daddy please come back! I'm not ready for you to go. You're going to miss everything. You're going to miss my whole life!!" I cried.

"I'll always be watching. You just won't see me, but you will feel me. I'll always find a way to let you know I'm here honey." my father's voice called out to me. "I love you dearly my sweet angel girl." and then it was silent again.

Just then my mother began to stir. She turned toward me and stretched. Then her eyes flickered open. She was startled by the sight of me and jumped nearly to the ceiling. She quickly sat up in bed,

"Oh my god Ava... You scared the shit out of me! What are you doing?" she asked.

"I just wanted to make sure you were okay mom." I replied.

Then I leaned over and kissed her on her cheek.

"I'm fine" she suggested. "I'm...I'm just tired that's all!" she said trying to reassure me.

After looking her over for a few minutes, and when I was finally satisfied with my observations, I headed toward the door. I stopped for a moment with my hand on the knob as I remembered what had just taken place moments before. I turned to her

"By the way...daddy is worried about you. He wants you to take better care of yourself and us." I told her. "You are still our mother. You can't just forget about us when you're sad you know!" I shouted, and then I stormed out of the room.

I half expected her to run out after me and scold me for being so bold. I mean she was still my mother and I had no right to raise my voice to her that way. Normally, behaviour like that would've been met with some sort of lecture, but not this time. This time there was just... nothing. Was I really losing her too? I truly hoped not. I wondered just how much my life was about to change, now that my father was no longer going to be a part of it. Nothing could have prepared me for what traumatic events I was going to have to face for years to come. Losing my father was just the beginning of this nightmare.

A Journey of a Thousand Miles – A Reflections Saga

Chapter Thirteen

A week or so had passed since the funeral, and we began to get a daily visitor. It was my father's friend Allan. The one I had met that day when he just so happened to be at the diner where my father had taken me as per our usual tradition. Since after my birthday party, my father had brought him by the house a handful of times. They often sat up and shared a few drinks together, told stories and reminisced about the things they had encountered throughout the course their friendship. Allan seemed like a decent enough man. He was however about thirteen years older than my father. Nothing alarming about that, as my father was a very old soul and often preferred the company of older individuals rather than those his own age.

"They're older and much wiser. They don't like trouble." I remembered him telling me numerous times.

Being an old soul myself, I understood exactly what he meant by that. The two of them were great friends. Allan had been in the picture a few months or so at the time of my father's passing. However, I don't remember if he attended the funeral. I'm not sure who called him after my father's funeral to this day, but somehow he knew that things were falling apart in our home, and he stepped up to help my mother as much as he could. He became like a part of the family I guess you could say. He was the father type figure that I was now missing in life, yet he and my mother never shared any romantic type of feelings for one another. She was just relieved that he had offered his help. Being that I was the youngest in the home and had recently lost my father, he seemed to focus the majority of his attention toward me. He was very much like an uncle to me. Ever since my father's passing, he would dote on me and often took me to the park, out for ice cream, to the movies etc just as my father once had. He pretty much took on that role. I enjoyed his generosity and gentle affection. If there was ever a movie I wanted to see, all I had to do was tell him, and he would rent the tape and then copy it for me. I was seven. I had no idea that this was actually illegal. After a few months of him coming around, I had every movie I could ever want on VHS. I guess one might say that he completely spoiled me. My mother saw that I was once again that happy little girl she remembered and was so fond of. It seemed that the pain from losing my father was beginning to slip away. I won't say I forgot about him. That would be impossible. He was still very much a part of me. It was more about allowing myself to be happy again. We all were. Allan was a breath of fresh air. Things were finally going back to normal. You might say they were damn near perfect.

"One….two…three…four." I frantically searched for a hiding spot as my sister Anne continued counting out loud.

It was a Saturday afternoon. I had hoped to go outside and play in my new tree house that Allan had built for me, but the weather had other ideas. It had rained all night and was still coming down harder than ever, so today was sure to be an indoor activities kind of day. I glanced quickly out the window as I listened carefully to the sound of my sister in the middle of counting. I became lost in thought for a few moments, as I tried to determine just how flooded my tree house was, and I began to wonder how long it would be before I could play up there. I hadn't yet had the opportunity. We had spent all night working on it, but then it had gotten too dark by the time we had completed it. My mother had assured me that I would have ample time to play that following day. She couldn't have been more wrong.

"forty six…forty seven…forty eight." I could hear Anne's voice edging closer to me.

"You're cheating!" I shouted "You're supposed to stay in the living room on the couch and count." I told her.

"Ugh…Fine!" she said and headed back through the dining room to continue counting. "I'll just start over then. Hurry up and hide…geez!"

As I heard her begin the count again, I rushed into the kitchen trying to locate a good hiding place. I was always the best at hide and seek. Probably because I was so tiny. I could squeeze myself into pretty much anywhere these days. I can still remember my father scaring my mother half to death one day, when she had come over to his apartment to pick me up, and he had me hide in one of his suitcases leaned up against the wall. I still chuckle to myself whenever I think back to that day. She had called about twenty minutes before she was to arrive, to let him know that she was coming, and he suggested she come in and have a quick coffee or pop. He told her he wanted to show her something funny. Just before she was expected to arrive, he had told me the plan. I don't know why, but we always liked to startle her in the most fun ways. Maybe we were the cause of her always being on pins and needles. In either case, it was always hilarious to hear the initial screams and see her reactions, then the giggles that always followed when the initial shock of it all had worn off. It was all in good fun. My father always wanted to be playful with everyone. That day the plan was that I would lay quietly in the suitcase and try not to move or giggle too much. I was to sit and listen for our code word, and then start wriggling slowly to see if she would take notice. Our code word was *"firetrucks,"* It had worked out great. She was scared beyond belief and we all shared a good laugh. She nearly peed herself that day. It was always great to see those rare fleeting moments of happiness cross her face. She rarely ever smiled. I think she must've been worried about those dreadful laugh lines the older generations always spoke about. Thanks to my father she was almost certain to have an abundance of them.

"Forty five…forty six…forty seven..."

I was quickly snatched back to reality as I heard Anne nearing the end of her count. I didn't have long. I glanced in the direction of the cabinets under the kitchen counter and decided this would have to do. I quickly and quietly climbed inside. I didn't want to give away my hiding place. I managed to close the cabinet door just in time to hear her shout

A Journey of a Thousand Miles – A Reflections Saga

"Ready or not…here I come!"

I let out a little giggle then quickly collected myself. I was determined to not be found. I could hear her footsteps heading toward the dining area. We were home alone so there was an eerie silence throughout the whole house. I could hear every little bit of movement she made. My heart was thudding in my chest in anticipation and the excitement of it all. I closed my eyes waiting for her to whip the cupboard door open and scare the living daylights out of me, but then I heard her footsteps walk right past my hiding spot. I could hear her out in the hallway now and headed toward the bathroom. I heard the sound of the shower curtain being pulled open and then closed again. Was she really not going to check the cabinets in the kitchen? She knew I always hid in the smallest spaces I could possibly find. Why wouldn't that have been the first place someone would check? I was baffled and lost in my own thoughts at the same time. I listened carefully and determined she was headed upstairs now. I decided now was the best time to make my move. I was safe to head to another spot, but I probably only had a matter of minutes to make it before she would be headed back in my direction and sure to see me.

We didn't play by the typical hide and seek rules most people adhered to. We made our own. We didn't follow the rule that you had to stay in the same hiding spot and wait to be found. You were free to move about whenever the person that was *"it"* wasn't in the area. It made the game more of a challenge and we were always coming up with new ways to improve it. I stopped and listened intently. I could hear the sound of the floorboards upstairs creaking with each footstep she took. I quickly opened the cupboard door and froze in sheer terror. There in front of me was the face of the same woman that had traumatized me in the basement that day. I felt my heart begin to race faster. I couldn't move an inch. I was frozen. For a moment she just stared at me and then she leaned in as if sniffing me. I was sure that she could smell the fear radiating off of me. She seemed pretty pleased with herself. The smell of rotting flesh permeated the air again. It was enough to make me gag. Then she came even closer. I could feel her breath prickle against my cheek and smell the putrid sourness of it. She came in even closer, our foreheads nearly touching, looked me in the eyes, opened her mouth and yelled out

"BOO!"

I began to scream as loud as I could. I could hear the sound of my sister's footsteps running down the stairs frantically in my direction. I don't know why it took her so long to find me, but when she finally did, I was rocking back and forth with my head between my knees shaking and crying hysterically. I felt a hand reach out and grab me to pull me from the cabinet, but I was too frightened to look up. I hoped and prayed that it was her. After what seemed like an eternity I felt her pick me up from the floor and I finally lifted my head.

"What the hell happened Ava? Why were you screaming like that?" she asked with concerned undertones in her voice.

"It was….It was awful! There was a….a ghost!" I cried.

A Journey of a Thousand Miles – A Reflections Saga

"No….you must have imagined it. There's no such thing as ghosts." she insisted.

No such thing as ghosts?! Boy was she mistaken. If only she could see the things that I had seen. If only she could experience the things that I had experienced. I guarantee she would never be the same again. A part of me wished she would. Just once. Maybe then she would come to understand the frequent torment I endured on a daily basis. I can't tell you how difficult it is to be born into a family and looked at as a total whack job. As far as they were all concerned, I was suffering from severe delusions. Maybe one might even say that I had managed to lose all of my marbles. My mother was convinced I needed medication. It was either that or an exorcism. I remember praying everyday for God to take these gifts from me. They felt more like a curse and I was eager to be rid of them. Of course prayer did nothing for me. It was pointless. I knew I would be forever alone in my suffering. No one would ever know what it was like for me. They couldn't possibly understand any of it, which is why I spent most of my time isolated in my bedroom. It was obvious they were afraid of me and only interacted with me when they felt they had no other choice.

"Come on! You don't really believe in them do you?" she snickered.

"I know what I saw!" I shouted, pushing her away and storming off to my bedroom.

How was I going to explain this one to my mother? I knew she was bound to find out sooner or later. Even if I told her everything, she'd never believe me. She would be quick to dismiss it like always and I would be left feeling like even more of an idiot than I already was. I tried to work out the incident in my head. Every time I would close my eyes, I could see the image of that woman in my head. What did she want? Was she just trying to torment me or was there something more she wanted? I pulled out my notepad and began to sketch the image of her face. Surely my mother would look at this and decide that it was far too vivid to just be a figment of my young imagination. At least that's what I was hoping.

When she came home I could hear indistinct chatter going on downstairs between her and my sister Anne. I knew that Anne was telling her everything, and it wouldn't be much longer before my mother called me to come downstairs. I decided to beat her to it and headed in that direction.

"What the hell happened? Your sister told me the two of you were playing hide and seek and she found you screaming at the top of your lungs in the cabinet. Are you going to tell me what's going on here Ava? What did you see?" she demanded.

"I saw a ghost woman. It was the thing nightmares are made of mom." I told her while pulling my hand from behind my back to show her the picture I had drawn.

She took it hesitantly and then raised it up to have a look.

"What the hell is this? This is what you saw? What is it? Is it something you saw on TV?" she asked.

"NO! That is what scared me while I was hiding under the sink." I insisted.

A Journey of a Thousand Miles – A Reflections Saga

She looked at it again and then back at me before she spoke again.

"I really think you need to not watch those movies anymore. They're rotting your brain. I think they are causing you to hallucinate." she suggested.

Oh yes! That's exactly what this was. I was paranoid to the point that I was now having hallucinations. I imagined the whole thing. The feeling of defeat crept over me and I never felt more alone in this world than in that very moment. I didn't say a word. I just turned and walked away from her. I could feel my blood practically boiling. I was beyond frustrated. I decided to just not discuss the matter anymore. What was the point? No one believed any of it was truly happening anyway and at this rate I was pretty sure I was on the path straight to the psychiatric ward.

That night I ate dinner in complete silence. I was lost in thoughts about my father and how much I missed him. I knew he would've handled the situation differently. I wondered if he was watching me go through all of this. I pictured him saddened by it all. Watching his little girl grow up without the one person who ever truly understood her. The one person who could offer her solace in his embrace. I'm sure it was almost too much to bear for him, and yet there was nothing either one of us could do to change it.

I was destined to grow up without a father. To endure more pain and suffering than anyone should ever have to endure and worst of all, I would be forced to do it alone. The loss of my father was heart wrenching and yet, it would only be the beginning for me. There would be a lot more to come.

After dinner, I headed up to my room to spend some alone time with my thoughts. I tried to read a book to distract myself from the image of the woman who haunted me, but she kept appearing in the back of my mind. It didn't matter what I did, she just continued to show up there. I decided it was probably best to just go to sleep. Hopefully I'd wake up in the morning with a clear head again, and the events of the day before would long be forgotten. I laid down on my pillow and pulled my covers up to my chin. It wasn't long before I fell fast asleep.

There was a bright flash of light ahead of me, as I walked along a dirt path that looked like it could've gone on forever. It reminded me of those strobe lights I had seen in my brother's room before. It was so bright that it was almost blinding, and caused my head to pulsate with each flash. Something in my thoughts told me to turn around and go the other way. I don't know why, but I felt compelled to follow orders. As I was walking in the direction I was being guided to, I could hear the sound of something running behind me. The movement sounded too fast to be a person. It had to be some kind of animal. I turned around to glance in the direction I had heard them, but there were only shadows surrounding me. They appeared to be on all sides of me now. I heard another sound come from behind me, and squinted my eyes to see if I could see anything. Just then I could see that the air appeared to be moving. As if it were taking the form of something, although I couldn't quite make out what that was at first. I squinted a little harder at the energy in the air, and that's when I saw it. It was a dog that had transformed from the shadows.

It was sniffing around on the ground for something. Then it stopped, looked up and glanced in my direction. As soon as it saw me it began to growl and skin its teeth at me. This was definitely not a friendly dog, and now it was headed in my direction, charging at me full speed. I turned to run and that's when I heard the sounds of more growls piercing through the air surrounding me. More and more shadows began to transform. They all began to advance toward me. Growling and showing their teeth. It was clear to me that they were planning an attack and I was about to become their next victim. I let out a scream and darted in another direction away from them. Running as fast as my legs could carry me. My heart thudding in my chest. Eventually the fear took over and my legs began to feel like Jello. I was numb with fear. I screamed out for help, but my cries seemed to go unanswered. That's when I noticed a blue coloured light off in the distance, and suddenly I heard the voice of Emily.

"RUN! Hurry up! They're going to catch you. Hurry up! Run – *FASTER*!" she shouted.

"I'm going as fast as I can! I can't run any faster. I'm getting too tired. I ca – I can't feel my legs!" I whined.

Just then the blue light raced toward me. It moved so fast and then it began to swirl around me. It looked like I was in some type of vortex. It was like a bright blue tornado. Before I knew it that light lifted me up and right off the ground. I was sucked up into the center of it. I appeared to be levitating off of the ground. I looked down at my feet and could see the ground about fifty feet below.

"Oh my God!!! Put me down. I'm scared. Please put me down. I don't wanna die!" I shrieked.

"It's okay Ava. I've got you. You will be safe here. They can't get you this high off the ground. Don't worry. I won't let you fall, I promise!" Emily assured me.

After what seemed like an eternity, I began to feel myself descend toward the ground. The light swirling around me began to slow down and I was able to see through it once again. After a few minutes it came to a complete stop and there standing in front of me was Emily.

"Whew! That was a close one." she sighed with relief.

"What were those things? They looked like dogs but they formed from the shadows, and they didn't have skin! Why were they after me?" I asked.

"Those dear Ava are hell hounds. They feed on fear mostly, but their favourite thing to feed on is the purity of souls. They could smell you as soon as you entered this dimension and they were drooling for a taste." she explained.

A Journey of a Thousand Miles – A Reflections Saga

"Well thank you for saving me. I couldn't keep running. I went numb and they were catching up to me. I could feel them nipping at my heels. They would've caught me for sure….Thank you!" I leaned in and hugged her tightly.

"It wasn't me" she said.

"Well then who the heck was it?!" I asked.

"That was all you! It was a vortex created by your own energy field. Your heightened sense of fear and the realization of your mortal danger must've activated it."

"But – I don't understand what you are saying. I'm just a child. How could I possibly do something like that?" I was confused. I needed to know.

"We will get into the ins and outs of all that later. Right now we have more important things to discuss. Follow me!" she said, and then proceeded to skip off down the path.

I had to jog just to keep up with her. It was as if her seeing me use my energy vortex caused her to assume I had inherited some super speed powers too. Newsflash...I hadn't. Luckily she stopped skipping after a few minutes and walked off the path toward a park bench and sat down. She patted the spot next to her

"Come sit with me Ava. We have much to talk about." she insisted.

I obliged her and did as I was told. We definitely did have a lot to talk about and the topic of conversation infuriated me. What she told me couldn't possibly be true. How could it? She was so certain that the information she was giving me was completely accurate.

"It's another reason your father had to cross over so quickly. I think you know what would've happened if he was permitted to witness such things." she told me.

Yes, I knew exactly what would've happened. My father would've killed anyone who so much as harmed a hair on my pretty little head. This would've enraged him. Unleashed hell on earth so to speak. I cried after my conversation with Emily. She assured me that everything was going to be okay. I was in complete disbelief. I became so furious with her, and told her this was the end for her and I. How could she tell me such awful things and then sit back and just let it happen?

As far as I was concerned no one who cared about someone, would allow such things to happen to them. My anger was so intense that I was quickly lifted out of that place and transported straight back to my bed. I awoke in a cold sweat. I was breathing so frantically I was almost to the point of hyperventilating. I rolled over to look at the clock on my nightstand 3:05 AM. I reached for the water bottle I always kept under my bed, but it wasn't there. I decided that one of the cats must've pawed it under my bed and I knelt down on the floor to retrieve it. As I was feeling my way around in the dark, I heard a creak behind me. I glanced around to locate the sound, but it was far too dark to even see my hand in front of my face. I continued to feel around under the bed hoping to locate the bottle. Just then I heard my closet door creak open behind me.

Chapter Fourteen

"Ava!" it whispered.

What the hell was calling out my name? I quickly stood up and tried to jump on the bed, but something grabbed me by both of my ankles, causing me to fall. I screamed out for help. The grip tightened and then it began to pull me. HARD! I struggled against the force, but I was powerless to whatever had hold of me. It was much stronger than I was and it continued to pull me toward the closet. I continued to scream. Begging and pleading for someone to help me. Before I knew it I was dragged into the closet and the door slammed shut. I stood up and pushed on the door with all my might, but it wouldn't even budge. It was as if someone were on the other side of it holding it closed. I slumped down on the floor in the corner of the closet, burying my head between my knees and began to rock myself back and forth, crying hysterically. After what seemed like forever I heard the door to my room fly open, followed by the closet door.

"What? What's going on? What are you doing in here?! Are you sleep walking again?" my mother asked.

I wanted to answer her, but I couldn't catch my breath from crying so hard. All I could do was continue to cry and shake.

"Jesus Christ Ava! Look at you. Did you pee on yourself?! I don't know what's going on with you but I'm tired of this! Let's go!" she shouted.

I stood up and walked out of the closet. My legs still shaking with each wobbly step. I walked over to my dresser and pulled out a fresh night gown and underwear from the drawer and then followed her downstairs.

After washing up I crawled into bed with her and faced the wall. I was so ashamed that I'd wet myself, but I was scared beyond belief. This was the worst experience thus far. I didn't say another word to her. I was just happy that I wasn't going to be sleeping alone tonight. Who knows what may have happened if she hadn't come upstairs when she did. I didn't even want to think about it. I pulled the covers over my head and drifted off again.

The next day Allan came by for a visit. I was happy to see him. He was probably going to take me out for some lunch and ice cream as usual. I was surprised when he and my mother had a conversation about him taking me for a sleepover at Henry and Linda's cottage.

I was excited to get away from the house for a change. I needed to escape my tormentors for awhile. Allan told my mother there would be other children there too, as Henry and Linda had grandchildren and they were coming to stay with us for a few days. All I heard were the words *"sleepover"* and *"cottage on the beach"* and I was off to pack for the trip. I wasn't sure how to feel about other kids being there, because I worried they would be much like the others. Judgmental and standoffish with me. You would think by now I would be used to that, but I honestly don't think that will be something that any child can ever get used to. All I ever wanted was to be accepted by others. I had such a pure and kind heart and although I was different from other kids, people often lost sight of the fact that I really was just a kid at the end of the day. Allan and I headed for the road around 4:00 PM that day.

"It will be at least three hours before we get there." Allan informed me.

I gazed at the scenery flying past me outside of the passenger window. I always enjoyed driving through the countryside, because I loved to see the animals grazing in the pasture. I especially loved to see all of the horses. They had such a gentle spirit and I was drawn to them. Allan looked up and smiled

"There will be horses there too!" he boasted.

I was excited for that. I couldn't wait to go horseback riding. I was going to have two of the many things I loved there. Beaches and horses. It was sure to be a heavenly experience. I was certain of that. The hardest part would be when it was time to come back home. I was dreading that moment, but I didn't want to ruin my adventure by dwelling on something that was still a few days away. I decided to push that thought as far from my mind as I possibly could. I was determined to enjoy every moment of this experience.

As we were pulling up the drive I could see both Henry and Linda standing there on the porch to greet us. They both waved and I smiled as I waved back. I couldn't wait for the car to stop moving so I could run out and hug the two of them. Henry and Linda had become like a second set of grandparents to me.

Sure I still had my own, but I rarely even saw them anymore. It was only ever on special occasions like Thanksgiving and Christmas. I had only known Henry and Linda a short time and yet, I'd grown attached to them rather quickly. They treated me like family. Linda was my favourite. We would sit up and watch girly movies together while the men did whatever it was that men do. She would braid my hair and paint my nails. She even let me return the favour. She always had a warm smile and the energy to match. I had never heard her so much as raise her voice to anyone. I'm not even sure she had an angry bone in her entire body. She was kind to everyone and always welcomed new people with open arms. She was almost angelic to me. I felt completely at ease around her. When the car finally came to a stop I rushed to smother her with hugs and kisses.

"It's so nice to see you again sweetie. We are thrilled to have you. Why don't you go on inside and meet my two granddaughters Olivia and Sky. They are definitely excited to meet you. I've told them all about you! They're in the living room making bracelets." she said with a smile.

I rushed inside and bolted for the living room, although I had never been to the cottage before and found myself in the kitchen instead.

A Journey of a Thousand Miles – A Reflections Saga

"Hello….is anyone here?" I called out.

Just then two young girls rounded the corner to the left of the kitchen. They both had blonde hair and blue eyes. Their eyes were so big and bright. They had smiles that put even Linda's to shame. As if that were even possible.

"Hi there!" they both shouted excitedly. "It's nice to meet you" said the taller one. "I'm Olivia and this is my little sister Sky." she told me while motioning for a hug. "Do you wanna make bracelets with us?" she asked. "I'd love to. Are you using beads or something else?" I asked excitedly.

"Come see!" they both shouted. "We'll show you!" and they disappeared around the corner.

The living room was so warm and inviting, but it was no surprise. The whole house seemed to be warm and inviting. It definitely matched the energy of its owners. There was a large fireplace along the far right wall of the room. The walls were painted a soft Lilac and the trim a bright white. There were photographs atop the mantle of the fireplace. There was a large coffee table in the center of the room, and directly beside it was a toy box that seemed to be out of place. It was filled with your usual girly type of toys. Baby dolls, Barbies, stuffed animals, colouring books and little storage containers filled with various materials for different arts and crafts projects. It was everything a little girl could ever want or dream of. On the left wall was a large doll house and to the right of it sat a small wooden table and chairs. The table had been set for what appeared to be a tea party and there were various stuffed animals seated on each of the four chairs.

Olivia, Sky and I sat in front of the fireplace and made bracelets out of some type of plastic string I had never seen before. All of the colours were bright and shiny. They made beautiful bracelets. Afterwards we all headed over to the small wooden table and had a tea party of our own. Linda had even given us real tea cups to use, and she brought out plates of cheese and crackers as well as a plate of chocolate bars she had cut up into little squares for us to share.

"Oh my! Look at you ladies. Perhaps you should go put on your fancy dresses for the party." she suggested.

We all agreed that was the best idea ever. The only problem was, I didn't bring any fancy dresses.

"Oh no! I didn't bring any party dresses" I said sadly.

"It's okay. You can use one of my mine!" Olivia announced at she pulled me toward the bedroom they were staying in for the sleepover.

A Journey of a Thousand Miles – A Reflections Saga

Once we were dressed, Olivia suggested that we put on some of her play makeup. We all took turns dolling each other up. Thank goodness there are no residual photos of that day. I'm almost certain we looked like clowns! We arrived back in the living room looking like pretty princesses.

"Wow! You ladies look fabulous! You're all so glamorous. Just like beautiful princesses." Linda told us. "Just wonderful little ladies. Enjoy your party." she said with a wide grin and then she walked out of the room back toward the kitchen.

The tea party was a lot of fun. Afterwards we changed back into our regular clothing and went outside to play. The girls showed me around the place and soon I discovered the horses I was promised. I started jumping up and down with excitement.

"Oh I wanna ride one so bad! Oh please Linda, can we?!" I begged her.

"It's getting kind of late ladies. Maybe tomorrow. It will be getting dark very soon. Why don't you ladies go for a swim?" Linda called from the porch.

We quickly headed inside to change into our swimsuits and then ran outside again to enjoy what was left of the sunlight. Let it be known that I have a very intense fear of water, as I have mentioned before. I don't know why, but I was just born with it. I feel the need to emphasize just how big that fear actually is. Once I nearly drowned one of my friends. It wasn't on purpose. I was in a life jacket and it had taken me a long time to even get in the pool wearing one, but this friend decided that she was going to try and be funny and pulled me into the deep end. I completely lost it and grabbed onto her, but by doing so, I was actually pushing her under the water. My friend Jessica's mom had to jump in with all of her clothes on and save her. That was the last time I was allowed in their pool for awhile. The fear was still pretty strong for me up to this point although, on this particular day I was having too much fun to care. As long as we didn't wade too deep in the water I would be fine. We played there in the water together for about an hour. Running through the water to make a whirlpool and having a splash fight as we screamed and giggled with laughter.

I really enjoyed playing with these two. They weren't like the other kids I knew at all. They accepted me right away. Soon it was time to go back inside. Linda suggested we take the mattresses off the beds and build a huge fort in the living room. She had even appointed Henry and Allan to move the furniture to accommodate us. We draped and hung blankets strategically across the furniture that surrounded us, and even managed to wheel the television inside too. It was a sleepover paradise. Linda fixed us some popcorn and even some little trays with candy. We watched several movies that night, and then when we finally grew tired of that, we decided to switch off the television and tell scary stories.

Of course, I had several, but mine were far from just my childhood imagination. Theirs seemed more fantasized in nature. It was still a blast. For once in my life I was able to speak about the things that went bump in the night and not be scrutinized for it. Olivia was just getting to the part about the babysitter who received a phone call from an eerie voice asking if she had checked on the children she was tending to. It seemed like it was heading toward a very gruesome ending, and I began to giggle with the excitement and anticipation of it all. For some reason the blood and gore stories never affected me the same way the stories of ghostly figures did. Maybe it was because I had actually experienced those horrifying tales on a nightly basis for as long as I can remember.

"So the babysitter realizes she hasn't checked on the children in a very long time. The voice creeped her out so much, that she decided to go upstairs and check on them. As she's walking up the stairs she hears a thumping sound. *THUMP! THUMP! THUMP!* What could it be?!" Olivia asks as she leans in toward us and puts the flashlight she's holding in her hand under her chin so that the light begins to illuminate her angelic face.

Now she appears almost ghostly and poor Sky looks terrified of her.

"She gets to the hallway outside the children's bedroom door and slowly reaches for the handle. She starts to open the door, but then she stops! Because she hears the sound again!" she whispers and leans even closer to us while she continues on "*THUMP! THUMP! THUMP!* She quickly opens the door and hits something directly behind it! She opens the door to see what's in the way and there she sees her boyfriend hanging upside down covered in blood. The thumping she heard was his body swinging and banging against the door. She let's out the loudest scream ever when she sees the children are also bloody!" she tells us in a panicked voice.

"I….I don't like this story. It's SCARY!" Sky cried. "Please stop telling it now sissy." she whimpered.

"Don't worry!" Olivia tells her little sister and then squeezes her tight. "You gotta let me finish. It's not all scary I promise." she smiles and then continues. "Her loud screams wake the children and then they too start screaming because they don't know what's going on. The babysitter is confused. She thought the children were dead. At least that's what it looked like. She rushes over to them and hugs them all tightly. Just then she remembers her boyfriend's body swinging back and forth in front of the door. She quickly tells the children to cover their eyes so they don't get scared and begins walking them toward the door and out into the hall. Just as she is about to go through the doorway, something grabs her. She lets out another scream as she tries to find the light switch. That's when she hears him begin to laugh and she realizes it was all just a game her boyfriend had played on her!" Olivia squeals. "The end!"

I was relieved to hear the story had a funny ending, because at that moment I was beginning to question Olivia's sanity. I thought she may have been a bit disturbed going into such gory details for such a young child. Here I was again forgetting that she and I were roughly the same age. It was the old soul in me I guess. I may have only been seven, but I felt like I was fifty something. It was something I just couldn't seem to grasp. It was like being an old and wise woman that was trapped in the body of a seven year old girl. I still can't explain the things I came into this life knowing, nor can I explain the fears I was born with. They just were. I knew eventually I would be able to pinpoint where it all stemmed from, but I wasn't about to start worrying myself over it now. I let out a sigh of relief when she announced the story was over.

"Are you okay?" she whispered. "I didn't scare you too much?" she asks.

"Oh no way!" I chuckled. "That was nothing. It wasn't scary at all to me. We really should get some sleep though." I tell her. "We have a long day tomorrow! Goodnight girls. Sleep tight!"

A few hours later I'm skipping down a dirt road. The air is cool and crisp and prickly against my skin. It's dark on all sides of me. I can hear the sounds of cars whizzing by, but I don't see any cars.

What is this about? I wonder. I begin to notice a familiar figure off in the distance. It's Emily. She appears to be skipping toward me. So I too begin to skip in her direction. I can see that she's facing my direction, but for some reason she is moving farther away from me! I don't understand what's going on and I call out to her

"Emily! Emily what's going on?!" I shout out to her, but I'm met with silence.

I stop skipping and begin to analyze my surroundings. I scan to my left and I see an old ice cream store. It appears vacant and abandoned. The sign is dangling down over the doorway. The entire building looks like it could crumble any second. Seriously though, the astral could sure use some renovations. As I stare into the darkened doorway, I see what looks like some type of energy beginning to take form behind the counter. It seems to be beckoning me to come closer. I don't know why but a sudden feeling of terror begins to creep over my entire body. I can feel the hair on the back of my neck begin to raise. I can feel prickles in my skin.

Suddenly the darkness begins to flood out of the doorway toward me. I try to run from it, but I'm frozen in fear. The darkness creeps closer until it starts to swirl around me and then it begins to suffocate me. I struggle to breathe as it seems to pass directly into me and suddenly I'm being lifted off the ground. I struggle to free myself from it, but it's much stronger than anything I've ever felt before. I feel like I'm losing my breath and I begin to scream for help, but no sound comes out. As I'm being held in the air I begin to lift higher and higher and that's when the visions hit me all at once. I'm not sure what they mean exactly but they are dark and terrible images. Worse than any ghostly figure I've ever witnessed up to this point. These are not ghosts or demons. These are some familiar faces and they are trying to do horrible things to me. I struggle to get away from them, but it's no use. Suddenly a voice snatches me from my visions.

"Do you see?" it whispers.

"See? See what? What are you talking about? Who are you?!" I ask angrily.

"It doesn't matter who I am. I'm only here to reveal the truth to you. To warn you that you my child are in very real danger!"

Just then I am freed from the grasp of whatever this entity was, and I see a figure standing in the doorway of the store beckoning me to come inside. I glance in the direction I last saw Emily, but she is gone. I quickly scan my surroundings for any sign of her, but she appears to have vanished from sight. I take a deep breath and walk toward the door to the ice cream shop and step into the darkness. This time the fear I once felt is completely gone. I suddenly know that whatever awaits me inside is for my own good. It's something that I have to see and I also know that whatever it is this being is about to show me cannot go unseen. Once inside, I fumble around in the darkness trying to locate a light switch. I'm not sure why I even bother to. This is the Astral after all and though it is much like our world it still has its own unique differences. Light seems to be absent here. It's always cold and the colours are always very muted. It's a depressing place to say the least. I've never had positive vibes while in this place, and my experiences have always reflected that. I continue to stumble around through the darkness, trying to make my way through.

"You are the light." someone whispers. "Use your inner light to see." a male voice suggests.

I'm startled by him, as he seems to know what I'm thinking without me ever having to say a word. I close my eyes and imagine the entire store lighting up. I imagine tables off to one side with chairs and behind the counter about four or five ice cream machines. I see the image of a husky, balding man with a friendly smile. I'm not sure at this moment why I see the man behind the voice this way. It's as if the image of him is being projected into my mind by some unseen force.

"That's better! Now open your eyes." he tells me.

When I open them I am in a bit of shock. Everything I had seen with my eyes closed, is now exactly as I had pictured it, just mere seconds ago. The store is well lit and there, behind the counter is the man I envisioned. I'm not sure how I did it, but I definitely did something.

"Come and sit with me. There is much to discuss about your life." he says as he motions toward one of the tables.

As I sit and talk with him, he begins to project images into my mind. They are all very traumatic events. They are filled with much pain and suffering. I am shown how these things will deeply affect me for years to come.

"I'll let you sit with that for a minute." he suggests as he gets up and walks behind the counter to grab some ice cream for the two of us.

I am lost in thought as I sit in contemplation. The images are difficult to fathom in my reality. They are some of the most horrific things one could imagine could happen to a child and I knew they would all be in my future. Tears filled my eyes as I began to imagine how I was ever going to survive any of it. All I wanted in that moment was my father. I wished there was a way to reach him, but I hadn't seen him since that day after his funeral, when he had appeared in my mother's bedroom. It seemed like he was now gone forever. Maybe that was the very last time I would see him. I was still trying to come to terms with it all.

A Journey of a Thousand Miles – A Reflections Saga

"I know it's a lot to digest and that you think you couldn't possibly survive it all but you should know that you are far more powerful than you can even begin to imagine. You will overcome everything and you will be stronger and more courageous in the end." he told me as he placed a dish of mint chocolate chip ice cream on the table in front of me.

I was surprised that he knew. This man seemed to know everything about me and yet, I had no idea who he even was. Seeming to read my thoughts in that moment, he replied to my questions that were playing inside my head.

"My name is Seth. I am another one of your guides." he said. "I take it she never even mentioned me huh?" he asked. "No worries kid," he said chuckling. "she always was a little forgetful. Well anyway… I have always been with you, however Emily has been your main guide up until now. I've just been watching and waiting for the right time. I have a specific purpose in your life and was told I could only be revealed to you when the time was pertinent. That time is now! Everything I've shown you is what lies ahead in your future, but unfortunately these things will all be forgotten when you leave here."

"Why bother to tell me then?" I asked., frustrated.

"Because kid! These memories will remain deeply ingrained in your soul memory."

I wasn't exactly sure what he meant by that, and yet I had a feeling I would soon find out.

"You should know…there's a lot more I need to tell you kid, but I feel that you may not be prepared for more right now. I'll leave you to process what I've already revealed. When you are ready to head back…let me know."

When he was finished speaking, he got up from his chair and headed for the door. Did he really just leave me here alone to deal with all of this? I sat there for what seemed like lifetimes. Why hadn't Emily ever told me about other guides of mine? Why did she act like it was just her?! She was supposed to protect me. We were great friends. Weren't we? I sat in silence eating the last few spoonfuls of my ice cream and tried to clear my thoughts of all that I'd just discovered. It was no use. My mind was racing with the most horrifying things imaginable, and yet I didn't even come close to scratching the surface of the unimaginable pain I had yet to endure. I was quickly drawn away by the sound of Seth choking outside.

I got up from the table and rushed toward the door. I was running so quickly that I forgot to even push my weight against it and I ended up running straight through to the other side of it. I wound the corner of the building following the sounds of someone struggling for air in between coughing fits. I ended up in the alleyway but there was no one in sight when I got there. I began to survey the area with my eyes, glancing in all directions. Where had he gone? I know I just heard him and yet here I stood in the alley completely alone. Maybe I was hearing things. I began to call out his name and that's when I heard it again. I quickly snapped my head in the direction I had last heard the sound. I was just in time to see a puff of smoke materialize in the air. It was a medium sized cloud that just seemed to come out of nowhere, directly following a deep and hoarse coughing sound. I was confused. As I began to focus harder on the cloud I realized that he was smoking. I couldn't see him though. All I could see was the puff of smoke every now and then.

"Seth are you okay?" I shouted into the smoky air as I walked toward it.

"Huh? Oh…Yeah I'm fine." he assured me. "I…I just need to quit is all. You would think in death that I might get the hint, but here I am!" he laughed.

"I can…I can't see you! All I can see is the smoke in the air" I told him.

"Oh! Sorry little lady. I keep forgetting you're not one of us. My apologies."

Suddenly a figure began to form in the side of the wall of the building, and then he stepped toward me. It was both the craziest and the coolest thing I had ever seen.

"It takes a lot of energy to do that. I figured while you were inside I would take a load off." he chuckled as he threw the butt of his cigarette down and stamped it out.

"What takes a lot of energy?" I asked inquisitively.

"Shaping…ah forming…hmm what is it called again?! Sorry. It's been awhile since I've walked with the living kid. I forget your words sometimes. It just takes a lot of energy for me to show myself in physical form. That's why whenever spirits appear to people, the first thing those people tend to notice is that the lights will flicker. We need the energy to come through." he explained. "The reason I left you to be alone was because I was using energy from you and I didn't want to overwhelm you or drain you too much. I hope I didn't harm you in any way. Do you feel anything unusual? Are you tired kid?" he asked with concern. "Maybe I should take you back."

I could see him go into his mind at that point. *Does he even have any thought process?* I found myself wondering. If he was a spirit without a body…did he really have anything to think about?

"I know you were having a hard time with everything I told you. I know it's probably difficult for you to understand or even imagine at this time. Maybe it would be better if I just show you what to expect." he walked up to me and placed his hands up in the air as if he were in a surrendering position. "Close your eyes. I'll show you. You're going to see a great deal, but I want you to remember that this is not actually happening to you right now. It's just like a mini movie. Remember to keep breathing…whatever you do…just *BREATHE!*" he told me and then he placed both of his hands on my shoulders.

Everything went black and it got very quiet.

"I don't see anything!" I told him in a state of what seemed like hypnosis. I tried to open my eyes, but it was as if they were fused shut. Whatever he was going to show me I was going to have to see through to the end. I took a deep breath and focused. Soon the movie of my life began flashing before my eyes. I was watching my parents doting on me as an infant at first. Then it was like someone pressed fast forward and I was watching myself grow up. I saw the loss of my father and many others still to come. It was definitely a lot. I even saw all that I was set to endure throughout high school. The birth of my children. I saw all of the gut wrenching heartache I would have to overcome time and time again. Past life memories and I was even shown my own death. Can you imagine that? Seeing the very day you die, played out for you like an old movie? Every detail revealed to you? What would that do to someone mentally and emotionally? If you can imagine that, then maybe you can come to understand why as soon as I left that place my memory was completely wiped. I remembered meeting Seth and that he warned me about something that was going to change the course of my life forever, but that was all I remembered.

Chapter Fifteen

I arrived back home that following Sunday from my trip with Allan. My mother had been sitting on the porch awaiting our arrival. I wasn't sure if she was anticipating my homecoming, or if she was just contemplating something. In any case I was happy to see her. I couldn't wait to tell her how much fun I had over the weekend. I was dying to tell her about Olivia and Sky. I was so excited about making new friends, and they were of the few I could actually be completely myself with. I rushed from the car and onto the porch to tell her all about it.

"There was horseback riding, make overs, swimming, campfires and even roasting marshmallows!' I told her excitedly.

She seemed pleased that I had enjoyed myself. It had been a very long time since I was able to have fun and just be a child again. My father used to read me medical journals as bedtime stories, while most of the other children were busy reading Dr. Seuss. I had an advanced knowledge when it came to the medical field, and could give you the medical terminology for various diseases and conditions, as well as provide the related information to the diagnosis. Looking back now I think he always knew where I was headed or at least he hoped I would end up in the medical field somewhere.

"You were born to inspire. Born to heal. You have a very unique gift Ava." he would always tell me.

He had always been good at restoring my confidence whenever the other kids or adults in my life would make me feel inadequate or crazy.

"That's nice sweetie." my mother smiled in response to my ramblings.

I wasn't sure if she was enjoying my story wholeheartedly or if she just wanted me to shut up. When I got excited about something…I could ramble on about it for hours. I didn't blame her. I just wish that she got more excited for me or encouraged me to continue with whatever made me happy. I kissed her on the cheek and rushed inside to find my sister Anne. She always loved sitting and listening to my stories.

A Journey of a Thousand Miles – A Reflections Saga

"Anne, Anne where are you? I gotta tell you something!" I shouted.

"I'm upstairs." she called back. "What's up?"

I ran up the stairs skipping one at a time while holding on for dear life to the railing. My mother hated it when I did that. She always lectured me about how I could fall and break my arms, legs or worse my neck. I could almost hear her voice lecturing me in my head with each step I took, but I was excited and decided I was prepared to take that risk. I told Anne all about my adventures. She seemed excited for me. She suggested we watch a scary movie after dinner. We were definitely due some sisterly bonding time. Of course of all movies she could've chosen, she picked Pet Semetary. She giggled whenever I'd cover my eyes at certain parts. Rachel's sister in that bed just creeped me right out. It didn't matter how many times I had seen it either. I couldn't stand that creepy voice of hers. I'm not sure what it was about her that scared me so much besides that though, but she definitely reminded me of the lady from the basement. The one who had scared the living daylights out of me that day Anne and I played Hide and Seek. My mother was convinced what happened that day was all just my imagination. That I must've conjured up the whole thing out of my own anxiety and paranoia. It was a bit frustrating to say the least. It made me not want to tell her anything…EVER! In any case, I knew that after watching this movie I sure wasn't planning to sleep alone.

"Can I sleep with you tonight sissy?" I asked her.

"Yeah…sure. Why not? You're scared aren't you? There's nothing to be scared of! Scaredy cat…scaredy cat!" she taunted.

"Forget it!" I shouted angrily. "I'm not sleeping with you. You're mean!" I yelled as I stormed out of the room and headed back downstairs.

My mother was still sitting outside on the front porch. She was deep in conversation with Allan about whatever the latest news headlines were. I grabbed my notepad from the cabinet inside the entertainment centre and sat down at the table. I liked to write short stories mostly. My mother had read several of them and told me I had quite an imagination for my age. She told me she wouldn't be surprised if I became a writer someday. She also told me that it was clear to her that I had invented all of my experiences and hauntings as well. I found myself praying for her to go through even an ounce of what I had to deal with, but of course that never happened. Even though she had seen my father after his death, she was still living in deep denial. She didn't really even believe in ghosts. I think it was really her fear that wouldn't allow her to believe much of anything. She believed in God and that he never gave us more than we could handle. That he was always testing our faith and devotion to him. I wonder what test he gave me when he ripped my father away from my life. I had asked her about her thoughts on that once after it happened and all she could say was

"Pray about it and I'm sure you will get an answer. I think God just needed him more than us. There's always a good reason."

A Journey of a Thousand Miles – A Reflections Saga

Somehow I doubted that. I couldn't understand what I had done so wrong that would warrant that kind of punishment. Didn't he create us with free will? Why then would we be punished for using the very gifts he gave us? If you ask me…he sounded more like a hypocritical and judgmental god than anything else. I sure wasn't convinced that he was a loving god like I had been taught all these years. I found myself deep in thought, trying to recall my conversation with Seth. Trying to recall what Emily had told me that same day that my father passed, but it was all coming up blank. I could feel my hand start to move, as if someone had taken hold of it and was writing for me. I snapped out of my thoughts and glanced down at the page. I had written the words, *LOSS OF INNOCENCE*. Why the heck would I write something like that?! What does that mean? I quickly scribbled it out. I was scribbling so hard my pen had put a hole in the page and the ink had seeped through onto the next.

"Ava…Ava." a voice whispered.

It caught me off-guard. I snapped my head around but didn't see anything.

"I'm gonna twist your back…just like mine and you'll never get out of bed AGAIN!!Never get out of bed again!"

"Who…who's there?!" I shouted and suddenly I could hear a snicker erupt from behind me.

My sister was on the verge of tears from laughing so hard.

"You're too easy!" she chuckled. "You were so scared! Did you think she was coming for you?!" she asked while rolling around in hysterics on the floor.

"I'm telling mom! You're gonna be in so much trouble" I told her.

I got up from the table and ran to the front door. My sister bolted from the dining room and ran upstairs. My mother was less than pleased with her. She scolded her for a good hour and then assigned her additional chores for the entire week. She didn't stop there though. She took away her television privileges and even grounded her to the house. After she was finished with her firm lecture she sent her off to bed. I was happy that she got in trouble. What she did was downright cruel. The sound of her groaning and grumbling all the way up the stairs seemed to suggest that she wouldn't be pulling that stunt again anytime soon. I was satisfied with the punishment she received. Did it fit the crime? Probably not, but at least she was going to reflect on her actions now.

"You're going to sleep in the living room tonight." my mother told me. "Allan made a few tapes for you and I figured you would probably want to watch them." she continued with a smile.

I was definitely excited to see what he had brought over for me. He seemed to take notice of my likes and dislikes. He knew I loved movies of all kinds. I wasn't just your average Disney princess lover. I'm an old soul and my tastes have always reflected that fact.

"Look what I got for you!" Allan interrupted with a smile while holding the films out for me to read.

"Fire starter!" I shouted and started jumping up and down. I had seen it once played on TV but never in its entirety. Now I owned it! Allan lifted the tape up so I could look at the titles of the others printed on the label. I read them and got excited again. *Little Mermaid* was the title on the next line and *Beauty and the Beast* followed it. I was so excited to watch them all. I rushed into my mother's room to grab my pillow and blanket and set up camp on the love seat. My mother popped some popcorn for me and poured me a glass of juice.

"Make sure you brush your teeth after you eat this! You don't want to get a mouthful of cavities." she insisted.

"I won't forget mom. I promise. Goodnight!" I leaned in for a kiss and hug before turning my focus to the TV just as the opening credits were rolling for Fire Starter.

"I'll be right back" Allan told me "I need to go grab my stuff in the car."

He returned with a few blankets and pillows of his own and set them up on the living room floor. After the movie was over and I had scarfed down all of the popcorn, I proceeded to wash up in the bathroom and get ready for bed. I knew that we still had two movies to look at, but I didn't want to keep having to pause the movie every time I had something to do, so I decided I'd do it all at once. I think I made it halfway through Beauty and the Beast before sleep finally took over. The next morning my mother asked how our movie escapades went and I told her that it was a lot of fun and I was hoping we were going to do it again soon. It became our little ritual I guess you could say. It was still summer so there was plenty of opportunity and it became a nightly thing for awhile.

After a few weeks Allan had to leave to go back home and care for his mother. She had become ill and he was all she had. I had met her and interacted with her a handful of times. She was a very sweet lady and she adored me. She didn't speak English too well. I think they were Hungarian or Ukrainian and I remember Allan telling me that she had only been in Canada for maybe ten to fifteen years at the most. She still had a very thick accent when she tried to speak English, but the more time I spent around her…the easier it was becoming to understand her. She thought I was just the cutest little girl ever. It must've been my blonde ringlets. Everyone often commented that I looked a lot like Shirley Temple. I think that must've been my meme's intention all those years ago, when she began training my hair to curl into spirals. It was something she did every night for years. She would cut up old washcloths and twirl my hair into the spirals before tying off the curls at the ends. I would go to bed with a head full of washcloth pieces. What a sight that must've been! She was determined that she was going to train my hair to grow naturally that way, and over time that is exactly what happened. Or was it? As I would later discover, my hair was always going to have those curls, even without her help. My hair was already going to be naturally curly.

My curls were the first thing Allan's mother commented on when she first laid eyes on me. Then she started buying me clothing, shoes, candy and hair accessories. I think she saw me as the granddaughter she always wanted but never had. Allan was an only child and it was just the two of them in that apartment. His

A Journey of a Thousand Miles – A Reflections Saga

mother seemed pretty lonely whenever we would go by for a visit and then appeared to be saddened whenever we would announce that we were leaving. It seemed like she never wanted us to go. She would always pack up a bag for me to take. A care package of sorts. When Allan left that day to go take care of his mother, we didn't have any idea how long he was going to be gone for. I missed our movie nights mostly, but I also missed his company. It was like he became the father figure I had been missing since the loss of my own. I had grown quite fond of him. He returned about two weeks later. His mother had become so ill that she had to be hospitalized, but now she was back home and seemed to be doing much better by the sounds of it. He mentioned that he could only stay for a few nights here and there and that he would be leaving to check in on her from time to time.

"Come over here. I've got something to show you. I know how much you like arts and crafts, so I thought this might be fun to do together." he told me as he placed a plastic shopping bag on the table.

It was one of those classic model car sets that you build from scratch.

"I think that might be too old for her." my mother interrupted. "It says it's for fifteen plus." she pointed at the cover.

"I think you underestimate your daughter. I think she can handle it just fine. Besides, I'll be here to help her. This is a beginner's model anyway. Let's just see how she does!" he smiled, giving me a wink.

"Yeah…maybe you're right." she smiled in return at me and walked out of the room.

The model took a great deal of time to build. It was weeks before we were even able to get to the painting portion. I was excited for that part the most.

"What colour are we going to paint it?" I asked.

"Well I was thinking that you could decide that. I was thinking maybe blue. What do you think?" he looked at me and smiled.

Of course I chose blue and we painted two white racing stripes on the hood with black on either side to really make the white stand out. I was so proud when it was finally finished. My mother congratulated me, but I felt that she was more surprised than anything else. Did she really think I wouldn't be able to handle it? Every week he would show up with something new to work on together. My creative juices were flowing and there was no stopping me. I began to show an interest in painting. I started off simple, with paint by numbers and worked my way from there. I enjoyed the paint by numbers, but they were always planned out for you ahead of time and I didn't much care for that part of it. I wanted to have the ability to choose for myself. I would paint pictures of mystical creatures and lands mostly. Things that didn't exist in our reality. I was always drawn to them. I would paint pictures of angels with wings made of light and fairies riding the backs of unicorns. It was my own little fantasy world and I was happiest there.

Eventually, Allan began spending so much time at our house it was as if he had moved in. My mother seemed to welcome the idea. I had someone to look after me and keep my busy little mind occupied. One night we were having our traditional movie night. My sisters and brother had gone off to their father's for the weekend and my mother had gone out with friends. It was just he and I. He had been around for quite awhile now and I was comfortable in his presence. I remember him putting on the movie My Girl. The song in it reminded me of my father. He used to always sing it to me in the car. He also sang Be My Baby by the Ronettes. He was always singing and dancing. I remember the movie made me a bit sad because it made me miss him. Allan must have sensed it because just as the tears started to roll down my cheeks, he turned around and asked if I was okay. He asked if it was what happened to the little boy in the movie that had me so upset and I told him that although that was very sad I was just thinking of my father in that moment. It was the song that brought up old memories. He smiled and told me that he understood and that I should come lay down beside him so he could make me feel better.

As we lay there, he put his arm around me and we continued to watch the movie. I must've fallen asleep at some point, because I remember waking up to the sensation of being carried. It brought back memories of whenever I would fall asleep in the car or on the couch and my father would pick me up and carry me up to my bedroom. It was a comforting feeling. I always felt safe in my father's arms. I felt that no harm could ever come to me there. Now Allan had taken his place, or at least he tried to. I felt him lay me down on the bed and that's when I opened my eyes to see where I was. I instantly recognized that it was my mother's bedroom. I was happy that he cared so much about my well being, that he didn't want me to wake up with a stiff neck from sleeping on the floor. I thanked him for his kindness and then rolled over toward the wall to go back to sleep. I felt him get in the bed beside me and didn't think anything unusual of it. What seven year old would?! I awoke a few hours later to the sensation of my back being rubbed gently. It was a soothing feeling and I found it very relaxing. It was making me sleepy again. I remember hearing Allan whisper in my ear

"Shhh it's okay. Just go back to sleep sweetie. Let the medicine work." he had told me.

"Med…medicine? What medicine?" I asked groggily. I felt like I often did when my mother would give me Tylenol for a fever, but this seemed much stronger. It was hard for me to keep my eyes open. I struggled to fight it's effects as hard as I could, but it was pointless. I could feel myself being pulled deeper and deeper and then I was gone.

Chapter Sixteen

I awoke the next morning, alone in my mother's bed. Allan was no longer beside me. I could hear the sound of someone rattling dishes in the kitchen.

"Mom, is that you?" I asked.

"In here sweetie. I'm making breakfast. Are you hungry?" she called from the kitchen.

I sat up in bed and threw the covers off of me. My head felt like a truck had driven through it. I had a horrible headache. Something felt off to me, although I couldn't quite put my finger on what it was. I held my head in my hands and took a few deep breaths. I was feeling awful and I had a sick to my stomach feeling. Like I was going to throw up if I moved another inch. I must've come down with some type of bug.

"Mom! I…I don't feel so good!" I shouted.

She opened the door and quickly looked me over.

"You don't look good. What's wrong?" she asked while placing her hand on my forehead to check for a fever.

I wasn't sure how she did that. How she was always able to check my temperature by first placing her hand on my forehead and then kissing it. She was always able to determine with accuracy whether or not I had a temperature. Was this some type of freaky superpower only moms had?

"You don't feel warm. How about I bring you some flat ginger ale and chicken broth?" she asked while rubbing my back and looking at me with that concerned mom face all moms make whenever their children are ill.

"Yeah…sure…thanks mom. That sounds good." I tried to stand up, but I was dizzy and I slumped back down onto the bed.

"Oh god…I hope you don't have the flu!" she blurted out. "Here…let me help you stand up."

She grabbed hold of my arm and gently pulled me up to my feet.

I began to walk toward the door when I felt her reach down and tug at my nightgown.

A Journey of a Thousand Miles – A Reflections Saga

"How the hell did you manage that?" she asked. That's when I realized what she was talking about. Part of my nightgown had been tucked into the back of my underwear. I must've had a restless sleep to have accomplished that feat.

"Where's Allan?" I asked inquisitively.

"Oh he had to go check on his mother and run a few errands for her he said. He should be back around supper. Did you guys have fun last night?"

I wished I could remember all of the details, but they were blank after he told me to *"let the medicine work."*

"We watched My Girl," I told her, "and I fell asleep halfway through."

"Oh I haven't seen that one! What's it about?"she asked.

"Well…it's about a girl who lives in a funeral home with her father and he works on dead people."

"Never mind!" she interrupted. "You said you fell asleep so you probably didn't get into the main idea of it anyway." she laughed.

"It's called a plot mom…the main idea?!" I giggled back at her.

"How do you know so much and you're still so young? I guess we have your father to thank for that one huh?" she smiled at me. "Do you think you're okay to go by yourself now?" she glanced in the direction of the bathroom.

"Yeah…I think I'll be fine." I assured her, making my way down the hallway toward the bathroom.

I wasn't sure what had made me feel so sick, but once I moved around a bit the dizziness seemed to fade. I guess maybe I was still half asleep or something and yet the sick feeling was still with me. When I got back to her room she had laid out a cold washcloth and a glass of ginger ale on the table beside the bed.

"Soup is almost ready!" she shouted from the kitchen.

I lay there trying to collect my thoughts. Going over the last things I could recall over and over again in my head. Yet no matter how hard I tried to remember, it was all still coming up blank. Maybe Allan would be able to tell me. I decided I'd ask him once he got back.

It was around 5 PM when he finally showed up. I was helping my mother set the table for supper as he walked in. He smiled at me and pulled a plastic bag from behind his back.

"These are from my mother." he smiled.

It was a kit with beads and everything one needed to make bracelets, necklaces etc. I couldn't wait to start making something. I decided I was going to make something special for her to thank her for such a wonderful gift. I sat down on the floor and pulled the contents from the bag. Allan pulled up a chair and sat down to watch me. I was busy stringing the beads when I overheard my mother ask

"Was she feeling sick last night?"

A Journey of a Thousand Miles – A Reflections Saga

"No she seemed just fine." he told her.

"Well…she's not today. Did you let her have too much junk food again?" she asked, sounding a bit annoyed.

This definitely wasn't the result of junk food. I wondered what medicine he was talking about and why he had given it to me. My mother already seemed upset with him and I didn't want him to get into any trouble. I waited until she had walked back into the kitchen before asking him what had happened. He told me I had just fallen asleep about forty-five minutes into the movie and when it was finished he carried me to her bed. That was all he said. He didn't mention anything about giving me medicine. I decided to just leave it alone. Maybe I was dreaming that part, although I was pretty sure of what I felt, heard and saw. I hadn't told my mother anything about it, but while I was going to the bathroom it hurt really bad. It stung like a bee down there. When I looked at my private parts they were very red and almost irritated looking. Maybe she had used a new laundry soap. I have been known to have very sensitive skin, so it wouldn't be unusual for me to get a rash from it, but I had never had a rash there before.

After dinner I was feeling much better and I went outside to play with the little girl who lived a few doors away from us. Her name was Natasha and she had just moved in about a week ago. We had already become pretty good friends. We played dolls in the backyard at her house, and then we played dress up with her cat. I guess you could say we both had that natural mothering nature, even though we were only seven. When it started to get dark, I hugged her goodbye and we made plans to play together the next day. We also said that we would talk to our mothers about a sleep over that weekend. We were both super excited. When I got in the door, my mother informed me that she was going out again and that I would be hanging out with Allan. He told her he had brought some new movies for me to watch with him anyway, and that he didn't mind having to spend another night at our place.

About an hour later she left. I'm pretty sure she was dating again and I was happy about that. I saw her smiling again, much like she did when my father was still alive. I could see that she was starting to move on and I hoped that eventually I'd get to meet the man who seemed to be making her so happy. I popped some popcorn in the microwave and poured myself a glass of juice, while Allan set up the movie. He told me I could choose the first one, but that he had next choice. I was perfectly okay with that idea. He gave me three choices of movies. I had chosen Halloween. I rather enjoyed being scared. It was never even close to the fear I felt whenever I would see the horrible things that were haunting me every night. Maybe it was because I knew that these movies were fake and those ghostly things were not. I rather enjoyed Michael Myers' character. The way he seemed to stalk his victims and that mask he wore was spooky. I never understood why people ran upstairs to get away from him though. Why didn't they just run outside and scream their heads off?!

A Journey of a Thousand Miles – A Reflections Saga

I was only seven and it always seemed completely silly to me. Still, it was entertaining to watch. My heart raced much the same as theirs did I'm sure. I was always doing that. Even without trying. It seemed beyond my control. I was always putting myself in other's shoes and it was scary as hell sometimes. I was busy munching away on my popcorn, when I realized I was out of juice. Now everyone knows that you should never eat popcorn without a drink handy, because you have a strong possibility of choking on the little pieces of kernel that always seem to lodge themselves in the worst possible places. Like your throat for instance. I set the bowl of popcorn on the couch beside me and stood up to head for the kitchen. Allan immediately took notice, and asked where I was going.

"Oh, I'm just going to grab some more juice." I told him.

He paused the movie and then reached for my glass.

"I'm heading that way anyway…I'll get it for you." he insisted.

He returned handing me the glass and went back to his spot on the love seat on the other side of the room.

"Can you wait a few more minutes?" I asked. "I need to go to the bathroom."

After the movie was finished he got up to go through the tapes for the movie he had chosen. He told me to come lay with him on the floor where we would both be more comfortable and then he put the tape in. I can't remember what the movie was called now and at first it seemed like any other movie. However, after about five minutes or so it quickly changed into something not meant for kids. It was the type of movie where you were told to cover your eyes for certain parts. Only this movie seemed to have more of those parts than anything else. When I saw the people getting naked, I instinctively covered my eyes.

"Why are you doing that?" he asked.

"Because I'm not allowed to watch stuff like this. My mom doesn't let me." I said to him. "I'm way too young for this kind of movie." I continued.

"Well she isn't here now is she? It's okay. This is perfectly natural. It's nature. This is what men and women do." he replied. "Just watch! You will be a woman someday too. It's better if you practice now. Don't you want to be a good wife for your husband?" he whispered while pulling my hands down from my face.

"Yes," I replied innocently, "but won't I learn all of this stuff later? Like when I'm much older?" I asked. "No…this is where you start learning. All the girls your age do it…even the boys are practising." he started to massage my shoulders.

"Just relax…and watch…and learn." he whispered again and he began to run his hand over my legs while kissing me on the neck and sniffing my hair.

I honestly believed everything he was telling me. He was a very good liar. I had no idea that this wasn't normal. No one had ever spoken to me about anything like this. I hadn't even heard of such things, so I believed every bit of it. I started to feel drowsy again as I felt him grip my bottom and rub himself against me.

"What happened last night?" I asked him.

"Well, I gave you some medicine to help you relax…and then I played with you almost all night." he whispered.

"I hurt down there, why?!" I asked. "What did you do?!"

"I just played inside a little. Sometimes it hurts at first because you're not used to it." he explained as he began to run his hand to the front of my Pajama pants and then down inside them.

"Stop it!" I shouted. "It hurts! No Allan! That hurts a lot. Please stop it now." I began to cry.

"It's okay. I'll be gentle. I promise. You won't feel or remember a thing!" and then before I knew it...everything went dark again.

The next morning he told me everything that had happened that night while I was in a deep sleep. He told me he played a little and then gave me lots of kisses on my privates and then he put something inside of me. He told me that I was now a woman and that my future husband would be very pleased. He told me not to worry. That he had cleaned me up really good and that I shouldn't tell my mother because she'd never believe me anyway. He convinced me that I had an overactive imagination and that this was all normal but that it was our little secret and we shouldn't say anything to anyone about it. He told me that all the adults knew that kids were doing this kind of thing and that it was just never talked about. Secrets were important he said.

Eventually after about a year or so of just he and I, he had convinced me that other kids could benefit from this experience too. That I was depriving them of becoming men and women and how that was completely selfish of me. He told me I needed to get my friends involved. Natasha was to be the first. He had found out about our upcoming sleepover plans that weekend and he wanted to prepare her. Prepare her? For what? I would soon find out. Like me…her whole world was about to change. There would be others too. But for now, it would just be the three of us.

Chapter Seventeen

Seven years had passed since the very first incident. It had been almost a daily thing for me and for the others it was on weekends or whenever he could whisk us all away to go camping. That was when he would do things with all of us and have us *"play house"* with each other. He had me watch as he gave Natasha the same medicine and then when she fell asleep, he showed me how he had played with me that first time. It started with medicine so we would sleep through the whole thing, but then eventually, for a few of us, we were always wide awake. I think he enjoyed how painful it all was for us. He even had us play with each other and used to say how much he wished he had a camera. The son of one of my mother's really good friends was also one of his victims and he began hurting himself after about two years or so. He was cutting up his arms and pulling out his hair, eyelashes and eyebrows. He was screaming for help and no one knew what was wrong with him. It was assumed that he was troubled because of the split between his parents. It was so much more than that. Me and one of my good friends Jessica realized that something was very wrong with what had been going on. She too was feeling tormented by what had been going on all this time. It took her quite awhile to convince me to tell my mother what was really happening. Jessica told me that she had the sense this wasn't right and that she would be speaking to her parents about it later that evening after we dropped her off.

"We have to tell! I think he's hurting us. This isn't right Ava. I just feel it in my gut." she insisted.

"It does hurt when he tries to...you know. It's no longer a question Jess, it's a certainty. But I'm scared" I told her. "He said if we ever told anyone that no one would ever believe us over him and that he'd hurt our families and then come back for us." I cried. "and I believe him!" I shouted.

"They will protect us! They love us and they will always keep us safe. He can't hurt us. I promise. Just trust me!" she turned to face me and look into my eyes.

I could see the pain behind her own and I knew that no matter what…we had to say something. Later that evening, Jessica called me on the phone.

"Oh my God Ava! They are so upset." she whispered into the receiver. "They said it's very wrong what he's been doing to all of us and that…that he's probably going to go to jail! They want you to talk to your mom." she told me.

"I…I can't! She'd never believe me. He's right! I can't tell her!" I shouted.

"Well…then we will talk to your step dad about it. Maybe he can talk to her after that. We will tell him tomorrow okay?! I gotta go…My mom's coming." and then she hung up abruptly.

That night I barely slept at all. Everything up to this moment began to flash in my head…like an entire movie being played over and over. I was terrified. What was my mother going to say?! What would my step dad say?! I cried myself to sleep that night. The next morning Jessica showed up at my house as promised. My mother was out at the grocery store and Allan had gone to check on his mother again. It was if it was all by the Universe's design…It was just Bernie and myself at the house. Bernie was my mother's fiance. She had met him a few years back, after she had dated some real winners. Men who treated her like total shit actually. It was as if she was just so tired of being lonely, that she was willing to settle with just about anyone. When Bernie first entered the picture, I gave him a hard time. I was certain he had to be just like the rest of the men she had dated and I wasn't willing to see past his history of drug use. It took me a good year or two to warm up to him and let him in. I was so glad that I had.

When Jessica came inside, she looked like she too had been sleep deprived.

"Where is he?" she asked while scanning the living room and kitchen thoroughly.

"He's gone to see his mother. Are you sure you want to do this?!" I asked worried.

"It's either we do it or my parents will." she told me bluntly.

"Fine!" I shouted "Bernie... Bernie could you come in the dining room for a minute? Jess and I would like to speak to you about something please." I shouted toward my mother's bedroom.

He came out of the room pretty fast. As if he sensed the urgency in my voice and we all sat down at the dining room table. Jessica ended up having to tell him a great deal of the details as to what was going on, as my fear wouldn't allow me to get the words out. All I could do was shake uncontrollably and cry. Bernie had grabbed my chair at one point and pulled me in toward his own chair, as close as he could possibly get it. I felt a strong sense of protection coming from him. He didn't say much of anything at first. He seemed to be in shock. I couldn't even tell if he believed what he was hearing. He just sat there in silence for a long time and then he put his hand to cover his mouth and shouted

"Oh my fucking God!! This is crazy...I'm going to kill that son of a bitch!" and then the tears came like a river, flowing endlessly. After he composed himself he turned to her and I and whispered, "I'm so sorry." before breaking down into another fit of tears.

The emotion coming off of him was unmistakable. I felt powerful levels of rage and also deep sadness emanating from him. It was so powerful that it sent both Jessica and I into a fit of our own tears.

"Okay," he told us once he had collected himself. "here's what we are gonna do. We are going to have to tell your mother. I don't know how she's going to take this, but we have to tell her. So we will tell her tonight. We have to get you away from here...from him, so we can keep this matter private. Jessica, I'd like for you to be there also. Can you call your parents and ask if maybe you could stay for dinner tonight? I'm sure they know what's going on by now. Just let them know what the plan is okay?!"

Jessicaa did as she was told and got up from the table to call her parents to let them know what was happening.

"Okay thanks mom. I'll be home as soon as I can. I love you too. Okay bye." then she hung up.

She had the look of defeat written all over her face. It was like the severity of the situation...the weight of all that we had been through for the last seven years. Yes you read that right. We had been going through this abuse for seven very long years. And suddenly it all had just come tumbling down on top of Jess and I in that very moment and we felt like we were both about to be crushed beneath it all. Jess fell to the floor, covered her eyes and began to cry again. Bernie walked over to her and lifted her up. She cried into his shoulder as he carried her over to the couch. Just then the front door swung open and in walked Allan. We immediately all composed ourselves in that moment. It was as if autopilot had switched on.

"What's wrong with her?!" he asked concerned and began to walk toward Jessica and Bernie on the couch.

"She's fine! Just has a bad headache" Bernie lied. "We're just waiting for Vic to get home and then we are going out for dinner. We will drop her off at home on the way." he turned to face Jessica. "Does that sound okay with you Jess?" he asked while winking subtly at her.

She nodded her head. You could see her trying her very best to keep her composure, but the fear of Allan was very real and it was written all over her face. I was afraid of him too. Now that I had discovered the true monster he really was. He wasn't my friend at all. He was an evil man and he had taken so much from me…from all of us! I once looked at him as a father figure, a protector…someone who loved me. Now the sight of him made me sick to my stomach. How could I have been so stupid?! How could anyone think this was okay? He was extremely manipulative and a master at lying. He wore a very convincing mask. I wasn't the only one who trusted him and believed his lies. Every single one of us did. Soon we would discover just how many victims he had stolen the innocence from.

About an hour later, my mother came home. Jessica and I ran outside to help her with the bags of groceries, and carried them into the house for her. She was none the wiser as to the conversation that had taken place earlier that day, and just how much we were all holding back. Allan didn't have a clue either. After she was inside, Bernie motioned for her to follow him into the bedroom. They closed the door behind them and I could hear the muffled sounds of Bernie's voice telling my mother about our plans for dinner elsewhere and informing her that Jessica would be joining us that evening. He didn't let her in on the whole plan. Just that we were going for dinner. When he had finished talking to her, I heard her say

"That's fine…I really like Jessica. She and Ava are so close. They're practically sisters." then the door opened and they both stepped into the hallway.

"Are you girls ready?" Bernie asked with a smile.

Jess and I both nodded in agreement.

"Okay! Let's go then" he suggested.

As we walked through the dining room past Allan, he looked in our direction and informed us he was also going to be leaving for awhile.

A Journey of a Thousand Miles – A Reflections Saga

"Yeah it's probably a good idea if you don't come back until morning." Bernie suggested. "We're probably going to take Ava to a late show after dinner, so there's no telling what time we will be back." he continued while reaching past Allan for his car keys on the table behind him.

I think I must've been holding my breath in that moment, as my heart started racing and I gasped for air. I wasn't sure what was going to happen between them, but I could feel the tension in the air. My mother however, seemed completely oblivious to everything. Allan got a weird look on his face, and for a second my heart nearly stopped altogether, but then he nodded in agreement and walked out of the house ahead of us. I turned to Bernie and looked at his face. He seemed calm, cool and collected on the outside, but inside...well that was a different picture altogether.

When we arrived at the restaurant, my mother excused herself to go to the bathroom. Bernie took advantage of the opportunity for us to be alone and then he turned to Jessica and I and told us that we would wait to tell her any details until after we were all finished with our meals. He didn't want her to be upset on an empty stomach. I ordered my usual...fish and chips. Jessica got the same as me and my mother ordered a seafood platter. She always did love shrimp. I think she must've been the one to get me to love it so much. She would eat it every day if given the chance. So would I for that matter. After we were finished eating, Bernie turned to her and reached for her hand.

"Vic...Sweetheart...The girls have something they need to tell you." he said while turning toward Jess and I, and attempting to clear his throat. "Girls...you have the floor!" he announced as he twisted in his chair and began watching her very closely.

He watched her reactions as he listened again to the story we had told him just an hour or so prior. Hearing it a second time didn't seem to affect him any less than when he had heard it the first time. He looked deeply into my mother's eyes, as if he were trying to read her. Yet she wasn't looking at him. She wasn't looking at Jessica or I either. When she realized how horrible this story was becoming she had turned and looked away from us. Her eyes had started to water and she seemed to have shut down completely. She now appeared to be staring off into something in the distance, although when I turned to look in the direction of her stare there was absolutely nothing there.

Have you ever heard the expression, *'the lights are all on but nobody is home'*? Well that's exactly what it looked like. She had checked out. Jess again told the majority of the story, and I filled in the gaps where she got choked up and broke down into tears. We both took turns doing that for each other. It was the most difficult moment of my life...of our lives, and yet I knew we'd have to tell it again and again and again. When word got out about this I was sure he would be arrested and that we would all be forced to relive every single minute detail as we told and retold the story. I could only imagine the countless hours we would be questioned about this.

A Journey of a Thousand Miles – A Reflections Saga

Once we had finally gotten through the painstaking task of telling my mother all that we had been through, the lights seemed to flicker in her eyes and she checked back in…almost in a flash. She turned to Bernie first and began shaking her head side to side.

"I don't believe it Bernie. I don't know if I can believe this shit!" she shouted at him.

"They're not making it up, honey. Look at them! Look how terrified they are. Look in their eyes and then you tell me they're both lying about this!" He demanded. "They're not and you know it. We will take care of this." he assured her. "I will handle it!" he shouted, grabbing her hand and then the tears rushed from her eyes as she looked at Jess and I.

"Oh my fucking God girls! I'm so so sorry. How did this happen? Why did I let this happen? I should've protected you! I'm sorry…I failed…I'm worthless." she cried, and then she called us both over to her side of the table and hugged us tighter than I ever remember being hugged by anyone.

Her embrace was so tight. It was if she were holding onto us both for dear life. She looked both of us in the eyes and kissed our cheeks.

"We're going to get this bastard!" she said with absolution.

"Okay! So it's settled then and we are all on the same page. I think we should go." Bernie suggested.

"We don't want to cause a scene here." he said, then he flagged the waitress down and asked for the bill.

I don't remember exactly what the total was, but I do remember he left a fifteen dollar tip. My mother had become so distraught and Jess and I couldn't stop crying. People in the restaurant had drawn their full attention toward our table and Bernie was in a hurry to take us out of that spotlight. Once we were outside it was as if my mother suddenly became weak in the knees. The stress of the situation had seemed to overtake her. I hadn't seen her that upset since the death of my father. Bernie helped her to the car and told her to take a few deep breaths. He kept reassuring her that he was going to take care of everything. I found myself wondering exactly how he planned to do that.

I watched as Jessica walked up her front porch and waved goodbye as we pulled out of her driveway. She told me she would call me in the morning to discuss everything that had happened that day. It had been a long day for all of us. I found myself wondering if Allan returned to the house, how that was all going to play out. Especially now that the secret was out and both my mother and Bernie were livid. I wasn't sure how he would be received, but I knew it wasn't going to be too kindly after all of that. I had heard my mother mumble under her breath that she was going to murder him if he showed up anytime soon. Judging by the look in her eyes, I would say that wasn't too far off.

When we pulled into the driveway, my mother suggested we all watch a movie together to take our minds off of the whole thing for the time being. Of course they chose *My Girl*. I guess my mother forgot that I had watched it with Allan before. It wasn't as if I could avoid every movie I'd ever watched with him, plus I hadn't even seen the whole thing anyway. I was hoping to destroy my original memory of the first time I watched it and replace it with a new and happier one. I finally saw the movie all the way through this time. It was pretty good and I rather enjoyed it. It was sad, but still good. My mother was the one who fell asleep first this time. She always had a habit of doing that though. It was like an automatic thing for her. You turn on a movie, switch off the lights and she passes out within ten minutes or so. She would always argue that she wasn't sleeping though.

"I'm just resting my eyes!" she would argue.

And then five minutes later she would be snoring. It always made me laugh hysterically. Was it a common occurrence for old people? I wondered. Although she wasn't exactly old. Just older than me, and that always made her and everyone else seem ancient by my standards. After the movie ended Bernie turned to look at her and laughed.

"I'm going to get her to bed." he chuckled. "Are you going to be okay down here by yourself or do you want to sleep in our bed and I'll take the couch?" he proposed.

"No I'll be okay here. I'll just leave the TV on. Can you make sure all the doors and windows are locked though please!" I pleaded.

"Of course! I'll double check everything before I head there myself." he assured me while leaning over to kiss me on the forehead and heading off to bed.

That night I tossed and turned. Sleep eluded me. I kept having nightmares that Allan was going to break into the house and kill us all. I kept waking up and looking at the windows, as if I expected that he would be standing there looking in at me. I found myself wondering if he even knew what was going on. My mind was racing with thoughts of what was to come. Before I knew it, the sun was coming up. Now I definitely wasn't going to get any sleep! I reached for the remote control to flip the channel on the TV to check the time. 7:38 AM. I started flipping between the channels until I found something I might be able to fall asleep to and finally closed my eyes again. For some reason I felt safer now that it was daylight out, which really didn't make any sense to me since I knew Allan was supposed to be coming back soon. I was so mentally exhausted that I slept straight through everything. I didn't even hear the sounds of Bernie in the kitchen preparing brunch for us. I awoke to the gentle nudge of my mother.

"What time did you go to bed?!" she asked with concern. "Were you up all night?"

"Kinda," I said yawning. "I couldn't really sleep mom. I kept having nightmares."

"Oh! Well you're okay. Everything is okay. We are here. You're safe!" she squeezed my shoulder. "Now come and have something to eat." she got up from the edge of the couch and walked into the kitchen to fix our plates.

A Journey of a Thousand Miles – A Reflections Saga

"What time is it?" I asked.

"It's almost 1:00PM." my mother replied.

Wow! I had slept nearly five and a half hours, and yet I felt like I had just closed my eyes. I was hoping to catch a nap after brunch, but I somehow knew this day was going to be one the longest days of my life. I didn't know exactly why that was. I just felt it. Allan showed up a bit later that day, around 3:00PM and everyone put on an act for him. It was as if nothing had ever changed. Bernie had even invited him to go for dinner with him that evening. I thought that was completely unusual. Was he really about to go to dinner with the enemy?! Panic instantly set in. Did they not believe any of it now? Why were they being so nice to him? Didn't they hear the pain Jess and I were going through, as we were reliving everything he had done to us? Was he really going to get away with it all? My mind was travelling to some very dark places. I couldn't understand what was going on. I pulled my mother to the side, making up a lie about needing her help with hanging pictures in my room. When we were upstairs and out of earshot I asked her what was going on.

"Bernie is just taking him out for a quick bite to eat. I think he wants to ask him some questions. I don't really know sweetie. He just said he wants to take him out of the house and to ask him some questions...that's all." she replied.

"Do...Do you guys not really believe us?!" I shouted.

"Shhh! Keep your voice down!" she pressed her finger to her lips. "We never said we don't believe you. We're just trying to get to the bottom of it. That's all." she said as she tried to reassure me.

I couldn't believe what I was hearing. I became very upset. I felt anger, defeat and a deep sadness all wrapped up into one.

"It didn't happen, huh? He never did anything to me?!" I screamed at her while bending down to pull out the bottom drawer to my dresser.

I yanked the drawer out as hard as I could and ripped the cotton underwear I had taped to the back of them off the backside of it and pushed them into her hands.

"What is this?" she asked with astonishment while staring down at the fabric in her hands.

"Just look at them!" I shouted. "Maybe then you will figure it out. Look at the size they are too." I pointed furiously.

She began to unfold the underwear just enough to expose the tag on the inside.

"These are your underwear from when you were seven. Why would you keep them?" she asked, but suddenly it was like a light bulb went on in her head and she knew the answer.

She got teary eyed as she continued to unfold them the rest of the way and saw the old blood stain I had desperately tried to scrub out of them. For seven years I had kept them hidden.

"What is this? You were...you were bleeding?!" she fell to the floor and started to cry.

A Journey of a Thousand Miles – A Reflections Saga

"That, mother, is from when he forced himself inside of me. I woke up in the middle of it. You weren't here. I was screaming and you weren't here to protect me. It hurt so bad I nearly passed out. Now you know the secret I kept hidden all these years. Are you happy now?!" I was blind with – I don't know what – not really anger. Maybe. But maybe I was just heartbroken. I'd held that for so long with the end in sight and it just seemed like all of it, everything, was going to be taken away again. *SNAP!* Just like that.

I was sinking with the feeling no one believed it ever happened. That I was brutally assaulted by a fifty two year old man. Alone. Helpless. Terrified even. And no one was there to stop it. I began to flash back to that horrifying night and the morning afterwards. He told me it was completely normal for it to hurt that way. That it hurts everyone the same their first time. He also told me that he was disappointed that he could only get part of the way in. That next time he was going to make sure I laid there and took it and then it wouldn't hurt so much every time after.

"It'll hurt a lot at first. You can scream, cry, bite me and do whatever you need to do to get through it, but after that you won't hurt ever again okay?"

The fucker actually treated me like I was a woman of his, like a girlfriend or something in his twisted ass mind. I don't know what the fuck he thought, really. How could I? A Nightmare on Elm Street was happening in my home. The only thing was that the prick wasn't burned or horribly disfigured. To think about it again, it was sickening.

I quickly snapped out of the flashback as my mother grabbed me and hugged me so tight and cried so hard. I wanted to cry too, but I couldn't. Now I was filled with a deep seeded anger. I was mad at the world for what happened to me, but most of all I was mad at myself for letting it happen. Even worse I had allowed the same thing to happen to my friends. What kind of friend was I?! They were sure to never speak to me again after all off this. I didn't blame them one bit. I was just as evil as he was, or at least that's what I thought. After my mother had composed herself, we headed back downstairs. Allan and Bernie were just getting ready to leave. I studied their faces to determine whether or not they had heard us upstairs.

"Is everything okay?" Bernie asked. There was my answer.

"Yes, everything is fine. Ava just made me cry that's all. She made me a beautiful painting." she lied.

"Oh that's nice. I can't wait to see it later. Anyway ladies, we're heading out." he walked toward the door and motioned for Allan to go first.

"After you sir." he smiled and then he turned to both my mother and I and winked.

He kissed us both on the cheek goodbye and whispered in between us, *"I'm going to kill this son of a bitch..."* then he smiled an eerie smile and headed out the door.

My mother and I couldn't say a word. We just stood there in utter shock as we watched them pull out of the driveway and wave goodbye before driving off.

Chapter Eighteen

It wasn't too long after they had left, that I heard a loud knock on the door. Somehow I knew that this knock had something to do with Bernie and Allan. I wasn't sure what had happened, but I was sure that it would affect us all. It was a strong feeling in the pit of my stomach…something I would later come to call intuition. The knocking continued for a good two minutes or so, as my mother and I looked out through several windows that faced the driveway, before finally determining it was the police. My mother had a very concerned look on her face. I could hear her thoughts racing just as much as mine were, as she began to unlock the deadbolt to the front door.

"Good afternoon Ma'am. I'm officer Blount. There's been an incident with your husband Bernie and another gentleman by the name of Allan. We're going to need you and your daughter to come down to the station to give a statement as well as answer a few of our questions." the officer notified us.

My mother and I didn't say much at all. We just glanced oddly at each other as if trying to read each other's mind. I wondered what had happened between Allan and Bernie. Was everyone okay? Where were they both and why were the police taking us in for questioning? Had Bernie done something to hurt Allan?!! My mind was buzzing with a thousand questions. Questions I knew I would soon have all the answers to. I grabbed my shoes and walked down the hallway toward the back of the house to make sure all of the windows and doors were locked. There was no telling how long we would be.

"Are you ready?" my mother asked. "Okay then let's go!" she hurried me as she pulled the front door closed behind us and reached for her key to lock it.

"This way, please." the officer ushered us toward his cruiser and opened the back door before gesturing for us to climb in.

"My partner and I will give you a ride there. There's no need to worry. You and your daughter aren't in any kind of trouble. We just want to ask you a few questions." he assured us.

A Journey of a Thousand Miles – A Reflections Saga

The trip took about fifteen minutes. My mother and I sat in complete silence the entire way. All we could do was look at each other with curiosity. What were we about to learn? When we arrived at the police station the officers told us to follow them. We were led into a room with two other officers and offered a seat on a comfy looking couch.

"Thank you both for coming down. First I'd like to ask you both a few questions and then I will fill you in on why we've asked you here." the female officer spoke gently.

"Mrs. Ducharme, I was wondering if I might have a word with your daughter alone? My partner will escort you to another location to speak with you. Would that be alright?" she asked.

My mother didn't speak a word, she just nodded before standing up and walking toward the doorway to meet up with another officer. He actually had a suit on and didn't look like a police officer at all. He wasn't wearing the typical uniform the rest of them were.

"Don't worry sweetie. I'm not going far okay. I'll just be down the hall." she reassured me before walking out of the room with the other officer.

I knew these questions were probably the type that were of a more private nature. I guessed that was why they had my mother and the other officer leave the room. As soon as they left, the female officer began to ask me simple questions at first, then they became more invasive as time went on. She asked me how I knew Allan. How long he'd been in my life. If he had ever lived with us. How long ago he started touching me in a sexual way. Why I never told anyone. If I ever asked him to stop etc. I answered each of them and yet she always came up with more. It soon became clear that I wasn't just being asked a few questions. This was now beginning to feel like a full on interrogation! Just when I thought I might break down into a puddle of tears, my mother and the other officer returned. I was so relieved to see the two of them. The officers sat my mother and I down and finally told us why we were there.

It seems that Bernie had taken Allan to dinner as planned. Everything appeared to be going normal, but then Bernie had excused himself to go to the washroom. He actually went to find the kitchen and once he made his way inside, he grabbed a large butcher knife and proceeded to return to the table and place it up to Allan's throat while screaming for anyone in the restaurant to call the police immediately or he was going to kill Allan right there in front of everyone. He was arrested soon after and they were all set to press charges against him, until he started talking and he told a very convincing story about how he felt it necessary to protect me from that monster. The charges were all dropped once the police had questioned both my mother and I and determined that he was in fact telling the truth. They called it a *"crime of passion"* and he was released.

Apparently, it's when someone is brought to a state of heightened emotion and they just sort of lose control. After hearing the story, I began to picture how all of that must've gone down. I kind of wished I had been there to see it all. I'm sure everyone was frightened and probably thought Bernie had lost his mind. Allan must've been scared shitless too. Perhaps he got a taste of what that kind of fear was like for all of the kids he had victimized. I wondered what was going to happen now. About fifteen minutes later, we were finally able to see Bernie. He was released and brought into the room with all of us. Shortly after that, I was pulled out of the room by a woman in a business suit. She didn't look like a police officer at all either. She took me into a room and asked me to tell her about what had happened to me. She even asked me to act out the scenarios using dolls she had placed in front of me. I wasn't really sure why she asked me to do that, but I was sure it had something to do with her being able to better understand what took place. Just as we were finishing up, I noticed a familiar face walking down the hallway and just past the window to the room we were sitting in. It was Jessica.

'*What's she doing here?*' I wondered. The woman looked up to notice me staring out the window at Jessica.

"It's okay. We're finished here for now. You are free to go. I'll take you back to your parents now." she said with a smile.

"I'm going to ask your friend Jessica a few questions now…Come with me." she said gently as she opened the door and motioned for me to walk through it first.

"Come on inside Jessica and have a seat. I'm just going to take Ava back to her family and I'll be right with you." she informed her. Jessica waved as the lady closed the door, and then we continued on down the hallway. Once I was back in the room with my mother and Bernie, my mother informed me that the detectives had all they needed and we were free to leave the police station. She informed me that Allan would be spending the night in jail and that they would be releasing him in the morning. I wondered why that was.

'*Why only one night? Shouldn't he be spending a lifetime there for what he did?*'

I was terrified of what might happen when he got out. Would he come looking for me…for us?! The car ride home was complete silence the entire way. I just sat back in my seat and stared out the window. Wondering what was going to happen. I wasn't sure how these things worked, and I had never met anyone who had been through a similar situation, so there was no one to ask either. It was brand new to all of us. That night I had the most restless sleep of my entire life. I kept seeing images of Allan's face in my dreams. The things he said to me played over and over again in my mind. Would he really hurt my family? I found myself wishing that things could just go back to the way they were before…when no one knew the truth. When Allan had just been the seemingly normal guy he appeared to be. Before he became the monster.

I didn't want him anywhere near me or my friends, but I also didn't want people to look at me weird either. I had already had enough of the awkward stares just for being *"different"* as it was. I was never the child who wanted to be the center of attention. I did my best to stay in the background of large crowds. I hated public speaking. I couldn't handle all of the eyes focused on me at the same time. Now I had a feeling the focus was going to remain on me for a very long time, and just the thought of that alone was extremely unnerving. I must've tossed and turned in my bed for most of the night that night. I remember the sunlight slowing creeping through my window before I was finally able to feel safe enough to close my eyes.

I was startled awake by the sound of a very loud **BANG! BANG! BANG!** I opened my eyes quickly and gasped in horror. I was expecting to be in my bedroom, but I wasn't. I don't know where I was but it definitely wasn't MY bedroom. There was a cool summer breeze blowing through the curtains that hung on my window. There was a canopy over the top of the bed I had been sleeping on, and the bed was rather large for such a young girl. It was made of some very old, yet polished looking wood. I quickly realized it was an antique. It was held together by slats cut into the posts and large bolts securing them in place. The room smelled musty with the smell of vinegar and a hint of floral. I could hear the sound of three male voices talking loudly amongst each other just outside my window. I listened intently to see if I could place who they might be, but they were not familiar to me at all.

'*Where the hell am I now?*' I wondered. '*How did I get here?*'

I glanced around the room and noticed an old looking rocking chair in the far corner to my left. On the far wall from the bed was a huge vanity with a large mirror at the top. There was a chair pulled up to it, and a fancy looking robe strewn over the top of the chair back. On either side of it were two very large antique looking dressers, which took up three quarters of the wall on either side. On the far right wall was an armoire that appeared to be custom built, and had two very large French doors attached to it. The room was still very dark, with just a sliver of sunlight entering through the window as the curtains continued to blow in the cool summer breeze. I could smell the scent of fresh flowers in the air and the aromatic scents of breakfast. The sound of gunfire or what I believed to be gunfire could still be heard outside. **BANG! BANG!** Now I knew this must've been the noise that startled me awake. I threw the covers off of me and stood up on the antique hardwood as quickly and quietly as I could. I was trying to be careful not to alert anyone downstairs to my presence. I wasn't even sure where I was at this moment or whether or not I might be in any danger. I gently tiptoed my way over to the window to glance at the activity outside. There were five men dressed in Navy blue suits carrying very old looking guns, and they were firing shots into the sky while herding a bunch of people into a large barn. I watched them closely and tried to determine what they were doing, but just then I heard what sounded like footsteps coming up the stairway outside of the bedroom door.

'*Should I hide or just stand here?*' I wondered.

I quickly decided to take my chances, and I rushed over to the vanity to grab the robe hanging on the chair. At this moment I was quickly alerted to a draft that blew against my skin, and I suddenly realized I was completely naked! A knock came on the door as I reached the chair.

"Just a moment please!" I shouted out.

A Journey of a Thousand Miles – A Reflections Saga

"Annabelle…Annabelle are you alright? I thought I heard you fall." the voice of a female called through the door.

Who the heck was Annabelle?! I wondered yet, I knew I had to play along. I couldn't sound suspicious.

"No mother I'm really quite well. I've just woken up. I'll be down in a moment. Would you mind the trouble of fixing some tea please?" I asked.

Whoa! I covered my mouth in shock. This was not MY voice. This wasn't the way I spoke. This voice was completely different from my own. It sounded older and I heard strong hints of a British accent. This definitely wasn't my body. I grabbed the robe and quickly wrapped it around myself and tied the sash around my waist. That was the moment I noticed that everything about my youthful body had changed. I appeared to be in a young woman's body now. I had breasts, a curvy waist, long legs and manicured toes. My hair was almost down to the top of my buttocks and it was so blonde it looked almost white. I also had lustrous spiral curls. I was curious to see what my face looked like. I walked over to the window to pull back the curtain and let the sunlight pour into the room so I could get a better look at myself. Then I slowly walked back toward the mirror and bent over for a closer look. I was completely taken aback by my appearance. I was beautiful! I had the most beautiful emerald eyes I have ever seen, rosy cheeks with high sculpted cheekbones and small yet perfectly shaped lips.

"Nathaniel has arrived. Do hurry it up darling!" the voice I assumed to be my mother urged me.

"Okay! I'll be down in a moment." I shouted back to her.

How was I ever going to get through this? I had no idea who I was, let alone any of these people. I still had yet to meet my own family for the first time, and now there was a man by the name of Nathaniel who was waiting for me too?! I reach into the top drawer of the vanity and pulled out a paddle brush, some hair pins and some rouge. I begin to pull my hair back at the crown and form two braids on either side of my head, pinning them together at the back. I remove my clothing from the back of the chair and begin to dress myself. My clothing appears to be from the Victorian era. I recognize the corset and hoop crinoline that goes under my dress. I seem to have no trouble with fastening it myself, at least I don't think so. How should I know how it's supposed to look? I'm not from this time. I quickly but carefully sweep some rouge over my lips and take one last glance at myself in the mirror before heading toward the bedroom door. I stop as I reach for the handle and take a few deep breaths.

"Well…here goes nothing!" I tell myself.

Then I reach for the doorknob and slowly pull the door open. I'm startled by the presence of my mother just outside in the hallway

"Good grief, Mother! You gave me a fright." I lean in to embrace this complete stranger and hope that she won't catch on that a real life invasion of the body snatchers incident has just occurred with her daughter Annabelle.

She seems none the wiser and squeezes me tightly before looking up at me with concern.

"Good heavens Annabelle! Are you certain you're alright?" she asks with a confused look on her face "You look a mess! Your dress isn't fastened securely and it looks horrid. Come in your room and I'll tend to it for you." she urges while dragging me by the hand.

She undoes the back of my dress and begins to yank tightly on the strings of the corset. I can feel my ability to breathe fading with each pull

"Good God mother! Not so tight! I can hardly catch air!" I shout.

"My apologies, but you know that it must be secure. We want you to look like the jammiest bits of jam, do we not?" she turns me around and looks sternly at me. What the hell does, *jammiest bits of jam,* mean? I have no idea, but I decide to go along with it anyway.

"Of course we do mother!" I reply heading for the doorway.

As we walk down the stairs, I can feel my heart begin to pound in my chest. I am super nervous to meet this Nathaniel gentleman.

"Deep breaths!" I remind myself. Everything is fine. There waiting at the bottom of the stairwell is the most gorgeous man I have ever laid eyes on. He is tall, native looking with a tanned complexion and definitely masculine in every sense of the word. He smiles at me as I reach the last step, and reaches out his hand to help me to the landing. I smile at him and give him my hand and gently step down to the floor.

"You look beautiful" he says with a smile that lights his face, and then everything begins to fade to black.

I watch as he struggles to catch me and I can hear the commotion going on around me. Then everything disappears.

Chapter Nineteen

I awake in my regular bed again. Not a single hint of the place I just came from. Everything is back to normal. Nathaniel is gone. I find myself saddened by this, although I'm not really sure why. I figure he and Annabelle must've been very close. Maybe he was her fiance or something. Whoever he was, he was beautiful. I sit up in bed and wipe the sleep from my eyes.

Who is Annabelle and why was I in her body? I wonder.

Something like this has never happened to me before. The dream felt so real. I can still feel the warmth of Nathaniel's touch on my hand. I still have the faint smell of the house in my nostrils. It was like I was actually there! I glance over at the clock on my nightstand beside my bed 3:30 PM. Holy cow! How did I sleep so late?

Usually my mother would've shouted for me to wake up hours ago, and yet, for some reason she didn't today. Maybe she figured I didn't sleep much last night, given the events of the day that I had. I jumped out of bed and started dressing myself

'*Annabelle…I love you…*' a voice whispered.

Huh? Who the heck was that? I glanced around the room to find the source of the voice, but I was alone. '*I'll always love you. Until we meet again my love.*' it continued.

Snap out of it Ava! You're losing it. I finished dressing and rushed downstairs. My mother was in the kitchen making something to eat for her and Bernie.

"Are you hungry?" she asked. "You sure slept a long time." My mother turned and walked out of the kitchen toward me, "Is everything okay? You look like you've seen a ghost." she walked over to me and placed her hand on my forehead.

"I'm fine mom. I – I just didn't get much sleep is all." I smiled and pulled her hand from my head, "No, I'm not really hungry right now, but thank you."

"Well, we have to head back to the police station tomorrow." she said hesitantly. "They want to ask you a few more questions."

"Haven't they asked enough?!" I shouted. "I'm tired of talking about this!"

"Just a few more." she gently rubbed my shoulder, "They want to make sure they have the entire story. He's probably going away for a very long time." she paused, recalling something, "Jessica called while you were asleep. I told her I'd give you the message when you woke up. She sounded like she really needed to talk to you."

I walked into the living room and picked up the phone to dial Jessica's number. There was no answer at her house. There was a loud knock at the door a few minutes later. It was Jess.

"Can we go somewhere to talk in private?" she asked as I opened the door.

"Yeah, sure. Come on in." I turned my head over my shoulder, "Mom Jessica is here! We're going up to my room for a bit!" Without hesitation we headed for the stairs.

As soon as we entered my room and I closed the door, Jessica wanted to talk immediately.

"My parents said the police told them that we aren't the only ones he's done this to." she began, "There are thirteen of us Ava!" she scoffed.

"How do you…How do they know?!" I was astounded.

I was so shocked and in complete disgust at the thought that he had done this to anyone…let alone thirteen children!

A Journey of a Thousand Miles – A Reflections Saga

"He confessed! He told them that he had done it to others in neighbouring towns from us." she cradled her head in the palms of her hands. "Can you believe that?! How could he do that? Those poor innocent little kids! I wonder how old they all are and where they're from." I could hear her devastation.

"I don't think I ever want to know" I told her. "This is completely INSANE!"

"My parents told me that we aren't allowed to speak to anyone about this. It's going to go to trial and we probably are going to have to testify."

"Testify?" I interrupted. "What…what do you mean testify?"

"We might have to get up and tell the entire courtroom what he did." she hung her head and started to cry. "People are going to look at us as freaks!" she shouted.

I leaned in and hugged her tightly "It's going to be okay." I tried to assure her, but even I didn't know if that was true.

There were weeks of repeated questioning for all of us. Numerous medical exams, blood work and a lot of poking and prodding. We were tested for sexually transmitted diseases and we were even tested for pregnancy. It was completely invasive. We were scheduled for weekly counselling sessions too, but I didn't ever talk much in any of them. I just wanted to shut the world out. To go back to the innocent young girl I once was, but it was impossible. That innocence had been stolen from all of us, and our lives were sure to never be what they once were again. It was heartbreaking to go through it all. The trial was held and Allan actually had enough decency to spare us from having to face a courtroom full of people. He had decided to plead guilty, which meant we didn't have to appear. I think we were all grateful for that. It was the least he could do. He was sentenced to twenty five years with the possibility of parole in ten years. Everyone was shocked at the thought that he had harmed so many. Changed so many lives and even after all of that he still might be able to walk free after ten years. Where was the justice in that?

The story had made the newspaper, but our names were removed to protect us because we were minors. I was beyond grateful for that. I can't even imagine what might've happened if people ever found out who we were. We were to continue our individual counselling sessions for the next few months, until we were deemed *"healed from the ordeal."* It would actually take me much, much longer than everyone else. For the first eight months, I didn't say a single word. I would just sit at the table and draw pictures while staring out the window. The counsellor would always try to engage me in conversation, but I would quickly inform her that I didn't care to talk about it. Couldn't I just be left alone? It was all I wanted. I didn't want to talk anymore. I felt I had talked more than enough already. People were always bugging me to talk about my feelings and I hated it. It was torture for me. I'd much rather be poked with a stick or a sharp needle than bombarded with question after question.

A Journey of a Thousand Miles – A Reflections Saga

"We need to talk about what happened to you." I remember her saying.

"No, actually, we don't!" I shouted back. "I think you have more than enough information about what happened to me on that paper you're holding. So why don't you just read that and leave me the hell alone!"

She didn't pry. She knew I had enough for one day and so she excused herself from the room to go grab my mother who was waiting in the lounge area. Jessica and all the others had finished their sessions months before me, and I couldn't quite understand why that was. I felt like I was being punished more than I was being helped. I just wanted to be left alone and to move on from everything. I just wanted to be myself again! Why couldn't anyone just grant me that one wish?

Now all I would ever hear my mother tell medical professionals was about what had happened to me. As if it somehow defined me. It made me so angry whenever she did that and then they pried. I had started isolating myself more and more. I spent all day, every day up in my room alone. Something else had changed too. I was no longer travelling in my dreams…in fact I didn't remember my dreams at all anymore. Even my guides had turned their back on me, and I couldn't understand why. All of my gifts seemed to disappear in a flash, and I had no explanation for any of it. All I knew was that a switch had been flipped. I couldn't feel ANYTHING anymore. Even the things that used to haunt me in the night were gone. It was all just – GONE!

A few weeks after my final counselling session I returned to school. Everyone seemed to be acting different toward me all of a sudden. Did they know? Jessica and I had told a few of our close friends, but we were sure they would never tell our secret.

'*So why was everyone acting so distant and giving me weird looks?*' I wondered.

I decided to ask Jessica if she knew what was going on, but as I walked toward her the bell rang. Inside I hung my coat up on the hook and bent over to pull my textbooks out of my backpack.

"Hey stranger! Haven't seen you around here in a while. What's up? You been sick or somethin'?" someone asked.

I turned to see a boy named Chris standing there with a big goofy grin on his face.

"No, just had a lot going on." I told him.

"Well, glad to have you back Ava!" his smile widened as he leaned in for a hug.

He fit the very definition of, *Class Clown*, in every sense of its' description. He was always getting into trouble for acting up in class. Doing the silliest things to make us all crack up. Even the teacher couldn't help herself sometimes. I was sure he was going to grow up and become a comedian someday.

"Ugh!" he said gripping his forehead. "I've got a bad headache!"

I reached over and touched his arm, and that's when I felt a stabbing pain shoot through my own forehead.

A Journey of a Thousand Miles – A Reflections Saga

"Ow!" I shouted, reaching for my own head. "Now I've got one too! The air is really stuffy in here. Maybe we can ask to open a window?" I said, heading for my desk.

Jessica sat in front of me and turned around to face me as I took my seat.

"Are you okay?" she asked. "You don't look good."

"I'm fine!" I told her. "I just have a bad headache."

Chris had asked to crack open the window and the teacher had honoured his request. About an hour in, we were working on some math problems and I started to feel very funny. All I remember is seeing black dots floating in front of my face and then my head got really fuzzy and that was the last thing I remember. When I came to, Jessica, the teacher and a few other students were surrounding me and looking very concerned.

"What…what happened?!" I asked the teacher.

"You lost consciousness, Ava. Your body was shaking and then it stopped. I think you had a seizure! I want you to go to the office and we will call your mother to come and get you."

She lifted me from my desk and asked Jess to take the other side of me. My legs were like Jello. They were extremely wobbly and shaky. As I stood up, they tried to buckle on me.

"No this won't work. Sit her back down." the teacher instructed.

"Melissa…can you go to the office and ask them to call Ava's mother please? I think she might need to go to the hospital."

"No!" I shouted. "I'm fine, really!" I assured her. "I promise I'm okay…I just didn't eat much breakfast today. That's probably all it is."

"Okay, but if it happens again you are going home." she told me firmly, then she got up and walked back toward the front of the room. "Jessica, please keep a close eye on her." she said calmly, but there were still undertones of concern in her voice.

I picked up my pencil and went back to working on the math assignment she had given us. The rest of the day was uneventful. I wasn't sure what that was that happened earlier in the day, but I was sure it was probably just from being anxious about returning to school, or maybe it was like I said…not enough breakfast. I returned home that day and told my mother what had happened. She informed me that the school had already called her to give her a heads up, and that they wanted to make sure I would be eating enough breakfast every day so it wouldn't happen again. She looked a little pissed off as she was filling me in on the conversation she had with my teacher.

"Did you tell them I don't feed you?" she demanded.

"No mom. Of course not! I just told them that I hadn't eaten enough breakfast today, and that maybe was why that happened." I shook my head, "I never told them you don't feed me enough. Where are you getting this from?" I folded my arms and looked down at the floor.

A Journey of a Thousand Miles – A Reflections Saga

"Well, that's sure as hell what she made it sound like!" My mother shouted.

"Okay, well, I'm sure it wasn't what she meant." I rolled my eyes as I walked past her heading up to my room.

"Where are you going now?" she asked following behind me.

"Up to my room mom. I'm a bit tired, so I'm going to take a nap before supper."

"Okay, I'll let you know when it's ready." she told me.

"Fine mom. Thanks."

I hugged her and walked upstairs.

My seizure episodes would continue off and on for months. I would spend countless days in and out of the hospital. My mother and Bernie would come and visit me daily, and I was thankful for that. I was not a child that enjoyed interacting with anyone, let alone all of these strangers. I truly hated spending much time away from home, except when it came to sleepovers at friends houses or when I would go away to summer camp every year. A hospital however, was quite different from being somewhere that you go to have fun. I had no idea that this last time I would be hospitalized, would be yet another pivotal moment in my life. Things were about to change drastically, for all of us.

Bernie always cracked me up whenever they would come to visit me. It was almost as if he could sense how difficult it was for me to be in this place. He would go out of his way and make a complete fool of himself just to see me smile. He had invented his own version of a silly song. He called it the *"Hawaiian Nose Hum."* It consisted of him blocking one side of his nose with his finger while humming away and strumming the other side of his nose at the same time. It was hilarious and he had gotten to be really good at it. It was our new thing. Every time they came to visit he would choose a new song to hum, and I tried to guess what song it was. This time they came to visit was very different though. I felt this overwhelming sense of dread and sadness. I wasn't quite sure what had created this feeling for me, but I knew his impending death was fast approaching. Despite his best efforts, I was unable to shake this feeling. It consumed me. When he was leaving to say goodbye I became inconsolable. I begged him not to go. I knew deep in my soul that it would be the very last moment I would ever see him alive. To this day I am still unable to explain to you how I knew these things. They came to me as easy and effortless as breathing. He hugged me and kissed me on my forehead and tried his hardest to reassure me that he would in fact be back to see me tomorrow. I continued to cry uncontrollably.

"No....*NO YOU WON'T*!!" I shouted. "This will be the last time I'm going to see you!" I told him.

He just shook his head in disbelief and took my hand in his.

"I promise Ava that I will be back tomorrow and you had better be ready, because tomorrow I'm coming with a really difficult song for the Hawaiian nose hum." he told me.

A Journey of a Thousand Miles – A Reflections Saga

I knew there was nothing I could do or say to convince him of what I knew to be true in my heart, as he probably figured I was just being paranoid, and that there was no possible way I could ever know he was going to die that night. I pulled him in close to me, kissed him softly on his cheek and told him I loved him and that I will miss him. As he and my mother left the room I turned over and curled myself into the fetal position and prayed that I was wrong about everything.

The next morning my mother and him never showed up around their usual visiting schedule, and I knew that something was very wrong. He made sure they were always on time, because he wanted to make sure that when I needed them, that they would always be there. The nurse came into my room to check on me.

"Good morning, Ava." she said with a smile. "And how did we sleep last night?" she asked.

"Where is my mom?" I asked suspiciously.

"Oh, your mom? She called just a little while ago. She told me to tell you that she would be in around dinner time because something came up that she needed to take care of." she reassured me.

"She?! Don't you mean they?!" I sat forward.

"She only mentioned that she would be coming in, so I'm not really sure if anyone else will be in with her." the nurse told me.

In that moment I felt a huge lump begin to form in my throat. It became difficult to breathe. I just knew she would be coming with the worst news, and I pleaded with my guides to see me through the horrific moment that would surely arrive with her. How would I ever be able to get through yet another loss?! I was sure I wouldn't be able to bear another heartbreak. My young heart had already been through so much. More than most people endure in their lifetime.

'Would my tender heart ever recover?' I sighed.

I didn't want to find out, but I knew that it would soon be inevitable. There was no escape. Nowhere to run and hide away from the pain of it all. I would have to be strong. I was going to have to stand and face it. To feel it. Every single heartbreaking, gut-wrenching ounce of it and worst of all...I'd have to go through it alone once again.

My mother arrived later that evening just as she had said she would. I honestly can't remember now if she was alone or if any of my siblings came with her. I think I have forever blocked this moment from my memory. I can't even recall the exact words she said to me. It's all just a blur now. All I remember is feeling like someone had ripped my heart and soul out and set it ablaze. Not like any ordinary fire. This was an eternal hell type of fire. One that burned right through me. An endless inferno of despair and anguish. One that would take countless years to heal from. I vaguely remember her face as she entered my room, even though I could've sworn

I felt her presence lingering there in the hallway for quite some time. Perhaps trying to put herself together enough so as not to raise an alarm in me.

It was bad enough that I felt alone in this place as it was, but now because the doctors couldn't find anything physically wrong with me, they had diagnosed my seizure episodes as being *"psychosomatic."* They pretty much implied that it had all been in my head or that I had been faking the entire thing. That made me feel even worse. I knew something was wrong but, *hey*, they're the doctors right?! It always baffled me as to why when doctors can't explain something they immediately go to, *"the person must be crazy or faking the whole thing"*, route.

As my mother entered my room, I immediately took notice of her dishevelled appearance. Her hair was placed into a messy ponytail, much of which had seemed to have fallen out of place. Her clothes were wrinkled as if she had slept in them for a week, her eyes red and puffy as if she had been crying for hours on end and the tip of her nose was red, which for me was always a dead giveaway that she had been crying. She glanced in my direction and tried to feign a half smile before completely losing herself to the sadness that was consuming her being.

"I'm so sorry!" she whimpered while holding back tears. "He's gone...I can't believe it! I don't know how to tell you this but...but Bernie is dead!" she cried out.

The moment those final words escaped her lips she completely lost it. She rushed over to me, wrapped her arms around me and began crying hysterically. Was this a joke? How could this be real? I had to be dreaming. Please somebody slap me, pinch me...I don't care what you do. Just please wake me up from this nightmare. I felt so many things in this moment. It was as if every emotion that we as human beings are capable of hit me all at once. I was glad in that moment that I was sitting up on my bed, because if I had been standing, I would've collapsed under the massive weight of it all. At this moment I felt like my life was officially over.

I told myself, *"It can't get any worse at this point."*

Boy was I wrong! I wish I could've foreseen what was coming. Maybe I could've prepared myself better, and yet the truth is, nothing could prepare anyone for the events that would follow.

Chapter Twenty

I can't even remember if I attended Bernie's funeral or not. I blocked so much of those things out. All I remember is hearing the story my mother had told me about how he had died. He was at work and had been up high cleaning those large trailers that transport trucks pulled on their flatbeds. Somehow he slipped and fell. He

A Journey of a Thousand Miles – A Reflections Saga

broke his neck on impact. In the papers it said, *"the harness was still hanging."* The company claimed that his harness malfunctioned and he slipped through, but the truth was they didn't have any harnesses there and I knew this from going on a tour of the place when Bernie first started working there. I immediately told my mother that the information they provided was conflicting. There was an investigation into the whole thing and the company was found to be at fault for not providing proper personal protective equipment to its' employees. I also remember my mother telling me the story of how that dark and rainy night, a stranger in all black clothing arrived on the doorstep telling her and my brother to get to the hospital. No other details besides that there had been an accident and they needed to get there as soon as possible. The hospital would inform us later that they did not send anyone and they hadn't even had the chance to call yet. So who was he? To this day we still don't have a clue who it was and he never appeared again. Maybe he was just a messenger.

My mother was absolutely devastated by the whole ordeal. She had gone from daily visits with me, to cutting the time she spent at the hospital, and only coming once or twice a week...then once weekly and eventually she stopped coming all together. Not even a phone call. I think the nurses sensed my sadness. They could see how lonely I was, and they decided to do whatever they could to cheer me up. They started sending volunteers into my room daily to talk to me, or even just to play a game of cards. Whatever it took to take my mind off of what looked pretty obvious...my mother had abandoned me in that hospital. She had grown into such a deep depression that I guess she lost any ability to even care for any of us. She had been consumed by her grief, and it had driven her to the point that she no longer wanted to be a mother. Or perhaps she was afraid of me in some twisted way. After all, she had been there the day I told Bernie that he was going to die that night. Maybe I was cursed! My mind ran wild with possible explanations as to why someone would abandon their own child, and yet despite every possible reason I could drum up, not a single one was justified. It had been three weeks since she had come to visit...or even picked up the phone to call. I wanted to be so angry at her for that, but part of me had empathy. I couldn't imagine what it was like to lose a man you love and yet, she was dealing with that pain a second time. How could I be so selfish? I needed to think of her and try to imagine what this all must have been like for her. It had finally become too much and she just cracked. She lost herself.

I remember a childhood psychologist coming to visit me one day. No-one bothered to tell me what was going on with my mother. They all just continued to make excuses for her, and tried to reassure me that she would be coming for me soon. Eventually I knew that was a lie. They were just trying to stall until a plan had been put into place. This seemed to be it. The psychologist came and introduced himself. His name was Dr. Doon. Might as well have been Dr. Doom! He came in and asked if we could go for a walk and just talk. I was hesitant at first, but it had been months since I had seen the outside of these four walls and so I was actually quite happy to oblige him...at least for a little while. He was nice at first and seemed to be a great listener. He asked me lots of questions, but it was more of a getting to know you type of vibe than one of genuine concern for my well-being. He was more like a friend than a doctor. He told me that he knew some great kids like me and then he asked if I wanted to meet them.

"Yes!" I exclaimed. "I'd love to meet some teens my age. I've been so bored in the pediatric ward and I think I'm probably their oldest patient. I could use a change of scenery if even just for a little while." I told him.

We got onto the elevator and headed up to what he called, *"The teen ward."* You mean to tell me that there was a teen ward this entire time, and they kept me on the floor with the younger children?! Apparently that was only because I had to stay on the pediatric ward while undergoing all of the tests they wanted to do, but once they had ruled everything else out and had deemed me a faker, they decided they needed the bed for a kid who was actually sick. As I would soon discover, this "friendly" doctor had diagnosed me with severe depression and placed me on an antidepressant which would go into effect immediately. It completely suppressed everything. I became a shell of myself. I was to remain in the teen ward until they found a proper home to place me in. The teens on the floor were actually kids with mental and behavioural issues. Problem children was what they used to call them. I didn't see any problems with them though. They were simply teens who had been through so much and were often misunderstood by others.

We all became great friends rather quickly, and every night we had so much fun. We would watch movies mostly. I remember this was my first introduction to the movie The Labyrinth with David Bowie. This place was so much cooler than home, and it definitely didn't look like a hospital at all. They had everything you could think of to do there. Art, crafts, TV, VCR, board games, a Nintendo etc, but as much as I enjoyed my new surroundings, I wanted nothing more than to wake up from it all and be at home again in my own bed. Oh what I would give just to be home. Unfortunately it would be awhile before I saw that place again. It seemed like all hope was lost and after awhile, the fun aspect had worn off for me and now, each day grew longer than the day before it. It felt like I was in there for years. I can't really tell you how much time had passed, as I was never really told nor did I bother to ask anyone. I was completely devastated and traumatized by the whole experience. I guess that people think if you take a child from everything they know, drug them and stick them with children their own age and then surround them with cool gadgets and accessories that it somehow suffices for their lack of social interaction with the outside world.

Children also have a need for love, stability and affection. We received none of that in this place. As someone who has lived through this experience, I can honestly tell you that it was like some kind of nightmare I couldn't seem to wake up from. The people who ran this floor were all very nice, but it was clear that they were doctors, nurses and maybe even counsellors of some sort. It was as if we were all being studied or something. The kids who end up in there lose themselves. They become more distant and socially awkward. They begin to lose faith in themselves. It destroys their psyche and any sense of self worth they may have once had. It is a surefire way to get a child to hate themselves and to have difficulties with trusting people. Don't even get me started about the medication they put us all on either. It essentially turned us into drones. It felt like someone or something else was in complete control. A robot of sorts and our mind was just along for the ride. We were powerless. Just going through the motions day after day. It seemed like I was caught in an endless loop. Every day felt like it was on repeat. I found myself wondering if this was going to be my new home. It felt like I was somehow being punished for something I wasn't even aware of.

'Was this because of my fight with God?' I asked myself.

I spent every moment in that place trying to reconcile what I did to deserve all of this. I even contemplated getting on my knees and asking for God to forgive me for ever forsaking him. To be honest, there were countless prayers sent to him and yet despite my best efforts, they seemed to always go unanswered. When had God been there for me in all thirteen and a half years of my life? I had finally given up hope and given into the darkness. There had always been this thick black cloud just off in the distance, but I used my belief in things turning around for the better, and this helped me manage to keep it at bay. Now I was welcoming it with open arms. I had decided on this day that I was finally going to give in to it all. I was going to let it consume me.

I can't really tell you what happened after I allowed the darkness to seep in. It seems to all be foggy now. Maybe this was due to the medications they had me on. Or maybe I sank so deep into the abyss of my soul, that I went into full autopilot mode. I have zero recollection of anything past the moment that felt like the end for me. I just remember the day the people there told me that I was going to go and live with my sister Kim. It was like an endless thunderstorm had finally and abruptly ceased. The clouds had receded and the sun was bursting forth like the flame to a freshly lit candle. It was as if all of the darkness had suddenly been sucked up into an unseen vortex of some kind. I cried out with gratitude. There was someone who still cared. I was saved! I started packing right away, even though they told me I would still be there for a few more days. I just couldn't wait to get out of this place. The people were nice and the kids I met there were even better, but this was not my home. It's not where I belonged. I belonged with family. I belonged back at school where I could see my lifelong friends. I wondered if they even knew where I was, or what had happened to me. I had no contact with anyone since I had gone into the hospital. I was eager to get back to my life.

That night I imagined what my life might look like once I was free from this place. What it would be like to live with Kim and Doug. Doug was Kim's husband. They were newlyweds. I felt almost selfish that I would now be intruding on their new life together. Within days of reflection, I had decided that it wasn't fair to them to have to care for me. They were just starting their life together and would one day be planning a family of their own. I couldn't be a burden on them. I refused. It was a difficult decision, but as the day drew ever closer for them to come pick me up, I had made the decision to go live with my sister Grace, her boyfriend and their new baby Mackenna. I figured this way I would be able to be more of a help than a charity case. I told the counsellors

A Journey of a Thousand Miles – A Reflections Saga

my decision, and they told me they would speak to both Kim and Grace about it. I didn't even know if Grace would want me, but I was really hoping she would. Otherwise I might've chosen to stay in that place.

Thankfully, by some miracle she had agreed with my decision and said that they would be happy to take me into their home and raise me as their own. I was unaware at the time as to whether I would ever see my mother again. Would she ever want me back? I didn't know, but I would make the best of my new living arrangements. Finally the day arrived for me to leave the hospital. I was both excited and a bit sad to be leaving my new friends. I hoped to see them again. We all exchanged contact information and vowed to always keep in touch with each other, as we had become like family in that place. I think our wishful thinking got the better of us though, because that would be the last time we ever saw or heard from each other again.

Living with my sister and her little family was quite different from living with my mother and siblings. There was no yelling, I had gotten all new clothes and everything. Grace had even arranged for me to go to a new school. One that was closer to her apartment, it was a public high school and up til this point I had always attended Catholic schools. Grace assured me that I would receive a really good education there and that it seemed to be the only one that was in district to us. I was terrified with this notion. It was bad enough that my life had already been changed in so many ways, a new school where I didn't know a single person was almost more than I could bear. My anxiety had taken over and when the day came for me to get ready for my first day...I couldn't even get dressed. It was proving to be too much. Needless to say, I never attended a single day at that school. I'm not sure how long I was living there with Grace and her little family, but eventually I was given visitation with my mother and siblings at my old home. The visits were always great. It felt like everyone and every thing had somehow shifted. Who were these new people? I didn't recognize them. Everything felt so foreign to me, but it was something I could definitely get used to. After a few months of these visits, I wanted to go back home with the family I was missing so much, but how? How was I ever going to change my situation? I started acting out in order to get someone's attention. I was screaming inside and eventually those screams became audible. It became clear to everyone that it might be better for me to be back with my mother and the rest of my family. Outside of this normalcy, I was becoming nothing more than an empty shell of the person I once was.

I'm not sure how much time had gone by, but eventually my voice had been heard and I was granted my wish. Had God finally answered my prayers? I didn't know but I was grateful. Now don't get me wrong, living with my sister was wonderful. She cared for me in ways I had never been cared for in my entire lifetime. We would even sit up and have conversations, watch movies and spend quality time together, but I never felt like I belonged there. It wasn't anything she did, and believe me she did her best to make me feel welcome, but it was always just a temporary home for me. It was not my true home. She gave me everything I could ever want or need, but I think she could feel it in her heart, that I just couldn't be present in those moments with her. There

A Journey of a Thousand Miles – A Reflections Saga

was too much, *"NEW"*, for me. It made me uncomfortable. I wanted to escape it. It started to become almost uncomfortable for me to be there because it was all just too new. Grace was wonderful about the whole thing.

I was beside myself with emotion when the day came for me to leave her home and return to my mother. On one hand I was extremely excited to get back to what I had deemed normal to me. To return to the home I had always known. The smells, the people, my old friends, the high-school we all planned to attend together etc. I was elated to get back to my old life. To get back to me. Yet on the other hand I was sad because now it felt like I was abandoning my sister and the relationship I had with her and the little family she had created. They gave me everything, and I just took it and tossed it all aside. Some may even view my actions and behaviours as coming from someone who was ungrateful for all they had been given. I was shown a new life, one that was very different from the one I once lived, and if I'm being honest, it scared the living shit out of me. It always felt like someone else should've been living it. It was just not mine. It would've been a beautiful life I'm sure, and yet I couldn't bear it. I probably would've grown up to be a doctor or lawyer had I stayed living with Grace. What the hell was wrong with me?! People would've killed to even have a single ounce of all that was offered to me, and here I was tossing it to the side like it was trash. Like it meant nothing. If I could go back right now, I'd tell her – I'd need Grace to know, that it meant absolutely *EVERYTHING*.

It wasn't long after I returned to my life with my mother and siblings, that I began to feel like myself again. Well kind of. I was actually quite indifferent to these people for awhile. I was angry. I was confused and I was still trying to put myself back together from the whole ordeal. Imagine you break a glass, shatter it into a thousand pieces, but then little by little work to glue it back together again. Is it ever really what it once was? Does the glue maintain the integrity of that glass? Or does the water poured into it eventually breach the cracks and slowly seep through? That was me. I appeared whole on the surface, but a closer look would reveal otherwise. I was far from fixed. The damage done was irreparable. Yet somehow I would gain very valuable tools through this experience, and I had absolutely no idea how this was going to shape me. How much this horrible experience of being abandoned by my own mother would prove to strengthen my resolve. It would take years for me to discover just how much a single soul could endure. I wish I could tell you that this was the end of my suffering, unfortunately it was just a small dose. I had no idea just how many trials and tribulations I was about to face. Things that most people would take their own life over.

After a very long year of constant struggle to regain any sense of normalcy, two fires and the loss of our home—it seemed like things were finally starting to turn around. I had just started at a new high school, began to make new friends and even met a new boy named Paul whom I would quickly grow to love. You might say things were greater than ever! I was finally starting to feel normal and hopeful again. The future was bright with what my new perfect union had to offer.

I had given him my everything, including that which was most precious to me, my virginity. He became my best friend and we were inseparable—my knight in shining armour. We had been together about a year when I moved in with him, his younger brother and his mother. We had so much fun together. He was the bad boy that most girls would've been drawn to. I felt completely safe with him and I knew he would give his life to protect me. It was the same level of safety I once had before my father's passing. He was my protector. I honestly couldn't be more grateful for him. I had even nursed him back to health when he had gotten into a fight while out on a walk with the dogs one day. I'm so glad I wasn't there to witness it firsthand, but I did see the aftermath and it broke me to pieces.

I remember it like it was yesterday. We had always taken walks together, but on this particular day something held me back from going with him this time. His brother Mark had come running into the house with the dogs, but no Paul. He told me there had been a fight and that Paul was in very bad shape, and that I needed to get to him right away as he was unconscious and bleeding on the side of the road just a few blocks from the house. I immediately told him to call 911 and rushed to get my shoes on. I don't even think they were fully on my feet before I took off running down the block. I arrived to a gruesome scene. Paul was splayed out in the street and his face was covered in blood. He was in and out of consciousness at this time, and I was still trying to make sense of the events that may have unfolded. The ambulance arrived and rushed him to the hospital, but they wouldn't let me go with him. I rushed home to call Paul's father to let him know what had happened. It was the longest moment of unknown in my entire life, as I anxiously waited by the phone for news on his condition. He had to undergo plastic surgery for a broken finger and a fractured nose. When he came home from the hospital, I was the one who cared for him. Even bathing him because he was in no shape to do it himself. I never left his side...not even once. His finger was so badly fractured that they had to put pins in to hold it together. It took months for him to fully recover from the ordeal,. It turns out that the guy he had gotten into the fight with was a professional boxer who decided to try out his talents on my helpless boyfriend. It wasn't long after the incident that the police found him and he was arrested and charged.

After Paul's recovery, I started to notice small cracks forming in his personality. The proverbial mask was beginning to slip. He became more angry and aggressive. It seemed to come out of nowhere. I was absolutely floored. At first the aggression was steered in his younger brother's direction and then his animals. It took awhile, but eventually that aggression began to turn towards me. My happily ever after...HA! My fairy-tale was on a one way roller-coaster straight into HELL!!! Nothing could have ever prepared me for what lay ahead. It started out with snide comments here and there. Subtle words at first, but ones that lingered long afterwards. It seemed that nothing I ever did was good enough. I was always doing something to piss him off, although to this day I can't tell you what that was. Paul started getting angry at almost everything. He would yell at everyone and even started abusing his younger brother, whenever he would get mad at his animals for having accidents in the house.

His brother became his physical punching bag and I was his emotional one. He started kicking and punching his animals, and that should've told me to get out right then and there, but I always excused the behaviour as residual reactionary responses to the trauma he himself had endured in childhood. Even his mother would excuse it away as if it was just, *"not his day"*, and that things would go back to normal when he cooled down. For a while, that's exactly how it went, until one day the glimmers of the boy I met and fell in love with were all but erased, and in his place stood someone I no longer recognized anymore. I kept telling myself it must've been my fault and I would try to not piss him off and everything would be fine. I was being mentally and emotionally abused on a regular basis and I had no idea how we had gotten to that point. I began walking on eggshells daily. I had no idea what would set Paul off next, and I was sure to stay out of his way when he would rage. I remember countless times where he would get sick of me and tell me I needed to go stay with my mom or my sister until he was ready for me to come back. Never knowing what I had done to make him feel that way. I wish I knew then what I know now.

I wish someone had thoroughly educated me on what a narcissist was, and the red flags to watch out for. Here I was just sixteen years old and terrified for what the next day might bring for me. He made me feel like I was nothing without him, and it's sad to say, but I was totally convinced of that. I stayed and tolerated the abuse, thinking that things would eventually go back to normal, not knowing at the time that what I had recalled as our normal, was gone and never to return again. It was all a facade. None of it was real. It was all a ploy to lure me in and then tear me down to nothing so he could have complete control over every part of my life. He began isolating me from friends and family. Telling me that they were the reason I became the bitch that I was to him. Yet I had never even uttered an unkind word toward him. He convinced me that I was crazy.

He would gaslight me on a daily basis. Always discounting my feelings and when I would cry, it would make him absolutely livid. I remember countless nights of laying on the kitchen floor crying after one of his "episodes." There are a few in particular that stand out the most to me...even now. On one occasion he had gotten upset with me about the way I had cleaned up the kitchen. He stormed into the room, grabbed the trash can and emptied the entire contents onto the floor, then he started to throw dishes in my direction. He then grabbed me by my arm and threw me down to the floor, telling me to do it again, and if he didn't like the way it was done this time, he would make me clean all night until it was to his satisfaction. Thinking back on it now...maybe it was what created my OCD, or as I often refer to it "Obsessive Cleaning Disorder." I remember

Kimberley Hall   **127**

that night cleaning for hours, until I was absolutely exhausted and I collapsed on the floor and began to cry hysterically.

He came in and screamed at me, "Will you shut the fuck up?! I'm trying to fuckin' sleep bitch!"

I cried myself to sleep that night trying to do so as quietly as possible so as not to disturb him. Another time that stands out to me is when I had gone to see my doctor for a follow-up visit after recovering from a urinary tract infection. It was April Fool's day and I hadn't been feeling well for a week or so. I was throwing up quite a bit, and had convinced myself that I must have the flu. I needed a refill on my birth control pills, so I decided to mention that to her while I was there. It was routine to run a urine pregnancy test before refilling a prescription for any type of birth control. It came back positive! When she came in and told me, I cried for a very long time in her office. How the hell was I going to break this news to Paul?! He was still angry because his dog had recently become pregnant by her own son, during her most recent heat cycle. I couldn't get the image of him beating that poor dog to the point he could barely walk out of my head. He even picked him up and slammed him to the floor breaking the dog's leg. I was terrified at how I was going to tell him that we were now going to be having a baby. My sister Jane had been waiting in the next room for me while I was in the appointment, and I decided to break the news to her first. In the hopes that she could help me come up with a good way to break this news to Paul. I decided to keep quiet about it until I could come up with a way to break it to him gently. I wanted to give it a few days. Jane kept calling me that night.

"Did you tell him yet? What did he say?" She would ask.

Paul must've overheard our conversation because when he walked into the room he had this cold and steely look in his eyes. I told her I would call her back soon. As I hung up the phone, Paul whipped the remote in my direction.

"What the fuck was that about?!" he demanded. "Don't even fuckin' tell me your ass is pregnant!"

I lowered my gaze away from his in that moment, and suddenly he had all the confirmation he needed. To say he was angry would be an understatement. He was absolutely enraged by the news. Paul made me feel like I had gotten pregnant all on my own. As if somehow he played no part. He even asked me who the father was and insisted it wasn't his baby. Of course he knew it was. He never even let me leave his sight! Even when I would use the bathroom, I had to leave the door cracked and he would stand outside the door. He watched my every move. I had hoped that Paul just needed some time to calm down, and then we could talk about it, but he stormed upstairs and started packing all of my clothes.

Was he really throwing me out?!

He actually tried, heartlessly, until his mother intervened and told him I wasn't going anywhere because it was her house and I was there to stay. She told him if he didn't like it that he could pack his stuff and go. That

A Journey of a Thousand Miles – A Reflections Saga

pissed him off even more. So much so that I could almost feel his anger radiating from the depths of his pores. He decided to go and take it out on his brother. Even ripped the door off the hinges to get to him. There was no reason other than he was angry, and needed to release it on someone. I sat in the corner of our bedroom with all of my bags of clothing, my head between my knees crying uncontrollably. I could hardly catch my breath. He completely ignored me and slammed the door behind him, then he stormed off back downstairs. His mother came in to console me, and suggested I just give him some time to process the shock he was in. She ran me a bath and told me to go and relax, promising to keep him downstairs...though that promise would prove to be short lived. No sooner had she left me to soak in the tub, Paul came storming into the bathroom telling me it was over between us, and that since it was his mother's house and she was allowing me to stay, that I better not get upset when he brought other girls he wanted to date or screw over to the house. I couldn't believe what I was hearing. What had I done so wrong?! He stormed out yelling behind him

"Go unpack your shit and get your ass downstairs because I don't even want to look at you right now!"

I did as I was told, and hurried up to get away from him...wet feet and all. For the record, wet feet and wooden stairs don't mix. I ended up and slipping and falling down the stairs. It all happened so fast and I had hit my abdomen on quite a few steps on the way down. Naturally I was in pain from the fall. His mother rushed down the stairs after me and quickly scooped me up and carried me to the car.

It was like a switch flipped in Paul in that moment and he shouted to me, "You better not lose this baby!"

What in the actual fuck was this guy on? I spent hours at the hospital waiting to find out if the baby was in any danger. Had I lost it? Luckily we received good news that all appeared to be just fine, and I was given instructions to keep an eye out for any spotting or strong abdominal pains. They dated the pregnancy at around ten weeks. I was lucky! Paul had even started to be the old Paul I once knew. There was hope for us yet. Or at least that's what I thought. For awhile things were good. He was sweet and incredibly attentive. Maybe this was the scare that would be his turning point. Was this really happening? I can tell you that the caring and attentive Paul only stuck around for maybe a matter of weeks, before the evil version of him reared his ugly head again. I remember him actually getting upset with me once, because I had chosen to stop smoking marijuana in order to give our baby the best chance at being healthy. It was completely absurd to me.

Why would he not want the same thing?! I would love to say that he became less abusive during my pregnancy, but that couldn't be further from the truth. Things actually began to escalate and the abuse that I had endured up to this point was just the tip of the proverbial iceberg. Albeit one gigantic ass iceberg! Paul had started becoming more and more aggressive and one day that aggression manifested itself in the physical form. I was in a complete state of shock. I mean I knew he had abused his younger brother and even his animals at times, but I never in a million years imagined that he would turn and do those things to me. What did I do to deserve this? There were times where I would just lay on the floor after a beating, and beg God to grant me mercy. There were times I prayed for him to just end my suffering. To call me back home and let me be at peace. Unfortunately, it looked like my prayers would remain unanswered. Was it because I had walked away from God all those years ago? Had he forsaken me? I didn't know, but on this day in particular, I prayed for forgiveness and I prayed to take it all back. Was anyone listening?

My pregnancy was super rough on me. I didn't just have morning sickness...I had morning, noon and night sickness. Paul loved to torture me with it too. He would say things to make me throw up. My stomach was extra sensitive, and he seemed to get pleasure out of my misery. Another form of control I suppose. As sick as I was, I still had to be Cinderella. There was no reprieve for me. I wasn't granted any sort of privileges. I still had to slave away with my daily chores, and there was zero compassion on my really bad days. He would make me scrub all the floors with a toothbrush. That was until my belly grew too big to get down on the floor anymore, and probably only because he didn't want the inconvenience of having to help me up afterwards. He truly lacked any sort of compassion. If I was too sick one day to do whatever he had assigned for me, he would just pile on extra work for the next day. He told me I was completely useless and lazy all the time. Now don't get me wrong...it wasn't bad every single day. There were fleeting moments where I honestly thought we had a case of invasion of the body snatchers, but those moments became less and less with each passing day. I had endured so much abuse, that I guess you could say I had grown used to it. I learned how to take the blows, how to stuff down my feelings and emotions and just keep moving. I truly had no other choice.

After the birth of our son Jaxson, things began to slow down a bit. I was actually able to rest when I needed to and boy did I need to. I was a young mother of just eighteen years old, and everything was brand new to me. I had a baby who always cried and didn't seem to want to be held too much. He also didn't sleep, unless we put him in his car seat and in front of the TV. Nothing else we tried ever seemed to soothe him. I didn't know what was wrong with him, but my instincts told me something was. I had been around babies for a great deal of my life and I had never encountered something like this before. He didn't seem to want to eat much. He was severely jaundiced and very lethargic. On our Mommy and Baby Wellness visit when he was just a week old, he ended up in the Neonatal Intensive Care Unit for failure to thrive. He had lost a pretty large percentage of his birth weight, thirteen percent actually and doctors were deeply concerned. I was strictly breastfeeding at the time, and blamed myself for all of it.

Paul made sure to pour salt in the wound too whenever we were alone in the room. He kept asking me why I didn't take better care of him. I felt like such a failure. I stayed every single day in that NICU with my son. I refused to leave his side. I prayed over him and begged God to not punish my child for my own faults. I just wanted him to get better so we could go home. The nurses at one point became concerned, because I wasn't leaving his side and therefore they knew I was not eating. In that moment, I was willing to lay down my own life in exchange for his. They eventually called my mother to come and take me away from that place, and to make sure I was getting enough to eat and that I was resting like I was supposed to be doing. I never wanted to leave him. I was afraid if I did, that it might be the last time I would see him again. It was a thought that plagued the core of my being. I knew he needed me. We needed each other. Despite the trauma I had endured up to this point, I knew that my son had come into my life at a point where I need him the most. He was what kept me in the fight.

Once we were finally able to take him back home, I thought it would finally be over. Somehow I had convinced myself that we were going to be okay. I was foolish to think that I could somehow change Paul, and make him into the image of the loving and adoring father/future husband that I had always dreamed he would be. There were periods which brought me hope. It was the hope that he really had changed, and that things were finally going to be good. We even got engaged. I was so happy then, but looking back now I can't really say why that was. I began to see the old boy I fell in love with resurface, and he seemed to stick around for quite some time, but eventually old patterns returned and when Jaxson was just thirteen months old, I finally got the courage to leave. I wish I could tell you that I stayed gone, but shortly after leaving, I had discovered I was pregnant yet again. The problem was that during a brief moment of weakness, while Paul and I were broken up, I had a fling with a man name Charles and I did not know who the baby's father was at the time. At this time I had moved in with my mother and my stepfather Greg.

I didn't know what I was going to do. How was I going to raise two kids on my own? Was I even capable? Who was the baby's father? Paul had laid on the grovelling pretty thick after I left. He knew how to say all of the right things, and even did things to convince me that he had changed for good. I don't know if it was the pregnancy hormones, or just the sheer fear I was faced with of having to raise my children on my own, but I went back to him. We had decided that we were going to do everything in our power to repair our relationship for the sake of our children. Coming from a broken home myself, I was determined to make things work with him, and for awhile they actually did. Twenty two months after the birth of Jaxson, I gave birth to a second son who I chose to name Aaron. He and Jaxson were inseparable from the moment they first met. It was beautiful to see the bond they shared. Jaxson was so protective over his baby brother, and he was always rushing to grab his pacifier whenever Aaron would cry. It was extremely loving and attentive. A beautiful bond to witness, and I just knew they would always be close. I was just thankful to have my little family back together, and I vowed to give my everything into ensuring it would last.

A few months after his birth, Paul and I decided to take a paternity test to find out once and for all if he was indeed little Aaron's father. The test came back showing 99.99% that Paul was the father. We decided to put the whole thing behind us and move forward together. Our happily ever after. Finally! The physical abuse had ceased at this point and I was working on healing all of the scars that Paul had inflicted on me. I knew it was going to be a long road, but together with our two boys we were sure to get there. Unfortunately it didn't continue to remain that way. It eventually started back up again, and it was as if the hiatus from being his typical abusive self had given Paul more time to think of all the things he could do to seize back the power he had returned to me for those brief moments. It seemed to start up overnight and escalated rather quickly. It was as if he was starving for the power to return to him, and he needed to eat as soon as possible. On this one particular occasion, I was preparing to go out for a night with some girlfriends.

It had been a while since I was permitted any time with them, let alone since I had been out of the house without Paul, and I was excited. Paul never liked to see me happy or excited about anything that didn't have anything to do with him specifically. I was not going to let him ruin this night for me. I was determined to get out and have a good time. I deserved that much! That evening I may have had a bit too much to drink. Maybe it was because I was enjoying myself. Maybe deep down I was trying to drown my pain in alcohol. I arrived home later that evening, Paul and the kids were asleep in our bedroom. I quietly tiptoed into the room, stripped off my clothes and got into the bed next to him. I was so grateful that I had managed to get in without him waking up, because I could just close my eyes and sleep off my intoxication without having to go through a lengthy interrogation. If Paul had woken up, he probably would've made me sleep on the floor because he was just so disgusted with me for whatever reason. He was cruel like that. He had done it countless times before. When I tell you that this boy held power over me...I mean it in every sense of the word. Mentally, sexually, physically and emotionally. He owned me and he made sure I never forgot it. My comfort and well-being were solely dependant on him, and just how much he was willing to allow me to have in any given moment. He was my keeper.

The next morning I was abruptly awakened by Paul. He was pissed off that I had come home so late, and that I hadn't bothered to announce my return. He grabbed me by my ankles and pulled me straight out of bed and onto the floor. He then grabbed me by my hair and pulled me up from the floor. Apparently I wasn't coming to my feet fast enough, but I was frozen in fear and utter shock. There was no warning. Just violence. He began screaming in my face and even spit on me. He slammed me down to the ground repeatedly and then pulled me back up by my hair. I had fallen asleep with my makeup on the night before and he told me that I looked like a whore. He dragged me by my hair and into the bathroom. He grabbed a washcloth and made the water as hot as he possibly could, before he proceeded to scrub my delicate flesh vigorously. It felt like he had rubbed my skin raw by the time he was done. He had also rubbed soap into my eyes while doing so, and when I screamed he told me to *"shut the fuck up and think about this the next time I wanted to go out looking like a whore."*

The abuse went on for mere minutes and yet in that moment, it felt like an eternity. He must've felt like he gained enough power and control over me after it was all said and done, because he finally released his grasp.

A Journey of a Thousand Miles – A Reflections Saga

I was permitted to wash the soap out of my eyes and he even showed remorse for what he had done to me. It was the strangest thing. How could he just switch back and forth at will like that? So bizarre. After the incident, I cleaned myself up and got dressed, then I headed into the kitchen to start breakfast for the two of us and the kids. Even though I was bloodied and bruised...my *"wifely duties"* were never dismissed. I wish I could tell you that our boys never saw any of it, but I'd be lying to you. They saw all of it. Little Aaron was screaming hysterically the entire time as he stood in his Jolly jumper.

Poor little Jaxson didn't know what to do. Should he comfort his baby brother or try and help mommy? They were both terrified and it broke my heart. I scooped both of them up in my arms and assured them that mommy was okay. Was I though? In either case, for the sake of my babies, I was willing to fake it any way I needed to, if it was going to provide them that security and comfort. I never wanted my babies to feel unsafe. How long could we continue in this hell? What kind of mother allows her children to bare witness to such violence? What was I teaching them for allowing this bullshit to continue?

Finally after five and a half years of horrendous abuse in every way imaginable, I had finally had enough and this was the final straw. The kids and I were going to leave together. I began to hash out my escape plan. I wasn't sure exactly when the right time would be, but later that evening I was quickly given that answer. I had been sitting quietly in the kitchen, and talking with my girlfriend Lynn on the phone. I had filled her in on the earlier events that had transpired and I begged her to help me get out of it. She agreed and together we began discussing a plan, but it was cut short. Paul must've overheard the conversation. I'm not sure how long he had been listening, but judging by the menacing look in his eyes, it had been long enough. He practically flew at me and demanded I hang up the phone. I continued to hold the receiver in my hand as it somehow made me feel safe. I had hope that my girlfriend on the other end would hear enough, and that she would then hang up and call the police. I was fairly certain I was about to die this time. I had never seen Paul this enraged. It was like something evil had completely taken hold of him. Surely this man was about to take me out. He pushed the table hard into my abdomen and pinned me up against the wall with it, while I still remained seated in the chair. I was completely cornered and at his mercy. I was terrified but I knew there was only one way I was getting out of this alive. He shouted at me, and suddenly this voice bellowed from the depths of my soul.

It sounded like Satan himself had entered me in that very moment and I pushed as hard as I could against the table. Paul went flying backwards in disbelief. Now the tables had turned, and for a change it was he who would become the one who was terrified. I was not going to allow this man to hurt me anymore! I was hellbent on serving up some good ole fashioned, *justice.* It was time for his retribution. It was time he got a dose of his own medicine. Time for me to take back my power. It was time and boy was I ready. I honestly can't remember a time where I saw Paul in fear. Did I feel bad for him? Not in the slightest. He had it coming for a very long time.

A Journey of a Thousand Miles – A Reflections Saga

I was going to make sure he knew just what it was like to live in that place. The fear of the unknown for what was to come. I stood up from the table with a newfound sense of courage and strength and in this moment I could almost feel the anger consume me. I was blinded by it. I took every single bit of what I had endured at the hands of this man, and I used it as my driving force.

He stared at me with a look in his eyes that I had never seen before. It was the look of sheer panic. He did not know what I was about to do. Hell I didn't even know myself. Something or someone had completely taken over me and this woman was absolutely livid. I was ready to unleash a wrath of fury on him to the likes of something he would not soon forget. He began walking backwards with such haste, that he stumbled over his own feet. I cannot tell you what he saw in my eyes that day, but I can tell you that it was something he would probably remember forever. I picked up the chair I had been sitting on and whipped it in his direction. Anything I could find in my path was hurdled in his path. I chased after him through the hallway and into the bathroom where he proceeded to lock himself inside. I used all of my anger and every ounce of my weight and forced myself into it. The door ripped off the hinges with a thundering ***CRACK!*** He was backed up against the bathtub, with nowhere to go and he knew it. I swung in his direction and landed a blow to his left jaw. I then proceeded to grab him by his hair and slammed his head back into the wall to our right. His eyes were wide with disbelief and terror. He pushed me backwards hard into the door and tried desperately to make his way past me so he could make his escape. But it was like I became a stone wall, and he could no longer move me. He yelled out for his mother and brother to help him.

"This bitch is crazy! She's trying to kill me. Call the police!" he shouted.

He eventually forced me into a position where he had just enough room to squeeze by me and into the hallway again. I went after him and slammed him up against the wall a second time, placed my hands firmly around his throat and began to squeeze as hard as I could. Mind you this should've been next to impossible as I was less than a hundred pounds soaking wet. He easily had fifty pounds on me and yet, somehow I was able to overpower him now. I watched his eyes open wide with desperation, and felt the sting of his nails clawing at me to let go and yet I couldn't. The rage had completely taken over me. I could not stop! I wanted him to know that he would never, ever put his hands on me again. I wanted him to feel the helplessness that I had felt all of those years he abused me. I knew if I didn't let go soon...I was surely going to kill him. Just then I felt pairs of hands pulling on me with force. Both his mother and brother were trying desperately to free him from my grasp. They were unsuccessful. Maybe it was the adrenaline running through me which made me this powerful. I honestly can't explain it to this day. All I do know is that something pulled me back. It was probably the only thing that could in that moment. It was the look on little Jaxson's face when he came to see what all the commotion was about. A look I can't shake to this day. My son was afraid of ME. It shattered me to pieces and I honestly believe he is what pulled me back and made me let go that day. Paul's mother rushed to scoop up Jaxson and get him out the room, as Paul started choking and gasping for the air I had deprived him of.

"You're fuckin' nuts! You just tried to kill me you stupid bitch! What the fuck is wrong with you?"

I calmly pinned him up against the wall again and slid my hands back up to his throat.

"If you ever try to put your hands on me again Paul...I will fuckin' kill you. Do you understand me?!" I shouted. "This is it Paul!" I huffed, "We are done! You have taken my whole life from me and if I stay...I'm afraid I just might take yours...literally!"

I rushed to start packing up what little clothes and belongings I could for both myself and the boys. I called my brother Tim, and asked him if I could come stay with him and his fiancee. They lived just downstairs from us and had surely heard what just happened. Paul would not allow me to take the boys. He said I was too hysterical for them to be safe leaving with me, and assured me that I could come up and see them whenever I wanted to, but he just felt they were better off with him for now. I agreed with him, kissed them goodbye and left to head downstairs. I needed to calm down. I had never done anything like this before and it scared the living hell out of me! It took me quite awhile before I could even stop shaking. I decided to take some time to cool off and make my plans to move out for good. I had decided after a week or so, to go and live with my mother and Greg again. It was the only place I had to go at the time. I was definitely better off there.

Unfortunately when the time came for me to leave for good, Paul would not allow me to take my boys. He claimed that I had abandoned them, and that he feared for their well-being and safety with me. His mother had even stepped in and told me she was going to vouch for him, and tell the police what had happened between us. I didn't want to deal with the police or child protective services so I just left. I still have deep regrets about it, but I felt I was given no other option at the time. I needed to get back on my feet, and once I was able to secure a place for us, I would return for them. Seems the universe had other ideas for me though. It was a constant uphill battle from that point on. One filled with more struggle than most people can even begin to imagine. When the time finally came for me to go back for the boys, Paul had once again accused me of abandoning them. He refused to give them back and it seemed no one was willing to go against his wishes.

I honestly thought about ending his life that day too, but after I had a chance to calm down and process everything, we agreed that I would have weekly visitation with them. But of course, Paul being the asshole that he had always been, he eventually pulled back to just weekends. I had finally left this man and he still held so much power over me. He used our children as pawns in his sick and twisted little games. Part of me wished that Aaron wasn't his, because then he would've had no say about whether or not I could see him. I had to practically kiss his ass to even be able to see my own children. I couldn't seem to ever be completely free of him or his tight grasp. It was a never ending battle and one that I fought so hard and yet, here I was feeling completely defeated by him. He won. He got it all and stole everything from me in the process. He was right. I truly was nothing without him.

Chapter Twenty-One

Eventually Charles and I got together. Yet it took me quite awhile before I was finally able to trust anyone again. He seemed to be the perfect man for me. A wonderful man. Something I was already incredibly weary of considering what I had just been through for the last five and a half years with Paul. About a year after we had been together, we discovered we were pregnant. I was extremely hopeful for this relationship, as it was the complete opposite of what I had with Paul. I was excited for our future together and all of the happiness that was sure to continue. We hit a bit of a snag when Charles became unfaithful. A night that would have serious repercussions. Charles had given me an STD!! I couldn't believe my ears when my doctor came in during one of my prenatal visits and told me that the urine sample which she had me do for an assumed UTI, came back positive for Chlamydia. I was in absolute disbelief.

There must've been a mistake. Here I was pregnant and now battling an STD. How dare he! It was one thing to put my life at risk, but our unborn son?! When I finally mustered up the nerve to ask him about it, he told me I must've been cheating on him, and that was the only way I could've gotten it. Surely he knew that couldn't have been the case, because I never even left home except to go to doctors appointments or to spend time with my mom and sisters for a few hours. Everywhere I went that man was right there by my side. He was the one who had spent time away from me. Claiming to be going out with his friends for a bit. Clearly that was not always the case. Things were up and down with us for a bit, but eventually I had chosen to forgive him. Our son Jason was born in October, just days before Halloween. Things were absolutely perfect. The labour was quick and only took about three and a half hours from start to finish once I was induced. I finally found my forever. This time I was sure of it and for that I was extremely grateful.

A Journey of a Thousand Miles – A Reflections Saga

I was just anxious to get married, raise our little family and live happily ever after. We decided we would just move on and put the past behind us. It was just going to be us and the three boys. Things were finally going great between us. I guess having a new baby tends to change people. We were living with Charles' parents and our new son. You might just say that things were better...no they were absolutely perfect. We even got engaged. I was so surprised when Charles decided to pop the question on Mother's Day in front of all of our friends and family. I should've known he was up to something, because his mother had been acting strangely for weeks. It was the fairy-tale I had always envisioned since I was a young girl. Cinderella had finally gotten her Prince Charming and together they lived happily ever after. I should've known better. My knight in shining armour turned out to be more like a reject in tinfoil. You would think I would've learned after his first transgression that he had a problem and would do it again, but I was trying to give him that second chance in the hopes that we could just turn the page and start a new chapter.

Truth is I should've just ended that story and started writing a whole new book without him. I decided I wanted more for us and our children, so about six months after Jason's birth, I decided to go back to school to try and make something of myself, since I had never even graduated high school. Sure I had taken some night classes awhile back after I had Aaron, but I had only managed to get a couple of credits for that. I was determined to get into the healthcare field, as that seemed to be the place I would thrive the most. My sister Anne and I actually went back to school together, and for the same thing but we were in separate classes. A few months into our course, she was forced to drop out of school because she had been so sick and had just learned some shocking news. She was pregnant with her second child. I was sad that she left, but I refused to quit. I was going to make something of myself, come hell or high water. Charles and I had recently moved into a place of our own, which just so happened to be close to the college I was attending, and was just across the street from Anne. I loved being that close to her because it meant we were able to spend a lot of time together. We had always been close as kids, even shared a room together until the day she got pregnant with her daughter Kassie and then she moved out leaving me to feel abandoned. It was truly a life changing experience for me. I tried everything to get her to stay, but there was nothing I could do to make that happen. I was completely helpless in the situation. I was so mad at her for the longest time but eventually I came to forgive her.

School was going very well for me. I was getting all straight A's and impressing my teachers with how much of a natural I seemed to be. One day after exams, the teacher decided to let us go home earlier than usual because there was nothing left for us to do. Charles was at home with our son Jason, and I decided instead of calling to let him know I was done early, that I would just walk home and surprise him. Oh he was surprised all right and so was I! Turns out that while I was at school, that my supposed best friend Krista had called him to go pick her up because she had another fight with her mother, and just wanted to get away for awhile. Charles had obliged her. I still remember what I felt when I opened the front door and saw the two of them there in my living room together. I was just frozen in shock for what felt like forever, before I was finally able to react. You see you might be wondering why I would be reacting this way because they were just sitting together on the couch right? Wrong! The two of them were bottomless and she was straddling his lap. They both jumped up so fast, and it was obvious they knew they'd been caught.

They both tried to comfort me with nothing but lies. It didn't matter what either of them had tried to tell me because those words were falling on deaf ears. I mean quite literally. I couldn't hear a sound. It was like being underwater and trying to make out someone's words. Everything was just a muffled bunch of gibberish. I don't think it would've mattered much even if I could hear them. I knew it was nothing but excuses anyway. The two people who I thought would always have my back through thick and thin, had just gone and done the unthinkable. My best friend in the whole world and my soon to be husband had committed the ultimate form of betrayal. How was I ever going to be able to forgive them? I honestly didn't think I could but even I managed to surprise myself. I found it in my heart not only to forgive him, but I chose to forgive her too. I just wanted my happily ever after and I was prepared to do anything to make that possible.

Another year would go by before I finally decided to leave him once and for all. Even though I had forgiven him after he slept with my best friend, I never really trusted him the same way I had before. I was constantly keeping my eye on him, and trying to catch him in a lie. He started spending more and more time on the computer talking to *"friends"*. Those friends turned out to be women he was flirting with on the internet and one of them he had even set up a meeting with. He lied and told me he was going out with his friend Brad and that he would just be gone a few hours and I believed him. Shortly after he left though, my phone rang. It was my best friend Krista. She called to ask me if Charles was still at home and that she had something important she needed to tell me. You see, after Charles had slept with her I could no longer trust him, no matter how hard I tried. I had gotten together with Krista and discussed a plan to catch him in the act once I expected he was still cheating on me with other women. She agreed with the plan and created a fake profile in which she would pretend to be someone else. We even found some pictures for her to use so he would be none the wiser.

It worked like a charm! We *cat-fished* my own fiance. Trust me, it's definitely not something I'm proud of but at the time, I felt it needed to be done. That night that he had told me he was going for coffee with Brad, he had been speaking to her and SHE was the woman he had made plans to meet up with. They had discussed going to a motel and doing the deed. He thought it would just be their dirty little secret. Boy was he in for the shock of a lifetime. I told Krista to get herself ready and meet me at the place they had discussed. I hung up the phone and called Charles' friend Brad. I asked him if Charles was with him and of course he lied and said yes but that he was in the bathroom. He really had me fooled into thinking he cared about me and my relationship with Charles. I got angry with him and told him to cut the shit because I knew he was lying. I demanded he come and pick me up and that he take me to go meet up with Charles and his dirty little secret. Within ten minutes he was parked outside. He knew by the tone of my voice that I was serious.

I can still remember the look on Charles' face after we pulled up to that motel. He knew he was caught, but still tried to come up with a way to explain his presence there. All bets were off once Krista pulled up and told a much different story. He had the look of a deer in the headlights, but one that knew it was soon to meet its' fate. I told him it was over and that he should stay out for the night. I went home to pack my clothes and left. I had rented a nice little apartment for Jason and I with an extra room for when Jaxson and Aaron came to visit. Things were finally starting to settle down and that's when I met a man named Wayne. Wayne was seven years older than me, but we hit it off almost instantly. He was working as a dispatcher and I was a customs broker. We both worked afternoons at the time, so it gave us the perfect opportunity to spend time together. We both had children from previous relationships and they were all close in age. It was going to be the perfect little family. To tell you the truth, I never spent a single night in my new apartment.

Jason was with his father and I didn't want to be alone so I would stay at Wayne's at night and went home in the mornings. For the first few months we decided not to introduce our children to one another, as we wanted to be sure it was going to be a lasting relationship between us first. Wayne was funny, charming and always knew the right things to say. We had discussed moving in together, getting married and possibly having a child of our own in the future. I was so unbelievably excited to spend my life with this man. The future was very bright. I remember the first time I had met his children. I was upstairs in his bedroom and he kept the children distracted while I snuck downstairs and quietly made my way out the front door. I rang the doorbell as if I had just arrived, and he introduced me as his friend. The children were still fairly young, so I don't think they caught on to us. A few months into our relationship we decided it was time to move in together for good. Everything was absolutely perfect.

We had introduced our children, family and even some of our friends to one another. Then once we were all settled in, Wayne decided to break the news to me that he had decided he never wanted to get married again, because the first one was difficult for him and he didn't want to go through that a second time if it ever came to that point. As if that wasn't bad enough, he then told me he also didn't want to have another child. I was absolutely heartbroken. Here I was with this man who had made me so many promises. Promises that bonded us because we seemed to be on the same page. I felt like he had tricked me. He waited until I was moved into his home, with no place else to go and then he dropped it all on me. Somehow, I thought it was something I might be able to change his mind about and so I stuck it out with him. Then we found out we were pregnant. We decided not to tell anyone just yet because we were still trying to figure things out ourselves. We both were shocked, excited and happy about it though.

A Journey of a Thousand Miles – A Reflections Saga

One day after we had gone for a nice walk together, I started bleeding. We rushed to the hospital to find out what was wrong, only to receive news that I was having a miscarriage. This was absolutely devastating to hear. I had done everything right to ensure a healthy baby. I had even stopped smoking. Still it didn't seem to be enough. I prayed to God to save this child. I prayed for him to grant me mercy, and spare me the pain of having to go through such a horrific ordeal. I was not even sure I had the strength to survive another miscarriage. Yes that's right...another one. You see when I was just fifteen years old I had become pregnant by Paul. It was two years before we had become pregnant with Jaxson. Shockingly Paul was actually happy about that first baby, but sadly at thirteen and a half weeks I miscarried. Paul and I were both devastated and I thought for sure the next time we got pregnant he would be absolutely overjoyed but we all know how that turned out.

After receiving the news that I was most likely miscarrying and that there was nothing that could be done, Wayne and I left the hospital. He brought me home and up to our bedroom to rest. I lay there crying and begging for everything to be okay. I prayed the doctors were wrong. I was very weak and the pain was like nothing I remembered ever feeling. I wish I could tell you that Wayne was right there by my side through the whole thing but he wasn't. He was actually downstairs playing video games with his friends while I lay there completely helpless just waiting for the miscarriage to be over. I had never felt so alone. It felt like Wayne didn't care that we lost the baby. He actually seemed to be more relieved than anything else. A few months after the loss of our baby, I asked him if we could try again. He informed me that we weren't even trying to get pregnant the first time, and that he sure as hell wasn't going to do it on purpose.

The anger I felt hearing that soon grew into resentment. It got to the point where the sound of him breathing became irritating to me. I realized that he and I were never truly going to be happy together, because he wasn't willing to give me what I wanted the most which was a child with him and to be his wife. I felt that I had given him every part of me and that I deserved true happiness. I decided I had to get away from him, and I couldn't even bare the thought of staying in the city, so I made plans and moved to another province. There had been a man that I dated briefly before I ever met Wayne who I got back in touch with, and he had made me an offer I couldn't refuse. He told me if I came there that he and I could finally be together and I was convinced by every word he said.

I moved out there just before my birthday, and had gotten a job at the hospital working as a personal support worker. Despite all I had been through up to this point, this was going to be it for me. He was what some might call the perfect man. He didn't have any children, had never been married and had a house of his own. He had a great head on his shoulders and even worked for a nuclear power company. Surely this would be the man I was going to spend the rest of my life with. He and I were a match made in heaven, except there was one little problem, he wasn't who I thought he was. He changed his mind like the weather, was constantly stressed by

A Journey of a Thousand Miles – A Reflections Saga

having Jason there and he didn't love me the way that I loved him. No matter how hard I tried to be the woman he wanted, I couldn't be. I finally grew tired of constantly trying to mould myself into the image he wanted, and decided to call it quits, but I still had to make arrangements to get back home.

During this time Wayne had reached out to me. He wanted to reconcile. He said he had been able to do a lot of thinking while I was gone, and had decided that he was a fool for ever letting me go. We talked about working it out, getting married and even having a child together. It was official. We had made up our mind about one another, and we made plans to get back together once I returned. There was just one thing I needed to be sure of first. The morning I left to head back home, I went into the bathroom and took the test. I waited for that pink colour to wash over the whole window and show just the one line, before I placed it down on the back of the toilet and walked downstairs to get into my taxi. At the airport my head was swimming with excitement. I could barely contain how giddy I was at the mere thought of us getting married and holding our newborn son. When I arrived at my terminal, Wayne was there waiting for me with flowers, balloons and outstretched arms. Maybe this time apart was exactly what we needed. It sure brought each of us a newfound appreciation for one another. I was grateful.

All those feelings of resentment seemed to just melt away when I saw him. I dropped my suitcase and went running into his arms. He picked me up in one fell swoop and spun me around while planting about a hundred kisses on me. The tears in his eyes said it all. I was finally exactly where I was always meant to be. It wasn't too long after my return, that we started planning for our future. Wayne had proposed almost right away after my return, and we began to start trying for a baby shortly after. About six weeks later we discovered we were expecting. We were the happiest we had ever been. It was our brand new start and I was loving every minute of it. Wayne however was a bit concerned about the timing and wondered whether the other man could be the father. Luckily an ultrasound to date the pregnancy would put those fears to rest for good.

Unfortunately news of our impending new arrival did not go over too well with a few people on his side of the family. I was crushed. Here I was in one of the happiest moments of my life, and it was treated like something that was a horrible mistake. To make matters worse, we would find out shortly after that there was a complication with the pregnancy, and I was placed on strict bed rest at sixteen weeks. There was a very big risk of premature labour due to my condition. I had never even heard of such a thing, but it was pretty serious. I was making too much amniotic fluid and as a result my uterus was growing well beyond the size it should've been. At just sixteen weeks I was already measuring full term! At any moment my uterus could decide it was time for the baby. I was ordered to stay off my feet until the pregnancy reached full term. This would prove to be quite the feat because we had Wayne's two kids every day and plus I had Jason there too.

A Journey of a Thousand Miles – A Reflections Saga

I needed help and I needed it badly. The only person I could think of was my mother, and well I hate to say it but that help came with more stress than anything else. Eventually after a few weeks of staying with us, the pressure of the constant nagging and bickering got to me and I snapped at her which caused her to leave, leaving me in tears and utter despair. What the hell was I supposed to do now? Wayne didn't seem to want to listen to the doctor, and he wouldn't even call his own family to come and help. He would go to work every day and I was left there to care for all of the kids. When my sister Grace had heard about this, she immediately flew into action. She told me to call Wayne at work and tell him someone needed to come watch the kids because we were dropping Jason off to his father, and I would be staying at her house from now on.

I stayed with her, her husband and kids five days a week and only went back home on weekends. My sister took the best care of me. Just as she had done all those years ago. She fed me three homemade meals a day and snacks in between. She was determined to make certain she did everything she could for me so that I would carry to term and have a healthy baby. Those eighteen weeks seemed like an eternity. The weekends always went by too fast and I was really missing the way things used to be. Never had I imagined that when Wayne and I decided to make this baby, that I would feel so alone. Without my sister, I'm not sure our son would've made it into this world. I had become physically uncomfortable early on in the pregnancy, due to my ever expanding uterus. I mean I was tiny to begin with and my belly just kept getting bigger and bigger. I was afraid at one point that I might actually burst open. I thought for sure once I was pulled off of bed rest that I'd go into labour soon after, but that was definitely not the case.

I had to be induced about five days early. I didn't sleep too well the night before. I hadn't spoken to my own mother in months and was feeling a bit sad that she was going to miss the birth. She had been there in the delivery room when Jaxson was born but not when I had given birth to Aaron. Heck even the doctor wasn't there for that arrival. Everything happened so fast that the nurse had to be the one to catch him. I really wanted her to be there for this birth and Wayne knew it. I thought for sure that the baby would come fast once I was induced but no such luck. That little guy gave me a run for my money. It was thirteen and a half hours of hard back labour. I was becoming impatient because all the women who had come in around the same time as me, had already had their babies. I watched as two different doctors came and went...then a third, They couldn't get over how big my uterus was measuring either.

At full term it measured a whopping sixty one centimetres! It seemed like an eternity of continuous pain. I barely had time to breathe through contractions and the epidural they attempted to give me twice never bothered to take. The nurse had come to check me and told me I was only at eight centimetres. Just when I felt like I was about ready to throw in the towel, my mother walked into the room. It turns out that Wayne felt bad because he knew how much I really wanted her to be there, so he had called her somehow without me knowing about it. I was grateful that she was there with me, and she got to see her newest grandson be born. We named him Christopher. It took him forever, but he finally made his grand entrance into this world and I knew in that instance he was going to be the kid that would come around to anything in life when he was good and ready to. I'd like to tell you we all lived happily ever after, but as my luck seemed to have it, things began to deteriorate between us when Christopher was about six months old.

Chapter Twenty-Two

I had nowhere to go when I left, and so I had to stay in the Hiatus house with Christopher and Jason until my sister Grace had found us a place to call home. It was a nice two bedroom apartment in a quiet neighbourhood. My landlord was living above us which made me feel safe. I was so happy to be in a place of our own. Finally we were going to have a fresh start in somewhere that was not only close to my sister, but comfortable as well. I remember the day Grace took me to sign the lease. It was the first time I was meeting my new landlord. He seemed nice enough. An older gentleman from Trinidad. He said his wife was out of town on business, but that she would be returning in a few months. I signed the lease and he handed me my keys. After staying in the Hiatus house for a few weeks, I was happy to be somewhere where I wouldn't be surrounded by a bunch of strangers. Later that day I had to go shopping for all new dishes, silverware, appliances etc. I had left Wayne's with nothing but clothes that day so I was in need of quite a bit. I felt accomplished as my sisters Grace and Marie helped me unpack, wash everything and put it away.

The next morning I went out on my back porch for a cigarette and then my phone rang. It was my landlord welcoming me again, and letting me know what days garbage and recycle pickup would be. He also told me I shouldn't smoke so much. *Ummm okay,* but what business was it of his anyway? I decided to ignore his intrusive comments and went back inside. About ten minutes or so had passed when there was a knock on my front door. It was the landlord and he was standing there with another gentleman who looked like a maintenance guy or something. I was just getting ready to jump in the shower so I had just removed my shirt. I quickly pulled it back over my head and rushed to open the front door. It was a constant and persistent knock. I was kind of annoyed at this point, because he had just called me and didn't bother to even mention he was coming to down to my place. And he certainly never mentioned that he would be coming with company either.

I quickly opened the door to see what they were there for, and that's when he began to apologize almost immediately for not notifying me of his visit. He must've read the annoyance on my face. He told me the maintenance guy needed to check a few things and also wanted to look at the vents to see if they needed to be cleaned. I went into my bedroom and waited for them to leave. I didn't want to be in anyone's way. I heard the door close behind them after about twenty minutes or so, and then I proceeded to get ready for my shower. I wondered why he hadn't taken care of all of this prior to my moving in, but decided to shrug it off. I had probably only been in the shower for about five to ten minutes and then my phone rang again. I decided to let the answering machine take the call this time since I wanted to shower before Christopher woke up.

Have you ever had an eerie feeling that you were being watched before? I felt it almost instantly as soon as I stepped out of the shower. I could sense the presence of someone, and it felt like they were in my home! I decided it was probably my new house paranoia kicking in, and proceeded to towel off and get dressed. I could hear that Christopher was awake and babbling away in his crib. Jason had been with his father to make the move a bit easier, since it was just me and my sisters doing all of the work. We were alone in the house at this time, but were expecting him to arrive home just after noon. I quickly rushed to towel dry my hair and make my way toward the bathroom door, but as I went to reach for it...my blood ran cold. I don't really know how to explain the feeling I got, but it made the hair on the back of my neck stand up. My veins felt like they were filled with ice water again. I knew in that moment that it wasn't just me being paranoid. Someone was in my house and they were just on the other side of the half cracked doorway. I felt a lump in my throat as I reached for my hair dryer to brandish as a weapon, and then for the handle readying myself to pull it open as fast as I could. I could not believe my eyes when I finally came face to face with the intruder. It was him. It was my landlord!

"Wha...what the hell are you doing in my house?" I firmly demanded.

His eyes grew wide and he stumbled backwards with both of his hands up.

"I...I didn't mean no harm miss. I tried to call you but yo phone went to yo machine." he replied. "I knocked but you didn't answer either so I got worried cuz it's jus you and yo baby down ere. I just wanted to tell you that I do my laundry on Wednesdays." he stated.

"ummmm okay...well...uh...thanks for letting me know." I said sheepishly.

About a thousand thoughts were running through my head at the time. I was still in shock. This man had just let himself into my apartment and was standing just on the other side of the bathroom door. Was he trying to spy on me or something? Was he a creep like that? I wondered so many things and my head began to swirl with all different types of scenarios. I shook them loose and ushered him toward the door. Why would he need to enter my home by using a key in order to tell me what days he does laundry? What the hell do I care? The whole situation was just off to me and I was rattled by it all. I decided to call Grace and talk to her about it. She was appalled by what I had just told her, and it didn't take long for her to arrive at my place. She was quick to go upstairs and knock on his door to ask what the heck was going on. I could hear the sounds of their muffled voices carrying on a conversation. I texted her and asked her if she could also find out how to turn on the central air because I was so excited to get into the place, I had completely forgotten to ask those little things. When she returned she rushed right past me and down the hallway toward my kitchen without saying anything. She had her gaze focused on a mysterious door in my kitchen that was locked from the other side.

A Journey of a Thousand Miles – A Reflections Saga

That's when she turned to me and said, "Okay...well this is my fault because I'd never heard of this before, but apparently it is in your rental agreement that you and him share the washer and dryer."

"What do you mean?" I asked.

"There is only one set in this place and it's that one right there" she pointed at the corner of my kitchen where my washer and dryer sat.

I could not believe what I was hearing.

"And that door right there..." she said while pointing behind me, "That door leads up into his house."

"Wait a minute!" I shouted. "Are you telling me that not only am I to share a washer and dryer with this strange man, but he also has access into my apartment?!"

"Yes Ava, that's what he just told me. He said he won't ever come down though unless it's laundry day and he will call you beforehand."

She was trying to calm my fears and reassure me that everything would be alright. It definitely wasn't working. The more she went on about the details of the rental agreement, the more I cringed. She tried to calm my nerves and told me that perhaps after all I had been through in life, I was simply being paranoid. I wasn't so convinced. I didn't tell her he had entered the apartment earlier uninvited. I just told her about him showing up with the maintenance guy and then him showing up again to tell me about his laundry. If there is one thing I could tell you about Grace, it's that she doesn't play around with creepers, and I didn't want to jump to conclusions because I couldn't prove that I had even locked the front door. She honestly would've lost her shit on him and I know it. I didn't want to start any trouble for anyone. Especially if it was unwarranted. I decided to just leave it be. She informed me that he also had told her he would be controlling the central air and the heat and that I just needed to call him and ask anytime I wanted it turned on. My apartment was a basement apartment and you may or may not know this, but it tends to get cooler in those places, but given that it was the spring when we moved in, I wasn't too worried about it being cold until at least the fall. It was however hot down there at this time, for some reason which is why I wanted the air turned on. Almost as soon as I thought about the fact that he hadn't yet turned it on, I felt the sudden gush of cool air blow through the vent above our heads.

"Well I guess that takes care of that." Grace said "Hopefully he won't need to bother you for anything else but if he does just give me a call."

I walked her to the door and kissed her goodbye. Grace seemed to know me better than I even knew myself sometimes. She knew about my ADHD and the anxiety that sometimes came with it. The anxiety that seemed to be amplified whenever I had to talk to strangers. I wasn't the best at communicating, but I suppose it may have been residual PTSD from the traumas I had endured in life. It was definitely something I wanted to work on. That evening the boys and I watched Finding Nemo and headed to bed early. Wayne would be over to pick up Christopher around 9:00 am, and the ordeal from earlier that day had left me feeling exhausted. I tucked

A Journey of a Thousand Miles – A Reflections Saga

Jason into his toddler bed and carried Christopher into my room to lay in bed and snuggle with me until he fell asleep. He always liked being near me. So much so that when he was born, I had to page the nurse to come sit with him just so I could take a shower or even use the bathroom. He never wanted me to leave his sight. I didn't mind though. He was still a baby after all. Once he finally drifted off to baby land, I moved slowly toward his crib and gently placed him on the mattress. Any sudden movement and he would wake right up. I definitely didn't want that. I lay down in bed, set my alarm and went to sleep.

I don't know why, but something startled me awake around 4:00 am. At first I thought I was dreaming, because I could hear subtle sounds in the hallway which was right next to my room. I lay there in the dark and listened intently, as I tried to make out what I was hearing. It was a new place of course, so I still had yet to get used to the typical house sounds. Not to mention I had someone living above me now, so I needed to get used to that too. Maybe that was what I was hearing. After a few minutes of not hearing any movement, I drifted back off to sleep. It felt like I had just closed my eyes when my phone vibrated to wake me up. It was a very rough night's sleep indeed.

At one point I thought the lack of sleep was making me delusional, because I could swear I heard someone coming into my house at night. Not only that, but I started noticing things seemed to have been moved, certain articles of clothing I had left in the dryer overnight suddenly began disappearing, and it was all just super weird. By the time summer came around, I had started dating a man named Kevin. He was ex military and was now working a security job in the USA. He was divorced and had two little girls. We decided to take things slow, but we were excited to be able to spend some time together. We had been dating about a month or so at the time, It was a whirlwind romance. Funny thing is I had always said I would never date anyone who was in the military and definitely not someone from the USA.

Kevin was from Michigan. It's amazing how fast you can change your mind when it comes to finding your person. Kevin had come over to visit a few times, but this was the first time he was going to be spending the night. The boys were with their fathers and so it was just going to be the two of us. I was ready for some adult company! That evening we ordered pizza and wings, and went to pick up some beer. I had started a load of laundry before we left. I didn't want to get behind on the things I had planned to do around the house just because Kevin was over. When we got back, I went into the kitchen to put the leftover beers into the fridge and to grab some plates and napkins for the food. I walked into the kitchen and froze. I called for Kevin to come into the kitchen.

"Did you see me leave this open when we were leaving? No I closed it right? Didn't I?!" I asked confused.

A Journey of a Thousand Miles – A Reflections Saga

"Honestly Ava?! I can't really remember!" he said laughing. "We were in such a rush to pick up the food and grab the beer that I wasn't really paying it much attention. I'm pretty sure you closed it though." he told me.

He scratched his head and looked puzzled before stating that maybe we both were losing our minds since neither one of us could remember. We both laughed it off about how clueless we were and went back into the living room to enjoy our food. We ended up watching the movie, *Ghosts of Girlfriends Past*, and then wound up falling asleep snuggled up together on the couch. We were both awakened by the heat in the house. It was stifling hot and we could barely breathe. I went and checked the other rooms to see if they were just as hot. I had to turn my head away from the vent in Jason's room, because the heat was blasting through it. What the hell?! Why would my landlord have turned on the heat?

It was summertime and definitely not cold down there. I checked my phone to see what time it was, 8:00 PM. I decided to call the landlord and ask him if he could please turn off the heat. He didn't answer. I tried a few more times before going to open the front door and rushing to close all of the vents. We decided to go outside for a cigarette so we could cool off. It was actually cooler outside than it was inside my apartment. Imagine being in a sauna with the heat cranked up to max and that was pretty close to how sweltering it was inside. Kevin seemed to be on edge. He felt that the landlord had done this on purpose. I began to think this too. We knew he was home, because we could hear him walking around on the floor above us and yet he refused to answer my calls. About an hour or so later, my phone rang. It was the landlord and he told me I needed to open up the vents. He told me not to ever close them again.

I explained to him that we had to close them because it had become so hot in there that we were ready to pass out. He seemed to ignore my concerns, and demanded I leave the vents open. I was told that I was not to open any windows or doors either, because he was paying for the bill. There was absolutely no way I was going to stay in that. I opened up some of the vents but left the ones closest to where we were closed. I didn't care what he said. I was not going to be miserable in my own place that I was paying good money for. We managed to trap the heat in the other rooms we were not using, by closing all of the doors to them. It had cooled down only slightly, but I ran a fan to make it more tolerable.

We decided to make the most of it and Kevin suggested I call my sister Grace in the morning. While we were in bed that evening I was awakened by some sounds coming from my kitchen. I attempted to wake Kevin to go and investigate the noise, because it was clear that someone was in the apartment. Upon his investigation he didn't find anyone but swears he had just seen the door in the kitchen close as he was approaching. He was absolutely livid. I told him I would let my sister know first thing in the morning. We couldn't believe this was even happening. Why was my landlord doing these things? What was he so pissed about? I had been nothing but a good tenant. Even though I had children living with me, we were always as quiet as could be. I began to wonder about his previous tenants, and whether they had experienced similar issues with him. I drifted off to sleep again, but it wasn't a deep one. I was on edge and very aware of my surroundings.

Even with Kevin right there beside me, I no longer felt safe. There was one point where I was startled awake again by the sound of footsteps outside of my bedroom door. I nudged Kevin to wake him again, but he was in such a deep sleep he didn't even budge. It was so dark in the bedroom and yet, I could swear that someone was standing there in the doorway. Was I seeing things? I attempted to wipe the sleep from my eyes and adjust my vision to get a clearer view. When I finally looked up again, the figure was gone. Maybe I had been dreaming the whole thing. Maybe my fear and anxiety had made me hallucinate this shadowy figure. It must have been my mind playing tricks on me. After this incident there was no way I was going back to sleep.

I had tried to call Grace in the morning, but ended up having to leave a message on her machine. I figured she was probably busy with her own children and she would return my call whenever she was free. Instead of calling me back, she showed up at my front door around 10:00 am. She said I sounded terrified and she wanted to know just what the hell happened. Kevin and I went over everything that we could recall about the previous evening. Grace just sat there with her mouth open. Like she couldn't believe what she was hearing. This sounded like something out of one of those creepy stalker movies. These were the ones that scared her more than anything. She apologized to both Kevin and I, and told us she was going home to speak to her husband about the whole thing so they could come up with a plan. I knew that plan was more than likely going to involve calling the police. I didn't much care for them. At a very young age, my uncle Larry, my father's twin brother, had actually scared the living shit out of me about the police. So much so that when the police were called to our home due to a heated argument between he and my father, I ended up urinating all over the poor officer that decided to pick me up. He thought I was adorable with my little ringlets, and he had never seen a little girl who looked so much like Shirley Temple in all of his life. I bet you after that incident he didn't go around picking up any more little ones. Even to this day, I had never fully recovered from the trauma I had endured throughout my childhood. I preferred to keep them out of it for now. I would figure out a way to get through this. I had Kevin after all and surely he would have some ideas as to how to handle the situation. Oh Kevin had ideas alright, but they were not something I thought he would ever say. He asked me if I wanted to make my landlord go away. You see Kevin was in the military, he was trained on explosives and how to cover things up or make them look like accidents. I guess you might say that Kevin was a highly trained and efficient killer. Those words he said to me that day still linger in my mind.

A Journey of a Thousand Miles – A Reflections Saga

"Listen, I know that this guy isn't going to stop tormenting you. I mean just look at what he's doing now and you haven't even been living here that long. I could...I could make him go away if you want. I could make it look like an accident. You just gotta say the words and they'll never find him." he told me.

"Uh...Kevin I don't want anyone to get hurt. I don't know what his issue is, but I definitely don't think he deserves to die over this. You're talking crazy! Let's try to come up with a better solution that doesn't involve murdering someone okay?" I suggested.

Wow! In that moment I didn't know who I was more fearful of...my landlord or my current boyfriend. I mean I knew he was in the military, but I had no idea it was like this. Who was this man? Did I even truly know him as well as I thought I did? I mean we had met online on a site called *Plenty of Fish*. From the very beginning it was like a match made in heaven. It was like a real life fairy-tale. He was absolutely perfect for me and we had so much in common. His sister's name was even Ava, and she had a birthday that was just two days before my own. It seemed like we were meant for each other, and I was looking forward to spending our life together, because even though we had only been together a short time, I knew he was the man I wanted to be with. Everything was absolutely perfect and the way he made me feel was like nothing I had ever experienced before. He was sure to be my happily ever after, and yet hearing him talk this way made me question quite a bit.

Could we honestly be happy together? Was he really crazy enough to do the things he talked about doing? Something told me he was dead serious and that he could probably take someone's life without so much as batting an eyelash over it. Something told me he had done this before. Many times before! Could I really raise my children with this man? Was he trustworthy? Was I safe with him? So many questions, but my intuition told me that he was just being protective over me and that I had nothing to worry about. Kevin was planning to leave that evening, as the boys were due back after dinner, and we thought it might be better if he didn't meet them too soon. However, he could sense that I was still on edge, and no longer felt safe being on my own with them in this place, so he decided to stay just one more night. Even though we had agreed on him meeting the kids later, we decided that our safety was what was most important.

We had a great time with them that evening. We watched movies, read stories, played games and even got them ready for bed together. That whole evening was uneventful when it came to my landlord and his antics. We hadn't heard so much as a peep from him all day. Maybe Grace had come up with a plan. Maybe she had called and warned him that he was overstepping his boundaries. You see, Grace was a Paralegal, and she was feisty as hell. Definitely not one to mess with when it came to the legal aspect of things. She had definitely done all of her homework and had even started her own practice. I had even made her my *Power of Attorney* so that she would be able to handle certain details of my life that she otherwise wouldn't have been able to. I trusted that she always had my best interests, and that of my children at heart.

A Journey of a Thousand Miles – A Reflections Saga

I woke up the next morning and Kevin was no longer beside me in bed. I leaned over to check the time on my phone and jumped up when I saw the numbers on the screen. It was noon! I couldn't believe I had slept so long. Where was Kevin? Where were the kids? It was super quiet in the house. Eerily quiet, considering there was an almost five year old and an eight month old baby in the house. I jumped up in a panic and quickly pulled on my robe. A million thoughts were going through my head. I mean, I really didn't know this guy all that well and I had allowed him to be in my house with my young children. What the hell kind of mother does that?! *What if he's taken my children?* I shuttered at the thought of that, as I opened the bedroom door and stepped out and into the living room. There, kneeling down on the floor in front of the coffee table was Jason. My heart finally dropped back down into my chest at this precious sight. He was eating homemade pancakes and watching one of his favourite shows. There was still no sight of Kevin or Christopher. I could hear the subtle sounds of cooing and giggling coming down the hallway from the area of the kitchen. I was welcomed by an even more beautiful sight, as I crossed the threshold. There in his highchair was Christopher with a little plastic baby fork in his hand. He too was eating homemade pancakes and Kevin was making him giggle playing peek a boo with the towel as he attempted to finish making breakfast for the two of us.

"Good morning sweetie! Or should I say afternoon?" He chuckled. "I'm sorry. Please don't be mad. We didn't want to wake you. You were so tired and I figured you could probably use the rest, so the boys and I got breakfast started and figured we'd let you sleep in a bit."

I was so touched at how incredibly thoughtful he had been. Here was this man who hadn't even been with me for that long, and had just met my children yesterday, and yet here he was taking on the role of a loving step daddy. The boys absolutely adored him right from the start. It made me happy to see how he seemed to blend seamlessly into our little family. This was definitely going to work between us. He was extremely loving and attentive. After we had finished eating, we decided to get ready for the day and take the kids to the park for some fresh air. It was such a beautiful day. Grace had called while we were out, and told me that she had spoken to Michael, her husband about the whole situation between me and Harvey, my landlord. He told her that I should call the police immediately, and said it was important for me to start documenting everything odd that had taken place. He suggested that I continue to document everything going forward. Grace had informed me that she was currently working on a cease and desist order and that she was planning on serving him with it in a day or so. I agreed to document everything, but told her I wanted to hold off on calling the police for now. I was sure after she served him with the order, that I wouldn't be hearing much from him going forward, except when it came to the rent of course. I also asked her if she wouldn't mind taking me shopping for groceries later that evening, as Kevin was planning to head home soon and I wanted us to spend as much time with the boys as possible. Grace agreed and suggested bringing my niece over so she could look after the boys while we shopped. I told her I would give her a call when I was ready for her to pick me up, which would probably be within the next few hours.

As soon as Grace arrived, she put the cease and desist order directly into Harvey's mailbox, because of course he wasn't answering the phone or the door again. As we were in the midst of gathering the items I needed at the store, Grace's phone rang. She pulled it from her pocket and turned it toward me so I could see the caller ID on the screen.

"Looks like he got my letter." she said.

Chapter Twenty-Three

We returned to my place about an hour and a half later. Upon entering the apartment, we found my niece standing there with a puzzled look on her face. She told me she had gone to nap with the boys and someone must've come in while they were sleeping. At first, nothing she said was making sense.

"How do you know someone came in here? I asked.

"Because auntie...I went into the kitchen to warm a bottle for Christopher, and that's when I noticed your stove was gone!" she told me.

I couldn't even hold back my disbelief.

"What the hell do you mean my stove is gone?!" I demanded.

"It...It's just gone!" I don't know when they were in here because I had the door closed and the fan on so I didn't hear anything. The door was locked auntie I swear! I...I don't know how they got in!"

Grace and I just stood there dumbfounded and silent, for a very long time. We were both floored by what my niece had just shared with us. Then it was like we both snapped out of it and both headed toward the kitchen at the same time. We nearly bumped right into each other. It's like one of those things you get told, but that you actually have to see for yourself to believe. It was just that crazy. As we arrived in the kitchen, there was the empty space where my stove once sat just over an hour ago. Who the hell would come in and take my stove?! I mean what possesses someone to do such a thing? How could you rob a mother from having the ability to feed her own children? Had someone literally just walked through the front door and actually stolen it? What the hell was happening? Grace and I were frozen in place, just standing there and staring at each other. There was so much communication going on between us but there were no words exchanged. This felt like some kind of nightmare.

Was this real? How the hell was I going to feed my children now? We even ended up calling my sister Marie over to witness the craziness we were dealing with. None of us could make any sense of it. I mean, have you ever heard of such ridiculousness? It didn't take long for me to put two and two together and determine that Harvey was definitely behind it. How did a sixty something year old man remove a stove by himself? Not a single one of us could even entertain such an idea, it was just that insane. After the initial shock began to wear off, Grace reached down and pulled her cellphone out of her pocket, and then she began dialing a number.

"Who are you calling?" I asked.

"Ava...Enough is enough! I'm calling the police." she replied.

It was in that moment that I think my heart sank deep into the pit of my stomach. I was not ready for this, but I knew now that things had gotten out of hand and this needed to stop. Grace had attempted to contact Harvey numerous times while we waited for the police. But of course she was met with no answer. She left him several messages on his machine, but didn't go into much detail as to the reason for her call. The message just stated that she needed to talk to him as soon as possible. After what seemed like the first attempted contact, I decided to go out and check the mailbox after all of the craziness, because I hadn't had a chance to earlier in the day. My mailbox was of course on the front porch, which also just so happened to be positioned right next to Harvey's front door. He hadn't been answering, so I figured now was my chance. I didn't even want to see his face. I pulled the various sizes of envelopes from the box and proceeded to peruse through them. One envelope was handwritten but there was no return address on it. I wondered who it could be from. I decided to open that one first. I slid my fingers into the corner of the flap and pulled back to tear into it and reveal the contents within. Inside, there appeared to be what looked to be a handwritten letter. It was dated for today's date. I sat down on the front steps and pulled it open to read it. I stared in shock at the words on the page and felt the tears begin to fall. It was a letter from Harvey, my landlord. It appeared to be a handwritten eviction notice. The words seemed to blur together on the page as I attempted to read it through the midst of my tears.

To Miss Ava Ducharme,

A Journey of a Thousand Miles – A Reflections Saga

Please be advised that you are being asked to vacate the premises within 30 days upon receipt of this notice. The reason for this eviction is as follows:

-You have willingly interfered with the reasonable enjoyment of other tenants in the neighbourhood.
-You are in direct violation of your lease agreement by having unauthorized persons residing in the premises with you.

Thank you for your understanding and prompt attention to this matter.

Sincerely yours,
Harvey A. Blackburn

    I didn't understand where this was coming from, as he didn't exactly give any details highlighting how I had disturbed anyone or interfered with the reasonable enjoyment of their own property. I began to think that maybe when he met me he had gotten certain ideas about what the two of us would be. Maybe he thought we would develop a relationship other than landlord and tenant. In that moment everything that had transpired thus far suddenly began to make more sense. I was being evicted because I had a boyfriend, and Harvey had finally realized he didn't stand a chance in hell with me. I don't even know how he even got such an idea in his head. I was twenty seven years old and he was in at least his mid sixties. This confused me even more because it was my understanding that he had a wife. I hadn't yet met her or even seen her around, but he kept going on and on about her while Grace and I sat in his dining room that day she took me to sign the lease.

    I folded the letter back up and wiped the tears from my eyes, as I slowly walked back toward my apartment. Grace could tell I was crying and she of course asked me what was wrong. I didn't say anything. I just handed over the letter and watched intently as her eyes began to scan the page. Her jaw almost hit the floor and she too was confused. I had done nothing wrong other than date someone. It was utterly insane.

    The police came soon after, but they were less than helpful. The ironic thing about it was, I could hear them knocking on Harvey's door before they had even come to knock on mine. We had been the ones to call them and yet they went to him first. They basically told me I should just move. They didn't seem to care that he had taken my stove or that he illegally entered my unit without my consent. It was almost as if he paid them off. Maybe he knew them. Harvey seemed to be well loved and respected by everyone in our neighbourhood and I was sure no one would ever dare speak out about him, but that's also probably why he got away with things like this. My sisters and I thought the whole thing was odd. Things continued to escalate after this incident, and it got to the point where I couldn't even walk Jason to the bus stop in front of our house, without having someone on the phone at all times. I also had to ask my mother to come and stay with us for a week or two, because I was absolutely terrified to be alone at any time in that place.

At this point, Harvey decided instead of blasting the heat he would now blast the air instead. It got so bad we had to tape garbage bags over the vents. We all got sick and I ended up with pneumonia which is practically unheard of in summertime. I think it was a combination of my chain smoking in the heat due to the stress, and then coming into a freezing cold apartment. I was so stressed at this point, that my blood pressure and heart rate were dangerously high. I also wasn't eating or sleeping much, and even my ADHD medications were no longer working. I was constantly on edge, and wouldn't even go to the mailbox for days on end just to avoid that man. He knew no boundaries, and had made constant unacceptable comments toward me. I remember one time in particular when he was in my apartment one day so the plumber could fix my leaky toilet. I was in the bedroom playing with Christopher, and he stood in the doorway to my bedroom staring at us and said:

"I should be getting all that attention!"

The plumber quickly cleared his throat as if to remind him that he was still there with us. He too looked uncomfortable with the whole thing. This man didn't seem to care who was around. At one point, he even tried to fight Christopher's father Wayne. He had come by my place to pick up Christopher and Harvey assumed that he was the one I had been dating or something. It was absolutely shocking how one minute, Wayne and I were standing by the car getting ready to put the baby in his car-seat, and the next thing we know, Harvey was pushing Wayne and cussing at him. He had even gotten into Wayne's face and continued to push him, even while Wayne was holding our infant son in his arms! At this point, Grace had already served him with the cease and desist order and she had even given him a verbal warning.

He was told that he was no longer to contact me in any way, and if he needed to reach me for something, he was to do so through her from now on. Despite all of that, he didn't seem to care. If anything it only seemed to anger him more and his behaviour was becoming more and more erratic. He was still coming into my apartment every night, and had even gotten brave and started stealing my panties out of my dryer. One night he came in and took the lint filter from it. Only to come in the next night and replace it after I had accused him of taking it. He made me feel like I was truly losing my mind. Maybe I was.

My mother left us after about a week and a half of staying there, because she had become too sick to stay and needed to go home. Being that she is diabetic, I understood. As I was walking her out to her taxi, I turned to see Harvey glaring at me through the window. I tried my best to ignore him and kissed my mother goodbye, before closing the door to the taxi. As I turned and tried to head back toward my apartment quickly, Harvey came out onto the porch and stopped me.

"You have mail you know." he informed me.

I politely thanked him and walked cautiously up the front porch steps and made my way toward the mailbox. He then went back inside as I approached and slammed the screen door. He remained standing there in the doorway and just stared at me like a creep. I hastily opened the mailbox and noticed a delivery slip from the post office, as well as a few bills. The slip stated that they had tried to deliver a letter to me, but apparently they had gotten no answer. No one had even come to knock on my door.

I called Grace and asked her if she wouldn't mind running me by the post office quickly so that I could retrieve the letter. As I stood there glancing at the envelope, I recognized the handwriting immediately. It was most definitely Harvey's handwriting based off of the letter he had sent me just a couple weeks ago. It was covered in about ten dollars worth of stamps. I opened it as I made my way back toward Grace's car. Immediately after unfolding the papers inside, I stopped dead in my tracks. I felt my legs growing weak and I decided it was best to wait to read it until I was back home.

Once I finally had a moment to read the contents of the letter, I pulled my cellphone from my pocket and dialed Grace's number. As soon as she answered we both blurted out at the same time:

"You're not going to believe this!"

It turned out that not only had she received the exact same letter that I had just received, but it too was covered with the ten dollars worth of stamps. Just looking at the letter was like getting a small glimpse into the mind of a psychopath. To make matters even worse, Harvey had shown up to my sister's house while we were gone. Let's just say that her husband was less than impressed. Apparently, Harvey and Grace had been corresponding through emails and over the phone periodically. We aren't even really sure how he had gotten her address, because neither one of us had given it to him. Michael, Grace's husband had confronted him and asked him what he thought gave him the audacity to think it would be okay for him to show up at their home. Apparently, he told Michael that he had tried calling Grace earlier and had even emailed her. I guess when he didn't get a reply within fifteen minutes, he decided to go over to her home. Grace forwarded me the email he had sent her, just so I could get a feel for his bizarre choice of words and the condescension of his tone that he had used in writing it. It read exactly like this:

Dear Grace,

A Journey of a Thousand Miles – A Reflections Saga

I have received your correspondence with much gusto with regards to the accusations. Strange you have failed to mention the Fire Officer and The Building Inspector all to whom I gave ample notice (more than 24 hours) to Ava as well as the plumber. Ava do not understand the culture of the conversations she and I have shared now does she understand the conversation that transpired between myself and the plumber in regards to the makeshift spray bidet that he wants nothing to do with it for I was asking him to remove same. This house belongs to my wife and I, it is not the projects. You fail to mention who is smoking anyways some of us have short memory the carpets was cleaned by me personally.

If Ava feels threatened by me it is best she starts looking for another place to rent considering you have said that you are her representative and personal confidante. Formal vacate notice have been in train since the visit from the building inspector which will be delivered as per page 2 section 8 additional terms. In this connection. All the required payment will be the outstanding $150.00.

Best wishes to you both.
Harvey and Julie Blackburn
"Live Loving Live Long"
Victory has no Mother
Failure is an Orphan"

Now I think is when Grace finally realized just how crazy this was getting. Enough was enough. That day, after he had left her house, she started making some phone calls to various places to find out what we needed to do about the whole situation. She gave me the number to the investigative services for housing, and told me to call them and explain what's been going on. I wish I could tell you that they were able to help me, and that everything was fine after that, but unfortunately for me...that was not the case. The gentleman I spoke to told me that my case was extreme and that they didn't handle these types of situations, however he did make a few recommendations. He told me I should contact the Landlord and Tenant Board and file a harassment claim against Harvey. He also advised me to install cameras in both the kitchen and hallway, so I could record the activity going on in there at night. After hanging up the phone with him and the Landlord and Tenant board, I called Grace to let her know what they recommended I do.

She and I decide that things had escalated well beyond our control, as Harvey was still not abiding by the cease and desist order and therefore we felt we had no other choice but to call the police...again. We tell them that it's not urgent, but that we would like to file a report, so we request for them to send an officer at some point in the next couple of days. The next morning, as I am heading outside to smoke a cigarette, I happen to notice something taped to my door. It's another slip from the post office that reads: Sorry we missed you!. The description for the package, indicates that it is another letter and once again no one had knocked on my door. I decide to wait until after breakfast, and then I call Grace to ask her to take the kids and I once again to the location given on the slip. The boys sleep in pretty late that particular morning, because Harvey had decided that at 5:30 am that he was going to wake everyone in the house up by stomping his feet heavily, dropping things repeatedly on the floor and had even gone as far as to slam doors. By the time I was finally able to get them back to sleep, it was already 7:30 am. I was absolutely livid and felt he was doing all of this on purpose in order to push us out faster.

As the clerk at the post office handed me the letter I had missed, Grace and I just stood there, our eyes wide with disbelief. It was the EXACT same letter we had both received just a day ago. I mean exactly the same! It even had the ridiculous amount of stamps on the front just like the other one. Now I had received four eviction notices in the span of less than a week. This was absolute madness.

Later that evening, the police finally arrived to take our statements and file the report. I explained to them everything that was going on and even showed them all of the letters I had received, telling me I needed to vacate the premises. I showed them the door in my kitchen and mentioned that the police had already been here once before. They had zero record of that ever taking place. It was as if the documentation just suddenly vanished. Both officers agreed that Harvey's behaviour was completely out of control and informed us that they would be going upstairs to speak with him immediately. They asked for his name and as soon as they heard it, they both looked at each other and said, "yep...same guy!"

I began to wonder what they had meant by that, but I was certain this wasn't the first time he had terrorized a tenant. It was my understanding that the previous tenant was also a single mom of two and she had just outright moved one weekend while Harvey was away visiting his wife. He didn't have very nice things to say about that poor woman. He seemed to be very angry with her, and at the time, both Grace and I felt it was justified. Yet now I was beginning to wonder if he had scared her off.

After about fifteen minutes or so of the officers going upstairs to speak with him, one of the officers knocked on the door again to let me know that they had spoken to him and ordered for him to immediately change my doorknob in the hallway that led into my kitchen. They told him that the twist lock must be facing inside my apartment so that it cannot be easily accessed from the other side. He was also told that he needed to give me both keys to the new doorknob. The officer seemed to be concerned and suggested I install a camera. He tells me not to hesitate to call should there be any further issues with Harvey. He tells me that he and his partner have both issued a warning to Harvey that they will be returning tomorrow evening to ensure he had done what he was told. I say goodbye to the officers, as well as my sisters and my niece and thank everyone for all of their assistance. I tell Grace that I will call her later on this evening or sometime tomorrow morning. Both of my sisters seem to be satisfied with the way things were handled by the police this time around. Grace hugs me goodbye and tells me if I need her for any reason at any time, that I can just call her and she will leave her ringer on so that the line of communication between us will always be open. Somehow, this provides me a bit of comfort. Not even five minutes after everyone's departure, Harvey calls me to let me know that the locksmith will be coming by tomorrow afternoon to change the doorknob. He makes sure to tell me that this is him giving me more than 24 hrs notice. I thank him and quickly hang up.

After dinner, I head outside to have a cigarette to try and calm my nerves. I notice there is yet again something taped to the outside of my door. It's in a sealed envelope and I'm almost afraid to open it at first. It is a notice to enter. The first formal letter I have received from him since I first moved in. I guess the police must've given him a very stern warning.

Later that same evening, Harvey called me yet again, but this time I let it go to voicemail. The message he left on the machine said, *"Hi! I just wanted to ask you if it's too warm or cold down there. If it is, please call me and I will adjust it."*

I felt like maybe he's being nice now because he's trying to make me feel guilty for pursuing any further action against him. The temperature is fine. Funny thing is, it only became fine after the police went up there. I was surprised he didn't turn it back to freezing right after they had left. I decided I would take any small victory I could get. I mean, is it unreasonable to ask someone controlling your thermostat to keep it at a comfortable temperature? Would you really consider it as a win, or just a basic human right? I knew that night that I was going to be alone again and the police had given me some ideas about what to do with the door in the meantime until the knob was changed. They had suggested I put a wedge under the door and even put something standing up on the knob, leaning it against the door to ensure he wasn't trying to come in that night.

I didn't understand why they would just leave me in this situation, knowing how it had been a living hell for me ever since the day I moved in. I guess maybe they just wanted me to feel safe and they knew I was alone in the apartment with two small children too. I decided to take them up on their suggestions and placed a folded piece of cardboard under the door near the hinge and then I placed a cereal box on the knob, leaning it against the door just as they had shown me. It would do for tonight. At least tomorrow, Kevin would be with me for the weekend. The boys would be away with their fathers. I couldn't wait to fill him in on the latest insanity that had become a daily episode of my life. After putting the boys in bed, I decided to take a nice long, hot shower and try to wash off the ick from the day. Energy was always something that I had been extremely sensitive to and this energy sucked.

A Journey of a Thousand Miles – A Reflections Saga

The next day, I was extremely excited to see Kevin. It had been close to three weeks since we were together, and I was really looking forward to spending more time together. Just the two of us. When the boys left that afternoon, I decided to call him to discuss the previous day's events. He was completely blown away by all that I had shared with him and that's when he proceeded to make me the same offer he had the first time.

"No that's okay Kev...I appreciate how much you care...I really do! I think the police may have put the scare into him that he needed." I told him.

"Okay...if you're sure then I guess that's that." he said sounding a bit disappointed.

We continued our conversation, and made plans for the weekend we would be spending together soon. We continued to talk off and on throughout the day and then again about an hour before his shift ended. He was going to be heading home quickly to change after work, and then he would be headed over to my place around 11:00 pm. I could barely contain my excitement. I was definitely looking forward to not being alone in that place anymore. A little over an hour past the time Kevin was due to arrive, he still had not shown up. I texted him to see if maybe he was running behind or got caught up at the border, but got no answer. A few more texts....okay more like thirty texts later and still...nothing! I was really starting to get worried at this point, and finally decided to call. I waited patiently for the line to ring and was anticipating him answering and telling me something like he had just been running behind a bit later than he intended or maybe that he had been pulled in at the border, but all I got was the machine.

Weeks went by and still not a peep from Kevin. I got really worried and began to think of the worst. It just didn't make any sense for him not to answer my calls or texts. He had never done something like this before. What the hell happened? I continued to try texting and calling him every day, but all I got was complete silence. I eventually became depressed over not knowing what had happened. I even began to overthink the whole thing and wondered if I had pissed him off or something. I went through every possible scenario I could possibly think of, but none of them ever made any sense. Eventually, I tried to call his sister Ava and left several messages on her machine. I had no choice, but to be completely alone with my children in that hell. I even asked Krista and her son to come over and stay a night, just so we wouldn't be alone. She agreed, and after they arrived, she and I decided to just have a nice, relaxing evening and maybe have a couple drinks together. By 8:30 pm however, Krista decided that she wanted to go back home. She said she didn't feel comfortable sleeping over with my crazy landlord upstairs.

'Gee, thanks for nothing!' I thought.

Here I was, at a time when I needed my best friend and she was abandoning me. She offered for us to go with them for the night back to her place, and I happily agreed. The three of us took a taxi back to her place. I figured it was probably better than staying in mine. At least here, I knew I would be in a safe space.

A Journey of a Thousand Miles – A Reflections Saga

When I returned home a couple of days later, I noticed yet again that something was taped to my front door. As I moved in for a closer look, I noticed that it was a newspaper clipping that had ads for apartments for rent. This guy really wanted me out of there and he didn't care who knew it. I mean, what gives someone that level of comfort that they completely go against a cease and desist order countless times and then even has the audacity to ignore what the police have said? I decide to pull out my phone, open my notepad and document the incident, then I call Grace to inform her. Once Grace and I hung up, I decided to call my mother and check in on how she is feeling. I really didn't want to be alone anymore at all if I could help it. Thankfully my mother tells me that she is feeling much better and has recovered from her illness. I ask her to come back and stay for a couple of weeks with us and she agrees. She asks how things are going between Kevin and I, and I tell her what happened and that I'm very worried because he hadn't shown up or even called. I explain that any of my texts or phone calls just seem to go unanswered. She tries to reassure me, but even she can feel that something is off about the whole thing.

About a month or so goes by and my mother is over for a visit. I am in the kitchen making dinner for everyone and suddenly she comes rushing into the kitchen. Apparently she had recognized the ringtone and knew instantly that it had to be Kevin calling.

"That's your ringtone for Kevin isn't it?!" She asked excitedly.

I smiled and took a deep breath as I lifted the phone to my ear and hit the button to answer. I was going through a series of emotions all at once. I could barely get the word *hello* out of my mouth. It almost sounded caught in my throat.

"Hell...hell...hello?" I answer.

"Hey sweetheart! I'm so sorry I didn't call. I wanted you to know that I'm okay. I was so excited to see you that night, and when I went home to change like I told you I was going to, they were waiting for me at the door!" he explained.

I had no idea who he was talking about and almost as quickly as that thought came to me, I was blurting it out.

"Who Kevin? Who was waiting for you? What do you mean they were waiting for you?" I asked.

"The military!" he continued, *"I wasn't even allowed to call you. I had to leave with them immediately. I've been deployed and am once again on active duty."*

I was very confused with this news. As far as I knew, he was done with all of that. He had been honourably discharged after he had sustained a gunshot wound to the side of his neck. He nearly died the day it happened. I didn't know much about anything when it came to the military and I certainly didn't know anything about what he was telling me. When he and I first met, he showed me his top level clearance card which had no expiry date on it. This concerned me and I asked him if it was possible for him to be deployed again and he always said that he didn't think so. Now here we were, my worst fears realized.

"I'm sorry sweetie, but I can't talk much longer. I just called to let you know that I'm okay and to tell you how much I love and miss you and the kids. They are getting ready to move us out again soon and I have no idea where we are going, but I will call you again soon okay? I love you sweetheart. Goodbye."

After the call, my head was spinning in circles. My thoughts going a mile a minute. I was just happy that I finally got the opportunity to hear from him, and to know that he really was okay. I figured his sister must've gotten in touch with him. I wanted to call and thank her. Finally I could rest easy knowing that he was indeed okay and that he would be returning soon. He said it would be in about a month or so. When I called his sister Ava this time, there was no answer, so I decided to leave her a message.

"Hi Ava, I just called to thank you for getting in touch with Kevin for me. I was so worried, but he called and told me about his deployment and now I know that everything is okay. I'm feeling much better now. Thank you so much!"

After leaving the voicemail, I hang up the phone and breathe a very deep sigh of relief.

I started sending Kevin messages every day, just letting him know that I was thinking about him. After about three weeks or so, he called again. This time, I was not met with the happy, caring and excited Kevin. This man was completely foreign to me. He was angry and even called me clingy. He told me that he wasn't even supposed to tell me where he was, and now I had gotten him in a lot of trouble. He told me he didn't know when he would be back, but that it would be a week or so and then he instructed me not to call or text him again until he got in touch with me. I was deeply saddened by this, but I also didn't want to get him into more trouble than I already had. I chose to respect his wishes.

A week went by and then that week turned into two. Eventually after a month went by, and still no word from Kevin, I decided to reach out to sister again to see if she could get in touch with him and ask him to call me. My heart was beating fast for some reason as I began to dial her number. I really wasn't sure why. Ava, Kevin's sister answered on the second ring.

"Hello?" she said almost sounding annoyed.

"Hello, Ava. I'm sorry to bother you, but I haven't heard from Kevin in a very long time. He told me, when we last spoke on the phone, that he would be home from his deployment weeks ago and I still haven't heard anything so I'm starting to get worried now. Do you happen to know how I can get in touch with him or could you maybe ask him to call me...hello?!"

A Journey of a Thousand Miles – A Reflections Saga

There was a long pause on the other end of the phone. I then heard the sound of her clearing her throat, then she said the words I will never forget.

"I'm not really sure who you are. Kevin has never even mentioned you, but you sound sweet and I do think that you deserve to know the truth. Kevin was not deployed, so I'm not really sure why he told you that he was. He's actually at the boat right now with the rest of the family. I'm headed there now. I can tell him to call you, but you should know, he has a girlfriend. I'm very sorry." and then she just hung up.

I was absolutely stunned by what I had just heard. How in the hell could any of this be true? Had he had this girlfriend the whole time he was with me?! I started to wonder about all of the excuses he had used before when he couldn't honour the plans we had made. Was he lying this entire time? I couldn't even contain myself. I fell down onto the floor and began to cry hysterically. I was crying so hard that I could barely catch my breath. It was a pain I had never felt before. This man had made so many promises for a future together and now I was learning I probably wasn't the only one he was saying those things to. Once again, I was completely alone. There are no words that can describe how painful that whole process was for me, but eventually I found the will to move on.

Months had gone by since I last spoke to Kevin's sister Ava. Kevin hadn't even bothered to call me and apologize. I guess that was it between us. I had met someone new. His name was Doug. He was an incredible man, who was thoughtful, caring and a true gentleman. He even opened doors for me and took me out on several dates. He managed to sweep me right off of my feet and eventually it became...Kevin who? This man spent every day with me. Whenever he wasn't at my place, we were at his. He didn't care too much for my landlord either. When I had told him everything that had gone on, it devastated him. He had such a heart of gold, and he couldn't stand the thought of me and the boys living that way. Harvey had even called me up one day after Doug and I had been dating a couple of weeks and decided he was going to yell at me.

"You told me when you moved in here that you weren't getting back together with him. You are in violation of your lease because you have someone staying with you almost every single night and we agreed on just you and the two children. You better start looking for somewhere else to go!" he shouted into the phone.

Really?! It became very clear to me that my assumptions about what he thought we might have together were always spot on. When I told Doug about what he had said to me, his only response was,

"We really need to find you a place to go. As a matter of fact, we will make arrangements and you and the kids will come and stay with me for the time being."

I didn't want to burden him. My mother always taught us to never burden others and as a result, I had suffered in silence many times throughout my life. Hell, it's probably the very reason I never wanted to tell her about the sexual abuse. Soon after our discussion about the kids and I staying with him, we packed up our things and we were gone by the end of the month. Shortly after moving out of that place, Grace had learned the shocking truth about Harvey and his wife. There was no longer a marriage. It only existed on paper. She had moved away years ago to get as far away from him as she could. He was controlling and abusive toward her and he had in fact terrorized their previous tenant.

Chapter Twenty - Four

We stayed with Doug for about a week and he and I ended up finding a place for the kids and I to live that wasn't too far from where he resided. Doug even helped with the moving expenses and helped me to come up with first and last month's rent. I guess you could say that he had rescued us all that day.

A few months into our relationship, we discovered that we were pregnant. It was a shock to us both because I had been on the pill and never missed a single dose. At the time, I had also gone back to school and was working on building a better life for us and the boys. We decided roughly six months later, that it was time to move in together. We found out that we were expecting a baby boy. We decided to name him Mathew, after Doug's late grandfather. Things were great between us and shortly after moving in together, we got engaged. We had plans to marry the following year in June. Everything was on the right track.

Our son Mathew was born just a few days after Christmas, and we were both happier than either one of us had ever been. At that time, we also decided that our family was complete and so we made the decision that since this was baby number five for me, that I would have my tubes tied. Doug and his family never even thought that he would ever become a father and now there were five boys. I was finally content, our not so little family felt whole. Doug was absolutely great with the kids. He wasn't even their real father. He was so much more than a father to them. He was their best friend. They all adored him. We often took family trips together and had many adventures. Things were perfect between us and we couldn't have been happier, however one night something happened and it changed our lives forever. It was something that would shake the very foundation our relationship stood on. It would shatter us to pieces.

It was a Saturday evening, and I had decided to go out with my friend Krista. We had been friends for years. I had met her awhile back when I was dating Jason's father and she was dating his cousin Gerry at the time. She was actually the same woman that Jason's father had cheated on me with. I know what you are probably thinking, but honestly it was so long ago and I had completely forgiven her. We were best friends again and that was never going to change. I hadn't been out in so long since the pregnancy, I was happy to have a fun night out with just the two of us. We decided to go to our favourite spot, a local karaoke bar to have a few drinks and sing some songs together. At the time, she had been talking to a guy named John, whom she had met there a few weeks back. John only lived a few blocks over from the bar.

When we arrived, both John and his friend Jesse were seated at a table and we decided to join them. I made it very clear that this was not going to be a double date or anything because I was happily engaged. Jesse agreed to just being friends and told us to sit down and join them for a drink or two. The two of them even got up to sing some karaoke. They weren't any good, but it was all in good fun. After Krista and I had sang a few songs together, she told me that she wanted to go outside for a cigarette. Whenever she did this in the past, it usually meant there was something she wanted to talk about and she didn't want other people knowing about it. I figured it was going to be about this new guy she was seeing. Before we left the table, the guys had ordered another pitcher of beer and she and I filled our glasses up, took a sip and headed for the door. I asked Krista if the guys would be okay around our drinks, since I was very weary of bars and strange men near my drink at anytime. That's because I had been drugged once while out with Jason's father during the course of our relationship. It was honestly the worst feeling ever.

The drugs apparently weren't even meant for me though. Some guys Charles and his friends were hustling in a pool game, decided to retaliate by putting something in one of their drinks. Since we were all drinking the same thing, I must've grabbed one of their glasses by mistake at some point toward the end of the evening. I also didn't know at the time that I was pregnant, so the drug hit me that much harder. I never wanted to experience anything like that again. Krista assured me that the men would look out for us and that I had nothing to worry about. Once outside, she confirmed my suspicions about what she wanted to discuss. She had indeed wanted to talk about John, and her relationship with him. She told me that she had only been to his house a couple of times, but based on what she observed while there, she believed he might have a girlfriend or a wife.

"I just don't know what to do Ava! I mean, I really like him a lot, but I think he's been lying to me. What am I going to do if I'm right and he does have a wife or even a girlfriend?!" she asked, sounding disappointed.

"Well if it turns out to be true then you really need to leave him alone. Either way, you're going to have to find out and go from there." I suggested.

"I know! I'm just...ugh I don't know what to do. Like should I confront him?!"

"Um yeah! You need to do that like yesterday! You can't continue on like this. At the very least you need to talk to him." I told her.

"I know...I know! I'll talk to him tonight. Maybe all of us can go back to his place for a bit after this and I'll bring him in the other room and then I'll bring it up."

I could see that she was lost in thought at that moment.

A Journey of a Thousand Miles – A Reflections Saga

"I really don't like that idea Krista. I mean, I don't even know these guys!" I added.

"I know you don't, but I do and they are both really nice. I will say though, John's friend seems to have a crush on you." she chuckled.

"Well I guess this guy isn't very observant, and clearly failed to notice the engagement ring on my finger. He also clearly wasn't listening when I told him that I was not looking for a date. I have zero interest in him and you know that!"

I was actually starting to get pissed.

"I know!" she shouted. "I was just sayin!"

At this point, she almost sounded annoyed by me or something.

"Anyways...we should get back inside." she suggested. "We don't want them to wonder where we are." she tilted her head back and laughed.

Once back inside, we both headed for the bathroom and then made our way back to the table. Both John and Jesse were sitting there watching the latest karaoke performance. They both seemed mesmerized by the music and appeared to be staring off into space. They both quickly perked up when they noticed we had come back and taken our seats across from them. I decided that I was just going to enjoy the moment, as I hadn't been out in a very long time and I just wanted to enjoy myself. I picked up my beer and swallowed it down, as I bobbed my head to the music. We would all finish off a pitcher and a half of beer by the time the night was over.

I decided to go back with Krista and the guys so she could have that talk with John. Jesse and I stayed behind in the living room as the two of them proceeded into the bedroom. We both just listened to the music and talked a little bit, giving them time to have their talk. We both figured they might be awhile so we decided to make the most of it. When Jesse offered me a beer, I took him up on the offer. At this point, I was already feeling pretty buzzed. It must have been all of the time I had gone without so much as a single drop of alcohol and now it really seemed to be catching up to me. I used to have such a high tolerance, but on this night it was hitting me pretty hard. No – it was kicking my ass! Jesse and I struck up a conversation while we patiently waited for Krista and John to emerge from the bedroom. Jesse began to tell me about his children and how his ex was refusing to let him see them. He said she was using them against him, and he believed she was going to continue using them as a pawn to get whatever she wanted out of him.

I felt for him. I knew all too well the pain that one experiences from going through that kind of thing. Jesse seemed like he just needed someone to talk to. I was not surprised he was drawn to me, because this was something that seemed to happen throughout my life. Anytime I had been through something, I tended to draw people in who shared similar experiences to me. I guess part of me thought it was because I had become what they often referred to as the *"wounded healer."* I had the ability somehow, to help them. Maybe it was because I had lived it and therefore I had the ability to navigate such murky waters. I really didn't know what it was and yet, it continued to happen again and again. I just wanted to be there for Jesse, by hearing him out. He seemed to be in a lot of pain and it tugged at my heart strings. He seemed to be such a loving and devoted father. One who would give his life in a heartbeat for his children. He told me he hadn't seen them in roughly three months now, and it was killing him inside.

"I'm not even big on drinking. Or at least I wasn't up until three months ago." he scoffed. "That bitch destroyed my life! She took my kids and left me for someone else. She had been cheating on me for at least a year. Of course when she told me," he paused, "I just lost it man. I freaked the fuck out. I mean, what was I supposed to do?! Not only did she cheat, but she did it with one of my really good friends, man. It was so fucked up!" he leaned forward and placed his head in his hands.

He started rocking himself back and forth and I thought I heard him sniffle a few times. I didn't know what to do in that moment. I just did what always seems to come naturally to me. I rubbed his back and told him that I was here to listen. I offered him words of encouragement and comfort, then I suggested he go in the kitchen and grab us another drink. He agreed that he could probably use another and got up to head for the fridge. Sitting there on the couch, and waiting for him to return, I began to hear some banging sounds on the wall. It almost sounded like someone was literally bouncing off the walls. I got up and headed toward the noise to investigate what it might be. I finally managed to locate the source of the sounds, which happened to be coming from the bedroom. I knocked lightly on the door and asked if everything was okay. I didn't get a reply so I knocked again.

"Hello?...Is everything okay in there?" I asked.

"Yes...everything is better than okay. We will be out soon!" Krista shouted.

I then heard more sounds, followed by the sounds of pleasure. It was then that I figured out what was happening behind that door and I didn't want to be anywhere near it. I quickly headed for the kitchen to see what was keeping Jesse. He was in the midst of stirring the mixed drinks he had made. I leaned over and smelled the contents to determine what kind he had made. It was Rum and Coke.

"I hope you don't mind...I just needed something a bit stronger than beer."

"No, that's okay. I don't mind at all. I'm feeling pretty sick of beer at this point anyway." I laughed.

The two of us just stood there at the kitchen counter and sipped our drinks then.

"Thank you for listening to all of my bullshit." he blurted.

"Oh no problem at all! It's pretty fucked up what she did to you and you seemed to have a lot on your mind. I was happy to talk you through that." I told him.

He turned toward me and smiled.

"I really, really appreciate it." His eyes scanned me up and down, "You're an awesome chick."

A Journey of a Thousand Miles – A Reflections Saga

Jesse extended his arms, reaching for me to hug him in that moment. I don't know why, perhaps it was how sincere he was. Or, how lost he seemed. I felt for him. And just for that moment I felt the need to oblige him. At the time, I felt like we were going to be great friends. Then something shifted. I felt his embrace loosen and his arms slide from around my neck down to my waistline. His hands tightened around my hips as he pulled me in closer to him. The back of my neck grew warm when I felt his lips press to mine.

At first, and maybe I was being a little naive, it seemed like something unplanned. You know, the heat of the moment. The atmosphere. The vulnerability. Jesse even pulled away immediately afterwards, apologizing profusely. I understood. Shit happens sometimes. I forgave him. With everything, I could imagine how overly stimulated he was. I turned back to my drink, awkwardly sipping until our attention was drawn to the sounds from the bedroom growing louder.

"Oh boy!" Jesse laughed. "He's really giving it to her, huh?"

I nodded, averting my eyes to my drink. "At least we know they're enjoying themselves. Safe to say they've made up."

"For sure!" he continued to chuckle as he leaned over placing his glass on the counter top.

I swallowed my drink quickly, trying not to choke on it as I couldn't help but laugh to myself.

"We should probably go back to the living room." he suddenly suggested.

I'd like to tell you that was the long and short of it. But, it seemed as he spoke those words I began to feel strange. I didn't know why exactly. Everything just became hazy. My legs were tingling like crazy. That feeling like your foot just fell asleep – but my legs. The room started to spin on me in full revolutions as if I was twirling.

"I – I might have overdone it tonight." I grabbed my head. "Think I drank too much. I need to lay down."

"Hey," Jesse appeared concerned, "is everything okay?" he reached for me. "Ava! Ava! Are you okay? What's going on?! Hey, come ... talk to me!" he threw my arm up and around his shoulder. "Let me help you to the couch." he said as he scooped me up into his arms.

I felt the sensation of weightlessness as he carried me. The ceiling passing above me as I floated, drifting away until everything faded to black. I can't say how much time had passed before I was startled awake by the feeling of my pants being removed followed by the sensation of fingers prodding inside of me. I couldn't move. I couldn't speak. I was paralyzed. Trapped in some kind of waking nightmare, completely powerless to stop what was happening to me. I managed to clear the blurriness of my sight enough to make out a shape, the figure of the demon tormenting me like the night terrors that plagued my childhood. But this demon was no spectre or horned devil ... it was Jesse.

A Journey of a Thousand Miles – A Reflections Saga

He was too preoccupied to pay me any real attention. He didn't see me me looking at him. He had his sights elsewhere, on my body, kissing me all over. His tongue roving. Lips sucking. And worst of all, I could feel him violently push himself inside of me. Desperately, I tried to muster any strength I could to will my body ... my arms ... my legs ... any limb I could to push him off of me to no avail. My body was completely limp like I was suddenly boneless. This fucking incubus had planned this the entire time. He sucked the soul out of me as I lay there helpless at his mercy. Laying there, in my daze, I was still aware of what was happening. Son-of-a-bitch put something in my drink and timed it so that he could take full advantage of me. Left me to wonder, was anything he'd said to me true.

Jesse was so efficient, I had to wonder if he had done this before. Was this his game? I was in no-man's land. I didn't know either of these men, but I knew Krista. Never in a million years did I think she would put me in a situation like this. Friends look out for friends. They protect one another. I had to believe that there was no way she could have known something like this was even possible. My mind wandered as Jesse continued to have his way with me. That out of body experience you hear so much about. That coping mechanism. The mind drifts – something that may last minutes while your mind plays every one of your greatest hits like a matter of hours.

He was completely unaware that I was conscious. As if that would have even stopped him. He had gone in for the kill and gotten what he wanted. What was I to do to stop him? After what felt like an eternity, he finally finished to my utter disgust and horror. He cleaned me up and dressed me. I guess he could suddenly feel my eyes staring at him because it was then he noticed that I was awake. Fucker actually seemed surprised to meet eyes with me. Not that it mattered. He put on his act, goddamn wolf in sheep's clothing. Pretended as though he was taking care of me after I had gotten sick. For a moment, and only the briefest of moments at that, I wondered if I had imagined the whole thing. He was that good with the act.

He kissed my cheek and raised from the couch. If I could have shuttered in that moment, I would have. The icy chill that travels through your body like the shock of an electrical current. That's what I felt. He returned with a glass of water with a straw sticking out of it.

"Here," he held it up to my lips, "drink this."

He knelt down beside me to ensure I did just that. I tried my hardest to suck through the straw but only managed to get a few sips. Everything was off. Perhaps my taste too. I nearly vomited after tasting what had to be the most godawful tasting water I've ever had in my life. But then, the grogginess began to set in again followed by that spinning sensation. What – *the* – fuck! I felt his lips draw close to my ear. And then he whispered,

"You're so fuckin' hot." His hand slipped down my top into my bra, *"I'm not finished with you yet."*

A Journey of a Thousand Miles – A Reflections Saga

He began caressing my breast and moved his hand down toward my stomach. He then raised from the couch again and proceeded to unbutton my jeans. The last thing I remember, was him climbing on top of me and stroking himself in between my legs. That was the moment that everything went black again. I couldn't believe it. He must've given me more drugs! I assume that in his overwhelming excitement to get what he wanted, he must've miscalculated how much to give me. I don't think I was ever supposed to wake up. It didn't seem to be what he intended. As my mind began to wander and my soul prepared to leave my body again, I couldn't help but think that he had done this to someone before. He was too calm, too calculated and he moved like someone who knew exactly what he was doing. Yes I was pretty certain that there wasn't just someone else, but more than likely countless someones.

I'm not quite sure how much time had passed between then and the moment I was awakened, but all I remember is the sound of someone screaming into my ear. It was enough to send me flying through the ceiling, and yet, I struggled to even open my eyes.

-*Ava! Ava wake up! Come on we gotta go. Ava!!!! Let's go!* I heard a female voice say.

Still I struggled to pry my eyelids open, but she started shaking the shit out of me.

As I finally began to gain control over my body again, I could hear her shouting off in the distance.

"I can't fuckin' believe this shit! Are you guys kidding me right now?! Was this some kind of sick plan between the two of you?" Krista shouted.

I could hear the sounds of someone being hit, and then a few minutes later, she rushed over to me and helped me to sit up on the couch. She quickly rose from the couch and went rushing toward the kitchen. I watched her silhouette disappear a few seconds later. Only to return holding a glass of water in her hands. She held the glass up in front of me and took my hands to wrap them around the glass. I was much too shaky so she held my hands in hers and helped me raise the glass up to my lips.

"I'm so sorry!" she told me. "I should've never left you alone...he raped you! I can't believe this. I'm so sorry. Please forgive me." she pleaded.

After a few more glasses of water, I was finally beginning to get my bearings. I was still trying to make sense of all that had happened over the last few hours...or was it more? It was all very hazy. Almost as if I was having some sort of nightmare. And you know, I probably would've believed that had it not been for my shirt not being buttoned properly or the way my jeans and panties were twisted. There were also semen stains on the couch beneath me and the smell of sex still permeating the air. No, I had not imagined this. It actually happened. What the hell was I supposed to do now?

Neither Jesse or John weren't anywhere in sight.

A Journey of a Thousand Miles – A Reflections Saga

"Where did they go?" I asked.

"They left!" she paused for a brief moment to compose herself and then she continued. "They were scared because I said I'm calling the cops. So they just...took off!" she looked down at the floor and then raised her head up again. "I'm so sorry. I never should've left you alone with him, but I didn't think he was gonna do something to you. I definitely didn't think he would rape you!" she cried for a minute or so and then pulled herself back together. "We gotta get you home!" she pulled her phone from her pocket and began to dial.

About fifteen minutes later, the taxi arrived to pick us up. I honestly thought that she would suggest we go to the hospital and maybe have them contact the police. Instead though, she just suggested we both go home and get some rest. As we pulled up in front of mine and Doug's house, she leaned over and hugged me.

"I'll call you tomorrow okay? We can talk about what happened then." she suggested.

I agreed and made my way out of the backseat before closing the door and waving goodbye.

Krista and I had been through some shit together, but this was next level. Now it was time for me to put my best acting skills to the test. I walked up the front porch steps and entered the house, acting like everything was fine and that I had just gotten too drunk and spent the night out at Krista's recovering. Eventually though, Doug took notice of my strange behaviour and the slight edginess I had developed. He knew instinctively that something was wrong and so he asked me about it. I didn't know what to say. How was I supposed to tell him what had happened to me? I didn't want a repeat of what I had to go through when I was younger either. All of the questioning I had to go through at the hands of the police back then, and then there were the seemingly endless counselling sessions. Nope, I definitely wasn't willing to go through any of that again, but how was I going to get out of it? I decided to do the unthinkable. I lied. I told Doug that I had made a horrible mistake and slept with someone else. I mean, that part could be seen as the truth, but I left out the major detail of it being against my will. I left out the part where I had been drugged and repeatedly raped by a man that Krista assured me could be trusted. I just wanted to be normal. I wanted to be happy and just enjoy my little family. This would turn out to be one of the biggest regrets of my life.

Eventually, things between Doug and I began to fall apart. I had destroyed the one person whom I loved and cared for dearly. I just couldn't bare telling him the truth and that lie tore us apart. I had broken his heart. Shattered it into a thousand pieces, even began to self sabotage our once happy relationship and began dating someone else. All because I couldn't live with my own secret and I could not bring myself to tell the man that I loved dearly, that I was now *"damaged goods."* Why didn't I just tell him the truth? He was supposed to be my future husband and yet, I couldn't tell him this. I guess it's something that you yourself have to go through in order to understand exactly what goes through your mind. There is self blame and shame—a lot of shame. You just don't want to see that look on people's faces the moment they learn your dirty little secret. It's a look that speaks volumes and not one that will soon be forgotten. It stays with you. You carry that secret everywhere you go. It becomes just another part of you. Like that ugly wart or an extra appendage that you spend your whole lifetime trying to hide and get rid of. Doug never knew the truth of what happened that day. I let him and everyone else think the worst of me, because well it honestly couldn't be any worse than I thought of myself. No one ever knew the truth except for Krista and I.

I'd love to tell you that after that night, Krista stopped dating John. That she never went back to that place again, but that was not at all how things went. She continued to date him, even after she learned that her suspicions about him being with someone else were in fact confirmed. She became his dirty little secret. You have to wonder though, how much does one have to dislike themselves to be okay with remaining a secret in someone's life? I hate to say it, but Krista went through men like crazy. I often referred to them as *"flavours of the week."*

I'm still not really sure what it was about her, why she never bothered to stay with anyone for very long. Maybe she just got bored easily. Maybe she couldn't resist the temptation of other men who came onto her. Krista was beautiful, but as long as I had known her, she had been extremely promiscuous. One day, that lack of self control on her part, gave way to her getting something she definitely wasn't looking for. It was something that would stay with her for the rest of her life. Sitting here and thinking back on all the shit that she and I had been through together, I could probably write a book on just those things alone. Things that would've torn any decent friendship apart and yet we remained close. For people on the outside it didn't make any sense. After all that had happened, all that we had been through...I still couldn't let her go. We were like sisters, and the things we had been through only seemed to bring us closer together. I guess you might say we shared a trauma bond. Something I would learn about much later.

As things slowly began to disintegrate between Doug and I, we finally decided to call it quits for good. We both agreed that the kids and I would continue to stay there with him, until I was able to save up enough money for another place to live. We had been broken up for roughly six months and yet, we decided that we were going to continue to keep up appearances with friends and family. Both of us were afraid to deal with the disappointment on everyone's faces. All of this time...at least up til that point where it all came crashing down, I honestly thought he was going to be the man I would marry, but it seemed the universe had other plans for us.

In the spring of that year, Doug and I would part ways for good. The boys and I moved out and into a new place of our own. Doug and I remained civil, and continued to raise our son on a co-parenting basis. We agreed to keep things out of the courts and decided that it would be best for Mathew, if we shared custody of him. Shortly after moving out, I began to date a man named Derek. Things seemed to be going great between us, it was the honeymoon phase after all. We would spend nearly every day together, just as Doug and I once had early on in our relationship. After about a year of dating, Derek and I made the decision to move in together. It wasn't long afterwards that our relationship became quite rocky, in the months following the move. I mean, I saw the red flags early on, but I just excused everything away. I told myself that I could be a bitch sometimes and well Derek was just reminding me of that. I think I could've dealt with being called a bitch all the time, hell I was used to it from the five and half years I had spent with Paul. What I couldn't deal with though, was Derek's sex addiction. He was always going to strip clubs and spending all of our money. When he wasn't spending the money there, he was online watching cam girls. It got so bad, that he eventually lost his job. I became the sole income in the house.

Being with Derek, was more like adopting a child. I would go to work full time and come home to a pig sty. He didn't do much of anything around the house, except make more of a mess for me to clean up when I got home. I was constantly having to pick up after not only the kids, but him too. I of course appreciated that he looked after them while I was working, but I often wondered what he did with them all day. Eventually the stress for me became insurmountable, and my health started to drastically decline. I figured it probably also had something to do with me being overtired. My menstrual cycle had turned wonky, and I was not only bleeding every month, I was hemorrhaging. Things got so bad, that I was falling asleep at my desk in between patients. Luckily, I had been working in a walk-in clinic at the time, and was able to see the doctor there to get some answers. They soon found that both my thyroid and my iron levels were dangerously low. I was placed on iron supplements, but due to the massive bleeding I was having, my iron levels could not recover on their own. Eventually things got so bad, that I ended up needing IV infusions.

Despite all of this, doctors still couldn't quite figure out what was causing the bleeding though. We of course knew that I wasn't pregnant, as I had my tubes tied shortly after the birth of Mathew. Still, the bleeding had continued. It got to the point where the pain got so bad, I ended up passing out one day while I was at work and they had to call an ambulance. Once in the hospital, doctors promised me that they would get to the bottom of it all, but that was a lie. Instead, they gave me and x-ray and ran some blood tests which of course showed nothing unusual. They came to the determination that there was nothing wrong with me, and flagged my chart at the hospital for *"drug seeking behaviours."*

When I learned this from the doctor at the clinic where I had been working, it made me feel completely hopeless. I was ready to just give up. Thankfully though, there happened to be a female doctor working there at the time who refused to give up on me. She made the decision to send me to a specialist, who didn't do a single test on me aside from your typical pelvic exam. That so called *"specialist"* informed me that it was most likely being caused by a small cyst on my ovary and sent me back to the referring physician. None of this made any sense to the doctor who was still trying to help me, as she had ordered a CT scan which had come back with a comment on how bulky my uterus appeared to be. Finally she decided to send me for a white blood cell scan, which showed that my white blood cells were migrating to the pelvic region, indicating severe inflammation. She knew this had to be more than a cyst or a urinary tract infection and decided she would send me back to my regular gynecologist, whom I had seen throughout all of my pregnancies with the boys.

My doctor took one look at me in her office and said that clearly something was wrong given the amount of pain I had been in. She booked me in for surgery so she could take a look around inside. She knew I was definitely no sissy when it came to pain. She had never even heard me so much as wince during any of my labours, and now I was doubled over in excruciating pain. She was determined to get to the bottom of it. Not only did I have intense pain, but my abdomen was also swelling on the days leading up to my cycle coming on, and that swelling made me look about seven months pregnant. I still remember, one day I had to go into my old place of work for some pre-op lab tests. My old boss truly thought I was expecting, She was in absolute shock when I told her that I wasn't and that the doctors were still working on figuring out what was wrong.

The day before the surgery, I decided to send the boys to go and stay with their fathers. I knew that Derek was going to give me a hard time about him having to look after them during my recovery, so I felt it was just better if they stayed with their fathers instead. I remember that day so clearly, it broke my heart to see them go. I began to have fears that the same thing might happen as what had happened with Paul when I had to leave Jaxson and Aaron behind with him. I also knew that Derek would do a minimal job caring from them and they definitely deserved better than minimal attention and care. I knew it was only a temporary arrangement and I hoped that they would forgive me for sending them away. They had never spent more than a weekend away from home. I was going to miss them dearly. That night, after the boys left to stay with their fathers, Derek was less than compassionate about how the whole ordeal was affecting me. He just wanted to have sex, simply because he knew that after surgery, I wouldn't be able to do anything for at least six weeks. To be honest with you, I don't think he ever really cared about anyone but himself. Even though I had told him I was in immense pain. He just shrugged his shoulders and told me to go and smoke some marijuana because he needed to get off.

The following day, we arrived at the hospital and the nurses prepared me for the procedure. I changed into a gown, put on those funny blue booties and a cap to cover my hair. As we waited for me to be called down to the operating room, Derek seemed restless and like maybe he had something better to do. As I sat there in the chair next to him, he seemed consumed by whatever was happening on his phone screen. He honestly couldn't have been further away in that moment.

"Derek! Derek!!!" I shouted. "Can you please look at me so I know you're at least paying attention?" I asked.

"Ugh! What?! What the fuck do you want now Ava? I'm busy. Can't you see that?!" he scolded.

"I just...I just wanted to tell you that I spoke to the doctor earlier and asked her to come speak to you afterwards okay? So you have to tell them that when you go to the family waiting room. I want to know how things go and if she finds anything in there. So please make sure you stay in that waiting room okay?" I said practically pleading with him. "She's going to come out and look for you, but if you're not there then she won't be able to wait around for you. So just make sure you are there please!"

"Okay...okay! I heard you. God! Why do you talk to me like that?! Do you think I'm stupid or somethin'?" he asked angrily.

"No. Not all all Derek. I'm just trying to tell you that this is important to me okay? Like I've been waiting nearly two years to get to the bottom of it, and if you're not there then I will have no other choice but to wait until I see her at my six week post op appointment in the office. So pleeeaaaaseeee...please make sure you are there is all I'm asking." I told him.

"I heard you Ava! My god, you sound like a goddamn broken record sometimes. I am going to be in the room the whole time." he assured me.

I would've asked for my mother to be there in his place instead, had it not been for her disowning me after my break up with Doug. I had no one. No other choice. Just Derek. I had no choice but to trust that he would honour my wishes and just do what I asked. Surely he wanted to know what was going on too. I trusted him to do the right thing, but I never should've.

He of course didn't listen to me at all and once he saw on the board that I was finally out of surgery, he decided that would be the best time for him to go and get a sandwich. He simply could not wait until after he spoke to the doctor. She had come to look for him in the waiting room. They had even tried to call him, but got no response. He was even carrying a pager they had given him, yet he never even bothered to answer the page. I spent the next six weeks completely in the dark, wondering what the hell was wrong with me. I guess he figured that since I had gone this long without answers, what would another six weeks be. That night when we got home from the hospital, I was really hoping to get some rest. After all I was in a lot of pain and it was exactly what the doctor had ordered for me to do. Derek didn't seem to care though. He wanted me to get up and cook for him. Like I said before, he was just another child. There was very little compassion on his end. If I laid in bed longer than a few hours, I was lazy.

A Journey of a Thousand Miles – A Reflections Saga

Once I had finally recovered, I assumed we would go back to our regular intimacy, but it turns out that during my recovery, he had been busy flirting with cam girls online and was paying them for shows. He had very little interest in me at all anymore. Even getting him to kiss me was about as painstaking as trying to pull teeth. As the days turned into weeks, and weeks into over a month, I began to realize that he was no longer attracted to me in the way he once was and eventually my anger grew to resentment and then resentment turned into being absolutely fed up with him and his shit and we fizzled out. I found out that he had even been speaking to a supposed friend of his and telling her what was going on in our relationship.

He failed to tell anyone about how I took care of him after he had surgery though, or how he had acted like a spoiled child one night when I wanted to go out for my sister Anne's birthday, since it had been months that I had been able to leave the house other than to go to work or grocery shopping. We were staying at his parents' house at the time, and he had a nurse coming there to change his dressings twice a day. This was only because I still needed to continue to work so that we would have money to live off of for the month. I wasn't available to be there to do it every day. That night as I was getting ready to leave for the party, he had thrown a fit because I was leaving him. It was completely ridiculous. He had even tried to guilt trip me into staying with him, claiming I was always gone and never there for him.

A month before our two year anniversary, I had finally had enough of his shit and decided to leave. I only took the necessities for both myself and the kids. I left him with everything else. I had definitely been no stranger to starting over, but to be honest with you, I wasn't looking forward to doing that again. Unfortunately as my luck would have it, I wasn't able to bring the boys along, due to having to sleep on friend's couches for quite awhile. I had left Derek and had no place to call a home of my own. I needed to save up money for first and last month's rent, which proved to be nearly impossible given that Derek had spent all of our money on strippers and cam girls behind my back.

At my six week post op follow-up appointment with my doctor, I was finally given the answers as to what had been going on with me. It turned out that I had a condition that caused me to bleed into the muscle of my uterus, and unfortunately the only cure was a hysterectomy. I was beyond exhausted at this point and still in so much pain, we scheduled the surgery that day. I would have to wait a little over three months though. I wanted it to be as soon as humanly possible, but the operating room wouldn't be available until the date I was given, so I had no other choice but to remain patient. As much as I hated waiting, I felt that maybe my loved ones on the other side had been looking out for me. Like they were trying to protect me or something. I've always been a firm believer that everything happens for a reason.

A Journey of a Thousand Miles – A Reflections Saga

The day I had left Derek, I went to stay with Krista and her son Ryan. I still remember the day she found out she was pregnant with him. It was like yesterday. At first I was so happy and overjoyed by the news, but that all quickly turned to sadness as I realized she wasn't in the right kind of head space to care for another living person at the time. She had been contemplating an abortion. She was single at the time, since she had recently broken up with the baby's father, a much older man she had met at the same bar she and I were once very fond of. She told me that she didn't want to have to figure out how to raise the baby on her own and how it would be easier to just terminate the pregnancy. I'm so glad that I was able to convince her to keep him.

I agreed to help her as much as I could and told her that no matter what, I would always be there for her. Ryan turned out to be such a great kid, and that little guy had the purest of hearts. So much love and adoration for his mommy. I don't think I had ever witnessed that kind of unconditional love from a child for their mother, other than with my own children. A few months passed of me staying there with the two of them, and things were going great. I had even gone back to work, and had even been giving her money to help with the cost of bills and food. She and I would go out occasionally on weekends whenever Ryan had been visiting with his father. I was finally able to see my own boys as well. Unfortunately the space was so small, that there was not enough room for us to have sleepovers.

I started out sleeping on her couch for the first few weeks in the beginning, but eventually I made my way into her bed. No it wasn't that kind of sleeping arrangement. We were just the best of friends. Like two peas in a pod. More like sisters than friends. Krista was a few years younger than me too. But I often forgot about the age gap between us. Since I had first come to stay with her and Ryan, Derek had reached out a few times. I hate to admit it but at the time I was so lonely, I ended up hooking up with him a few times during my moment of weakness. He continued to beg me to come back, but I refused. I had made the decision the day I left him, that I wanted better for myself and the boys, and I refused to settle for less than we deserved. I was slowly beginning to find myself again. For once in my life, I was beginning to love myself too. Life was great. I had been working and working on saving money so that I would hopefully be out of Krista's in a month or two. I was finally going to have my boys back in my care, and together we would be starting a brand new chapter. I was excited about all of our future prospects.

Chapter Twenty-Five

I had been searching for apartments, but never could quite find what I was looking for. They were either too small, dishevelled in sketchy neighbourhoods, or asking too much. I also began to have this sense of deep longing. It wasn't for Derek, or any of my exes. I longed to find my person. The man who would sweep me off of my feet and keep me there, safely in his arms. I longed to find that once in a lifetime kind of love. The love that fairy-tales are made of and written about. The kind of love that gives you butterflies and makes you weak in the knees. The one where those feelings never fade, no matter how much time has passed. I wanted to find my soulmate. But where was he? What was taking him so long? Would I ever find him?

I spent countless days and nights, just daydreaming about my dream man. I remember when I was a little girl, and the love that my parents' had once shared together when they were still living in that happy, blissful bubble. Dreaming of my perfect man, I was often drawn back to my early years. My mother would be in the kitchen fixing dinner or washing dishes. My father would see her there and just stare at her with a look on his face of pride and adoration. I would watch him as he watched her. Seemingly lost in the grace of her movements, mesmerized by her. He would then walk over to the old record player and pull out his Elvis record, put it on and rush to dance with her. He would start with the songs Can't Help Falling In Love, Love Me Tender and then switch over to The Righteous Brothers' Unchained Melody.

He played them over and over again just for her. He would walk into the kitchen, wrap his hands around her waist, and serenade her while spinning her around in the kitchen. It was as if he literally swept her off of her feet...every time. At first she would act like she was upset with him, and then she couldn't help but giggle. I'd stare at the two of them, watching her face just melt into a warmth that I had only ever seen when he was near her. I could feel the love they shared for one another. It was such a tender moment between them. Eventually, at a certain point in the song, he would spin her around and dip her, and I would just laugh with delight. He would then turn to me and smile, walk over and scoop me up into his arms and dance with me too. As small as I was at the time, I had never forgotten that moment. I held onto it with every fibre of my being, and I promised myself that one day, I too would find and marry the man who danced with me in the kitchen. I found myself wondering if he was indeed out there somewhere, and whether or not he even knew of my existence.

After weeks of reflection and daydreaming, I finally got inspired and decided that I should make a list of all that I had wanted in my, *"perfect man"*. I poured every ounce of my soul into creating him for myself. I felt like it was something straight out of the movies and giggled to myself as I was drawn back to the scene in the movie *Practical Magic*. It was the part where the character Sally is a little girl and she sees other women being heartbroken by love, so she decides to conjure up the man that she knows couldn't possibly exist in order to protect her heart. As it would later turn out, that man did in fact exist after all so her foolproof plan actually backfires on her. The two meet and fall madly in love with each other. I wanted that.

I wanted a man who was creative, talented, someone who could cook, who was handsome, loved his mother, was charming, had a great sense of humour, could carry on an intellectual conversation with me, was spiritual and not attached to any kind of religion and who was someone that would make me feel safe and comfortable just being me. It was also important to me that he would be as passionate about me as I was sure to be with him. I wanted the man I couldn't stop kissing, or manage to keep my hands off of. It was absolutely vital that he fit seamlessly into my family and of course that he was great with kids. I just wanted someone who would make me feel the kind of intensity that I had never felt with anyone else. I too wanted to be serenaded by him. I wanted to dance in the kitchen with the love of my life. I wanted someone that I could see myself growing old with and yet still be a kid with from time to time. Yes, that was sure to be the man I would marry someday.

I had spent a great deal of time both learning everything about myself, as well as unlearning the things that I was told or that made me believe I was something I was not. I was curious to learn all of my past lives, or at least the ones I could manage to uncover. I decided during this period of deep reflection, that I would book something called, *Past Life Regression Hypnosis*. I was however a bit disappointed after my session, because it hadn't met my expectations. While I was under, I couldn't remember seeing anything and I didn't recall anything after waking up. This was supposed to be something that would help me to remember who I had been in other lifetimes, I was initially so excited and now, I left feeling like I had been scammed. The hypnotherapist explained to me that sometimes, nothing comes up at first, but then later there would most likely be dreams and memories that would come flooding back to me like crazy. He told me not to get discouraged, that everyone went through the recollection process differently and that in my case it might just take some time. I decided to give it a few weeks, and if nothing happened, then I was planning to ask for a full refund. I mean, it definitely wasn't cheap for the session and I wanted to get what I had paid for. Wouldn't you?

It took about three to four days and then, the floodgates opened. When it all first started to come back to me, it began with a lot of lucid dreaming, similar to the one I had had when I was a teenager. I started getting visions of that same man I had seen before. The dream where I had awakened in the body of that girl Annabelle. I think the man's name was Nathaniel. The visions appeared to be somewhere in Europe. I saw my relationship with Nathaniel and how deeply in love the two of us were. We were absolutely head over heels for each other. This was one dream I had never forgotten.

One night, shortly after the memories began to flood back to me, I was asleep and had been awakened to the sound of horse hooves outside of my window. I could hear a man calling my name from the ground below.

"Annabelle it's me! I've missed you so much my love. Please come down here so that I may hold you in my arms this instant." the voice insisted.

A Journey of a Thousand Miles – A Reflections Saga

Who the heck was this Annabelle? Could this truly have been me? I got up from the bed and made my way over to the window. I peered down to the ground below and gasped.

Standing there and looking up at me was a handsome native man. He stood directly to the left of a white horse. The sun was shining brightly and he had his hand shielding his eyes as he continued to look up at me. It was definitely the man I had seen in my dream all those years ago. The sight of him standing there, radiating in the sunlight suddenly drew me back to the memories. I had lived in the English countryside during the 1800s, my name was Annabelle, I had curly blonde hair, green eyes, and I was hopelessly in love with a man named Navarro. Only when we first met, it was during a time where racism was so prevalent, and I guess he somehow felt safer passing himself off as a white man named Nathaniel.

I somehow always knew the truth though, but I myself came from a racist family and knew that they would never approve of a relationship between us if they knew the truth. That Nathaniel was actually Navarro and he was not white, but native. My mother always seemed to be more accepting of people, however my father and brothers were not. Seeing this man standing there before me that day, there was this deep sense of familiarity between us. Like we had met somewhere before. There was something in his eyes, and the chiseled jawline he wore so well. It was a face I had kissed before. His beautiful dark hair and even his spirit. It was just something about him that spoke deeply to my soul. I decided to keep the truth from Nathaniel, about just how much I truly knew about him. I thought that one day, I might tell him after we had grown old together. At the time he and I met, my family and I had been living on a plantation, and my father even kept slaves in the barn. I was instructed by my father to never speak to them, but I did so anyway. I didn't understand what everyone's problem was. They were people too. I never approved of the way they kept them like animals. I simply couldn't understand it.

Some nights, I found myself sneaking off under the cloak of darkness and making my way into that barn. I loved to read to the children. They seemed to be filled with such joy whenever I read to them. Maybe it was the emphasis in my voice as I read, or the faces I made during times of expression. I just absolutely adored them all and was excited about the day I would have children of my own. I loved Nathaniel dearly. He and I were going to ride off into the sunset together and live happily ever after.

One day, the truth of who Nathaniel really was, had gotten out and made rounds quickly around town. My father and brothers were furious. They wanted to kill him. Nathaniel's own family wanted him to marry within his own tribe, but he couldn't help loving me anyway. Despite the wishes of both of our families, we were young and madly in love. No matter what anyone else wanted for us, we wanted nothing more than to be together. Nathaniel was the puzzle piece that completed my very soul. His every word like the sweetest harmony blessing my ears. He was the true embodiment of perfection – in my eyes at least.

A Journey of a Thousand Miles – A Reflections Saga

Recovering these memories of the life we shared together brought tears to my eyes. There was this overwhelming sadness that seemed to linger just beneath the surface of the deep love we had for one another. I suddenly remembered the pain I had felt back then, when I was terrified that our families would tear us apart. That fear of losing him. I couldn't bear to live without him. The two of us had so many plans for our future, but that was all cut short when a horrible accident had occurred. It all came flooding through me, the memories and the pain of it all hit me like a massive wrecking ball. It all flashed before my eyes then, like watching a movie where everything is sped up. I remembered that fateful day. The day my father and brothers had set off to look for Nathaniel after learning the truth about him. He and I had made arrangements to meet beneath the big willow tree, located between my home and his. We were to meet in the middle and then ride off into the sunset, never to be seen or heard from again. We were going to run away together and live out the rest of our lives until we became old and grey and died two old people, lying in bed and holding onto one another. After we had met up, we shared a loving and warm embrace. The promise of forever.

Suddenly, they appeared to be closing in on us and I saw my brother creep up from the side of us. Both Nathaniel and I, quickly hopped up onto his horse and took off like a bat out of hell. After what seemed like an endless pursuit, it looked as if the coast was finally clear. Nathaniel and I were safe. We were free to be together now, and we were both overjoyed by the thought of that. I wondered if this was the elation the people that were kept as slaves felt when they were finally free. They should've always been free anyway. What audacity people had back then to think that they had the right to own human beings as if they were animals. The mere thought of it even to this day, disgusts me. I often found myself wondering where the idea of such atrocities even came from. My mother, back in that lifetime with Nathaniel, was very similar to me in that way, except that she still allowed my father to keep them anyway, despite her moral compass screaming at her that it was wrong. I knew it was very wrong, and I would've freed them myself, except I knew the fate that would befall them if they were ever caught walking around without a master. I had made it my personal mission to keep them safe, and to make them as comfortable as possible. I treated them like they should've always been treated...like humans!

Nathaniel and I paused for a brief moment, as he leaned back for a kiss. I was more than happy to oblige him. His kisses tasted like sweet nectar and he gave me butterflies every time our lips met. As we sat there on the horse, basking in the warmth of our love, I suddenly felt my heart skip a beat. This of course wasn't unusual for me to feel, especially whenever this man was within ten feet of me. This time however felt different. This felt like panic. It felt like danger. I slowly pulled my lips away from his and glanced around us, trying to locate the source of my anxiety. It was a feeling of being punched in the gut and I knew it all too well. As I turned my head

A Journey of a Thousand Miles – A Reflections Saga

back toward Nathaniel, that's when I saw him. Out of the corner of my eye, I was just barely able to see a dark and shadowy silhouette. It was my brother!

BAM!! There was no time to react. Something had hit me in the side of my head. There was pain and a loud ringing in my ears and then suddenly, there was nothing but darkness. I was suddenly drawn back to the here and now, wondering what the hell had just happened. I found myself trying to recall what had happened after the blow, but I'm assuming that I must have died. Would I ever be able to fill in the gaps of my past? Little did I know...I was soon to get all of my answers and then some.

I remember that day so clearly. It's like it all just happened yesterday. Just another ordinary day. I had been bored and looking for something to do, so I decided to go on social media. As I skimmed through my notifications, I took notice that my friend Lynn had added me to a few groups on the platform. They sounded interesting enough, and so I decided to check them out. I remember there being one group in particular that caught my attention more than any others. It seemed to be a group of like minded people who were discussing everything from the mundane and surface level stuff to the more deep and intellectual conversations. It wasn't your typical group though. They were a lively bunch, and definitely had no issue fully expressing their deepest desires and sharing their thoughts, even when it came to more of the adult topics that people wouldn't typically discuss on social media. I began perusing though the various posts and topics, before stopping on a few to comment. That's where I first saw him. He was the most beautiful man with the most incredible energy. I mean the sight of him alone gave me a sense of giddiness. His profile picture kept popping up under the *people you might know* section on the platform.

"Um, yes please!" I thought to myself. *"I'd love to know him."*

There was just something about him and yet, I just continued to scroll past his picture. I figured a man that beautiful, would surely be taken, and well I wasn't up for more disappointment. No matter how many times he kept popping up in front of my face, or how many times I chose to ignore his profile, he just kept showing up! I finally decided to peek at his profile, and that's when I noticed that we shared a mutual friend in common. It was Lynn. There were also a couple of other people I knew too. I took notice of the fact that this man had a daughter and based on the pictures of the two of them together, he looked to be an amazing father. Another thing that seemed to jump out to me was that he was an author. This drew me back to the memory of Lynn, when she would talk about her author friend, and she would tell me how incredible he was at his craft.

I found myself wondering if this could in fact be the same man. I myself had always wanted to be a writer, ever since I was young. Even though I had enjoyed writing immensely back then, someone had come along and shot that dream right out of the sky long ago. I had been told countless times that although my writing was good, it was sub par and would never amount to much. I had so many hopes and aspirations for my future as a writer and in one instant it had all gone up in flames. Now here I was staring at the profile of a man who was not only a writer, but an intriguing individual as well. I just couldn't stop looking at him! He had the most beautiful, piercing eyes and there was a look of mysterious about him. I wanted to know more. Although I hadn't so much as spoken a word to him, he felt oddly familiar to me. I was dying to know everything there was to possibly know about him.

Kyle Reed. The sexiest man I had ever laid eyes on. While admiring his beautiful self, I also happened to notice that he was in the same group that I had recently been added to and as it turns out had actually commented on one of the posts. How could I have missed him in there? I left his profile and quickly made my way back to the group page to locate the post in which he had left the comment. I decided to reply to a comment he had made and the next thing I knew, the two of us were going back and forth in the comment section of the post. We had completely hijacked the post unintentionally. Every word he wrote only added to my curiosity of him. He was deeply intriguing. I loved his personality and the way he worded things. He was definitely funny and could hold a conversation with me quite easily. Something I had longer for my entire life. Someone who I could be completely myself with and not have to hold back any part of me or the things I was passionate about.

Sure I had been in relationships with others before, but I never truly felt like I could be myself completely with any of them. With Wayne, I had been deeply religious and he happened to be atheist. With Doug, I had become spiritual and he and his family were Catholic and seemed to be quite religious. They couldn't even begin to understand anything that I was. With Kevin, he seemed to be afraid of me and my gifts and had even called me a *witch* on more than one occasion. He and his family were deeply religious, yet they were some of the most prejudiced people I think I have ever met in my entire life. Up to this point, I had never met anyone that I felt I could be safe removing the masks, and just allow myself to be completely open and vulnerable with them and them with me. Yet here I was, talking to a complete stranger and going back and forth with him as if we were long lost friends that had moved away from one another years ago. There was this inexplicable level of comfort between us. I had never felt so free or seen by anyone. As we continued to go back and forth, I pondered whether or not to add this gorgeous man as a friend, but something told me not to worry, as he would soon be adding me himself.

I was impatient and continued to hover my cursor over the, *add a friend button,* for a solid twenty minutes. I mean, I had always trusted the Universe and all it had in store for me, but I was antsy to talk to him further. Just as I was about to click off of his page, he sent me a message in my inbox. I could not believe it. My heart raced with anticipation as I sat there staring at the unread message in my inbox. I was super curious as to what he might have said, but I also didn't want to come off as desperate or something like that, so I waited a full three minutes before I opened the message. I took a deep breath and clicked on it. I'm not really sure what I was expecting. At first I guess I just expected the typical male response I always seemed to get from men online these days. I was half expecting him to start off with how hot he thought I was, or something along those lines. But somehow I had hoped that Kyle Reed would be drastically different than all the others. As my eyes prepared to scan the message, I was pleasantly surprised. He had written me a novel and told me in the message just how intrigued he was by me, and he shared that he was definitely interested in learning everything there was to know about me. I was quite impressed. I gladly accepted his friend request and within minutes we were continuing the conversation.

Kyle: Thank you for accepting me into your circle

Ava: Of course

Kyle: How are you tonight

Ava: I'm good. Just relaxing. Had a long day at work. What about u?

Kyle: Just getting readjusted to home. I took my daughter on vacation and just got back this morning. I'm restless but exhausted at the same time.

Ava: Oh nice! Where did u go?

Kyle: We spent a week in Atlanta. Got to introduce her to family. We went to Six Flags. And just relaxed...took in some sights.

Ava: I'm jealous!!

Ava: Sounds like u enjoyed urself though so that's good!

Kyle: It was long overdue. I wanted her to get that experience...especially with the family. We have a rich history and I wanted her to see it for herself.

Ava: That's awesome. I haven't really been anywhere.

Kyle: I'm sure you will in time. It's just committing to the process really

Ava: I never have time lol

Kyle: That's what I always said lol. Just had to throw it all to the wind. What do you do for work?

Ava: I'm a medical laboratory technician aka vampire.

Kyle: Very interesting. Well, you're quite beautiful for a vampire.

Ava: Thank u :) I am though. I currently work at 4 different labs during the week. What do u do for work?

Kyle: I'm an editor/illustrator

Ava: Oh very nice

Kyle: I'm also an author, I'm on the cusp of securing a film option with Warner Bros. To bring my series to film adaptation.

A Journey of a Thousand Miles – A Reflections Saga

Ava: That's exciting

Kyle: Yet with obligations to editorial work I tend to get bogged down. Hardly any time to myself and very little sleep. Aside from my daughter I have two foster sons so I usually begin a larger portion of my work when everyone is sleeping.

Ava: Makes a lot of sense. I'm always busy too. Barely get any down time and when I do I'm sleeping because I'm so exhausted.

Kyle: I can definitely understand that

Ava: I'm lucky if I get 3 hrs a night lol and yet I'm amazing at my job.

Kyle: So if you're a vampire I'm a hybrid vampire/werewolf lol

Ava: U would be surprised how many people truly hate needles but I'm good with keeping them distracted

Kyle: You definitely sound passionate about it. I can't stand the sight of a needle

Ava: haha today I had a patient I had to draw 12 tubes from and he freaked out asking if I was going to leave him any... I told him I'd leave him with just enough to walk to Tim Horton's lol

Kyle: LOL

Ava: Then when I told him he had to have an EKG so I needed him to take his shirt off he got pretty nervous. He asked if I would be performing it.

Kyle: 12 tubes sounds like a lot

Ava: Each tube is equivalent to 5 mls or 1 teaspoon

Kyle: Hell I'm nervous and it isn't even me.

Ava: U have 5-6 litres lol u can spare some

Kyle: LOL. PASS. That's the only part of physicals I hate

Ava: He informed me that his heart was probably going to go crazy lol. Started sweating. Never a dull moment at my job.

Kyle: I believe it

Ava: I'm very gentle...most people don't even feel it

Kyle: Wish you drew my blood the next time

Ava: Lol Why?

Kyle: If you can make me forget what's happening I'd be all the better

Ava: Oh I'm really good at distraction lol I'm always talking to my patients

Kyle: I'm used to blood...just can't get used to it being drawn from my arm. I used to teach martial arts...I still do but at my daughter's school...so not as frequently as I used to. I've practised from the age of 2...something passed through my family. So with tournaments or people trying to test you all the time it becomes commonplace. It would seem a needle would be the least of my fears lol. But I believe you're awesome at your job...being a distraction. I'd welcome that

Ava: Then u would be just fine lol I'll even give u a sticker!

Kyle: Awe thank you. I can tell you're quite lively. It's awesome you enjoy what you do.

Ava: Yes I love what I do. Don't like hurting anyone though

Kyle: So many people hate their jobs

Ava: I know they do. Not too many people can say they love their jobs so it's nice that I can

Kyle: Truly. How long have you been a lab tech

Ava: Just over 2 years now. I can't even tell u how many I've poked lol. I run a lab on my own now but I'm currently bouncing all over the city. I'm wanted everywhere I guess

Kyle: That's a testament to your ability. I know we've just met but I'm proud of that

Ava: Thank u :) I am as well. It's nice to be wanted sometimes. Appreciated. That's a better word.

Things progressed pretty quickly between us in that first conversation. It was unbelievable how comfortable we were having just begun to message one another. So much so that it wasn't even awkward when the conversation suddenly turned sexual. Kyle told me all the things he would do to me. Things that made me feel alive. Things that made me feel warm and giddy. I was a teenager all over again. Only this time, someone actually knew how to light that fire that had been missing. All I could do at the time was imagine his touch. How his lips would feel pressed against my skin. I was so flushed. I wanted badly to feel him. I began to touch myself ever so slightly. Grazing my fingers lightly between my naval and my crotch. His fingers, as I closed my eyes. His touch. His caress. Who was this man? How had he opened me up so quickly? All I knew was, I was already yearning for him and all we had done at that point was share words through the messenger. I hadn't even heard his voice yet. And there I was, my shirt raised. My bra loosened. Sweat building. And his image right in front of me as I read his words.

And yes, we got a little naughty. I sent pictures to show him just how I felt. Was that bad of me? I don't think so. I haven't felt that kind of excitement in a long time. And again, if I'm being honest, I don't think I had ever been that captivated. Not truly captivated in that way. Not in the way that Kyle had me completely disarmed at the time. It was unbelievable. I didn't want that conversation to end. Even as I watched the time pass on the screen of my phone. As night turned into morning and it got later and later. Knowing we both had a day ahead of us, I didn't want to end it. It was just the beginning with this man, um, wooing me. He was charming. Articulate. Engaging. And dare I say, he was quite smooth. Sexy comes to mind. It all culminated in this beautiful man that desired me. For no other reason than for the vibe he felt. Even without a voice, his words spoke to me with clear sincerity. I believed him. If that wasn't enough, I soon found that he felt the same

Kimberley Hall   185

sentiments as he wanted to continue our conversation more personally. I was drawn from my fantasy as I read his next message.

Kyle: You've got my attention.

Kyle: (313) 526 – 0934

Kyle: That's my phone number.

I paused. Stunned ... no ... amazed at the fact that he had just dropped his number on me. It brought me back to reality. All this time I was so wrapped up in his words that it dawned on me that I haven't even actually heard his voice. I have to say, it also made me kinda nervous. We can say anything in a message. We can bolster all the confidence in the world. Project ourselves to be as provocative, as sexy, as alluring as we imagine ourselves through text. But to hear the voice made reality, that's new ground. And when I looked at how long we had been messaging with one another, I realized there was no wasted time or words between us. It seemed so accelerated yet natural at the same time. Like I divined this. Manifested it. Was Kyle too good to be true? How many chicks has he been laying his game on? I couldn't let my mind dissuade me. Wasn't gonna let something that was potentially good pass me. I had denied myself far too long. And this – it just felt – right. In fact, I smiled, ready to hear the sweet voice of my future man.

Ava: And I didn't even have to ask? Wow, u do like me!

Kyle: Of course.

Ava: U will have to come visit Lynn sometime lol and I will come hang out too.

Kyle: That's on my things to do.

Ava: U will have to meet me in person to see if u like me even better.

Kyle: I'm sure I will.

Ava: Probably even more than right now. I'm ok with that.

Kyle: I've never been so turned on by someone I've just met. Giving you my number actually reminded me I just met you.

Ava: Here's mine lol we can text if u want – (226) 545 – 7931

Ava: See now u don't have to feel bad about giving out ur number to someone u just met.

Chapter Twenty-Six

The entirety of our online conversation lasted hours before we decided to continue talking over the phone. Just hearing his voice gave me a giddiness I can't quite explain. It was a feeling like no other. Usually during phone conversations with men I had talked to in the past, there would be large periods of awkward

A Journey of a Thousand Miles – A Reflections Saga

silence, but with Kyle, there was none of that. The conversation just seemed to flow seamlessly between us. We came to learn quite a bit about each other that night, and eventually we even video chatted. I wasn't aware at the time, but the only reason Kyle wanted to video chat was to make sure that I was real, as he thought I might be catfishing him or something.

Here is what I came to learn about Mr. Kyle Reed during that very first conversation between us. He had a twelve year old daughter named Jaide. She was the spitting image of him from what I was able to ascertain from the photographs of the two of them. Kyle was also a foster parent, and had been caring for two boys who were brothers. He and the three children were living in the house together along with his mother Lorraine. I didn't mind this one bit, especially when he told me about how it all came to be. Years ago, his wife had cheated on him and left him for another man. He was left to raise their young daughter on his own. His mother had stepped in to help him care for her and to become that positive female role model to her. It was truly an inspiring story. I also came to learn a great deal about his writing. He was indeed an author and at that point had already published two books. He was also a journalist, and had written several articles which dealt with the trauma he had experienced when he found out that the person he had thought was the love of his life, had turned around and crushed his soul. It was the man's side of the story. The one we often never get to hear.

Kyle and Lynn had also been friends for about thirteen years at the time we met. I knew then, that he had to be someone special. Lynn was never much of a people person, so if you were a person who had the pleasure of being called a friend, she cared for you deeply. I was intrigued by all this man had accomplished so far, and found myself deeply fascinated by him. He also was not a person that attached himself to any sort of religion. He too was spiritual, and I could tell that he had a huge heart. He and I just clicked so well. It was effortless between us, and that first night, he nearly told me he loved me when we hung up the phone.

The thing that blew my mind the most though, was when the subject of past lives had come up. He asked me if I believed in that sort of thing, and wanted to know whether or not I had any memories of a life or lives I may have had before. I began to tell him the story about what I had uncovered after having the past life regression session. I told him it was fascinating to me because when the memories came flooding back, they aligned perfectly with a lucid dream I had when I was about fourteen years old. I told him I knew that it all had to mean something, but that I wasn't yet sure what that something was. I went on to share about the lifetime I had lived as a girl named Annabelle who lived in the English countryside in the 1800s. I told him about the man I had been in love with back in that lifetime, and the tragedy that I was certain had occurred as a consequence to that love. I told him as much detail as I could possibly remember in that moment, and then I began to laugh sheepishly when I realized just how insane I must've sounded.

"Pretty crazy right?!"

A Journey of a Thousand Miles – A Reflections Saga

My question was met with silence, and I began to think to myself, "Well isn't this just great? I finally find a man who I can truly be myself with and someone I can truly see myself falling for and now I've just gone and scared him off! Oh well, I guess....another one bites the dust. I prepare myself to hang up the phone.

"Hello?! Are you still there? I asked.

I was hoping he wouldn't hear the panic in my voice. After a long pause and what felt like an eternity, I heard him clear his throat.

"Is everything okay over there?" I asked, my voice trembling.

"Hello?! Oh, I'm sorry. I was just in shock there for a minute. Um....I don't really know how to say what I need to say right now. I think this might scare you, or maybe it won't...I don't know, but here it goes okay? You ready?" He asked.

"Yes of course! Go ahead and say what you need to say." I replied.

"Okay...Well...I don't know how to say this any other way but here it goes! I wrote this story!" he told me, the remnants of shock still lingering below the surface of his tone.

"I'm sorry. What? You what? What do you mean you wrote it?" I asked with surprise.

"I mean...I don't know how....or why but I wrote this exact story! I have been dreaming about a life I had with this girl named Annabelle. I wrote everything you just told me. This is crazy, but I think you are *THAT* Annabelle I wrote about. I mean, the similarities are just way too crazy to be a coincidence. Down to the finest detail, and I think I may be able to fill in those missing pieces you may have forgotten. I know you probably don't believe me, hell I don't know if I could even believe it had I heard it anywhere else, but this is really happening. I'm going to send it to you in an email okay?" he asked.

I didn't know what to think in that moment. I was just frozen, and I swear my jaw must've been on the floor. No way was this happening right now. This was absolutely insane! I simply had to see this for myself. He told me he had written it about a year or so ago. He felt deeply that his dreams were telling him the story of a past life he had once shared with this woman. She was haunting his dreams nearly every night. Beckoning for him to remember her...to find her again. When I finally had a chance to read the story he had told me about, I nearly passed out.

The names were exactly the same. He called the story, *Perpetual*. His name had even been Navarro in the story, but he had lied and told this girl Annabelle that his name was Nathaniel! I know there may be some people out there who might just chalk it all up to coincidence, but there were too many similarities for it to be concluded as such. Besides, I never believed in coincidence. It was clear to me as I continued to read, that this actually happened. It was a love story that transcended time, space and even reincarnation. I was speaking to the man whom I had shared that life with.

A Journey of a Thousand Miles – A Reflections Saga

It took about a week or so, just for me to process everything. This was some next level fairy-tale type of stuff. Only it wasn't a tale at all. It was our reality. It seemed that we had both crossed time and space, just to find one another again. I found myself wondering, given the tragic ending to our love story back then, whether or not we would finally get our happy ending. It was quite a lot to take in, I mean, you don't often hear about this kind of thing. This was absolutely epic. Kyle and I both agreed that from that point on, we simply had to meet. I needed to see this man. To feel his warm embrace. My soul knew him, and there was this deep sense of longing for both of us.

We had continued to text and talk on the phone every single day from that day of profound revelations. We both were completely consumed by one another. It was like some sort of puppy-ish high-school crush. You know the one where you hear their ringtone go off on your phone, and you just stare at the screen and smile? The one that gives you the butterflies in the pit of your stomach, and that warmth that creeps in and consumes you. We were growing closer to one another with every single moment we shared.

After about a month of our continuous conversations, we decided it was time for us to finally meet. The feelings that we shared for one another were so profound that there were simply no words that could truly encompass what we both truly felt. It was just this sense of soul recognition. After all this time since that lifetime we shared together, it felt like we had spent countless lifetimes searching for one another. It was as if some unseen force within the universe was conspiring to draw us back into each other's arms. It felt like Navarro and Annabelle were getting a second chance because their love story had been tragically cut short. We both seemed to come to the conclusion very early on, that we wanted to be together, and had even delved deep into what we saw for our future.

The day I finally went to meet Kyle at his home in the USA, I wasn't even nervous. I mean my heart was racing with anticipation, but there was no anxiety about meeting him. I felt like we had known each for lifetimes. It was pure joy and excitement. As if seeing a dear friend again after years of being apart. I was already feeling so much for him and I knew that when I could finally be in his presence and feel his energy, that was going to be it for me. I felt then that I had already fallen for him. There was no question and yet, I was afraid of how intensely I already felt about him. I never quite expected to feel this way about anyone. How could it have happened so fast? I remember it like it was yesterday.

When I first saw him standing there in the doorway, my heart skipped a couple of beats. His smile was so inviting, his skin like an endless river of the silkiest caramel mixed with copper tones, his eyes were brown with blue rings surrounding the pupils which made them even more intense and deeply mesmerizing. His smell was completely intoxicating. It smelled like a combination of Frankincense with a hint of Old Spice, but then there was also his natural scent, and that is what drew me in the most. Kyle also spoke with one of the sexiest American accents I had ever heard, which wasn't helping the intensity he was already exuding.

Though his energy was intense, his presence radiated a calming energy, which immediately put me at ease. He was absolutely beautiful. Now I could truly feel the intensity of his energy and let me tell you...it nearly floored me...literally. The conversation in person was no different than the one we had through text or on the phone. It was effortless, like a river reconnecting with its source. There was the discovery of more shared interests, values and we both felt a deep emotional resonance. Our connection was so palpable, and it left us both wondering how we ever lived without each other. We were magnetic. I didn't even want to leave his side. It just felt so natural...like breathing. Christine and I needed to get back home soon, and eventually she had to pull me from that world with Kyle. I had honestly forgotten she was even there. I think we both did. Being there in the same space together, we were captivated. It was as if the whole world around us just disappeared and it gave me tunnel vision. All I could see in that moment was him. I could've spent a lifetime talking to him.

When it was time for us to part ways, Kyle walked us out to the front porch. Such a gentleman. He then almost instinctively wrapped his arms around me and leaned in for a soft peck on the lips. I was almost taken aback by the softness of his lips, and the way we moved together completely in sync. It was like the two of us had shared a thousand kisses before. We knew each other. It truly was a kiss to remember. A few moments into the kiss, there was a flash of light, and I began to see all of the lifetimes we had shared together. There were many. It was almost as if I were watching a movie...the entire movie, but in reverse. It took me all the back to the very beginning. There seemed to be an endless series of flashbacks, giving me a profound sense of just how many we had shared together. I nearly cried when he released me from his embrace. It felt like I had been forced to spend lifetimes without him, and I honestly didn't know how I was going to let him go. Somehow though, I knew I'd see him again and it would be soon. As we stood there, staring into each others eyes. Motionless and mesmerized by the view, it was like the sky gods suddenly heard my pain and unleashed tears of their own. It began to rain, as if to shield the emotions that were welling up inside of me that would surely give way any minute now. Little did either one of us know at the time, just how symbolic water and rain would turn out to be for us and for our relationship.

I left reluctantly, and hoped he didn't see the pain I was feeling from having to leave his arms. I was almost certain that he felt the same way. That kiss shifted something inside of both of us. It was the feeling of something finally locking into place. The feeling of searching lifetimes for something, finding it and then being forced to lose it again. As Christine and I pulled out of the driveway, I felt my heart sink into my stomach. It was as if something was off. Something was missing. It seems the universe decided to lighten the mood a little bit with some humour. When Christine instructed the GPS to take us *"Home"*, it tried to take us around the block and straight back to Kyle's place. He and I had already called each other on the phone the moment we left, we both just chuckled when we figured out where the GPS was leading us. Was the universe trying to tell us something? Was he truly about to be my home?

Our conversations only seemed to intensify the weeks following that first meeting. Kyle and I had grown closer than ever, yet when he asked me to be with him, I said no. I'm not really sure why I rejected him that way. Maybe at the time, I believed that things were just too good to be true. I mean, can you even imagine what that would be like? I think my heart was still very guarded at the time. I wanted to open up to him and give him my all, but I was terrified of being hurt again like I had been in past relationships. Despite me downright saying no to him, he wasn't going to give up that easily. Nothing seemed to change between us, we were still continuing to talk each and every opportunity we had. I was really looking forward to seeing him again. I just didn't feel like I was ready to start a relationship at the time. I still had a great deal of processing to do from the hurt I had endured with Derek and I felt like my heart still had a lot of healing that it needed to go through. It would've been unfair to Kyle if I was only able to give him half of me. He deserved the best. Yet, every time I managed to talk myself out of a relationship with him, my feelings for him only grew deeper with each passing day. I knew that I was becoming powerless to the way I was falling for him. Finally one day, I had made up my mind. It was abundantly clear to me that I just couldn't live without this man. The profound way he touched my heart, broke down my walls and invited me to bare my soul. No one had ever gotten through to me the way he did. I realized that not only did he deserve the best, but I did too. And the best for both of us was each other. I was going to surprise him the next time we were together and agree to his proposal. Kyle Reed and I were about to be official.

It was a few weeks after we had officially met, and things were great between us. There wasn't a passing moment where I didn't want to be near him in any and every way possible. I wanted to hear his voice, his laugh, and see that beautiful smile again. I just wanted to be in arms. I would wake up to his "Good morning beautiful" texts and fall asleep to the sound of his voice every night. I never stopped thinking about him. Could you? He had completely consumed me.

On this particular day, I had just hung up from a long conversation with him. I needed to shower, do some laundry and make something to eat. Krista had been out for the day with Ryan. I stayed behind to do some things around the house and of course talk on the phone with Kyle. I never really liked her being around and listening in on our conversations, so I was always trying to sneak in a few private moments with him whenever I could. That day, we had talked for hours. I could've talked to him all day, but eventually my stomach became the boss and growled to remind me that I hadn't eaten that day. We made plans for both of us to go and take care of what we needed to, and then we would talk again in about an hour or two. As I made my way into the kitchen, I thought I heard my phone ring. I was eager to do what I needed to do as soon as possible, so that I could get back on the phone again. I decided to ignore it. As I'm spreading the mayo across a slice of bread, I hear the phone ringing again. This time I stop dead in my tracks, as I listen closely to the ringtone that is playing on the phone.

"Nah...couldn't be." I tell myself. *"I must be imagining things."*

Nope. There it goes again. An all to familiar ringtone. One I never thought I'd have to bother getting rid of since I was certain to never hear from this person again. The ringtone goes off one final time, and I toss my butter knife into the sink and make my way with my sandwich into the living room. As I stand over my phone, and glance down at the screen, I am in complete shock. It was the man who had walked out on me all those years ago. The man who took my heart and shattered it into a thousand pieces...no....more like millions of pieces. It was Kevin! I could've sworn my eyes and ears were playing tricks on me.

"Why would he be calling me after all this time?" I contemplated.

I had even heard from his sister a few years back, that he had gotten married...on my birthday of all days, just to pour more salt in the wound I suppose. What the hell did he want now? Had he not hurt me enough? I cursed at the caller ID on my screen as I held the phone in my hand, then I took a deep breath and answered.

"Hello?!" was the only word I could manage to get out.

A million different thoughts and emotions had taken over me. It felt like I had managed to take every possible human emotion one person could feel, and then I rolled them all into one. I felt physically ill.

"Hi my sweetheart! Ugh...sorry, I'm just so used to saying that whenever I hear your voice." he said apologetically. *"God how I've missed your voice. I've missed you!"* he told me. *"I'm sorry that I never reached out to you after I got back. I just felt like I wasn't good enough for you. I felt ashamed that I left things that way, and honestly, I didn't know if I was ever going to make it back."* he continued.

I couldn't take another lie. Not one more minute.

"Kevin! Your sister told me the truth! I know you had someone else. Probably the whole time we were together and I know that you never left!" I interrupted angrily. "You lied to me and broke my heart. I waited for you like some desperate and devoted housewife and then I find out it was all just bullshit!" I asserted firmly.

"What?...What are you talking about Ava?! I was deployed. My sister didn't even know about it. No one did because I wasn't allowed to say anything until we got to our final destination. What are you talking about? I was never with anyone else! She was just a friend of mine. Her name is Kelly, and we were hanging out on the boat one day and my sister just assumed we were dating...like she always has anytime she has seen me with a

girl anywhere. I was with you and ONLY you. I only thought about you, the boys and our daughters the entire time I was over there. I kept a picture of you in my vest. You all kept me alive, because for once I finally felt like there was something worth coming home to. I wanted to marry you!" he insisted. His voice dripping with undertones of desperation.

I wasn't having it. I didn't want to hear another line of bullshit. I couldn't. It was time for some accountability.

"Your sister told me Kevin. She told me you were there at the boat with that girl and how she was going to meet up with you and the rest of the family. Then I find out that you ended up getting married to her and on *MY* fucking birthday of all days!" I shouted into the phone.

I could feel my blood beginning to boil. How did he expect me to believe this girl was just a friend if he went on to marry her?

"She probably lied to you because she thought you were some crazy chick that was looking for me. I told her about you tons of times, but obviously she wasn't paying any attention to me. I'm gonna call her and make her set the record straight." he assured me.

"Kevin...she told me you got married to Kelly a few years ago. I'm not stupid you know. It does not take a rocket scientist to figure this shit out!" I reminded him.

"No. I never said you were but I swear to you that I'm telling the truth! Let me call her and have her tell you the whole truth okay?" he pleaded.

"Fine! But I want the WHOLE truth!" I demanded.

We agreed to carry on this conversation once I had a chance to speak with his sister. It wasn't long after we hung up that his sister Ava called me. She let me know how deeply sorry she was for lying to me before. It turns out that she was the reason he hadn't bothered to reach out to me when he returned. He had in fact been overseas on a mission, and she just figured he had gotten into one of his depressive moods again and that he had been isolating himself from the family. She told me the lie about him having a girlfriend, because she thought I was another girl he had dated briefly before me. A girl named Alyssa, who turned out to be extremely clingy and had eventually gone on to stalk him when she couldn't accept that their relationship was over. She apparently, had eventually gone on to stalk several members of his family and his ex wife who was the mother of his two daughters Cassidy and Candice, and had been living in Colorado at the time.

I thanked her for letting me know what happened and helping to clear the air once and for all. She went on to apologize again and told me how much Kevin truly loved me. She told me that he had been absolutely heartbroken when she told him that I was angry with him for what he had done, and that I never wanted to speak to him again. It had been all he was looking forward to once he returned. He had waited a couple of months in the hopes I would reach out to him and eventually he had gone back to my apartment to try and talk to me there, but when he arrived, it appeared that I had moved out. He was devastated by the whole thing. It took him awhile to move on she said but eventually he fell for Kelly, since she had been the one who was there for him during that time. Hearing all of this from his sister, made me feel awful. I asked her before hanging up the phone if she would ask for him to call me as soon as she spoke to him. She seemed to be very happy with that request and assured me she would tell him immediately.

When Kevin finally called back a few minutes later, we ended up speaking for about an hour and a half. He told me that he and Kelly never planned to get together and that it just sort of happened. She was there for a shoulder to cry on and somehow one night, they had ended up in bed together. It was one night that led to her becoming pregnant. The two of them went on to share a son together, and decided to get married. Over time though, things fell apart and as of six months ago, they had officially gotten a divorce. I honestly didn't know what to feel about everything he had just told me. He had always been a man with all of the right words to say, yet he seemed to be sincere when he professed his undying love for me. He made it perfectly clear that no matter how hard he tried, he just couldn't forget about me.

My mind was spinning in a million different directions. Here I was, having a deep connection with Kyle, and now, after seven years, the man I had fallen madly in love with all those years ago had returned and wanted to be with me again. He wanted to marry me. We had talked about having a child together all those years ago and that too was in the offering. I thought that at the very least, I owed him an opportunity to set the record straight once and for all, so I agreed to meet up with him and talk. I found myself wondering a lot of things in that moment. Would I still feel the same way about him when I saw him again? I didn't know for sure, but one thing I did know was that I was now standing at a crossroad. I was faced with the decision of a lifetime and it could go either way. Was I going to get back together with Kevin and live the life I had always dreamed we would? Or, was I going to risk everything and start a new life with Kyle? I figured the universe was definitely trying to tell me something. This truly felt like some kind of fate. Had I made this decision before...perhaps in a past life? I mean what are the odds that this man would return seven years later and profess how much he still loved me? Nothing about this felt like a coincidence, and surely it wasn't something I was just going to be able to ignore. I knew then what I had to do. I had to tell Kyle about what had happened, and I knew it wasn't going to be easy.

I broke the news to him as gently as I could. I told him that although I cared deeply for him, the man who I believed to be the love of my life had returned after seven years, and I thought that it was something I needed to explore further. Kyle sounded disappointed. It was like someone had taken all the wind out of his sails and he was just left to drift alone on the ocean. It broke me. We agreed to be friends and swore that would never change. With each passing day, I felt him begin to slip further and further away from me.

A Journey of a Thousand Miles – A Reflections Saga

I had spent some time with Kevin at a party with a few mutual friends that following weekend. He was the same old Kevin I had remembered. We talked about where life had taken us and where we saw the two of us going. I had also finally met his entire family, and discovered that not a single one of them were who I had thought they would be. They seemed to be deeply religious and also very prejudiced at the same time. Kevin told me that he was not okay with me being spiritual and at one point he had even called me a witch. It cut me very deeply when he told me I was going to have to change my ways and bring myself back to religion. He wanted to mould me into something I was not, and would never be again. Despite all of this, things seemed to be going rather well for us. There was just one very big problem. I felt like a huge piece of me was missing. It was sort of like that feeling you get when you know that you had something to do that day, but you can't for the life of you think of what that is. Then it hits you, and you're running around screaming, shit! Shit! SHIT! It didn't take long for me to pinpoint what was missing for me. It was Kyle. I could not for the life of me stop thinking about that man. No matter how hard I tried, he was consuming my every thought. Here I was with the man who had hurt me so deeply that it took me years to get over him, and Kyle had never so much as uttered an unkind word toward me.

He had been repeatedly offering me words of reassurance regarding our friendship, but I felt it in my heart that it wasn't going to last. I mean, how could it? I knew how much he still cared for me and how much I still cared for him. It wasn't something that was just going to fade with time. It was clear that this would never just be your typical type of friendship. Despite having everything in this moment that I had always dreamed of, it just wasn't with the right man. I wanted all of those things with Kyle. I think that Kevin began to sense that something had changed with me. I was not the same person anymore. Not even a little bit, and my heart was given away that day that I first met Kyle. Kevin began to slowly pull away from me.

There were suddenly less texts and phone calls and eventually he had stood me up twice, coming up with the lamest of excuses. I'm pretty sure he had started seeing someone at some point too. What the hell was I doing? Why was I wasting all of this time and energy chasing after a man who clearly didn't mean the things he had said. Maybe that was his game. I had such a great thing going with Kyle and then this asshole had to show up and fuck everything up. He was the ultimate fuck up of my life, besides Paul of course. Despite everything going on between Kevin and I, Kyle and I continued to talk on a regular basis. He was always there for me no matter what. What an incredible man he was.

I don't know how he did it, or why, but he just sat there and listened to me telling him about how shitty things were going between Kevin and I. He had all of these feelings for me, and still he sat there and listened to stories about me and some guy that I had walked away from him for. All because I thought it was like some real life fairy-tale or some made for the movies type of shit, and all it ever truly was was more bullshit! It had to be infuriating to listen to all of that and to want nothing more than to be with me. On this particular day, Kevin had once again stood me up. I had gotten myself all dolled up to go out with him, and hadn't heard from him all day. Suddenly Kyle was texting me, as if he sensed my sadness and disappointment. We ended up speaking on the phone the whole day, with still not a single word from Kevin. I honestly didn't care at that point. I was done wasting my breath on him. If he wanted me, he knew where I was. That night, after I had broke down to Kyle and told him what had happened, I remember his words to me so clearly.

"So...let me get this straight. You halted things with me because this man who disappointed you years ago came drifting back into your life." He paused, just then, I heard him take a sip of whatever he was drinking. Then he cleared his throat and continued. *"And now you mean to tell me that this dream stud. This man of movie magic can't even make the time for you after he interrupted your life yet again...Okay...makes sense."* I could hear the agitation in his voice. *"Now what I will say is this...Let me try to appeal to your better senses here. Why spend time waiting for something that was clearly not for you when everything you could ever want is already here talking to you?"*

I was equally stunned and at a loss for words just then. *"Appeal to my better senses"*? What the hell was that supposed to mean? That was the first time I had ever heard him get cocky with me. Or was it just agitation and frustration? Still, I knew he wasn't done yet. I took a deep breath...

"Um...wow....okay. Is that everything you have to say?" I asked.

"Actually, no...I've made it abundantly clear how I feel about you. It's never been a secret what I wanted. And by no means am I a chaser. I'm at a stage in my life...I'm not interested in making new friends. I want a partner. And against my better judgment...I'm listening to my best friend right now. So you have HIM to thank for that. If you were anybody else...we wouldn't even be having this conversation...so here it goes. Not once have I ever played with your emotions. Nor have I made you any false promises. And I stood aside...for a minute. But I think you know...I'm not willing to do that anymore. So yes, I have a lot to say!" his voice was steady and firm. It almost sounded like I was being scolded...like a child.

I had to steady myself and take a few deep breaths. I could not believe he was going in on me like this, but worst of all...he was right. How could I have been so stupid?! All this time, this man was right here in front of me, offering me everything I had always hoped for. The two of us had shared a deeply profound connection and I had just tossed it all to the side for a piece of shit who could probably write a handbook on how to lie to your woman when you need to go see another one. I knew by Kyle's tone, by his energy...that something had shifted in him in that moment. He was going to say what he needed to say and then he was going to walk out of my life for good.

"You're right! I made stupid choices all because I thought it had to be fate. I mean who wouldn't think that way? I had to see if there was anything left there between us. I felt like things had ended so messy and needed some kind of closure. Still, I should've just hung up the day he called. It was stupid to entertain him. He's not at all what I want. He asked me not be spiritual anymore and I could never give something like that up for anyone. And I don't think I should have to. Anyways enough about him, fuck him. His loss. I'm truly sorry Kyle...for everything." I told him, trying to hold back the tears.

"*It might sound crazy. We've only seen each other once and yet with all the time that we spend talking to each other, I could fully envision something special with you. And to think that was put in jeopardy all due to chance.*" he scoffed. He took a deep breath and then continued. "*Don't you think that the universe is always going to test you? You have the thing you've wanted most right in front of you, and then it throws an obstacle in your way to see how badly you want it. And you my dear...took that bait. But you remind me of a song. Hold on a sec...let me send it to you.*"

Just then my phone vibrated and I see that Kyle has sent me a song by Gerald Levert called, *Mr. Too Damn Good.*

"Go ahead and listen to it, I'll wait." he tells me.

I hear the words start and Gerald begins to sing "*Guess you never know a good thing when it's right in your face...*" That very first sentence alone was disarming. I honestly didn't know what to say at that point. Was Kyle trying to speak to me through the song? It sure sounded like it. I press play again and hear the words "*You've been abused for so long, love gets jaded and it all seems the same.*" I was quite impressed. He managed to find a song that encapsulated our two dynamics. I couldn't help but feel in that moment that I had wasted so much precious time with Kevin, when it could've always been with Kyle. I could tell that Kyle meant every word in the song as it continued to play in my ear. Suddenly, it was like Kyle had taken over and I swear it was almost as if I could hear him singing it to me. Just as I was becoming lost in the melody, Kyle's voice broke my trance.

"*So it seems like we have quite the predicament. We both want something, and we need to do something about it. I'm not going to ask anything of you again, except this...Let me come and spend the weekend with you and we can sort this tangled mess. It's all up to you. Wherever you wanna go from here.*"

In that moment I knew. This was it. I had a massive decision to make and if I didn't make it soon, Mr Kyle Reed was about to leave my life for good. This was sure to be the last conversation we would have. I had already rejected him twice. Was I really about to do it a third time? He and I had built such a strong connection. We had both come to know one another on a level, that would take most people years to achieve. This man even knew me on levels that Kevin never did. The thought of him not being in my life scared the ever loving shit out of me. I could not imagine a single moment without him in my life. He had only been there for a short period of time, but he had stolen my heart from day one.

A Journey of a Thousand Miles – A Reflections Saga

I began to have flashbacks of fleeting moments I had spent with Kevin. The conversations he and I had back when we first dated seven years ago. The promises he made. That we made to each other. I had been the only one to honour them. Losing Kyle would absolutely shatter me, far beyond what Kevin could ever do to me...or anyone else for that matter. Losing Kyle would've been equivalent to the pain I felt when I lost my father. There was a bond between us. Something that could never be broken. If he walked out of my life, I honestly didn't know how that would affect me, but one thing I knew for sure...I was already feeling that pain beginning to seep into my soul and it hurt me...deeply! My mind began to wander. I knew this was a do or die moment. It was all or nothing. The cards were on the table. Was I in or was I out?

Despite the good times I had spent with Kevin on the rare occasions I did see him, and with the possibility of a future between us, the future I thought I had wanted, I just couldn't bring myself to commit to him. It was as if a huge part of who I am was missing with him. I can't really tell you exactly why that was, but what I can tell you beyond a shadow of any doubt, was that I realized that evening, exactly what the right choice was. I knew right then and there, that I was head over heels, hopelessly in love with Kyle, and I couldn't even fathom a life spent without him. I never wanted to find out what that would even be like. I knew in that moment that Kyle had given me the push I had so desperately needed, that I, Ava Ducharme wanted to be with Kyle Reed forever, and I wasn't willing to spend another moment without him if I could help it. I made a vow to myself that evening, that I was going to make plans and spend the weekend with him. I had planned to tell him my decision. I was choosing him. Now, forever and always. And that...is exactly what I did.

Chapter Twenty-Seven

The next day, I ended things between Kevin and I, and made the decision to cut off all contact with him for good. I was finally ready to be happy. I was ready to choose myself for a change, and most of all...I was ready to have the love that I deserved. That weekend, Kyle came to visit me at Christine's house. To see the pictures she took of the two of us that day, you would never believe it was in fact only our second time meeting. We appeared to be completely comfortable with one another, and the sexual chemistry...was off the charts! From the moment he got there, we couldn't keep our hands off each other. I don't know how we were able to breathe as often as we were locking lips, at what seemed to be every passing moment.

Christine tried to be a good hostess, playing movies and pouring wine, but it seemed the screen was just looking at the two of us. I don't even remember eating, even though Kyle had ordered an extra large pizza fo the three of us. As the night wore on, and the sounds of *Dirty Dancing* played in the background, I couldn't help but feel like Baby in the movie, the way Kyle would just lift me in his arms and kiss me so passionately. His lips. So soft and supple. I still feel them tracing my neck. Pressed into my cleavage. His strong arms as he lifted me and braced me against the wall in Christine's kitchen. He kissed me with such hunger. The more he kissed me, the more I wanted him inside me. I didn't even care what kind of conversation Christine was trying to carry on. The world just fell away when we were together. I couldn't keep my hands to myself. I remember distinctly saying when we finally came up for air,

"I can't stop kissing you."

I don't really know what words were shared between us that night. Our bodies seemed to be doing all the talking. I just knew we needed privacy. I had never felt such an intensity with anyone before this. The later it got, the more impatient I grew. Was he here just to tease me? I wanted him to tear my clothes off damn it! He must have felt my sense of urgency. It wasn't long, that he was on the phone booking a hotel and calling a taxi for us to leave. Finally I would know what it was like for us to be truly lost in one another.

When we arrived at the hotel, I could feel my cheeks warm, as I blushed when he was handed the room key. I couldn't wait another minute. We could've gone right there in the lobby. This type of urge was foreign to me. Usually I'm able to contain my composure, but this wasn't about control. This was about some kind of primal lust. The lion and the lioness. And the room was our jungle, and I was ready for Kyle to explore all of my secret garden. Let's just say...the moment the door opened and before he could get it closed behind him...it was on. He threw me down on the bed, and tore his shirt over his head. I could barely scoot up into the bed, before he had removed my pants completely. Oh yes! There was no pussyfooting around this. We were engaged in the most intense and passionate embrace. As Kyle became ravenous, how did he know my body so well? We've done this for lifetimes. Our souls were finally reconnecting. And while many may have seen this as intense sex, we were making love. It was equivalent to an out of body experience. When he pressed his forehead against mine...as his gaze met mine, we both said it in unison.

"I love you."

The words they weren't hollow. I felt my soul become ablaze. Orgasmic doesn't begin to describe it. It was more than that. We didn't just make love with our bodies...our spirits became entangled. It was so much more than lust, it was an emotional liberation. We made love until it was nearly time for the sun to come up. Hours passed, as I lay trembling beneath him. Every orgasm moved the earth. Time didn't seem to exist. Wrapped into each other, we folded into the fabric of our own space. If only just for that time being. I knew it to be true then, as I had no doubt before...I truly and deeply loved this man.

A Journey of a Thousand Miles – A Reflections Saga

After a night lost in the throes of passion, we awoke to the sound of the phone ringing in the room. It was the front desk calling, because we had slept through our check-out time. And even though we may have only slept a couple of hours, I awoke feeling so refreshed. The sun shone just that much brighter. As I watched Kyle leave the bed in tow for the bathroom, I looked back and noticed the headboard. I chuckled to myself thinking of that scene in Twilight. You know, the one when Edward and Bella made love for the first time, and Edward broke the headboard? Yes, it was just like that. As I scanned the room further, I giggled to myself. It looked as if a cyclone had come through the room. But then again...damn! This man actually broke the headboard. I had never, in all my life, been made love to like that before. I could still feel him throbbing within my body. My legs were still numb...all of me was.

That evening together in the hotel, was like nothing either of us had ever experienced before, and it was all the two of us could think about. Intense doesn't even begin to cover it. No...it was enlightening! Our energies had been drawn together like magnets. As we both rushed to get ourselves together, and stood at the sink side by side, we both just started laughing hysterically at the disarray the room was currently in. It was as if the intensity of the two of us together, was just too much for the room to hold. I had decided later that day, when Kyle was to return home, that I would go with him. Now that we were together, there was so much to make up for. We weren't willing to waste another minute. I was dying to meet his mother. He had told me so much about her, and I was eager to meet the woman who had raised such an incredible human being. Sure, I had been to his house once before, but she had stayed in the bedroom the whole time to give us some privacy.

As we entered through the back door of Kyle's house, his mother was there in the kitchen cooking something. She immediately turned to greet us. Although she had been cooking something on the stove, that didn't stop her from turning her undivided attention toward me the minute she saw the two of us together. She was instantly very warm and welcoming, and had the biggest smile on her face. I wondered in that moment if he had told her about me. I felt like I just wanted to stand there and talk to her forever. I didn't want to seem rude or rushed, but she assured me we would have plenty of opportunities to get to know one another. I think she always knew, I was there to stay. She could probably see and feel the love between us from the very first day she had met me in that kitchen.

From that moment on, from the very first day I came home with him, Kyle and I had become inseparable. We began to spend every single weekend together. During that very first week together as a couple, I had already met his father, stepmother, a few of his cousins, and one of his aunts. They all seemed to think that we were perfect for each other. Some of them even commented on how comfortable we appeared to be together. Things began to get pretty serious between us from the very beginning and at one point, Kyle's mother swore that I had to be pregnant. She told me I had that unmistakable glow about me. Oh it was a glow alright. Kyle had breathed new life into me. I assured her that it was just happiness, as I couldn't possibly be pregnant since I had my tubes tied years ago after giving birth to Mathew.

Surgery was now fast approaching, and I had even decided to spend the next few days leading up to it, with Kyle and his family. At this point however, part of me thought of cancelling and having my tubal ligation reversed. I wondered what it would be like for Kyle and I to have a child together. I wished it could've happened. Kyle and I had discussed the possibility of having a child in the future, but he knew I was in far too much pain, and he couldn't stand having to watch me suffer that way. His primary concern was about me, and how another pregnancy might effect me. Despite having had quite a few surgeries before, this time around I found that I was extremely nervous. It didn't make much sense to me at first, because I was no stranger to the process. Yet this time around, I had been having visions of what was going to happen afterwards and they shook me. Eventually, the day I was to leave and head back home had arrived. I decided to open up to Kyle about my fears, and tell him about my recent visions, as well as the dream I had the night before. I was absolutely terrified to go through with this surgery.

I knew this feeling had to be significant, because I had never felt this level of fear before. It was far worse than the fears I had experienced in my childhood. In these particular visions, I had seen that something went very wrong with the surgery and I saw myself dying. I saw my mother, whom I hadn't spoken to in a couple of years at this time, crying over me. She was begging me not to leave her. It was so vivid and I tried so hard to push it from my mind, but I just couldn't seem to shake it. I just knew this had to be a premonition. I felt it in my gut. There was this gnawing feeling, followed by a sheer sense of agony. It felt like I was never going to see Kyle, my children, my friends or family ever again. There was this lingering sense of loss. I felt it deep in my soul. When I confided in Kyle, he was so attentive and reassuring. He told me that it was natural to be afraid, and that I had nothing to worry about because he didn't see anything bad. He too had the gift of seeing and knowing things, so his words were revered by me. After our conversation, I decided that maybe this was just my subconscious fears playing themselves out. I mean, I was more afraid of this than I had ever been about anything in my entire life. That had to be it. It was just nerves. Talking to Kyle made me feel better. His words of reassurance brought comfort to my soul. I was ready. Shortly after we finished our conversation, Christine had pulled up in the driveway. I kissed and hugged Kyle goodbye, told him I loved him and headed for the door.

A Journey of a Thousand Miles – A Reflections Saga

We spoke that night from the time I got back home, until the time I had fallen asleep with him on the phone. I can't believe he didn't hang up. I think he must've fallen asleep too. The thought of us sleeping on the phone made me chuckle. Although, this was never something that was foreign to either of us. We had both taken turns falling asleep on the phone together countless times. Yet this time felt different. It was sort of like when you get a bad feeling about something and you can almost sense something bad is about to happen, so you are afraid to hang up with that person because it just could be the very last time you ever speak to them again. It's almost as if you just want to burn their words and the sound of their voice deep into your brain. That morning of my surgery had come so fast. It was as if someone had snapped their fingers and here we were. I told Kyle that as much as I would love to sit and talk with him, I had no choice but to get ready. I promised to call him when I wasn't so groggy after surgery. Truthfully, I wanted him to be there with me at the hospital, so his face could be one of the first I would see when I woke up, but understandably he had other obligations to take care of at home. The children always came first, being a mother...I understood that. He wished me good luck, told me he loved me and that he couldn't wait to talk to me later.

"You're going to be just fine baby. I'll be here waiting for you when you wake up. I love you." he told me reassuringly.

"I love you too baby. We'll talk soon my love." I whispered sweetly before hanging up the phone.

Surgery had only been about an hour or so. Christine had been waiting there in the family waiting room the entire time. She waited for me to come out of recovery and then again until I was moved to my room upstairs. I was just so happy to see her face when I opened my eyes. It meant that I had made it through the surgery. I think I distinctly remember asking her groggily to pinch me a few times, just so that I could be sure. She seemed more than happy to oblige my request. I was alive! All of that fear was for nothing. I was so grateful. Kyle had been right. I couldn't wait to hear his voice again. Christine sat there at my bedside for quite awhile, and waited for me to start falling back to sleep. Then she got up and hugged me goodbye, telling me that she was going home to do some laundry so that I would have some clean clothes for tomorrow when I went home. I had been staying at her place for a few months now. We had reconnected about three or four months ago, after quite a few years, and at that time she asked me if I wanted to come and stay with her. I decided that her place would probably have more room than Krista's since she had a house and Krista only had a small two bedroom apartment.

Christine had much more space and it would finally be possible for me to take my children for sleepovers. We also knew I would be having surgery, and I would be needing someone to look after me as I recovered. Christine being in healthcare...seemed like the perfect person to do it. My recovery time was six to eight weeks and I wouldn't be able to do much. She offered to take care of me and for that, I was eternally

A Journey of a Thousand Miles – A Reflections Saga

grateful. I guess since I mention Christine so much, I should probably give you a little backstory on our friendship. She and I actually met back in high school. I was friends with her sister Chelsea.

At the time, Christine and I didn't say as much as two words to each other, but ten years later we got reconnected through a mutual friend and began to hang out at a local bar on Thursday nights. That was the first time we actually spoke to each other and realized that we actually got along great. I hate to say it, but at first, I had let others tell me who she was as a person and I never bothered to give her a chance. She had a child out of wedlock when she was just fifteen years old, and I was a very different person back then. I was still pretty deep in one religion or another and as a result of that I had judged her unfairly. I saw her as promiscuous and wanted no association with such people. But once we reconnected, everything changed. I was happy now that I had finally given her the chance she deserved to prove to me that she was far more than the reputation she had been given by others. I often think back to that very first day I met her, and I have deep regrets on how I handled things. If I could take it all back, I would.

After she had left to go back home, it took me a long time to fall asleep, despite being very groggy from the anaesthesia. I found myself suffering, and in immense pain. This was a pain I had definitely not expected, and to make matters worse, my nurse was a straight up sadist with control freak issues. After the surgery, my doctor had ordered IV pain medication, and yet this nurse decided that she suddenly knew what was best for me and figured I couldn't possibly be in that much pain. Um....they had cut me from inside and pulled my uterus out through my vagina. How would you feel? No matter how much I pleaded with her, she argued with me and tried to give me an oral dose of Percocet, which she already knew was going to do absolutely nothing for the pain I was in. I mean why else would the doctor order IV pain meds if an oral dose would suffice? The nausea from the anaesthetic was also pretty overwhelming for me. I had to scream at her and threaten to call my doctor in order for her to agree to give me what was ordered. She seemed surprised that the oral medications hadn't worked, but then when she saw my mother come in...she changed her tune rather quickly.

Christine had called her and she turned up for a visit shortly after. I was absolutely exhausted. I mean just imagine...you have just had surgery and can't even get up out of bed. You are in agony and all you want is for your pain to be managed and for this psycho to stop arguing with you about what pain medication you needed. My blood pressure had gone through the roof at that point. Probably a combination of the excruciating pain I was in coupled with the fact that I needed to argue with a nurse over what the doctor had ordered. The pain was honestly all I could think about. I could tell my mother felt helpless sitting there and watching me suffer. She was completely powerless to the situation. I was powerless to it too. Soon after the nurse finally gave in and administered my medication, my doctor arrived to tell me how everything had gone with the surgery. She told me that I had developed a post-op hematoma during the procedure. It was on the right ovary and was about the size of a big mac. She said it appeared to be high risk for rupture, so she decided to cauterize it. I was definitely glad she would be keeping me overnight now. She was too. She told me that they were going to be keeping a close eye on me, and watch for any signs of bleeding. My mother and I were relieved that she had got to it in time. She assured us that everything would be just fine. Just as she was about to leave the room, she stood there for a minute and watched me. She could tell by my blood pressure and the grimace on my face that I was still in a lot of pain.

"Have they come and given you anything for pain?" she asked, a concerned look on her face.

"Yes..but I told the nurse that it hadn't worked and she said she needed to speak to you about it." I told her as my hand clenched my abdomen.

"Well...it's clear to me that you are still in a lot of pain. I'm going to change the orders to ensure that you are comfortable." she smiled at me just then, and then she turned and walked out of the room.

A few minutes after she left, my nurse had returned with another dose of Morphine. Finally! It took the edge off just enough for me to be able to get some sleep. I had a chance to speak with Kyle earlier, when my mother had first got there. He too had heard how much pain I was in and even heard me going off on the nurse. I think he too must've felt completely helpless in that moment. He definitely didn't care for the way the nurse was treating me, or for the thought of me being helpless and suffering needlessly. I'm sure if he had been there, none of that would've ever happened.

Later that evening, I had a few visitors. Jane, Anne, and Anne's boyfriend Mark had come to see me and make sure that I was alright. During their visit though, my pain returned with a vengeance. It had become far worse than before. I also noticed that my abdomen was beginning to swell. It had gone from flat to looking like I was about five or six months pregnant. It was very uncomfortable. Almost like going through a normal pregnancy but without the gradual growth of the belly. I noticed that it was also beginning to feel like a brick wall, instead of the soft and squishy it had been just hours earlier. I decided to bring this to the attention of my nurse, and even told her that my pain had become much worse. She didn't seem to care much and even went on to remind me that I had just had surgery. She spoke to me in a condescending tone, telling me that I had just had surgery so of course there would be swelling and pain.

She must've grown tired of watching me squirm, or maybe it was the incessant ringing of my call bell, but she finally gave in and had given me a small dose of pain medication before allowing my visitors to return. It was only about half of what was ordered and I honestly think she had only done that simply because I had visitors, and she had wanted to appear caring and compassionate. I don't think she had a compassionate bone in even her pinky finger to be honest. When my visitors finally were permitted back into the room, I was beginning to feel very drowsy. I remember my sister Anne laughing at me because I kept slipping in and out of

A Journey of a Thousand Miles – A Reflections Saga

consciousness, as Jane attempted to feed me some Jello. One minute my eyes would be open and I'd be talking, and then the next minute my eyes would grow heavy and I'd fall asleep before the spoonful of Jello had reached my mouth. I was completely out of it and they could all see it, I think they just assumed it was because of all the medication the nurse had been giving me. A short time later, everyone decided to leave and let me get some much needed rest.

Once I was alone again, I called Kyle to say goodnight. My nurse was going to be coming to give me more pain medication, because my blood pressure had gone into the danger zone. I was well beyond exhausted at this point. It had been a very long day and all I wanted now was to hear Kyle's voice one last time before falling asleep. I was just glad that I was going home the next day, because I was certain that I would be much more comfortable there. Plus I wouldn't have some sadistic bitch withholding my pain medications until I was in agony and it was too late. By that point it only ever took the edge off. I could barely keep my eyes open for longer than two minutes at this point. It was clear that I desperately needed to rest.

The next day, two nurses got me up in the morning and helped me walk to the bathroom so they could remove the catheter that had been in my bladder all night since the surgery. I didn't feel any pain at that time and they were commenting on what a trooper I was. They had also given me a top up on my pain medication before attempting to get me up to walk. I figured that was why I wasn't feeling much of anything. I did however take notice that my legs were very wobbly and I felt lightheaded and dizzy. I knew this was to be my new normal for the time being. I don't know why I had expected anything different this time around, as I had been through this rodeo quite a few times. You always feel like shit after surgery. Expect no less. I continued to walk with the nurses to the bathroom without any issue whatsoever. Having that catheter removed was a massive relief. In just a few hours, I would be heading home.

I couldn't wait to talk to Kyle again. To see his beautiful face. To hold him. To see the kids again. It was all I could think about in this moment. Just after they had removed my catheter, one of my nurses was paged to another room. The other one stayed close by but had left the bathroom to give me some privacy. She told me to pull the red cord next to the toilet when I was ready for her to help me up. I was not permitted to do any sort of weight bearing and yes that meant pulling myself up off of a toilet. I hated that but I understood the importance of following those orders to the letter. A few minutes later, I remember pulling the cord, standing up with her assistance and taking a few steps...then all of a sudden, I got very very dizzy and everything faded to black.

I must've only been out for less than a minute before I woke up in bed with about ten nurses surrounding me.

A Journey of a Thousand Miles – A Reflections Saga

"Call the doctor right away!" one shouted to the others.

There was a cacophony of sound all around me, but it was slowly beginning to fade out. Almost as if I had been plunged under water. Before I knew it they rushed out of the room while one nurse stayed behind to check my vital signs.

"What....what the heck happened?" I asked groggily. It almost sounded like my words were being slurred.

"You passed out!" she told me, concern in her tone.

"What? I did? Why?"

"We aren't too sure. That's what we are trying to figure out right now. The nurse had to catch you. You nearly fell face first into the floor. Judging by your blood pressure, I'm guessing that might be why you lost consciousness." she continued.

"Oh....is it high again?" I asked. Now I was concerned too.

She didn't reply to my question. She just turned and bolted out of the room like a bat out of hell. Something wasn't right. I could feel it. But no one would tell me what was going on. Next thing I know, the lab is rushing into the room and taking blood from me. Not even ten minutes later, I am being rushed down for an emergency ultrasound on my abdomen. My new nurse was just the sweetest. So caring and attentive. Students are always the best. That's during the time they are filled with passion and still care deeply. She made sure to give me pain medication just before they rushed me down for the test. She wanted to make sure that I would be comfortable, and that my pain was well managed so there would be no issues during the scan. I remember them wheeling me down in my bed. They seemed to be in quite the hurry. I saw the ultrasound tech within a few minutes and felt her place the wand on my abdomen, and then....everything faded to black again.

I awoke this time to the feeling of someone tapping my hand gently and caressing my arm. I could hear my name being called, but it sounded like it was off in the distance. It was a warm and soft female voice. It sounded familiar to me. I followed the voice back to my body and struggled to open my eyes. I was just so tired. It was my doctor who had been calling me. She looked very concerned as she glanced at the screen. Then she spoke softly. However I was still able to pick up the seriousness in her tone. She told me that her worst fears. That OUR worst fears were just confirmed. That the hematoma had ruptured and I had massive internal bleeding. I was dying. She let me know that she had to take me back into surgery and that she knew the news was scary, but she assured me that she would do everything in her power to see me through this. I was given multiple blood transfusions, as we waited for them to prepare the OR. I called my girlfriend Christine to let her know that I didn't think I was going to be going home any time soon.

A Journey of a Thousand Miles – A Reflections Saga

"Something bad is happening Chris... You need to get here as soon as you can. Can you please call my family and let them know that they need to come? This is life or death. They are about to take me back into surgery and well....I'm not sure if I'm going to make it out of this one."

Christine could tell by what I was saying to her, that the situation was critical. She immediately hung up and called my mother to let her know what was going on. She explained to her the severity of the situation and that she needed to get to the hospital.

When everyone arrived, the doctor pulled my mother into a private room and spoke to her about what was going on. It was a race against time, and most certainly a matter of life or death. I was allowed to see everyone for a few brief moments, while we waited for my doctor to run and scrub in. And that was the moment that I saw the vision that I had before come to life. My mother leaned over, kissed me on the cheek and rubbed my forehead. She tried to remain strong and not show any emotion but there was this look of being terrified I won't soon forget. I needed to call Kyle. He needed to know. I needed to speak to him one final time before they rushed me in there. I don't really remember much of that conversation. Kyle could probably tell you word for word. It was very brief.

"Kyle? It's me. Something is wrong. I can feel it. I need you....to come here. Okay? I NEED you. Please come. It's very bad. I'm about to go in for another surgery. I'm bleeding. I'm not doing well. I love you. I have to go now. Please come."

"I'm right here baby. You're okay." he reassured me.

"No Kyle. I NEED YOU!" I told him sincerely.

I think in that moment, hearing me say those words, and hearing the sound of me slowly slipping out of consciousness. He knew.

"I'm sorry Kyle. I have to go now. They are here to bring me into the OR. I love you baby." I whispered into the phone before hanging up.

Just as I hung up the phone, my doctor came up to my bed and told me that it was time to go. Once inside the OR, everything seemed to be moving very quickly. You could feel the urgency of the situation. It was written across everyone's face. The room was absolutely freezing! Was it always this cold? I could feel myself beginning to slip away. At this point, I no longer had the strength or the capability to stand or even lift my head from the pillow. They had to grab onto both sides of the sheet on my bed and transfer me to the table that way. I could feel the cold steel of the table, through the sheet beneath me and this was quite scary to me because it reminded me of those tables they keep in the morgue. Was this where I was headed? I didn't remember it ever being this cold. I was given two more units of blood. An IV in each arm and then hooked up to all of the monitors. It all happened so fast. I knew this was serious because that room was filled with people, and there wasn't a calm or collected energy to be found. One of the nurses had been moving so quickly to hook me up to everything, she nearly punched me in the face as she attempted to put the oxygen tubing into my nostrils. My doctor had scrubbed in quickly and she appeared ready to go. She had called another doctor for assistance, because she knew it was about to be a race against the clock and she was going to need all of the help she could get. I remember her walking over to the side of me, pulling down her mask and then taking my hand in hers.

"I got you Ava. Don't worry okay. You just go to sleep and me and Dr Sorensen will fix everything. I got you. I promise." she whispered to me softly.

I tried to nod my head to show her that I understood what she had said, but I was far too weak. I felt like all of my muscles were beginning to shut down. There was this terrifying feeling of paralysis beginning to set in. Just as she had said what she needed to say to me, it was like someone had suddenly lit a fire under everyone's ass and it became almost chaotic as they prepared for me to go under. I stared groggily at the mask that was now descending from directly above my face, and waited for them to ask me to start counting down from ten to one. There was no countdown though. It was just lights out!

No sooner had I fallen into a deep sleep, that I found myself floating above my body. It was the weirdest experience I had ever had to date. One minute I'm there floating in the operating room, watching all of the medical staff, and the next...I'm somewhere else completely. Sitting there on a bench and talking with my father. It truly felt so real. I could smell the scent of flowers in the air surrounding us, and could even make out the distinct scent of his Old Spice aftershave. I was certain that I had died. This had to be the place they call heaven. I even saw my little nephew that had passed away years ago, while I had been pregnant with Aaron. I gotta tell you, that was truly the saddest funeral I had ever been to.

Everyone there was a mess. Even the people who worked there were in tears. My nephew had only been two years old at the time he died. A seemingly routine surgery had resulted in dire consequences. He had suffered from sleep apnea, and the doctors had told my sister Marie and her husband that this problem was an easy fix. All they needed to do was go in and remove his tonsils and adenoids. Everything had gone well with the surgery, but he was sent home that same day and had sadly passed away that night. We were all in complete shock, but I don't think any of us felt the pain as intensely as my sister and her husband had. My heart was breaking for the two of them. I cannot even begin to imagine what the loss of a child must've been like for them and I pray that I never have to find out. I'm sure at the time, many people wondered whether or not their relationship would be able to sustain such a tragedy. But they actually grew stronger and are now one of the strongest couples I know.

A Journey of a Thousand Miles – A Reflections Saga

So here I was, sitting on the bench and talking to my father. He looked as handsome as I had remembered him. He was wearing a white suit with a blue tie. Do people dress up in heaven? I wondered. I guess he had heard my thought just as I thought it because he threw his head back and chuckled to himself before saying,

"No Ava. We don't dress up in heaven...in fact...we don't even have a physical form here because there is no need for anything like that in this place. You are just creating the image of me that you want to see. The one that makes me most memorable to you. Hey! Look over there!" he said, raising his finger and pointing in the direction to someone just off in the distance from us.

I couldn't quite make out the figure, until it started to get closer to us. Then I watched in amazement as one figure turned into two. As the figures approached, I began to see some familiar features to them. One of them was my paternal grandmother and the other... was the little girl who had shadowed me throughout my entire life. It was Emily! She appeared differently from how I had last remembered her. She was no longer in the form of a child, but that of an elderly woman. Her hair which was once blonde, had now faded to a beautiful grey which sparkled in the sunlight. Her eyes still looked the same, but were now adorned with laugh lines and crows feet. The skin on her cheeks hung loosely on her jawline, but that smile...was exactly the same as I had always remembered. It always reminded me of a warm, summer day. Where the sun would shine so brightly that you often felt like you might have to shield your eyes away. You couldn't stare directly at it for too long, but it warmed you up inside nonetheless.

"Hi there!" she said. Greeting me with her typical bubbly and upbeat personality.

"Fancy meeting you here." she continued. "I knew you would be coming so I wanted to make sure I got here in time so we could have a little chat. I take it you got my message?" she asked, as she motioned for me to scoot over so that both she and my grandmother could sit.

"I know...I know! You're probably thinking this is it right? You think that you are on the other side or heaven as most people tend it call it. Well...it's a bit hard to explain what this place is but let's just call it the in between of sorts. People come here when they are under anaesthesia for surgeries or other types of invasive procedures that require sedation. Also...sometimes people end up here when their soul is sort of jarred out of the body too fast. Kind of like if someone had been involved in a horrific car accident or something." she paused, making sure I was absorbing this new information before continuing.

"They come here to wait but also to meet up with loved ones. Think of it sort of like your soul has gone on vacation...kinda." she explained.

"They come here and talk with their loved ones about their earthly mission and how things are going. Their loved ones often offer them advice and guidance to assist them on their journey. Then when it's time for them to go back to their body...they are drawn back in." she continued.

A Journey of a Thousand Miles – A Reflections Saga

"Oh okay so it's similar to when a person goes into a coma right?" I asked inquisitively.

"Yes! Yes! That's a great way to explain it. The soul goes on vacation for a bit and during that time the person is faced with a choice. Albeit the biggest they decision they will ever make." she stated with serious undertones cascading off of her words.

"See those lights off in the distance?" she asked while pointing all around her before continuing. "Well those lights all lead to somewhere different. There is no telling where they will take you as each one is like a portal to another reality. That big one over there in the center...well that's home and no I don't mean back to your body. That light leads directly to the other side. It is actually zero point field. It is the one people often refer to as source or God, but we are all a part of that. I won't say any more because I don't want to confuse you. I'll let you visit with your family. You don't have much time." she whispered and then she stood up, and began to fade off into the air around us.

I guess the best way to describe it is sort of like a whimsical mist that was blue, gold and purple and then the colours began to fade and there was nothing in the place where she once stood. I spent quite awhile catching up with my father and grandmother. Various relatives of mine that had passed on showed up to say hello too. Some of them I had never had the chance to meet in this lifetime, but they most certainly knew me. I can't remember too much about the things we discussed. It just seemed more like a homecoming party. Emily had told me that I ultimately had a decision to make. Would I choose to stay there and wait to go back to my body, or would I make my way back into the center of the light source? It was not a difficult decision for me to make. I had so much left to live for. The decision was made within seconds of my awareness of it. I decided to sit there with my father until it was time to go back. It seemed like he and I were really getting into the depth of our talk when suddenly he motioned for me to get up and follow him.

We walked through the beautiful, lush gardens and he went on to explain where each light source would take me. There were portals for travels through time and space. There were some to bring me to all sorts of alternative versions of myself and the lives attached to them. There was even one that he didn't know where it might take us, as he had never bothered to explore it himself. He explained to me that since I already knew my choice, that I would know it on a soul level when I had come to the right one. This would ensure that there were never any mistakes. My soul would always choose the right way back, so I didn't need anyone to show me.

"You will just feel it." he explained.

Soon it was time for me to head back. I kissed and hugged both he and my grandmother goodbye and headed for this beckoning bluish, green light. Yes. This had to be the right one. Inside, it was very dark. Like a long and winding tunnel. The air in there felt like a cool summer breeze brushing ever so slightly against my skin, and yet it was becoming warmer and more inviting the deeper I went through it. Then the air shifted. I fel it prickle ever so slightly. Sort of like the feeling someone gets whenever you get goosebumps. I must've walked for miles, and suddenly, everything seemed to turn upside down without warning. I was falling. It was such a jolting experience and not one I wanted to have again anytime soon. Suddenly I was back. I could hear the faint sound of my heart monitor...beeping somewhere in the distance. I opened my eyes as I felt a gentle and warm hand graze my own. There, next to me...was Kyle.

Chapter Twenty-Eight

I was so overjoyed to see him. I suddenly had this rush of energy wash over me. I realized then that it was his love. I was feeling the warmth of his energy. He had called me back to him. Somewhere...lost in that tunnel...he had found me. He reached in with the purity of his love and pulled me out of it. Our two week whirlwind romance had sure gotten off to a tumultuous start. My life had been hanging in the balance, and I was fighting for my survival. My spirit had been hovering between worlds. As I was walking through that dark tunnel, before everything had flipped upside down on me, I saw a faint light flickering in the distance. Sort of like the flame of a candle flickering rapidly just as the flame is about to go out. I didn't know it at the time, but what I saw there in that tunnel and what had led me back to my body, was the love and connection we shared with one another. After speaking briefly to him on the phone and telling him how much I needed him, he came, He felt that inexplicable pull and heard the desperate call to be by my side. I'm quite sure this man would have moved mountains that day if that was what it would take for him to reach me.

He sat there beside me on the bed and held my hand, pouring all the love that he could into me. He refused to let me go. It was the power of our connection that drew me back. He breathed life back into me...again. We both knew at this moment that our love was not just a chance encounter, but that of a cosmic reunion. A connection that had been forged across lifetimes. It was in that instant, that we both knew our bond was unbreakable and it ignited a flame that would only burn brighter with every challenge we might face in the future. This near death experience awakened the two of us. It became a testament to the transformative power of our love, which would serve as a beacon of hope in our darkest moments. It cemented our commitment to one another, to cherish every moment we shared and to never let go of the love that had saved us both that day.

My mother had a look on her face of utter shock and disbelief. She had just witnessed something truly miraculous. She witnessed the power and purity of our love for one another and she stared in awe as it drew me out of an unconscious state. She was amazed as she watched the colour begin to wash over my pale skin again.

A Journey of a Thousand Miles – A Reflections Saga

She literally saw my skin slowly begin to pink up. The nurses had later told me that I had been out for quite some time and they weren't really sure if I was going to come out of it. My body had been through so much trauma. It was basically a watch and wait sort of situation. At this point, I had even managed to sleep through the entire time I had been in the recovery room. I was just gone. My heart was still beating, and I was breathing of course, but no one was in there for a long time. Kyle sat there holding my hand until he had no other choice but to go. Visiting hours were over. We both knew that I was going to be okay now, yet he still seemed hesitant to leave at first. Everyone had assured him that I was going to be watched very closely now and I promised I would stay in touch as much as possible. That seemed to provide him enough comfort to finally be okay with heading back to the States.

I later found out that my doctor had gone in on the nurses once it was discovered that I was bleeding internally. It was their job to watch me for those signs specifically and all of that went ignored. She was absolutely livid with them. I actually kind of felt bad though because it wasn't their fault. It was the nurse I had the night of the first surgery. She was the one to blame. She nearly killed me. I was just glad that they got to me in time and were able to save me. The thought of Kyle and the children having to live without me was difficult to even fathom. Luckily, they wouldn't have to.

The following day, I was sent for another ultrasound to check on the hematoma. It was discovered at that time that I had developed yet another one and a decision needed to be made. My doctor came to speak to me about my options, and explained the risks involved in both scenarios. Together we made the decision to watch and wait. There was the hope that it would just simply resolve on its' own with time. She helped me to understand the risk involved, should we have to go back into surgery. There was a high probability that I would not come out of that one alive. My body had endured far too much shock already and an additional surgery could cause dangerous complications. The hematoma appeared to be stable so we decided not to to risk surgery at all. I had not come back after all of that just to put myself back in that place that I may never return from. Why risk it if we didn't need to? I even prayed to the god that I don't believe in and any other gods that might hear my plea. The nurses were watching me like a hawk. We were all on edge and feared that it might happen again, They wouldn't even allow me to get up out of bed for about a week. Due to my being bedridden for so long, I was at very high risk for blood clots, so they had to put these air boots on me to avoid that.

Finally, after all I had been through, it was time to go home! The hematoma was checked one last time and was deemed to still be stable. Things were beginning to look up. Kyle didn't want me out of his sight. He asked Christine the day I was discharged from the hospital to bring me to him. He wanted to be the one to care

A Journey of a Thousand Miles – A Reflections Saga

for me. After all that happened, he wanted me near him always. I stayed there in the States with him for roughly a month or so. My recovery was a bit slow at first, but then as each day passed, I began to get stronger and stronger. Kyle was so incredible through it all. He was so loving, caring and attentive. He became my strength, and I leaned on him for support. For the first time in my life, I had found someone who loved me unconditionally and who was willing to do anything to ensure my safety and well-being. I wasn't permitted to use any stairs for the first eight weeks, so this man would pick me up and carry me to avoid them completely. He carried me up and down flights of stairs...day in and day out. Multiple times a day. It was one of the sweetest things anyone had ever done for me. He also catered to my every need and made sure I was always comfortable. When it came time for us to part ways...it was one of the hardest things I've ever had to do. To make matters even worse, I was now homeless. Well kind of.

Christine had decided to throw me out of the house a few weeks before I was to return. It turned out that she had rekindled an old relationship with an ex and they had made plans to move in together. Luckily, my friend Lynn stepped up to help me out. Something that almost didn't even happen because I didn't have the heart to ask her for help. That was when Kyle had to step in and ask her on my behalf. A friend I had since childhood. Someone I had always been close with and I was still too ashamed to ask her for help. I would've rather went to live on the streets then to swallow my pride and ask her for anything. When Kyle spoke to her, she had agreed without hesitation and had even set up and area in her basement for me. She made sure I had whatever I needed and that I was comfortable. I had only been staying with her for a little over a week at the time, and that is when I got the phone call that would change everything.

It was every mother's worst fear come true. I recognized the caller ID as the phone number to the local hospital.

"Hel...Hel...Hello?" I said shakily.

"Hello...is this Aaron Gadby's mother?" the voice on the other end asked.

"Ye... Yes...This is Aaron's mother. What's going on? I...Is everything okay?" I asked shakily.

"Hi Mrs. Gadby. I'm a nurse here at St. Luke's Hospital. We have your son here and the doctor asked me to call you to ask if you could come in so he can speak to you about your son." a female voice continued. I could detect concern in the tone she was using.

"Is...Is everything okay?" I asked again. This time a bit more frustrated.

"I'm sorry ma'am but I can't discuss any details of that with you over the phone, but I will tell you that you should get here as soon as you can." she suggested before hanging up.

I sat there with the phone in my hand, shaking from head to toe. My mind going about a mile a minute. Trying to decipher the phone call I had just received. I didn't even have the strength in that moment to press the button to hang up. I was just frozen there in fear. In shock. My mother's instinct kicked in. I knew something had happened. Something was wrong with Aaron. I immediately called a taxi and rushed to the hospital to be by Aaron's side. It had been well over a month since I had seen him last, but I barely recognized my own son when I walked into that room. He was as white as the sheet on his bed, his eyes were sunken in and it was clear that he had lost a significant amount of weight and quickly. It was obvious that something was very wrong. Being in the medical field, I knew more than the average person would know. I carefully surveyed the monitors showing his heart rate, blood pressure and oxygen saturation.

It was not looking good. His doctor must've been informed that I had arrived, because not too long afterwards, he came into the room and introduced himself. Then he asked me if he could speak to me in the hallway. As I followed behind him, I knew I was about to get some of the worst news a parent could ever hear. Standing there looking at my son, I could feel him starting to slip away from me. A mother always knows. There is just something inside of us. An inner knowing when something is very wrong with any of our children. We know when they have a tummy ache, the sniffles or even a fever. It is not something that can be easily explained, but it is very real. I call it mother's intuition. I knew by the tone of the doctor's voice, and his unwillingness to speak in front of everyone else in the room that this was serious. Once we were out into the hallway, we stepped to the side and he began asking me a few questions regarding Aaron's health before he got right down to business.

"Your ex has told me that you work in healthcare. Is that correct?" he asked.

"Yes sir. That's correct. I'm a medical laboratory technician." I told him.

"Oh good! Then you will be able to understand what I'm about to show you. Here is a copy of some tests I have done on Aaron. Do you understand what this means?" he asked, handing me the sheet of paper he had been holding in his hand.

I glanced at the page and struggled to read the numbers that were there. Suddenly they all began to get jumbled together and blurred as I felt the tears well up in my eyes as I attempted to free myself from this temporary blindness. I scanned over the page a few times, just to ensure that my eyes weren't playing tricks on me. I couldn't believe what I was seeing. Surely there must have been some kind of mistake! According to these numbers, I was looking at a person who by all indications on this report should no longer be alive. And these were the numbers for a twelve year old boy!

"Yes sir...I do. This looks to me like Leukemia." I replied, narrowing my eyes to the floor as the tear drops began to fall like rain from the heaviest cloud. I could not contain them. He paused for a moment to let me collect my thoughts and reel in my emotions before continuing.

"Yes. That's what we think is going on here. Mrs. Gadby, your son is very ill. We aren't quite sure if he will make it much longer, but I'm not giving up on him. He's going to need the best care he can possibly get, so

A Journey of a Thousand Miles – A Reflections Saga

I have ordered for him to be transferred to London Sick Kids Hospital. There you will meet with one of the top pediatric oncologists in the country. He will take over his case and advise you from there. They may need to do a bone marrow biopsy to confirm the cancer, but to also determine what type of Leukemia he has. We are pretty sure this is the correct diagnosis. The paramedics who will be taking him there, should be here momentarily." he informed me, and then he turned and walked back into Aaron's room.

The moment he was away from me, I could barely feel my legs, and I began to slide down with my back against the wall until I was seated on the floor with my head resting against my knees. Paul and I were all too familiar with London. You see, three years ago, Aaron had given us the biggest scare of our lives. He had gone into diabetic keto acidosis. He had never even been diagnosed with diabetes up to that point. We had no idea and yet when he was finally diagnosed, he was doing very bad. His kidneys had started to shut down and they had to rush him to London. He wasn't expected to survive that crisis. They had even told us to prepare for the worst. He was my little warrior, and he fought with all he had.

Shortly after that whole ordeal, he was diagnosed with Type 1 diabetes. We still aren't sure how it managed to go undetected all of that time. We had managed to overcome that traumatic event and now here we were again. I couldn't believe this was happening. My poor child was suffering, and just when he had managed to fight his way through one thing, he now had to be struck with something even worse. Prior to his Type 1 diabetes diagnosis, he had absolutely hated needles of any kind. Now he was a pro and would even help us give him his insulin. He didn't even flinch anymore when it came time to test his blood sugar multiple times a day. He was a trooper. This child had defeated the odds once before and I was certain...or at least I was desperate for him to do it again.

Soon after the doctor had walked away to prepare all of the paperwork for the transfer, the paramedics showed up to take him. Paul and I were not permitted to ride with him in the ambulance, as there wasn't enough room for us, so we followed behind them in Paul's car. They went lights and sirens the entire way and we were directly behind them. I absolutely hated being alone with this man, but I began to wonder how I was going to tell him that our son had cancer. My heart broke for him. He was terrified because he didn't know what was going on. He just knew that Aaron was very sick and it wasn't good. I tried to prepare him the best way I could, and eventually broke down and told him what to expect. He didn't want to believe me, but I could see from his expressions that he knew I was going to be right.

"We can't tell Aaron...We just can't. Even if we call it Leukemia, he will know it's the "C" word. He's not dumb you know." he said in a condescending tone. I could've told him off at that point, but my empathetic nature took the driver's seat instead. I had felt compassion for him. I didn't understand where it was coming from, but there was this overwhelming sense to comfort him. I was completely devastated by the news, and I could only imagine how he was going to handle hearing those words out of the doctor's mouth.

No sooner had we arrived at the hospital, that we were greeted by a slew of hospital staff. We met with the hematologist and he explained what he felt was going on based on his review of Aaron's test results. He tried to assure us that Aaron was in the best hands and that he would do everything in his power to see to it that we would all get through this together. He ordered some more blood work and a bone marrow biopsy. Everything was happening so fast. Much like it had been when I was lying on the operating table on the brink of death. We got to be in the procedure room with Aaron until he fell asleep. He was beside himself with fear. Normally parents wouldn't have been allowed in there due to it being a sterile environment, but this doctor didn't seem to mind one little bit. He wanted us and Aaron to be completely comfortable with what was happening. We just had to make sure that we washed our hands well, and had to wear gloves, a gown and booties into the room. I held Aaron's hand and reassured him that he was just going for a short nap and that his daddy and I would be waiting for him when he woke up. He managed to muster a smile and whispered,

"Well...That's good mom...because I'm soooooo tired."

It broke my heart to see my little boy in this state. He had always been so healthy and energetic throughout his life and now, here he was, lying there helpless and barely able to lift his head from the pillow for a kiss from his mommy. It didn't take long for him to go to sleep and as soon as he did, one of the nurses ushered us out and down the hallway into a waiting room where we could watch TV and try to take our minds off of everything going on for awhile. Easier said then done. Still, I appreciated her good intentions. We were greeted there by a social worker named Michelle. She was the kindest soul I had encountered since this whole nightmare first began. She sat beside me, took my hand and offered words of reassurance. She told Paul and I about the doctor's reputation and let us know how truly kind and caring he was.

His resume was impressive. He had been in the field of pediatric hematology for nearly twenty five years. He had saved countless lives. Even the children who weren't given a good prognosis and had the odds stacked against them. He wasn't quick to throw in the towel and call it quits. He was relentless in his pursuit of putting the cancer into remission and as soon as it was possible. He was even a father himself and had one of his own children go through the same thing Aaron was, so he had a deeper level of empathy and compassion for parents going through the process. It meant that he would know what we were going through. No matter how hard Michelle attempted to engage us, my mind kept drifting to that procedure room. I spoke to Aaron telepathically and watched over him the entire time. Another one of my many gifts. I have the ability to remote view, which means that I can use my consciousness to project my soul somewhere else and this in turn gives me the ability to see and hear things that I might not otherwise be privy to,. Although at this point, I hadn't done i for a very long time. I wasn't even sure if it was going to work. I had always had this deep and profound spiritual connection to all of my children, and I was eternally grateful for that blessing.

After what felt like an eternity, Aaron's doctor entered the room and confirmed everyone's suspicions. Aaron was diagnosed with A.L.L or Acute Lymphoblastic Leukemia. He told us that we were lucky we caught it when we did, because Aaron's bone marrow showed 99% Leukemia cells. The cancer had almost completely taken over. This meant that Aaron was no longer capable of producing his own blood cells anymore. The doctor notified us that there was one more test he needed to wait for results on. He was checking the chromosome of the cancer. He told us about one that he highly suspected Aaron of having, given the acuteness of his illness. It was something called the Philadelphia chromosome and it was also one of the hardest to treat due to its' track record of being so resilient and resistant to typical treatment. We all prayed that it was not going to come back positive for that one. He told us that it would be another day or so before we would get the answer to that question. He explained that once the results were in, he would come by and we could talk about a treatment plan from there. Aaron was given multiple blood transfusions due to his counts being so low. He didn't even have the ability to clot on his own if he was cut, because his platelets were so low. They were at a level so insane that the first doctor at the other hospital had told me he had never seen counts so low in a living person in his entire career. I can't even tell you how much blood Aaron received that day, but it was a lot.

The next morning, both Paul and I were antsy to hear the results of the chromosome test. Aaron's doctor had come in shortly after 10AM to give us the report. We all decided that it might be best if we had this conversation away from Aaron, as it was sure to be an emotional one and we didn't want to upset him. Paul and I both kissed Aaron and told him we were coming right back, before following the doctor out of the room and down the hallway. Maybe it was just me, but that hallway seemed to stretch on forever and then eventually we turned a corner and made our way into a private room that had a "Conference Room" sign on the wall beside the door. Before he took his seat at the table, he asked Paul and I if we wanted something to drink before we settled in. Paul and I both declined politely and took our seats at the table directly across from him.

"So it's as I suspected Mr and Mrs. Gadby," he began.

"I'm sorry to interrupt you doctor but I just want to clarify that the two of us are not married." I corrected him.

"Oh I'm sorry about that. I just assumed that you were. My apologies Miss..."

"Ava is fine." I told him.

"Okay, well, as I was saying, it's as we suspected. The results came in this morning and show that it is in fact positive for the Philadelphia chromosome. Now – What does that mean? Well it just means that your son is in for the fight of his life. It will be harder to treat, as this one tends to have a higher rate of being very resilient and it has been shown in a few cases to also come back. Based on your son's age, the type of cancer and his history of being a diabetic. I hate to say but the odds are only a thirteen percent likelihood that he will go into remission." he explained.

"But that doesn't mean we are going to give up. I'm willing to fight this aggressively and to ensure that I give Aaron the best chance for survival, but I just like to be completely honest and upfront with parents from the beginning. That way there is no room left for surprises. We will start treatment immediately. I'm actually going to take him down in a few minutes and inject some chemotherapy directly into his bone marrow. I will of course make sure he is asleep and comfortable." he paused to observe us, "Tomorrow he will have another procedure where we will surgically implant a port into his chest so that from this point on he won't need to get poked by the needles so many times." he continued. "Your son's diabetes will also complicate things further, due to the fact that part of his cancer treatment will involve the use of steroids which typically contain a lot of sugar. Not to worry though, as we will be monitoring him and adjusting his insulin accordingly. Tomorrow evening we will start the chemotherapy through the IV. He will also be kept comfortable with some morphine to help with any pain he might experience. This is a very painful process, but we will take it one day at a time and always make sure that Aaron remains comfortable and eager to fight. There are three different types we will be using to target the cancer. I feel very positive though that he will beat this. I do however recommend that you prepare your son for what is to come but we will take it step by step. I also feel it is important for my patients themselves to know exactly what is making them sick. Now, I can come in and talk to him as well, to explain things maybe in a way that all of you can understand, or you are definitely welcome to just have that private moment alone with your son. Please let me know whatever you both decide and I will be more than happy to honour your wishes."

I felt like in that moment, I couldn't breathe. It was as if the walls were closing in on us and the ceiling appeared to be getting lower and lower. Our son was in very deep water and it felt like we were too far away to reach him. I pictured myself throwing him a life preserver and hoping that it would get just close enough for him to grab onto. As a mother, I felt that it was my job to always protect him and keep him safe. I had done everything I could to ensure a healthy pregnancy and that a healthy baby would come into this world. I had stopped smoking and everything when I found out I was pregnant with him.

As a parent, something like this tends to be the most difficult thing for us. Especially as a mother, that facing the reality that no matter how much we do to keep them from harms way and ensure they are healthy, life comes in like a sledgehammer and smashes all of that hope, love, devotion, protection and reassurance a mother can offer her child. It just takes all of her efforts and smashes them into oblivion. Sitting there and thinking about all that was happening, it made me think that somehow I had failed Aaron. Was it due to me smoking when I didn't know I was pregnant? Was it the fights his father and I had in front of him and Jaxson? Did I feed him too

A Journey of a Thousand Miles – A Reflections Saga

much of that sugary cereal when he was younger? Was it because I couldn't breastfeed him for the full two years since his father was a selfish bastard who was jealous of the bond I shared with my newborn son?

He had actually made me stop breastfeeding because he became insanely jealous and wanted the chance to feed him from a bottle. Surely there had to be something I had done wrong. Did my children feel abandoned by me all those years ago when I was forced to leave them with their father? Had they buried their feelings until they began to rot from the depths of their soul? So many thoughts rattled through my head and yet, I failed to come up with a good enough explanation as to why this was all happening to my baby. All of his life, I had been able to kiss away the scrapes, bumps, cuts and bruises and yet here I was, completely and utterly helpless. We had just heard the worst news of our lives. It felt like someone had just come into the room and sucked all of the air and with it, the sound. My vision became blurry again and I felt my heart pounding in my chest.

I could feel the doctor's concern, and knew that he wasn't letting on just how bad this was. Paul brought his hands up to his face and began to cry hysterically. I had never in my life seen this man cry this way. I rushed over to him, and wrapped my arms around him. I was trying to offer any words of comfort that I could manage to choke out. This man had beat the living shit out of me, for five and a half years of my life. He had ripped away my self esteem and torn it to shreds, leaving me a broken and empty shell. He had done some of the most unforgivable things to me. Atrocious things, and yet here I was, letting him cry on my shoulder. I was all he had at the time and he knew it. He even gave me weird looks, as if to ask me on a subconscious level whether I was crazy or not for wanting to be there for him. I just felt it in my heart. This was something I needed to do. Our son needed us. He needed both of us equally, and I was prepared to remain civil with Paul, for Aaron's sake. Aaron had seen enough fighting. Even though it hadn't been since his younger years that Paul and I had fought, somehow I knew he had never forgotten it. That was not the kind of thing that just leaves you. It was surely something that would remain with him forever.

Once Paul and I managed to compose ourselves, we wiped the tears from our eyes and headed for Aaron's room. The news had been heartbreaking. It tore me apart, and yet I had to turn around, put a smile on my face and go back to pretending that everything was fine. When children are sick, they often look to their mother for comfort and support. It's as if the mother holds some kind of secret powers and she can somehow make it all better. I felt in this moment, that I had failed him as his mother. This was one boo boo I wouldn't be able to fix with magic kisses and chocolate ice cream. I was completely powerless to this and it killed me inside.

Every single day in that place, brought more trials and tribulations. Paul had taken the only extra bed in the room and forced me to sleep sitting up in a plastic chair at Aaron's bedside. I was forced to sleep that way every night, and even slept holding onto Aaron's hand. Part of me was afraid to ever let him go. I had this crazy thought, that somehow if I let him go, I might just lose him forever. Paul was a total asshole to me. He had turned back into the same old Paul just a few days into our stay. Even the nurses couldn't believe his lack of care and compassion for the mother of his child. My sister Kim, had decided to start a fundraiser for Paul and I, so that we would have money to afford being able to stay there in London with Aaron. I had to split half with Paul, which I was fine with, but then like the selfish and greedy son of a bitch he was, he had his family start one too and he never offered me a dime. That's just who he was to his core. He only ever thought of himself. I'm honestly not sure why I ever thought things would be different this time. Nothing had changed for him. He was all about himself and put his own needs above all else.

I remember when we were together, he had run out of weed and was going through major withdraws. It was Christmas time and he went to return some of the gifts we had bought for the boys so that he could have his weed. I'm not sure why I ever agreed to that. I guess I just didn't want to deal with the monster he would become without it. Besides, it's not like I ever had a choice in the matter. I was just glad now that I would never have to put up with his bullshit again. We were there together with our son and were supposed to be supporting one another, but I don't thing he was ever really there for me, even when we were together. I had never felt so alone then I did there in that hospital room. All I wanted was Kyle. I wanted him next to me, and to feel his warm embrace. I needed him there. He was my rock and somehow, I managed to get stuck dealing with this douche bag instead.

Kyle had been devastated by the news about Aaron too. We spoke every day through text and then briefly at night before I would go to sleep. I told him all about Paul and how he had been treating me. He was not impressed to say the least. If he could've been there, he would've and Paul damn sure wouldn't have been treating me the way he had been. Of that I can be sure. Still, part of me wanted to see Paul cower like he had made me do all those years we spent together. I still don't know what made Paul the selfish prick that he was, but he had even talked Aaron into asking for an Xbox One as his wish, which Paul had actually been wanting for a couple of years but couldn't afford at the time. The people from Make a Wish Foundation had shown up to ask Aaron what he wanted more than anything in the world. They are the ones who come and grant a child's last dying wish. The sky is the absolute limit as to what they can ask for.

Aaron could've gotten the whole family together for a nice vacation anywhere in the world. He could've met his favourite super heroes. There was nothing they would've denied him, and instead his manipulative father had managed to talk him into asking for an item that he wanted for himself. He lacked any empathy for the fac that our son was dying and might not get another opportunity to do something special. It was his wish and his father had stolen it from him. To say I was livid that day, would be a massive understatement. That just goes to show you how truly selfish Paul has always been. To tell you the truth...I wanted to finish the job I had failed to complete all those years ago when he had put his hands on me for the last time. I wanted to strangle him. Even though we hadn't been together for years and I had comforted him in his time of need, he was still trying to control me and bark orders at me. We would head down to the cafeteria every day to eat, and he always made me pay for him, while he hoarded his money selfishly. Even after my funds had gotten low and I could barely afford to feed myself anymore, he told me to call up my family and ask for more money. He had more than enough to spare, but he wanted me to kiss his ass for it. We even had to go and smoke in his car because we were not permitted to smoke on hospital grounds at all.

One day, after I had finally taken enough of his shit and actually stood up for myself, we went outside to the car to smoke like usual. He had gotten into the car and locked the doors on me so that I couldn't get in. It was absolutely freezing outside but he didn't seem to care. He was still trying to establish some sort of control over me and he was determined to achieve this any way he could. He had also just bought a brand new car a few weeks ago. He was so arrogant and proud of it. Treated it like it was his baby. I mean, it was pretty pathetic. You had to be extra careful not to get too many fingerprints on it when you opened the door. That day when he decided to lock me out, I walked over to the front of the car and sat my ass right on the hood as I proceeded to light my cigarette. He rolled down the window and screamed for me to get off his precious baby, claiming that I was going to put a dent in it. I explained to him that some dickhead had locked me out and that I would be more than happy to honour his wishes if only he could manage to get the fuck over himself. I told him that it was his choice and that as long as he continued to remain a dick, I wasn't budging. That was when I saw a supposed grown man throw a full on temper tantrum, He even turned on the windshield wipers so they would continuously hit me because he knew he couldn't and would never do that again. He had now become the one who was fearful, but he still managed to have his moments of bravery from time to time. I just wasn't the woman he remembered from all those years ago. This woman, was not taking shit from anyone.

After about ten minutes of us arguing back and forth, he turned off the car and got out. We argued all the way to the elevators and even once we were inside. The argument carried on past the nurse's desk until we were just within earshot of Aaron's room. I'm not sure if he heard us that day or not, but he sure didn't seem like he had. I should've been given an award for my impeccable acting capabilities. You would've thought that Paul and I were the best of friends whenever you happened to walk into that room. Truth was...I couldn't even stand the sound of him breathing and often thought of clever ways I might be able to stop his heart. I was a great actress. Although, I'm sure the tension was still palpable.

A Journey of a Thousand Miles – A Reflections Saga

Later that evening, we received word that Aaron's white blood cell count had come up and it was all looking positive. We were told that we could leave the hospital probably within the next day or so. They didn't want us going all the way back home though, as he was still going to be returning to the hospital for his tests and treatments. We were told about a place nearby, where families could stay while their child was still going through treatment. It would be far cheaper than any hotel. Aaron and I were so excited at the great news. Paul was too, or at least I think he was. He had been away from his weed for too long and this seemed to be agitating his soul. Shortly after receiving the good news, he spoke with me about him returning home for a few days because Jaxson had become quite upset being away from his parents' and brother for so long. I agreed it was probably best for everyone if Paul left for a bit and I told him that I would stay with Aaron in the room the nurses had set up for us in the Ronald McDonald House. Paul kissed Aaron goodbye and explained to him that he'd only be gone for a few days. He told him that he just needed to check on the dogs and let Jaxson know that his brother was doing okay.

Jaxson and Aaron had always been very close. They were not used to spending a single night apart from each other since the day we first brought Aaron home from the hospital after his birth. They were like twins and had become inseparable. Each of them had their own beds, but that didn't seem to matter to them. We would always find them snuggled in bed together by morning. Jaxson had been diagnosed with high functioning autism, and as a result he did not like any sort of disruption to his routine. He couldn't handle even the most subtle changes. I knew what this must have been doing to him and I was heartbroken that he was having to deal with that uncertainty. Sure we had called every night so that we could reassure him, and let the two of them talk, but for Jaxson, seeing was believing.

I still remember the day that Jaxson was finally diagnosed. It took them six whole years to reach one Early on, when he was just over a year old, I had taken him to the doctor because I noticed that he wasn't reaching his milestones like the other children we had been around. The doctor was completely dismissive of my concerns and told me everything was fine with him. I was told that I was just being a *"paranoid first time mother."* Boy was he wrong! My child didn't even begin to crawl until after his first birthday. He didn't start walking until he was nearly two years old. When he would speak, it was often very difficult to understand him At times he sounded like he was unable to hear himself talk. Aaron had learned to speak from us but gravitated to him as his role model first. Eventually we decided it would be best to have them both see a speech and language pathologist which thankfully helped correct that issue. Despite all of us adults speaking to Aaron normally, he seemed to want to follow the way Jaxson spoke. At first, there was concern that he too might be on the spectrum. Luckily that was not the case.

A Journey of a Thousand Miles – A Reflections Saga

I wanted Paul to get to Jaxson as soon as possible so that he could comfort him. I also wanted him out of my sight. Aaron at first seemed reluctant to let him leave, but I'm sure he was beginning to sense the tension in the air between his father and I. It had grown so thick in that room, you could probably have cut it with a knife. I was actually glad to see Paul go, but I was heartbroken for Aaron. He needed both of his parents now more than ever, and here was his father abandoning him in his time of need. He and I made the most of it though. The home we stayed at was gorgeous. Our room looked a lot like one of those fancy hotels rooms. They served breakfast, lunch and dinner and there was always coffee and tons of snacks, fresh baked goods and fruit for the guests to help themselves. Aaron especially loved their chocolate chip cookies and fresh fruit they offered daily. I was enjoying the peace and quiet away from the hospital and most of all...Paul. I finally had a comfortable bed to sleep in too. Life was grand.

Even though Paul had promised Aaron that he would only be gone for a few days, those few days quickly became a week, then two. Aaron would cry at night and ask why his father lied to him and why he hadn't come back yet. As his mother, I felt the overwhelming need to protect him and unfortunately that involved making all kids of excuses for the jackass he called his father. As much as I hated Paul, I was quick to defend him to our son. Paul had called every night after he left, but he never seemed to talk to Aaron for long. He always seemed to be distracted and had his attention away from where it should've been the most.

Chapter Twenty-Nine

After we had been staying at our new temporary home for about two and a half weeks, Paul called and promised Aaron that he would be returning for us in just a few more days. He told him that he was even going to bring the dogs and even Jaxson to see him. Aaron was so excited about that. He couldn't wait to get out of that place. Of course he enjoyed our stay, but he was just eager to get home again. He was doing so well now. Beating all of the odds. He was doing far better than anyone expected and after a month in London, we were finally ready to take him home. We were told that we needed to return in a couple of weeks for a checkup and so they could run some more tests to check his progress. We were so ready to get home. They didn't have to mention the word to us twice and we were off and packing.

A few days later, when Paul arrived, he was an even bigger asshole to me than I think he had ever been up to that point. He told me that although he had promised me a ride back, he was no longer offering one, and told me that I would need to call someone to come and get me because there wasn't enough room for me in the car. This bastard was planning to leave me stranded there. Had this been his plan all along? Over an hour and half's drive away from home! Knowing full well that I had no other way to get back. The day we had driven up there, he had promised me that he would drive me back. I was even going to call Kyle to come and get me that day we were sent to London. He and I could've driven up there together instead, but Paul had assured me that he would make sure I got home. What had suddenly changed from then to now? I could not believe the audacity he had. Was this paybacks because I wouldn't kiss his ass anymore or let him talk to me like trash? Sure seemed that way. After he had broke the news to me that he wasn't driving me back, I called Christine to see if she would come and get me. That asshole had even left me to pay the entire bill for mine and Aaron's stay at the Ronald McDonald house, which of course left me completely broke! He didn't want me to have any money left over it seemed. I couldn't even afford to pay Christine gas money to get home that day, but I promised her that I would give it to her the following week when I got paid. Thankfully she understood and told me that would be fine. She didn't want to see me stranded with no way to get back.

I was so excited to get back and see my boys. I was dying to see Kyle and his family too. It felt like years had passed since I had last seen or kissed his face. I was missing him something fierce. Even though he wasn't able to be by my side during that nightmare...he had come to me in my dreams a couple of times while I was there. I remember hearing his voice calling out to me and telling me that Aaron was going to be alright. He made sure I was certain of that. There was a time where things were so scary watching Aaron and his ongoing battle with the cancer. Kyle's words every night we spoke seemed to embrace my soul and provide comfort. They were exactly what I needed to get through it all. I was so terrified that Aaron might succumb to his illness and leave this world for good. I would fall asleep every night and then jump myself awake so that I could check to make sure he was still breathing. This was much the same as what I was like after we brought him home after his birth. I felt like I constantly needed to check on him. Maybe that was just part of being his mother. Even though we wanted to be together but couldn't, Kyle kept me from going insane with worry. He reassured me countless times and I appreciated that immensely. He truly was my rock. He and the children were my everything.

When I finally had a chance to see him again, I ran straight into his arms and cried so deeply. I felt myself just melt into him. I had missed him so much, and now after all of the ups and downs I'd been through with having to watch Aaron go through such a terrible illness, not knowing whether he was going to make it to his thirteenth birthday, I was finally home. Those first few nights after we had reunited were incredible. We had made passionate love countless times. My body yearned for him. And his for me. The two of us couldn't seem to keep our hands off of each other. I guess it really is true what they say, absence really does make the heart grow fonder. I was here now with him and as long as I could help it, I was never going to let him go.

After about two weeks since we brought Aaron home, we finally received the news we had all been waiting for. Aaron was finally in remission. The best Christmas gift anyone could ever ask for. Kyle and I celebrated. He wanted to make the day special. We decided to make a nice dinner and some dessert to honour this momentous occasion. Then Kyle got up and told me to follow him to the kitchen. He turned on some music and then took my hands in his. When I heard the song, it nearly had me in a puddle of tears. He smiled and gently pulled me into him and wrapped his arm around my waist as he held my right hand in his. Was this really about to happen? Slowly he moved and began to slow dance with me. We danced there in the kitchen to the song my father used to dance with my mother and I to. In that moment, I found myself wondering if Kyle had been sent to me by my father. I mean, this was just too much of a coincidence. There was something very profound taking place. Something I couldn't quite put my finger on. Later, I would discover just how profound it all really was.

Our love was like a story that you only see in those cheesy romantic movies. I had never even told Kyle the story about my father dancing with my mother in the kitchen before this. I wondered what he might think of it all. Would he agree that the similarities were crazy too? I knew...I always knew that he was going to be the man I was going to spend the rest of my life with. He was perfect for me in every way. We were perfect for each other. Our love very much reminded me of the love between my parents that I had witnessed as a young child. It was the kind of love I had been waiting lifetimes to find. When I finally got around to telling Kyle the story about my father and mother dancing in the kitchen, he began to ask questions about him. He seemed to be thoroughly intrigued by it all. Eventually, he told me that he believed my father had come to him one night. It was long before he and I had ever met, so it really threw him off as he had no idea who this person was at the time. The two of us weren't sure at the time if it was in fact my father who he had seen that night, but he told the story about what had happened that night anyway. He said a man came to him and said something like,

"I've looked after her all of her life. Now it's your turn to take over."

He said before the man appeared that he could smell stale cigarette smoke and was trying to figure out where it might be coming from because no one was smoking at the time nor had anyone smoked in there for ages. I thought the story was beautifully touching. It warmed my heart. It definitely sounded like something my father would do. I was a daddy's girl after all. I decided to show Kyle a few pictures of some of my male relatives. One of them was my father. Kyle recognized him immediately.

"That's him!" he shouted.

"That's the man who came to me. You and I hadn't even met yet so I was like what the fuck?"

A Journey of a Thousand Miles – A Reflections Saga

I was stunned. From that moment forward, not only did I believe that Kyle and I were destined to be together, but now it appeared as if my father had stepped in and hand selected him for me. He knew I needed someone to look out for me and it seems he had chosen Kyle to be that man. That night while Kyle and I were dancing in the kitchen, I swear for the briefest of moments, I felt my father take over. It very much reminded me of the movie Ghost. The part where Patrick Swayze uses Whoopi Goldberg's body so he can share one last moment with the love of his life. There had always been something about that scene that stuck with me.

Kyle and I had finally spent our first Christmas together. This seemed to bring us closer than ever before and by the time we were four months into our relationship, Kyle had asked me to marry him. Sitting here talking about it, brings me back to that night. On this particular evening, about a month after Christmas, Kyle, Jaide and I were sitting in the living room watching movies. I had been sitting in Kyle's lap and we were snuggled up together in our favourite chair. It was the same chair we first sat on together that first day we met. Kyle kisses me lovingly on the neck, and then remarks about how beautiful the earrings he had bought me for Christmas look on me. Then he turns to me and says,

"I was wondering...Do you think that scarf I bought you will keep you warm enough in the winter? Jaide, why don't you go and grab the box with the scarf in it for her? It's over there under the tree." he pointed.

Jaide trotted over to me with the box, and at this point I'm wondering what Kyle is up to, because clearly he is up to something. I take the box from Jaide's hands and pull the scarf out of it. As I do so, something falls out from within it. It is a small box. It looks about the size of a ring box. How the hell could I have missed this? I wonder. Had it been there all along or did Kyle sneakily place it there recently without my knowledge? As I open the box to glance at its' contents, all of the sound suddenly gets sucked out of the room. I can hear Kyle's voice, but it's so low and muffled. It almost sounded like he said,

"Jaide and I were wondering, would you like to join our family?"

I turn around to face him again and now Kyle is down on one knee beside Jaide. He smiles and asks me sheepishly, "Well....Will you?"

Is he asking me what I think he is asking? No, I must've heard him wrong. I'm at a complete loss for words and Jaide begins to giggle.

"What?... What are you asking me? Are you asking what I think you are? Kyle, Are you serious right now?!" I ask through a shaky voice as tears begin to form in my eyes.

Just then, Kyle stands up to hug me and I just can't hold it in anymore. I start crying on his shoulder and then it's like I can hear myself saying something, but I don't feel like I am in the driver's seat anymore and sound almost as if I'm stuttering.

"Is...Is...Is this for real Kyle?" I ask, trying to hold back the outpour of tears.

A Journey of a Thousand Miles – A Reflections Saga

He pulls me away from his shoulder and kisses me softly but passionately on the lips and whispers, "I'll take that as a yes?"

"Oh my god, I can't believe this. Yes! Of course I'll marry you!" I shout excitedly.

The next day when we woke up, I still couldn't believe what had taken place. Did I dream the whole thing? As I look down at my finger, I realize that it was indeed my reality. I was now the future Mrs. Reed! I was beside myself with excitement and happiness. I mean, Kyle and I had talked about getting married at some point in the future, but I figured a proposal was at least another year or two away. I couldn't wait to share our good news with everyone. I'd love to tell you that everyone was overjoyed by the news, but that didn't seem to be the case for some people. There were those who felt they deserved to have a say in my life and they believed it was too soon. Then there were the ones who never thought that things were going to work out for us, considering up to that point I had managed to earn myself a nickname given my past response in previous relationships. I was the "Runaway Bride." Most of our family members were delighted with our big news. At that point, Kyle had only met my mother and my sister Jane but my family was still onboard for us to get married. They saw how happy he made me and after our engagement, everyone was now dying to meet him. I on the other hand was so excited to be a wife, that I almost immediately started planning our wedding. Kyle and I looked at venues, bridesmaid's dresses, and even wedding decor.

Every night away we spent away from each other, we would often share pictures and websites back and forth between us for ideas as to what we both pictured for our wedding. Our anniversary was going to be that upcoming August, and we decided to set the wedding date for exactly one year from the day we officially started dating. We hired a wedding planner, and even put down a deposit for the venue. We were planning a wedding in Canada, at a special place that had always been near and dear to my heart. I wanted to share my whole world with this man and this would be the perfect place to do it. It was located just a few hours outside of where I was currently living, and we had decided that since it was going to be such a long way to travel for some of our friends and family, that it might be nice to make a little vacation out of it. Our guests would be able to sight see and enjoy themselves outside of the wedding.

A couple of weeks before the wedding, Kyle and I had to go and purchase our Marriage certificate. We had decided to purchase one in Michigan because the process was both cheaper and would take much less time than applying in Canada. Unfortunately for us, we discovered after obtaining the certificate that we could not use it in Canada and that it was only valid if we were married in the USA. We had no other choice. All of my dreams felt like they were crashing down on top of me...all at once. My fairy-tale wedding. The dream I had envisioned since I was a little girl had just been shattered into a thousand pieces. I was sad, because not only could we no longer get our deposit back, but none of my family members would be able to attend. Still, I wanted to marry this man more than anything, and he wanted to marry me just as bad. Together we faced the rain and made the most out of what we had. The glitz and glam didn't seem to matter so much when it came down to us and what we truly wanted.

That following Wednesday afternoon, Kyle and I were married in the court house. Our daughter Jaide, my father-in-law and his wife were in attendance. It was a very small, yet intimate ceremony. I didn't even have the chance to wear my wedding gown. Instead, I was compelled to choose a powder blue dress with white lace. Very much symbolic of the dress I had worn the day as Annabelle when Navarro and I had first met. Remember how I mentioned that it rained the day Kyle and I had met, and that soon I would come to learn the significance of the water? Well, the night before we were married, the pipe in the kitchen had burst and we had a flood. Kyle seemed a bit irritated by it, until I reminded him that water had been prevalent throughout the course of our relationship. Even on the days we would have to separate so I could return home, it would always start raining. It was as if the universe was trying to show the world the pain we both felt every time we had to say goodbye. On the night before our wedding however, it felt more like the universe was blessing our sacred union. After we were married, my mother in-law had a surprise for us when we returned home. She had rented us a hotel room for two nights so we could celebrate finally being husband and wife.

About a week after the wedding, Kyle and I returned to my home town in Canada, where my family was eagerly waiting to meet him. They had even put together a little gathering to congratulate us. It was very special and they all welcomed him with open arms. I was quite surprised how seamlessly Kyle fit in with everyone. I was like he had always been there with all of us. My family absolutely adored him, and he and I were even told by numerous people that night that the energy between us was palpable. There was no mistaking it. We were head over heels for each other. At the time we were married, I had been living with my mother and stepfather Greg. After the party, Kyle and I returned to stay with them for a few days. We also spent some much needed time with the boys and shared a few fun nights with family and friends. We shared some drinks and sang karaoke together. I can still remember the very first song we ever sang together. It had been the song from Dirty Dancing, which was perfect because it was one of the movies we had both always loved and one of the things that we bonded over, *(I've Had) The Time of My Life,* by Bill Medley and Jennifer Warnes.

Oh yes...most definitely! It was incredible how strong our bond was becoming. We had even begun to speak telepathically to one another very early on, and this connection was only intensifying. This was something I had never shared with anyone before. I know there have always been those couples who claimed to be able to

A Journey of a Thousand Miles – A Reflections Saga

finish each other's sentences, but it was obvious they were setting one another up for it. Kyle and I were nothing like that. We could read each other's mind. Sometimes he and I even came out with the exact same words at the exact same time. It was pretty wild. The way we knew one another completely, right from the word, *"Hello"*. I could just sit there beside him and think about something I wanted to eat or a show I wanted to watch. I didn't have to say a single word and he would just read it off of me. We were always able to do things like that. The first time it ever happened, I remember that we had both blurted out the exact same words during a conversation we were having with his mother. We all couldn't help but start laughing. It was just divine perfect timing...every single time. We had this thing we would say every time it happened,

"Get out of my head!"

It always made for a good bout of laughter. There were not very many moments in our relationship where you couldn't find us either lost in conversation, in each other or rolling around with tears in our eyes, dying with laughter. We were best friends. Definitely twin souls. One soul...staring at its' own reflection through two sets of eyes.

Despite us being married, Kyle and I were still stuck living apart from one another. We spent every waking opportunity to be in constant contact in one way or another. Whether it be through texts, phone calls or in person. We both just wanted to be near each other always. Each time we were forced to say goodbye was sheer agony for the both of us. Our souls didn't know that the separation was just temporary...it sliced through us as if it were a deep scar that may never heal. There are no words to encompass the gravity of the pain we both experienced.

After being married for about six months and not being able to see one another for over a month, Kyle and I had made plans to spend a nice romantic weekend together. I asked my girlfriend Christine whether she would mind bringing me across the border, and told her I would give her some gas money as well. She said she would be more than happy to do that, as it would give her a chance to see her fiance Felix who happened to live in the US as well. Felix was the man she had thrown me out for. The one who never even spent a single day living there. I think he only acted like he was going to move in, because he knew she would jump at the chance and this way he could be rid of me too. He knew I didn't care for him one bit. He had broken Christine's heart many times before and I honestly believed that she deserved better. It seemed like he was only ever calling her over for a late night booty call. Their arrangement was sketchy to say the least. For some reason, she could only come over late at night or when he called her to tell her she could come and they could never stay at his place. He would always get a hotel room, like she was a call girl or something. The thought of the two of them together, absolutely sickened me. Kyle and I were pretty sure that he was more than likely still married, because his behaviour was definitely indicative of someone doing things on the sly. Despite my distaste for that man, I knew that Christine was madly in love with him. As her best friend, all I wanted was for her to be happy and so if he was what made her that way then I would accept him. I mean, that's what friends do right? Yet there was still part of me that had tried several times to talk some sense into her. Nothing was going to get through. She had been sucked in by his charms and hung on his every word. To me, he was just another Kevin. A lying, cheating snake who preyed on women and made them believe they meant more than they actually did. I truly believed with all of my heart and soul that Felix was just stringing her along and that she was nothing more to him than a mistress at best.

No matter how many times she caught him in lies, she just couldn't seem to let him go. This man and her had discussed having children together. He had already had two daughters from a previous marriage, but he told Christine he wanted more. They had discussed a future together at length and he had even purchased a brand new home for them. It all seemed to be aligning perfectly and it seemed that they were going to get married and spend their life together. So I can understand why she was under the impression that they were going to have a child together and live happily ever after. The two of them had even gone and had a discussion with a doctor to talk about the process of reversing her tubal ligation procedure that she had after giving birth to her last child. Then Felix went and did the unthinkable! He actually went behind her back and got a vasectomy. Yup you read that right! I don't think he was ever planning on telling her either. He was most likely going to let her think that maybe her tubes had been tied for too long and that the reversal had failed. Who does that? Not someone who love you that's for sure.

The sad thing is...the only reason Christine ever learned the truth about what he had done, was because he wound up in the hospital after the incision site got badly infected. A little dose of karma one might say. Can you even imagine? You are dating someone and planning a future with them. The two of you even plan to have a child together someday and go as far as to talk with a doctor about a reversal procedure, then your so called future husband goes behind your back and gets himself fixed. You find out because he winds up in the hospital due to an infection...what is your next move? Bye Felicia! Right? Well...that's not what happened at all. Even after learning of his betrayal, Christine still went to visit him in the hospital. She nursed him back to health and even went on to meet his daughters. She had always been so caring and generous but that often left her with people who used and abused her. One of Felix's daughters was pregnant, so Christine being who she is, went out and bought gifts for her baby shower.

This man even went on to introduce her to his mother. After all of that, one might say things improved for them right? I mean surely if someone is introducing you to their family they have intentions to keep you around right? Still, even after all of that, their arrangements for when they would spend time together were still very odd to say the least. She was still only allowed to come late at night and only when he called her to say she could. She was never permitted to just show up and whenever she was there at the house, she had to keep her car in the garage. Felix's ex wife only lived a few houses away. The entire thing was sketchy to me. Eventually, Christine and Felix's daughter whom she had bought baby gifts for, had a falling out. Although it was never really clear as to why that had occurred. And still, even after all of that...she was still chasing after this fool. The absurdity of it all was downright maddening for me. If you think that's where it ends, that things couldn't possibly get much worse, well you would be wrong.

One night, the two of them had gotten a hotel together. Christine showed up first, and she waited there for Felix to meet up with her. They had planned to spend a romantic evening together, but there was just one little problem...Felix never even bothered to show up. He came to the hotel the next morning, apologizing profusely and claiming he got stuck working again. He was nice enough to bring her a muffin though. Then there was yet another time where the two of them had been spending another romantic weekend together in a really fancy hotel, but that weekend was cut short when Felix received a call from his brother...or so he claimed. He suddenly jumps up, tells Christine that something terrible had happened and that he needs to leave immediately. Apparently, his brother had an altercation with some guy at a gas station and someone got shot. She believed his mountain of obvious lies and had even gone on to tattoo his name on her body...not once....not twice....but three times! After her first time getting his name on her, they split up for quite awhile. She ended up having to go and get it covered up, only to go back to him and put it on her twice more. I have never understood people who do that. To me, putting a tattoo of the name of a person you are dating on your body is equivalent to staking claim on a piece of property. Some people think it's romantic, but I have never cared for it. To each their own I suppose. There is just no way in hell that I would ever do something that insane.

Now I'm sure by this point you must have figured it all out. None of those outlandish stories he told her were true. Felix had a wife...not an EX wife but a WIFE. In fact the called ex wife that lived just a few houses away...was in fact his current wife and the mother of his children. I don't think Christine would've ever learned the truth, had it not been for the wife contacting her about the relationship Christine had been having with her husband. To make matters even worse, Felix had also been talking with some other women and carrying on a relationship with them too. He had women buying him clothes, lavish gifts and paying for whatever he needed. The sad part about it all was the Christine only came upon this information after they had already gotten engaged and planned a life together. She thought she was the one and only, and she was more like number three or four. Felix of course denied everything. He claimed at the time that all of these women were lying...including the wife who had thanked Christine for the brand new patio furniture that she had bought Felix for his birthday.

Sadly, Christine still believed Felix and every word he said, despite catching him in several lies herself. She continued to carry on a relationship with him. To this day, I still don't know what it was about about him that made her unable to let go. I truly hoped she was going to wake up one day and come to her senses.

Chapter Thirty

As we drove to the tunnel entrance at the border, she was telling me how much she couldn't wait to see Felix. It had been weeks since she had seen him, and she was pretty emotional talking about how much she missed him. The two of them had made all of these lavish plans together and were leaving the state to go to one of those luxurious hotels where you have a private swimming pool in your suite. I knew how much she was looking forward to it all. I just hoped it would be drama free this time around. Kyle and I were looking forward to our own quality time together too. It was very much needed for both of us. This had been the longest time that he and I had ever spent apart, other than when Aaron had been in the hospital. At this point, things were the best they had ever been and I don't think either of us honestly saw them getting any better. All I knew was that I just couldn't wait to be in his arms again. It had felt like I had spent an eternity without him.

I often found myself wondering what it might have been like if Kyle and I had met sooner in this lifetime. Would we have a child together or maybe even two? As sad as it made me that it had taken us this long to find each other, I was just grateful that we did at all and that I had gotten the opportunity to have all of my boys. I wouldn't have traded them for anything. The boys just adored Kyle and I adored Jaide. I had tried to be there for her as much as I possibly could. You see, Kyle and his ex wife Angel had a whirlwind romance of their own too. He truly thought she was his forever person. Hell, the two of them had even grown up together. They had crossed paths early in life and it just seemed like fate that he was supposed to end up with her. They seemed like a match made in heaven, but soon the cracks began to form and their once match made in heaven eventually took a sharp detour straight into hell. Nothing could of prepared him or Jaide for the way she left things between them. She had been cheating on him and left him to raise Jaide on his own when she was still an infant. Luckily Lorraine had stepped in to become that positive role model for her. I still remember the gut punch I felt when I read the articles for the magazine he wrote for. They were all about everything that she had put both him and their daughter through.

Rather cryptic, you would have to know him to know what he was really talking about. I cried reading it. It truly broke my heart. I felt like I was standing there in that living room with them on the day she shattered his whole world. I wished in that moment, that I could turn back time and find a way to never let that happen to them. It was clear to me from every word on the page, just how deeply she had cut him that day. It was one of the saddest stories I had ever read or heard. Sure, we all hear the woman's side of the story when a relationship falls apart, but how often do we hear the man's version? The story made me angry. It was almost too much for me to bear. It may have been a sad story, but I realized that he had also gone through so much growth in that process, just as I had throughout the traumatic events of my own life. Everything serves a purpose, even though at the time we are in it, it just feels like hell. Despite all that Kyle and I had been through in our lifetime, and our individual journeys, each experience shaped us into who we had become. Still, I wished I could alter the past and make it so he had never even met her. Unfortunately though, if that were the case, he probably wouldn't have had Jaide. As much as I couldn't picture my life without Kyle, I couldn't imagine one without her either. She was the most precious gift for him and he cherished that little girl. I wish I could've met them both sooner though. I wanted desperately to take the pain away for both of them.

Jaide had only been twelve years old when Kyle and I first met. I remember how nervous I had been to meet her. I decided to have a dream catcher made special just for her and gave her a rose quartz necklace to help mend her broken heart. Rose quartz is a beautiful stone that helps to heal and reopen the heart chakra. I wanted this little girl to know just how much I would love her as my own. I already did, long before I had ever met her. To me, she was my daughter. Her mother may have given birth to her, but I would always see her as mine. Jaide and I had a special little connection. She was the daughter I had always wanted, but never had on my own. I loved my boys without a doubt and I was grateful for them, she was just the icing on the proverbial cake. Shortly after we met, I discovered that she too was an empath. She felt everything so deeply. She had many gifts of her own, and I was eager to help her navigate those waters. I was beyond grateful that she trusted me, and that she allowed me to be that confidante to her.

I was looking forward to seeing all of them. Jaide, Kyle and my mother in-law. I became lost in thought as I began to daydream about all of the fun we would all have this weekend. I thought about teaching Jaide one of my favourite intuitive games that really helps young psychics hone their abilities. It's a card game called Red or Black. Basically, one person holds up each playing card one by one but facing away from the person sitting across from them. The other person who is not holding the card then tries to see the card in their mind's eye and connect to what colour suit it might be. It's just a fun little way to keep your intuition sharp.

I pulled myself out of my daydream, just long enough for me to call Kyle and let him know that we were almost across the border and that I would be seeing him soon. After hanging up, I quickly shoved my cellphone back into my pocket. I didn't want the custom's officer to think that I was acting suspicious or being rude or something. They could be odd at times. It just all depended on the day that particular officer may have had before you showed up. They could be quite intimidating. Christine and I always tried to pick the one with my lucky number...seven. It seemed to be the fastest way through and with very little hassle if any. I could barely contain my excitement to see everyone. I was trying my best to pull it together, but the thoughts just continued to swirl in my head. I was caught up on all of the lovemaking that Kyle and I would be doing that weekend and thought about how much fun we would have with Jaide and Lorraine too. Kyle and I had always been that playful couple.

Sometimes it was like we were little kids again. There was always so much joy and laughter between us, that it could probably fill every room in that house. It was never just the soft giggly type of laughter either. It was the kind that made your cheeks and stomach hurt. The type that brings you to tears because you just can't seem to stop laughing. Kyle and I never stopped laughing and we have never had any issues communicating either. I've noticed this tends to be a pretty common issue among couples. Two people come together but can't seem to talk to one another. For Kyle and I, it always seemed to flow effortlessly. Despite all of the talking we did on a daily basis, we never seemed to run out of things to talk about. We also covered a wide array of topics every time we discussed anything. We would start off on one thing and end up somewhere else completely by the time we were finished. All of my life I had been unable to talk to anyone. I mean, sure I could talk. It wasn't as if I had lost my voice or anything. It was just that I never felt heard by anyone.

With Kyle, it was different. I was always seen and heard and man did I have a lot to say! He and I often stayed up all hours of the night, sharing in the most deep conversations. I can't tell you what a blessing it was to share that with someone. All these years I had felt like I needed to water myself down for others. I knew the things I could talk about with them and the things that I couldn't. Let's just say that for a great chunk of my life I had been running on autopilot. On the outside I would appear engaged in conversation and perfectly content but on the inside I was practically screaming. I can't do mundane. I'm a person with much depth. Surface level conversations were only meant for robots and computers. I've never fit inside any boxes either...despite people trying to shove me into them at every opportunity. The conversations between Kyle and I, were intellectual and so profound that he and I would always say that a fly on the wall would leave the room forever changed. Kyle was the only one I felt completely safe with and the only person who ever made me feel unafraid to reveal the true depths of my soul. There was no mask or representative necessary. We just got each other other. We loved one another for exactly who we were. There was never a desire to change one another. We wanted to grow together. To learn together. I loved absolutely every single thing about this man, even the quirky things he did like rubbing his feet together or rub the top of his head like a small child whenever he was tired.

I even loved the funny sounds that he made whenever he would get what I can only assume is an inverted hiccup. It sounded more like a loud gasp. Sort of the sound someone would make when they are surprised by something. It always managed to scare the shit out of anyone who heard it, but Kyle and I always thought it was great for a laugh. Kyle also loved music and often sang and danced in the kitchen while cooking food and sometimes you might even hear him singing in the shower. It had always been one of my favourite things to listen to, other than the sound of his heart beating softly as I lay my head on his chest. He was always just so full of life! Upon first meeting him, people would swear he was shy and reserved, but for those of us lucky enough to meet all of him...he was always the life of the party. Anyone who saw him living in his joy, knew that he was perfectly content with his life. We both were.

I was so lost in thoughts of him, that I barely noticed that Christine and I were fast approaching the exit to the tunnel. I was still finding it quite difficult to focus on much else. Kyle had completely taken over my thoughts. I just couldn't help myself. Kyle Reed had captured my heart and soul and I was deeply, passionately and irretrievably in love with him. He was the love that made my heart sing, my soul soar and the man who made my life complete. The missing piece that I never even knew I needed. His love was all consuming.

"Pull it together Ava! You have to get it together before you get to that booth!" I told myself.

I couldn't have myself being lost in fairy-tale land when we were getting ready to cross the border. One wrong look and the officers could take you for being nervous or combative. I quickly shook all thoughts from my head and leaned forward to grab my passport documentation. I glanced toward the cars ahead of us and took a long, deep breath.

Up ahead, the line was long and I turned my head toward the booths, looking for my lucky number, but there was a closed sign above it. Shit! We always use that one. It just gave me the best vibes and if you know anything about me then you would know how big I am when it comes to vibes. Today, unfortunately we would have no other choice because I could see that most of the traffic was being diverted to lanes three and five. As skeptical as I am about these kinds of things, I tried desperately to shake the feeling that was gnawing away at my insides.

"Everything is going to be fine!" I told myself out loud. "Just take a deep breath and relax."

Soon I would be where I had been dying to be forever. Mere minutes from now, I was going to be safe in the arms of my love. As the car got closer to the booth, I continued to try and calm myself and took a few long deep breaths, as I straightened my clothing so that I would appear tidy and kept. I never did understand why people felt the way they did about the border officers. Everyone seemed to be intimidated by them for whatever reason. I had crossed the border so many times and I guess maybe I was just used to their stern demeanour. I still understood why some might shy away from them, but at the end of the day I knew they were people too and never lost sight of the fact that they were just doing their job. The authoritative way they carried themselves was understandable given the nature of their work though. Your demeanour played a vital role in your interaction with them too. If you were polite and friendly, they seemed to just let you pass on through. It had to be a certain level of friendly though. If you were too friendly, well then that could be mistaken for the fact that maybe you had something to hide.

We were now the next car in line. My heart began to beat so hard, I thought it might come out of my chest. I glanced down at my sweaty palms and rubbed them vigorously against the fabric of my blue jeans.

"Get it together Ava!" I commanded myself.

"Huh? Did you say something?" Christine asked.

"N...No. I'm just talking to myself." I chuckled.

For some reason I was always nervous at the booth, but this time something felt very wrong. As we approached the window at the booth, a rather muscular man leaned over to grab our passports.

"Where are you headed?" he asked.

"I'm going to see my fiance and she is going to visit with her husband who lives over here." Christine answered.

"How long are you both planning to be gone?" he asked more gruffly.

"Just the weekend." she told him.

His eyes scanned the backseat of our car and then came back and locked onto mine. He appeared to be studying me quite closely for what seemed like forever, and then he finally spoke again.

"How much money do you have on you? He asked.

"N...Nothing sir." I replied.

"Well then how are you planning to support yourself while you're over here?!" he inquired.

I could feel my whole body begin to sweat. Could he hear the nervousness in my voice? Maybe he could hear the thunderous pounding coming from my chest. Christine was usually the one who did all of the talking. She seemed a lot more comfortable with them then I was. She would even flirt sometimes or make jokes with them. This time however, none of her Canadian charms were working. All eyes and interest seemed to be on me.

"Well I'm not currently working at the time, because I had surgery and then my son got ill. My husband supports me whenever I'm over here." I replied sheepishly.

"So let me get this straight! You're not currently working and you are coming into the country without any money claiming that your husband will provide for you? Well I'm sorry miss but I'm not satisfied with those answers. How do I know that you aren't trying to move here?" he asked accusingly.

A Journey of a Thousand Miles – A Reflections Saga

"Sir. I promise you that this is not my intention at all. I simply wanted to come and visit with my husband and our family for the weekend. I've not seen them in over a month, due to my son being very ill." I said in an almost pleading tone.

I had children, a job and family to return to. Surely that would be enough to convince him. Yet no matter what I said to try and explain the situation, he just wasn't satisfied. He leaned out of his booth and proceeded to slap a yellow ticket on the windshield.

"I'm going to need you ladies to pull in over there please." he instructed.

I could not believe this was happening right now. Was it that obvious that I had been trying to crawl out of my skin the entire time? Given what had happened to me as a child, I still struggled with being uncomfortable around strange men. Apparently the officer thought that I had something to hide. Clearly he couldn't read a room or a car for that matter if his life depended on it.

Christine pulled into the spot we were told to, and waited for further instructions. Just then, two hulk like men approached the vehicle and instructed her to put the car in park and turn off the engine.

"Ladies, I'm gonna need you to empty your pockets and leave the contents on the seats where you are sitting. This includes your cellular phones and purses. You may take your wallets with you, but everything else stays in the vehicle. Got it?!" one of them barked with authority.

This was going to be the first time I had ever been pulled into customs in my life. To say I was practically shitting myself, would be an understatement.

After we were allowed to exit the car, we were handed our ticket from the windshield and instructed to make our way inside the building. It didn't take longer than a few seconds or so for someone to approach us at the entrance. He took the ticket from Christine and glanced at us both multiple times before clearing his throat and ordering us to follow him inside. I felt my palms begin to dampen again, as I was led up to one counter and Christine another. I didn't like the fact that they had separated us at all. The female officer who was standing here in front of me, proceeded to ask the same questions as well as what Kyle did for work, where he lived and why we hadn't started the immigration process yet. Again I reiterated that I had just come to visit my husband.

"How long have you been married?" she asked me.

"Just six months." I responded.

"Oh. I see. Well congratulations!" she said, smiling from ear to ear.

"Um...The problem is though. You and your husband haven't filed any immigration paperwork. Who is planning to move where?"

"We have agreed that my husband will move to Canada." I told her.

A Journey of a Thousand Miles – A Reflections Saga

"Well that's great and all, but why have neither of you filed any paperwork to that affect?" now she was beginning to sound accusatory in her tone.

"We...Well...we just don't have the money for that just yet. I was sick and then my son got sick and I just...we just can't afford it right now!" I explained.

By this point, a huge ball of phlegm had worked its' way toward the back of my throat. I began to start coughing violently, trying to clear it away.

"I understand miss and I feel for you. I truly do, but you see why the officer was hesitant about letting you cross?" she continued.

"You haven't been working in about eight months or so now, you have no money and neither your husband nor yourself have filed any paperwork showing that you have plans to reside in you home eventually, except...All we have for proof is your word. We think that you may be trying to move here." she stated.

"Um...no...that's not the case at all ma'am. I have five children back at home, I have a job, a home and a whole life back in Canada. Besides we have free healthcare." I told her.

"We have better." she rebutted.

"Well I'm telling you the truth. All I want to do is go visit my husband and family. I am going to be returning on Sunday evening." I responded.

"Can you come with me?" she asked.

Finally I appeared to be getting somewhere. I mean she was a woman and seemed to be quite sympathetic to my story.

"At least someone has sympathy!" I thought to myself as I followed her into a room where we were met by two other female officers waiting.

That was the moment I was told that I was about to be searched and fingerprinted. The two officers in the room instructed me to remove my clothing and told me I was permitted to leave my bra and underwear on. I was absolutely flabbergasted by what was about to transpire. As I sat in the cold, sterile customs room, my dreams of reuniting with Kyle shattered around me. The agents' stern faces and accusatory questions made me feel like some kind of criminal, not a loving wife who was eager to see her husband. In a moment of frustration and desperation, I involuntarily unleashed my anger on the computer system, my fingertips pressed firmly against the electronic panel as I unwittingly brought the entire network crashing down. The silence that followed was deafening, the screens going dark as the agents' eyes widened in shock. I knew in that moment, I had crossed a line.

The strip search that followed was a humiliating nightmare, leaving me feeling violated and powerless. After all was said and done, the agents instructed me to get dressed and return to the waiting room, where I wa to wait to be called up to the desk again. I had to wait about an hour and a half due to the system crash, as everything had to be rebooted. The agents seemed dumbfounded as to how the whole thing had happened. I guess they had never experienced such a wide network going down. I guess they never had the pleasure of meeting someone like me. I was born during a thunderstorm, and on the eve of a full moon, surely everyone had to know I was going to be a force. Yet up to that point, I myself didn't realize just how powerful I really was. I too was in utter disbelief over the whole event. I had unleashed my wrath, and yet still managed to make things even worse for myself. When my name was finally called, I felt an intense sigh of relief. All I wanted to do in that moment was get to the love of my life. To let him comfort me in his arms, as I told him all about the ordeal I had just been through. Finally after going through all of this bullshit, I was going to be able to leave. As I approached the counter to the area I heard my name called, two officers I had never seen before let me know that I would not be able to cross today. They handed me a sheet of paper which stated all of the requirements necessary to make that happen. I broke down into tears right there. All I wanted was to be safe in the arms of my love, and now that wouldn't be happening. Kyle wouldn't even be able to hold me and reassure me that everything was going to be okay. What the hell was I going to do now?

Chapter Thirty-One

The days that followed were dark and isolating, depression's heavy force suffocating me. The days turned into weeks, and the weeks into months. The distance between Kyle and I felt like it was an endless road. I felt lost and alone, trapped in a never-ending cycle of longing and heartache. The memories of our time together haunted me, bittersweet reminders of what we had, and what we might never have again. The border that separated us seemed to grow wider and more insurmountable with each passing day. The deep ache in my heart became a reminder of the bureaucratic hurdles that were keeping us apart. Yet even in the midst of that darkness, Kyle's love was a constant source of light. A beacon of hope. His words of encouragement and unwavering belief in us, it all kept me going, even during the times where it felt like everything we had together was falling apart. And so we held on, to each other, to our love, to the hope that one day we would be together again, free to build the life we both wanted, without borders or restrictions or that suffocating grip of uncertainty. We held on, and we never let go, no matter how hard it got, no matter how bleak the future seemed. We held onto the one constant that we knew would never change.

A Journey of a Thousand Miles – A Reflections Saga

We loved each other deeply and though we felt powerless at times to the situation we were faced with, we would never let anything break us. We would never stop loving one another or fighting for each other. Eventually we both decided we could no longer allow this distance between us to remain, and Kyle came to visit me at home. As great as it felt to be able to see him again, every visit was a painful reminder of the life we had been wanting to build together, but couldn't. The uncertainty and frustration of it all simmered just below the surface, threatening to boil over at any moment. I felt like we were living in limbo, caught between two countries, two lives, and two dreams. I couldn't help but wonder if we would ever be able to close the distance between us, to wake up in the same bed each and every day, and to build a life without the weight of borders and bureaucracy holding us back. The tears I cried were endless, the pain I felt was unbearable, and the fear I had was suffocating.

Yet no matter how hopeless it all seemed, Kyle's love remained that source of light, a reminder that our bond was stronger than any obstacle, any distance, any border. Each and every time we made plans together, seemed like forever before they finally came to fruition. Kyle would come and visit for a few days every couple of weeks. I couldn't help but count down the days until I saw him again. They always seemed to pass by too quickly. If only we could stop time and just stay in these moments forever. We would often spend a day or so with my mother and stepfather at their place, and then the last couple of nights before he was leaving to go back home again, we would rent a hotel room so we could have some much needed alone time together. It wasn't ideal, but we were willing to do whatever it took to be together.

About four months after it all began, Kyle and my mother in-law Lorraine came for a short visit, with the intention that they were going to bring me back to the states with them. We all thought that we might have better luck if the officers could actually see the people I was so desperate to get to. Maybe sympathy would turn in our favour. Despite our best efforts that day, we were pulled in once again. This day turned out to be another emotional one for me. As the officer called me up to the counter, Kyle grabbed my hand and walked up with me. We told the officer what the plan was and discussed the circumstances.

I'm sorry Mr and Mrs. Reed. Mr Reed you are free to return to the US but I'm afraid it will have to be without your wife. She has not satisfied us that she has legitimate ties to Canada, and therefore we do not feel comfortable allowing her entry." the officer told us both.

I finally couldn't take it anymore. I balled both of my hands into fists and held them firmly at my side.

A Journey of a Thousand Miles – A Reflections Saga

"I don't understand! What seems to be the problem? All of this time I have been crossing every weekend without any issue and now suddenly you don't feel comfortable allowing me into the country? Oh I know what it is. It's because you have learned that my husband is black right?" I shouted angrily.

Just then, I felt Kyle squeeze my hand firmly but gently. It was as if he was trying to comfort me because he could feel me getting more and more upset. No sooner had I uttered those words, the officer took a step back away from the counter and put his hands up in protest. He looked as if someone had just hit him in the face with a baseball bat.

"No ma'am that is not true and I'm offended that you would make such an accusation!" he said sternly.

Just then Kyle had decided he too had had enough and before he could stop himself the words were flying out of his mouth.

"It's ridiculous the way my wife was treated here the last time. To be pulled in like a criminal and strip searched simply because she wanted to come and see me. How would you feel if that was your wife?" he said narrowing his eyes at the officer in front of us.

Just then a female officer who had been eavesdropping in the background, decided to get involved.

"That never happened!" she shouted out.

"Yes...it did!" Kyle told her bluntly.

He was so pissed at that point that his tone had grown louder. I wondered if anyone else had picked up on that. She didn't seem to take too kindly to his tone. Suddenly, I watched her pull her hand up toward the holster on her hip and rest her hand on her gun. Was this really escalating to that point that she felt threatened by us? Or was she simply trying to use intimidating behaviour to deter us from carrying on the conversation, which was now heading into an argument? I was absolutely livid at that point, and just wanted to be done with it all. I begrudgingly thanked the officers and squeezed Kyle's hand tightly, signalling for him to drop the whole thing so that we could just leave without incident. I definitely didn't want things to escalate any further than they already had. We could both speak quite passionately about something and many times it would come off to others as if we were yelling. Something else we shared in common. My mother in-law just sat there listening to the bullshit, yet I could almost feel the steam that was radiating from her toward the officers. You could tell she wanted to say a whole lot, but she knew that Kyle and I were handling it so she just left us to it. After we were finally able to leave, she and Kyle drove me back to my mother's place. I never felt more defeated. I was just ready to give up on ever trying to cross the border again. I had been traumatized enough by my previous experience with customs, and this had just poured salt in the wound. That night they dropped me off at home, I kissed Kyle goodbye and cried on his shoulder for a long time. I wanted to hold onto him as long as possible, to stay in his arms forever. But I knew he needed to get back to Jaide and the boys. The crazy thing is though, he and Lorraine were pulled in again on their way back across the border. Apparently, the officers wanted to check the trunk, thinking maybe they would try to smuggle me across the border anyway. The whole thing was completely ridiculous.

Kyle was relentless in his pursuit to get me across that border. A few weeks later, he and my father in-law drove across to Canada, and came to pick me up to try once again. My father in-law was hellbent that we were going to succeed this time. As we pulled up to the booth he was jovial and laughing with the officer. Everything was finally going in the right direction for once, and I felt a small glimmer of hope begin to well up inside of me. I became excited again. I was finally going to be able to go back to the US. After all of this time...it was finally happening! I gave Kyle's hand a gentle but excited squeeze. We were both excited. Just as I was beginning to get lost in fairy-tale land again, the officer leaned over to look at me sitting there in the backseat, and that's when I felt myself shrink. If I could've disappeared at the time I just might have. His gaze felt like it could burn a hole into my fragile heart. Just then he straightened up, and looked at my father in-law with a stern look on his face.

"Who's been smoking marijuana?" he asked.

"No one has been smoking marijuana!" my father in-law assured him.

"I smell weed." he said accusingly.

He then came right out of his booth and slapped a yellow ticket on the windshield. At that point I felt all of the wind go out of my sails and a feeling of despair began to take over me.

"Do you have a criminal record sir?"

"No...neither does my son!" my father in-law said while puffing out his chest.

"You sure about that sir? Do you have any weapons in the vehicle?" the officer continued

"What?....what the fuck he jus say to me?!" my father in law shouted angrily.

It was a mixture of disbelief but the undertones of rage were bubbling just below the surface. You could feel the tension building. You see my father in-law is from Alabama, and well... he won't take shit from anyone. Kyle told me the story once about how his father had gotten into it with a neighbour over something when Kyle was younger, and it ended up in the two men going to grab their guns and having a shootout. Any inkling of the smile that had crossed his face just moments ago, had now quickly faded and become one that was stone cold serious.

"Mutha fucka I'll snatch your heart out of your goddamn chest!" my father in-law shouted.

I couldn't help but giggle in the backseat. For just a moment, the car was erupting with laughter and we all had forgotten just how ridiculous it all really was. Once again we were told to leave all of our belongings and turn off the engine before exiting. Once we all stepped onto the pavement, we were quickly ushered inside. This was when I got a chance to see what racial profiling was. Both Kyle and my father in-law were treated like they had something to hide. They were treated like straight up criminals. The officers refused to believe that neither one of them had ever had any sort of run in with the law. Hell, my father in-law was a retired police officer himself, so he knew when they were crossing the line in their interrogation-style line of questioning, and he didn't hesitate to call them on it too. It gave me such joy to see that people loved and cared for me so much that they were literally willing to go to war over me. I had never really had that kind of love and protectiveness from anyone, besides my father when he was still alive. Still I found myself eternally grateful that Kyle and his entire family loved me the way they did. Although I really had no idea why that was.

The conversation between my father in-law and the officer continued, as Kyle and I listened intently. At one point it sounded like he had even managed to persuade the officer to let us cross without incident. Just as he was about to hand our ID's back to us and let us go across, the officer who had pulled us in, came in the door and made his way behind the desk. It turns out that he was the same officer who had pulled Christine and I in the day this shit show all began. He recognized me immediately and asked the officer who was talking to us to come to the back for a minute so he could speak with him.

"Can I speak to you for a minute officer Dole?" he asked.

"We'll be right back" the other officer assured us.

I knew right then that it was over. There was no way they were going to let me across now and I was right. As the officer who was assisting us came back in, he had a solemn look on his face. It was one that spoke volumes.

"I'm sorry gentlemen, but her passport has been flagged and she will not be permitted to cross into the US until she satisfies the officer's requests and proves her ties to Canada. I'm really sorry. I'd love to help you guys but it's out of my hands." he told us.

He too looked like he had been defeated in that moment. I wondered what had been said to him in the back room. I didn't know, but one thing I knew for sure was that the other officer was a dick and I was never going to forget his face for as long as I lived.

"Just my luck!" I thought.

I lowered my head and stared at the floor. I didn't want Kyle or his father to see the tears that were flowing endlessly like a river from my eyes. They noticed almost immediately however, and Kyle grabbed me and pulled me into his chest. That just seemed to break open the floodgates even more.

"I'll tell you what," the officer continued. "If she can get these things together that we have listed here." He pointed to the sheet, "I have no doubt in my mind that she will be permitted to cross again. It's just that....well you can see how it looks bad right?" he asked.

A Journey of a Thousand Miles – A Reflections Saga

Both Kyle and his father just nodded in agreement, we thanked him and made our way towards the exit to go back to the car. The drive back to my place seemed endless.

"We will figure something out baby." Kyle assured me as he held me in his arms. "I'll think of a way we can be together. I promise. You believe me right?" he said as he placed his fingers under my chin and lifted my head from his chest to look me in the eyes.

"Yes...I trust you Kyle!" I cried. "It just...it just feels hopeless. They won't let me across anymore no matter what we do!" I told him sounding defeated.

But then like a beacon of light through the storm, I found hope again. Six months into when the whole nightmare began, my mother in-law stepped in. Determined to reunite us and celebrate our love. She planned a family trip to a place that she knew was near and dear to my heart. A place that was a symbol of beauty and unity, to mark our one year wedding anniversary. It was a place I had been wanting to share with Kyle ever since the day we met, and best of all it didn't require me to cross the border. The trip was a dream come true. It was filled with laughter, tears of joy and precious moments with Kyle and our loved ones. My mother in-law chose to stay in the hotel room for most of the trip. I think she just wanted to see us both happy and together again. But those blissful moments were short-lived. As we attempted to cross the border again on our way back, the trauma and anxiety came flooding back. My heart raced, my mind spiralled and my body trembled. I was trapped in a nightmare, reliving the strip search, the attempted fingerprinting and most of all the rejection. The panic attack consumed me, leaving me gasping for air, my vision blurring. Kyle's arms wrapped around me, holding me tight as I sobbed uncontrollably. My mother-in-law's voice was a gentle whisper, reassuring me that I was safe and that I was loved. But in that moment, the border seemed to stretch out before me like an endless and rapid flowing river, a constant reminder of the pain and fear that I couldn't seem to shake.

The days that followed were a blur of tears, anxiety and desperation. I couldn't shake the feeling of being trapped, of being a prisoner of the border and it's cruel restrictions. Kyle's love and support were my lifeline, but even the gentleness of his embrace couldn't chase away the darkness that had settled in my soul. A one point I even contemplated ending it all, and by that I mean I thought about leaving this world. I truly felt like I was losing myself. Like the person I once was had been left behind in the chaos of the attempted border crossings and the bureaucratic red tape. Without Kyle there by my side, the panic attacks came frequently now leaving me gasping for air and trembling with an insurmountable level of fear.

But even in the midst of all of it, Kyle's love remained a steady anchor, holding me and guiding me through the storm. His gentle touch and soothing words brought a calm to my soul, reminding me that I wasn't

Kimberley Hall

244

A Journey of a Thousand Miles – A Reflections Saga

alone and that together we could weather any storm that might blow in our direction. He had become my lighthouse, standing tall and steady in the turbulent waters of my emotions. His love and support shone brighter than the sun, illuminating the darkest corners of my soul and guiding me through the relentless tides of anxiety and fear. With every wave of panic or doubt, he stood firm. Always providing me with calm and reassurance. His gentle words and comforting embrace helped me find my footing on the rocky shores of my heart, and his unwavering belief in me...in us, gave me the strength to keep pushing forward. Step by step. Day by day. One foot in front of the other. Together, we weathered the storms of my PTSD. Kyle's steady presence anchoring me to the present moment and helping me to navigate the treacherous waters of my past. For as long as I could remember, the fear of abandonment, and the belief that I wasn't good enough had haunted me, casting an ominous shadow over my relationships and my very sense of self-worth.

I always felt as if I were walking on thin ice, always waiting for the other shoe to drop, for someone to abuse me, leave me, or reject me. In order to protect my delicate heart, I had developed a defence mechanism and chose to hurt others before they could even have a chance to hurt me. But Kyle was different. He saw beyond my fears and insecurities, and with gentle patience and unwavering love, he helped me navigate the darkness that had muddied my own mind. He showed me that I was enough, that I was worthy of love and acceptance. Not despite my perceived flaws, but because of them. With every tender touch, every reassuring word, and every act of kindness, Kyle chipped away at the walls I had built around my heart all those years ago. He helped me to see that I was not alone, that I was loved and cherished, and to feel safe in knowing that I would never be abandoned by him. He became my safe haven, my rock, my forever home. He was my refuge from the battles that raged within, and with him by my side, I knew I could face whatever lay ahead. And as I let go of my fears and embraced his love, I realized that I had finally found my happily ever after. I had found a love that was not only strong enough to withstand my insecurities and fears, but also gentle enough to heal them. I had found a love that made me feel seen, heard, and loved for who I truly was. I had trekked my way through some of the most unforgiving terrain. It had been a long and winding journey, filled with twists, turns, ups and downs. I faced struggles that tested my resolve, my patience and my perseverance along the way, but I was finally home.

About four or five months had passed since we all took the much needed family vacation, and I finally decided enough was enough. I couldn't stand to be away from Kyle another second. I knew exactly what I needed to do. That day with Christine by my side, I finally found the courage to face my fears and take the leap. We set out early, my heart racing with anticipation and nerves. As we approached the border, my palms grew sweaty and my mind raced with worst-case scenarios. But I was able to calm my nerves by focusing on Kyle. On all that we had endured. With a deep breath, I handed over my documents and stepped forward, my eyes locked in on the image of Kyle's gorgeous face just on the other side of the border. The wait felt infinite, but finally the officer nodded and handed me my papers.

"Enjoy your stay ma'am" he said with a smile.

"Th....Thank you sir!" I said excitedly.

I had done it. I had faced my fears and crossed the border. From the moment Kyle opened the door, his eyes widened in utter disbelief as I emerged from the car, my passport still in my hand. A mix of pride and determination etched across my face. He had grown accustomed to my fears and anxieties, to the countless times I had faltered and doubted myself. But in this moment, he saw something different. He saw a woman who had found her inner strength, who had confronted her demons, and who had emerged victorious. His jaw dropped, and his eyes locked on mine, as he struggled to process the magnitude of what I had just accomplished. The woman he loved, the one who had been held back by her fears for so long, was standing there in front of him. He was shocked, amazed and overwhelmed with pride. Tears of joy and disbelief filled his eyes as he embraced me, holding me tight as if to say, *"I always knew you could do it."* Tears of relief and joy streamed down my face, as I let myself melt into Kyle. Basking in the warmth of his embrace. He had no idea what I had been up to. It was a surprise and I didn't want to get his hopes up if for some reason they turned me back again. But here I was, standing in his kitchen and holding my love. I had conquered a massive hurdle. One that had held me back for far too long. I felt free, empowered, and grateful for the love and support that had carried me through. When I turned the corner to enter the dining room, my mother in-law's face lit up with a mix of shock, joy and disbelief. You would've sworn by the way she reacted that she had just seen a ghost. Her eyes widened, her hands flew to her mouth, and she let out a gasp of amazement.

"Oh my goodness!" she shouted with excitement, tears of happiness welling up in her eyes. "I can't believe you are here! You did it!"

She rushed over to me and wrapped me in a tight embrace. It was one of those forever type of hugs. Like an I never want to let you go type of hug. I could feel her heart overflowing with pride and love for me.

"I always knew you could do it. I'm so proud of you baby girl." she whispered hugging me tighter.

Her reaction was soothing to my soul, a reminder that I had found not only a loving partner but also a supportive and loving family. In that moment I felt grateful for the love and acceptance that surrounded me, and I knew that I was exactly where I belonged.

A Journey of a Thousand Miles – A Reflections Saga

A few years had gone by and Kyle and I were now spending time together on a regular basis. We spent birthdays, holidays and our anniversaries together. There were family get-togethers and plenty of parties. Yet despite all of the moments of contentment that we shared, it became harder and harder to say goodbye to one another. Kyle and I were determined to find a way to bring he and his family to live permanently in Canada. It was clear at this time that we never wanted to have to say goodbye again. We had endured enough heartbreak. We wanted to finally be able to wake up next to one another. To hold one another every night when we went to sleep. As we journeyed on together, the struggles we faced only made our love stronger, more resilient and truly profound. We learned to cherish every moment, to appreciate the beauty in the imperfections and to find joy in the journey we had been on together, and not just the destination we were headed.

The littlest things that most people tend to take for granted in relationships, were moments of pure bliss and celebration for us. Our love became a lighthouse, a testament to the power of true love and its' ability to overcome even the most daunting of obstacles. There were times when the road ahead seemed uncertain, the struggles insurmountable, and when our love had been pushed to the brink of its limits. The very things that most relationships would've never been able to sustain. And yet we held on, to each other, through every storm, every setback, and every moment of doubt that would creep its' ugly head up from time to time. We drew strength from each other, from our love, and from our determination to make it work. There was so much joy and excitement as we looked toward our future. In a year or so, we were planning to start the process for Kyle and his family to move to Canada. Soon we could all be together as one big happy family.

We talked about putting Jaide in the medical program. As long as I had been in her life, she had always told me she wanted to become a doctor. There was no doubt in my mind that she was going to be a great one. That little girl was born to change the world, and though she often didn't think the world of herself, Kyle and I were always going to be there to remind her that we did. The plans were beginning to be set in motion, and finally after years of Kyle and I being separated by borders...we were going to have the chance to bask in our happily ever after. It was just going to be a little while longer. We had to keep telling ourselves that. We were excited and could not wait for that day to arrive.

The weekend finally came and I rushed across the border to be with them all. The boys had been spending the weekend with their fathers, and Kyle and I had made plans to take Jaide to a small amusement park. She was surprised and absolutely thrilled when she saw where we were. The park had roller-coasters, laser tag and lots of fun games to play. The three of us ending up having a blast together. We would've taken the boys that were in Kyle's care too but Kyle was no longer the foster parent to either one of them. Something had happened and Kyle nearly lost Jaide over it. I remember it so vividly...even today. The oldest boy had gotten into a fight at school. He had been quite the little trouble maker, and didn't seem to respect anyone...especially other kids. One day he said something smart to another boy about the boy's mother and let's just say the boy didn't take too kindly to that and had beat him up. He came home that day from school, I had just happened to be there visiting and we noticed he had a mark on his nose and a small bruise under his right eye. Kyle was informed by the school about the incident and grounded him to his room. The two of us proceeded back down to the basement. All of a sudden we could hear him yelling and carrying on upstairs. Kyle went up to address it and sent him back to his room. Apparently the boy had gotten pissed off with Kyle for that and decided to lie and tell child protective services that Kyle had punched him in the nose.

There was an entire investigation opened up, and even though Kyle explained to the caseworker what had happened with the boy at school, she refused to even speak to the school, and was actually going to try and charge him for something he didn't do. They had sent someone out to the home to interview everyone that had been present that day. Despite being told the truth of what had happened, this worker took it upon herself to escalate the matter and the shoddy investigation continued. The boy and his brother were removed from the home, and at one point the caseworker tried to intimidate Kyle by telling him they might take Jaide out of the home too. Kyle was not having it and the next time a caseworker showed up and tried to bully him into signing a confession, he refused and threw her out of the house. The entire thing was unbelievable and yet we lived it. It took months for the investigation to conclude, and eventually Kyle had to go to court. They made sure to give him very little notice of course, and because of that he had no time to find proper representation. He was left with no other option but to represent himself. It was like a modern day witch hunt.

They seemed out to get him at every turn. They had even ignored what the emergency physician had told them after he had examined the boy, which proved Kyle's innocence. I think they were just looking for someone to pin it on to be honest. Needless to say, the judge was appalled by the way Kyle had been treated, and he threw the entire case out. The charges were dropped completely. However, the judge wasn't just going to let what they did to an innocent man slide so easily. He issued a stern warning to child protective services about knocking off the shenanigans.

As much as we all missed the boys, and as hard as Kyle and his mother had tried to care for them, after what we all had just gone through...we all thought it was best that they be placed with someone else. Kyle nearly went to jail over the whole thing and it was enough to shake everyone. After all that had transpired, we all just wanted some semblance of normalcy. Getting out with Jaide was just what we needed. We stayed there at the park for pretty much the whole day, and then headed back home to rest and get out of the sweltering heat. We were all exhausted, and Kyle said it was too hot to cook anything, so we decided that we would order something and he and Jaide would go and pick it up. I stayed behind with Lorraine, which gave us more of a chance to do some more bonding. She and I talked about our own childhoods and all that we had been through. She shared with me just how much of a blessing it had been for everyone to have me around. We talked a bit about Kyle and what had happened with his previous marriage. After she had finished letting me know about her distaste for her ex daughter in-law, she leaned in toward me.

"I knew from the day I met you that the two of you were meant for each other. I've never seen him so happy. Thank you for loving him the way that you do. I have no doubt that you will take care of them always and I know they will be safe and happy with you in Canada." she said smiling.

"Huh? What do you mean, Ma? You're all coming to Canada. Not just Kyle and Jaide." I reassured her.

She leaned in a little closer and took my hand in hers. "No baby...I'm not coming." she told me.

What the hell did she mean she wasn't coming? Of course she was coming! We all wanted her there and Kyle and Jaide would never even think of leaving her behind. Neither would I for that matter. I didn't understand where any of this was coming from. It all seemed so sudden. Her words sounded so certain. They sent a chill down my spine. It was if she knew something that I didn't. Had Kyle and her discussed this? Up until now, the plan had always been that all three of them would come to live in Canada with me and the boys. Why was she suddenly excluding herself? I decided to shake it off. At least until I had a chance to discuss it with Kyle. Maybe he would be able to get to the bottom of it.

That night, the four of us ate dinner together and then Kyle and I sat up with Lorraine sharing a nightcap. It was always one of my favourite things to do together, because we all got to share stories and just reminisce about the past. Lorraine had bought a few different types of alcohol for us to try, but on this particular night we chose to go with the Apple Pie Moonshine. I was definitely excited about it because this would be the first time I had a chance to try it. It was absolutely delicious but potent as hell. One of those drinks you could easily get drunk on because it tasted so innocent. Jaide had gone to bed and the four of us were seated there at the dining room table sharing several funny stories. I especially enjoyed the ones that pertained to Kyle in his younger years. One in particular that stood out to me was that when he was a baby, his father had gotten drunk and almost laid right on top of Kyle after he had passed out. Kyle's mother walked in to find baby Kyle looking annoyed and using his tiny arms to hold his father up who was fast asleep. He looked at his mother as if to say,

"Get this muthafucka off of me!" Lorraine chuckled as she got to that point.

Then she went on to tell me about the time Kyle as a little baby had gotten all of the items together to change his own diaper. She found him laying there on the floor fastening the tabs. He had actually managed to change himself. She had so many funny stories to share about him growing up, and I was completely fascinated by them all. Kyle seemed to be some sort of super human. He definitely wasn't like any other typical child that age. From that moment on...he became my Superman. Jaide and his mother had always seen him that way and now I was beginning to as well.

A Journey of a Thousand Miles – A Reflections Saga

Things couldn't have been going better between Kyle and I. It seemed the universe had finally conspired to bring us together again, and we were going to be sure to make the most of it. Once we finished up with our bonding over stories, we all decided to call it a night and head to bed. I waited until Kyle and I were alone in his room and then I told him about the bizarre conversation Lorraine and I had earlier that day.

"It was so strange Kyle. You should've seen her face. She was dead serious and adamant that she would not be coming with you guys to Canada." I told him, feeling a bit concerned.

"I'm sure that's not what she meant by it. I'll talk to her tomorrow about it baby." he reassured me.

"Okay baby, but I just hope that she didn't say all of that because she feels like a burden to us or something. I can't even imagine her not coming with us. She's not a burden at all. I get the impression that she feels like she's stepping on toes or something and that is not the case at all!" I continued.

"Don't worry baby! I'll talk to her and make sure she understands that she is part of our life and she always will be. She's not a burden at all and I'm gonna make sure she knows that. Now come here and let me hold you already." he whispered.

I felt his arms reaching for me across the mattress. He wrapped his arm around my waist and pulled me into him. Then he propped himself up on one elbow and leaned over for a kiss.

"It'll be okay baby. Everything will be okay." he reassured me.

I nuzzled into his chest and breathed in his intoxicating manly scent.

"I love you baby." I whispered softly.

"I love you too baby." he replied.

At this point I was feeling the buzz from the alcohol we had consumed. We both were and there was only one way to solve the need that we both felt in that moment. I leaned into Kyle, my hand tracing the curve of his jaw, my fingers grazing his skin with a tender touch. Our lips met in a kiss that spoke volumes of our desire. Our hearts beating as one. The world around us just melted away, leaving only the two of us, lost in the depths of our passion for one another. Every moment was a promise, every touch a vow of forever. It was just the two of us there, lost in each other's eyes. Our love a flame that burned brighter with each passing moment.

We began to move together in perfect harmony, our bodies swaying to the rhythm of our love, and as our lips met once again, I felt my soul soar...leaving my body behind. It was as if our love had transcended the physical realm, becoming a force that connected us on a deeper level. Time stood still, and all that existed was the two of us, lost in the expanse of our passion. It was truly an out of body experience, one that left us both breathless and yearning for more. Every moment with Kyle was a journey, deep into the unknown. An exploration of the uncharted territories of our love. In Kyle's arms, there was always the feeling of floating, as if I were on a sea of pure bliss. Our love was a symphony of sighs, whispers, and tender touches. A sweet serenade that echoed through every fibre of my being. It was a fantasy I never wanted to wake up from. Kyle and I alway had a way of making love that defied the physical boundaries of the physical world. Our bodies entwined, our hearts still racing together as one. Our souls had taken flight, and were slowly beginning to descend back down from the cosmos. Our love making was like a psychedelic journey that transcended both time and space. Every moment we shared together, wrapped up in one another was a profound and explosive union, a fusion of our very essence. Once our soul dance had come back down to Earth, we snuggled closely.

Our bodies still entwined, we both drifted off into a deep sleep. But even in slumber, our souls would continue their journey. Meeting in the astral realm, where our love would continue to explore the depths of the universe. There in the astral realm, our souls danced among the stars, our love shining brighter than any celestial body. We explored the vast expanse of the universe, our hearts filled with wonder and our spirits with joy. We visited distant worlds, meeting ancient beings, and uncovered hidden secrets of the cosmos. And when we returned to our physical bodies, we both woke up with a sense of peace and connection, our love stronger and more profound than ever.

Kyle and I both knew that our love was not just an earthly bond, but a cosmic connection that transcended any and all boundaries. That evening as we were both transported to the astral, at one point Kyle and I had gotten separated. One minute we were dancing among the stars and the next it was like someone reached in and yanked me to another location. This was a place I definitely had never been before. I was outside somewhere. The surroundings were really quite pleasant. There before me stood a grey and blue two story house. The house looked a bit old and a tad run down, but it seemed to add to its character. There were light grey shutters on the windows and an old wooden porch that looked like it could use a bit of love. I could smell the very distinct scent of pies and cookies as they permeated the air and wafted into my nostrils.

"Mmmm something smells yummy." I said aloud. As I began to make my way up the porch steps, I was interrupted by the sound of Emily's voice calling my name off in the distance.

"Ava....hey there how's it going?" she asked.

"Really well! Kyle and I finally got those border issues resolved and can now spend all the time we want together now." I told her.

"Oh that's great! I knew eventually you would learn the lesson." she told me.

I wondered what she meant by that statement, but I figured that would be a conversation for a later date. I wanted to get down to business as to why I was brought there to the house. As I stood there outside the house, taking it all in, Emily came and stood beside me. Her skin radiating with a soft, ethereal glow and her eyes shining with knowledge.

"Why have I been brought here? I asked her, my voice barely a whisper.

A Journey of a Thousand Miles – A Reflections Saga

"There is someone inside who needs your help." she replied in a soft and gentle voice. "A grandmother figure wise and kind. She has been waiting for you."

I felt a surge of curiosity, my heart beating with anticipation.

"Who is she?" I asked, but Emily just smiled.

"You will know when you meet her." she said. "Trust in the universe, trust in yourself!"

With that, she vanished, leaving me alone standing there outside of the house. I took a deep breath, feeling a sense of purpose wash over me. I knew I had to go inside, to meet this grandmother figure and help her with anything she needed me to. It was my destiny. I had been called here for a reason. As I took a deep breath and swallowed hard, I pulled the door open slowly toward me and stepped into the entrance-way. A warm light enveloped me. The house was old, but it felt alive. I could feel that the walls were infused with love and laughter. I turned to my right and walked down the hallway, my feet bare and silent on the creaky floorboards. As I came to the end of it, I turned to my left. That's when I saw her. She was sitting there in a rocking chair, her eyes fixed on me with some sort of deep wisdom. She smiled, and her face lit up with a gentle grace.

"Welcome child," she said, her voice like a soft breeze on a summer day. "I have been waiting for you."

I felt a sense of peace wash over me, as if I had finally come home. It was odd though because this was the first time I had ever seen this place.

"Who are you?" I asked, my voice barely above a whisper.

"Never you mind that now child. Just know that I am da guardian of this house." she replied, her eyes twinkling with secrets. "And you my dear, are da key to all of it." she whispered. "Come, come with me child. I could use some help here in da bedroom."

I followed her down another hallway on the opposite side of the house, and into a large bedroom. My heart began to beat with curiosity again. The room was cozy, with a large bed, a nightstand on the left hand side as well as a small antique dresser with a lamp resting on the top of it. I also took notice of a patchwork quilt on the bed, that seemed to shimmer in the dim light. The grandmother figure walked over to the bed and gestured for me to come and sit down beside her.

"I need your help." she said, her eyes serious. "Someone is coming soon, someone who will need our guidance and support." she paused, her eyes locked on mine now. "A female in Kyle's family is going to be crossing over soon, and she will need our help to transition peacefully."

I felt a surge of shock and sadness, but the grandmother figure's calm demeanour reassured me.

"We must prepare da way for her!" she said, her voice soft but urgent. "We must create a safe space for her to let go and move on. She's not going to be too happy when she gets here...not at all."

She took my hand in hers, her grip warm and comforting.

"Will you help me, child?" she asked, her eyes shining with a deep and ancient wisdom.

Kimberley Hall

A Journey of a Thousand Miles – A Reflections Saga

"Of course I'll help!" I told her.

The grandmother figure smiled and winked at me.

"I knew I could count on you!" she said. "We must work quickly now, for time is short. She is a stubborn soul, and she will need our guidance to let go of her earthly world." she stood up, her movements graceful and fluid. "Come now, let us prepare da room. We must create a sanctuary for her spirit."

Together, we worked in silence, our movements synchronized as we smoothed the quilt, lit candles and brewed a soothing tea. The room was transformed into a peaceful oasis, a haven for this female relative's journey. Once we were finished, the grandmother figure turned to me, her eyes shining with an even deeper wisdom.

"It is done." she said. "Now we wait."

As we waited, I could feel the energy in the room begin to shift. The air was thick with anticipation, and I knew that this female who would be crossing over soon was very close. The grandmother figure took my hand in hers again. "Remember child..." she said, her voice low and soothing. "This is a sacred moment. We are here to guide her home."

Suddenly, the room filled with a bright light, and I felt a presence standing behind me. I turned to see the female and gasped in utter disbelief. Her eyes were fixed on me with a deep sadness. The grandmother figure stood up, her arms open wide.

"Welcome, dear one!" she said, her voice again like a gentle breeze. "We are here to guide you home."

The female took a step forward, her eyes locked on mine. And in that moment I knew, that our journey was far from over.

As I stepped outside, it felt like someone had gut punched me in the stomach. All of the air felt like it had been sucked out of me. I needed to find Kyle. I focused in on his face in the hopes that I would be transported back to where we were last together. It worked, but Kyle was nowhere in sight. I searched for him, my heart racing with urgency. I had to find him. I had to tell him about what I had just witnessed. I needed to tell him about the grandmother's words. As I continued to frantically search for him, I felt a gentle tap on my shoulder. As I whipped around to see who it was, I nearly bumped heads with her.

"Emily! What are you doing here? Oh my God Emily, I have to find Kyle! I have to tell him about what I saw. He needs to know she's going to die. They all do!" I shouted.

"You will have plenty of time for that. But right now, I need to tell you something Ava. You may remember some of what you saw and heard here, but you will not remember who it was." she told me.

"What?! What the hell do you mean? Of course I'm going to remember! How could I not? This is going to break them all. Jaide, Kyle, his mother, sister...just everyone. I'm definitely not going to forget something like this!" I shouted.

A Journey of a Thousand Miles – A Reflections Saga

Emily turned her head and looked down at the ground.

"I'm sorry Ava, but that's not how this works this time. In this case, as soon as you leave here...you *ARE* going to forget almost everything. You may remember a few details but not who it was. Eventually, this will all come to make sense though." she assured me.

She leaned in and gave me a big hug.

"It'll be alright. Just prepare them all." then she walked away and disappeared into thin air again.

I hated how she was always doing things like that. She was always showing up, saying cryptic shit and then just leaving me there to digest it all. Like why even bother to say anything at all? I swear she had sadistic tendencies sometimes. It was almost as if she enjoyed the mindfuckery of it all. Even though she was often cryptic, she always turned out to be right. I absolutely hated that part too.

I decided it might be best to wait a bit before I told Kyle about my experience in the astral the night before. I was still trying to process the whole thing myself. Later that afternoon when we were finally alone, I decided that I should talk to him about it. I looked into his eyes, my heart heavy with a secret. I knew I had to tell him. I needed to share not only the experience, but also what had been revealed to me.

"Kyle, baby, I need to tell you something." I told him, my voice barely above a whisper. "Something happened last night. Something that will change everything."

His eyes narrowed, a hint of concern etched across his face.

"What is it baby?" he asked, his voice soft but concerned.

I took a deep breath, the words sticking in the back of my throat.

"Someone is leaving. I mean...they are going home....as in...they are going to die." I began, my eyes locked on his. "Someone whose passing will cause great sorrow." I lowered my head.

Kyle's eyes searched mine, a mix of confusion and fear in his own. I knew there wasn't much more I could reveal. At least not yet anyway. Emily was right. I didn't remember much more than what I had just shared with him. All I knew was that I had to prepare him. I had to prepare all of them.

"I can't remember all of the details, but it's a female on your side of the family. Her death will be unexpected and shocking. It's going to rip the family apart, but I need you to know one thing. When she passes on, I was there to greet her on the other side." I told him.

For some reason, I felt compelled to tell him that. It was important that he knew that.

"And you can't remember who it is that's leaving?" he asked inquisitively.

"No. I'm sorry! I thought I would remember, but as soon as I got back in body, that part was gone!" I replied, frustrated.

"Well...What else can you tell me? Maybe I might be able to figure it out based on something you saw or heard." he suggested.

"Yeah okay. Maybe you're right. Let's see now. I was in a house with someone who I'm going to assume was your grandmother or something like that. She was definitely a grandmother figure. We were in this house, and she asked me to help her prepare for this female's arrival. I remember that we had to have this special quilt on the bed too. She said it would offer this female who would be crossing over soon...*some* comfort. She said that this female wasn't going to be very happy upon her arrival." I explained.

Kyle and I were not able to determine who it was at the time, but we did manage to narrow it down to two people. It was either his great grandmother who everyone often referred to as Big Mama or a woman named Tina who had been the paternal grandmother to his sister and had come to see Kyle as her grandchild too. She had come to spend a great deal of time with Kyle and the two of them grew very close. She was one of the reasons why Kyle enjoyed baking so much. She was also a very loving and caring woman. She helped out at the local community centre, cooking and serving meals to underprivileged children. Tina always put a lot of love into everything she made. including her food. Nothing was ever done halfheartedly. Kyle's mother, Lorraine had even patterned herself after Tina quite a bit, so although I never had the pleasure to know this woman, I felt like somehow I already did. Kyle and I went back and forth between the two women, but we couldn't seem to settle on a definitive conclusion. Perhaps the grandmother figure I had met in the astral, was an amalgamation of the two. We racked our brains trying to figure out who the female that was passing on might be, but we couldn't seem to figure that out either. A few weeks later, we would receive a phone call that would finally put our confusion to rest.

Chapter Thirty-Two

It was a Saturday afternoon. Kyle, Jaide and I were sitting together in the living room, watching a movie. Kyle and I were snuggled up together in our favourite chair, and Jaide was seated on the carpet next to us. Despite there being plenty of furniture to sit on, she always seemed to want to be as close to us as possible. I always thought that was so precious. It was as if she could feel the love between us and it just drew her in. We seemed to have that effect on everyone in our presence for some reason. I guess there was just something about the two of us together that made others who were around us, happy. Even early on in our relationship, people often mistook us for being a married couple. Maybe it was that perfect level of complete comfort that we shared with one another. It just seemed to be felt by everyone.

The three of us were sitting there, our eyes glued to the TV. We were all so completely lost in the story line of the film, that we almost didn't even hear the telephone ringing on the table right beside us. Then it was as if we were all suddenly drawn away at the same time. It was as if we knew this was an important call. After a few more rings, Kyle leaned over to answer the phone, but noticed that Lorraine must have answered from her room at the same time. We all went back to watching the movie, and thinking nothing more of it. After about twenty minutes or so, Lorraine came into the living room. A look of shock and disbelief on her face. I stared at her intently as she stood there, trying to study her face and read her non verbal cues. There appeared to be a deep sadness hidden in the depths of her eyes. Something was wrong. I could feel my own heart begin to race and my palms grow sweaty as we all braced for the news she was preparing herself to share.

"I...I just can't believe she's gone." she began, her voice trailing off as she uttered the word "gone."

"What Ma? Who's gone?" Kyle asked, sounding almost panicked.

"Your cousin Vivian!" she replied narrowing her eyes to the floor.

"What?! What do you mean she's gone? Where did she go?" Kyle continued.

"She's dead Kyle. I was just talking to your aunt Mae. Vivian is gone!"

For a moment, there was nothing but an eerie silence that filled the room as the shock of the news began to set in. It was completely unexpected for everyone. Vivian was only seventeen years old! She was the adopted daughter of one of Kyle's aunts.

"What happened?!!" Jaide blurted out.

"I don't know all of the details of that yet baby. All I know is your aunt Mae said she had been complaining of a really bad headache. She went to her room to lay down and then she just....died. Aunt Mae found her this morning." Lorraine explained. "I just can't believe this. I need to call everyone."

She rushed out of the room and back in the direction of her bedroom. Jaide was so upset. We all were but Kyle and I were trying our best to console her. As she sat on Kyle's lap and cried on his shoulder, Kyle and exchanged a look with each other that seemed to say, *"I guess now we know who the female was"*. Vivian' death came as a massive shock to the family. Everyone attended her funeral except for me. Hell, I hadn't even met everyone yet, and I sure wasn't going to feel comfortable doing it on these terms. I mean how comfortabl would you have felt if your loved one had just passed and now here was this strange woman whom you had never even met before, offering you condolences? Kyle and I agreed that it would be best to let me meet them al on more positive and lighthearted terms.

A Journey of a Thousand Miles – A Reflections Saga

I decided that I was going to spend the remainder of the summer with Kyle, Lorraine and Jaide. The boys had been away for the whole summer with their fathers and there would be nothing left for me to do back home. Weeks of sadness passed, but eventually everyone seemed to be processing their grief in a healthy way and things were slowly getting back to normal. Kyle received a sudden and unexpected phone call from his nephew Bradley, who had moved away and was living in Georgia with his wife and children at the time. Kyle had not heard from him in years and he seemed to be happy to be able to catch up with him. He was excited to be able to fill Bradley in on the latest events of his life. He told him that he and I had gotten married, and that he couldn't wait for him to meet me someday. I was definitely looking forward to it. At this point, Kyle and I had been married for nearly four years and I still had yet to meet his best friend Dexter. A man I had been dying to meet ever since Kyle and I first got together.

Dexter had been the one to convince Kyle to hang in there, when Kyle was going to stop talking to me because I had told him I felt like I needed to explore things with Kevin all those years ago. Dexter had told Kyle that things weren't going to work out between Kevin and I, and that he and I were going to end up together. He even saw us getting married and living happily ever after. Thankfully, he had managed to talk some sense into him because had it not been for him constantly being in Kyle's ear and reassuring him that everything was going to work out, Kyle and I never would've ended up together. We never would've had the chance to experience the love that we had. I felt like I owed Dexter so much. Kyle had told me so much about him, how they were like brothers and he told me just how much they had been through together. Both men had been in each other's weddings, and even became the godfathers to each other's children. It was very clear to me early on just how much Dexter meant to Kyle, and loving Kyle as much as I did, I was eager to meet the infamous character who had played such a vital role in my husband's life. The hardest part about meeting him though, was that Dexter lived so far away. Years ago he had moved away with his wife and children to South Carolina. He still had family left in Michigan though, so he came to visit at least a few times a year. Yet somehow, I always seemed to just miss him. Eventually I would meet this mystery man. I had no doubt about that.

A few months after Kyle had received the call from Bradley, we all became aware that Bradley and his family were not doing so well in Georgia. They were facing homelessness, so Kyle and Lorraine decided that it would be best for everyone if they came to stay with us for awhile in Michigan. The plans were made and in a few weeks time, they would be coming to join us in our home. Kyle and I decided that we would go back to Canada and celebrate our fourth wedding anniversary with my side of the family.

Shortly after our arrival, we all decided to meet up at a local pub to share some drinks and sing some karaoke. We had only been back in Canada for about a week or so when Kyle had gotten a phone call from

A Journey of a Thousand Miles – A Reflections Saga

Lorraine back in the US. He broke the news to me that he, Lorraine and Jaide needed to fly out to Georgia as soon as possible. They needed to help Bradley and his family get packed for the move to Michigan. Apparently they were being evicted from their home and needed to be out as soon as possible. I was a bit upset with this news because Kyle told me that I would not be able to go with them, as there wouldn't be enough room and we couldn't afford the extra plane ticket at the time.

As soon as we returned to Michigan, the three of them packed for the trip and left the next morning for Georgia. I stayed behind with Kyle's cousin J'Von. I had only met him once or twice up to this point, so things seemed to be a bit awkward at first. Eventually though, we managed to hit it off very well. As much as I enjoyed getting to know J'Von, those three or four days without Kyle by my side seemed like an eternity. The time seemed to pass by at a snail's pace and I missed him exceedingly. I felt like I was living in an eternal loop of the movie Groundhog Day. It just felt so odd to fall asleep every night without him there to hold me. I tried to keep myself distracted with social media, phone calls with friends and family and I began to sleep a lot too. But no matter what I did to take my mind off of Kyle, the thoughts of him wouldn't leave me. Like a thief in the night, his absence had came and stolen my joy. My happiness. Despite J'Von being in that house with me, I had never felt more alone. As I stood in the empty silence of our home, the weight of Kyle's absence began to crush me like a boulder. The shadows on the walls seemed to mock me, reminding me of the laughter and joy that was now missing. Every room felt like a cold, dark cave, devoid of the warmth and light that Kyle's presence always brought.

The silence was deafening, a constant reminder that my partner, my best friend, and my soulmate was thousands of miles away. I felt like a part of me had been ripped away, leaving a gaping hole that seemed impossible to fill.

The loneliness was suffocating, a heavy blanket that wrapped around my heart and squeezed tight. Every breath felt like a struggle, as if the air itself was thick with the weight of my sorrow. I felt like I was drowning in a sea of despair, unable to find a lifeline to cling to. Even the thought of J'Von's presence in the next room felt like a cruel mockery, a reminder that I was stuck here, alone and adrift, while Kyle was living his best life without me. The pain was a constant ache, a throbbing wound that refused to heal. In that moment, I felt like I was losing myself, like I was disappearing into the darkness of my own despair. The world outside seemed to fade away, leaving only the bleak and barren landscape of my own broken heart. But then, like a ray of sunshine breaking through the clouds, I finally got to speak with Kyle. His voice on the phone was like music to my ears, a sweet melody that soothed my heart and lifted my spirits. We talked for hours, our conversation a lifeline that connected us across miles. But as the hours ticked by, my depression deepened, and I felt like I was losing my connection to the spiritual world. I couldn't hear my guides anymore, and I felt like they had abandoned me. The silence was heart wrenching. I felt like I was walking through a forest without a map or a compass. I was lost and alone, drifting on the stormy seas without an anchor. I cried out for help, but my voice was swallowed by the void. I felt like I was drowning in my own despair, and I didn't know how to keep my head above water.

J'Von, Kyle's cousin, tried to comfort me, his kind words and gentle presence brought a sense of calm to my soul. He listened patiently as I poured out my heart, my tears, and my fears. He offered me a sympathetic ear and a comforting embrace. We became closer, our bond strengthening with each passing day. We spent hours talking, sharing stories, and supporting each other through the ups and downs of life. I found myself opening up to him in ways I never thought possible, and he did the same.

But it was when I started receiving messages from beyond the veil that our connection deepened in ways I never could've imagined. I began to sense the presence of his deceased fiancee, and I could feel her love and devotion to him still strong. I shared with him the messages I received, and he was amazed at the details I was able to reveal. I told him things about his fiancee that I couldn't possibly have known, things that only he knew. I described her personality, her quirks, and her love for him in ways that brought tears to his eyes.

It wasn't just his fiancee that I was able to pick up on. I also began to receive messages about J'Von himself. Things that he had never shared with me before. I knew about his fears, his dreams, and his desires, and I was able to offer him guidance and support in ways that he never thought possible.

Our connection had transcended the physical realm, and we had entered a realm of spiritual understanding and connection. We had become spiritual siblings, connected at the soul level. And as we continued to support each other, I realized that our connection was not just limited to this lifetime. We had known each other before, in past lives. It was obvious.

As I slowly began to come back to myself with the help of J'Von, I heard a faint whisper in my mind. It was the soft and gentle voice of Emily, reminding me that she was always with me, even when I couldn't hear her. She told me that I was never alone, that I was loved and supported, and that I would get through this. Her words became the lifeline I clung to. A reminder that although I had felt as if I were adrift on a stormy sea at times, I was being guided, even when I couldn't feel it. That brought me a great sense of relief. It also brought greater clarity for me on how certain levels of stress or deep sadness brought me to such heightened emotions, that I could switch off the spiritual world in a heartbeat. I knew that this was definitely something I would work on again...and again.

A Journey of a Thousand Miles – A Reflections Saga

After four long days, like a dream come true, Kyle returned. Seeing him walk through the door, his smile lighting up the room, was like a ray of sunshine breaking through the clouds once again. I felt like I was home again, like I was finally where I belonged. We embraced, our hearts beating as one, and our love shining brighter than ever before. In that moment, I knew that I was never alone. That Kyle would always be there to comfort me, to support me, and to love me. And with J'Von's kindness, Kyle's love, and my guides' guidance, I knew that I could face anything life threw in front of us.

As we finally pulled back and stood there gazing into each other's eye, I knew that I would never let him go again. I would hold onto this man forever, through thick and thin, through good times and bad. We were two souls, destined to be together, and nothing could ever change that.

"Come upstairs baby." Kyle whispered as he peered into my soul. "I want you to meet the family."

Bradley and his wife had six children. It was about to be a houseful. I was just thrilled to see that everyone had arrived home safely. This was going to be great. Lorraine seemed happy. Her heart was full. It seemed to bring her so much joy to have everyone safe, happy and together again. She was especially fond of having her great grandchildren there with all of us. Although the house was going to be overcrowded for awhile, we knew that we would all find a way to make it work.

Eventually though, things began to crumble. Bradley and his wife's representatives had left the building. We were beginning to see their true colours, slowly seeping through the cracks of the facade they had fooled everyone with. It honestly should've come as no surprise to any of us. When they had first arrived, the children were absolutely filthy. They appeared as if they hadn't been bathed in weeks. It was so bad that after the final child had been bathed, there was a thick, black ring around the tub and Kyle ended up having to bleach it. Despite their appearance, we all chose to give Bradley and his wife the benefit of the doubt and had chalked it up to them just not being able to bathe them in the last couple of days. We should've known better.

The two of them were becoming quite lazy. They didn't even bother to cook for their own children. Kyle, his mother and I were having to prepare meals for the entire household every single night. If we didn' feed them, the children would not eat. We always made sure they were fed first. Some of them even appeared to be quite malnourished. Lorraine also made sure that they were all bathed every night and even went to buy them all new clothes and toys. She was just that kind of woman. So loving and caring...especially when it came to children.

From the stories that Kyle had shared with me, Lorraine was always caring for other people's children. She could always be found raising one family member or another. I absolutely adored her love, kindness and compassion. She reminded me so much of myself in that way. As a child, I would often take in stray animals, she was doing that with people. She despised the system, and never wanted to see any child end up in foster care or living on the streets. She always went above and beyond to ensure that people had everything they needed. She would probably even give you the shirt off her back. Both she and Kyle were humanitarians at heart. Kyle had even given Bradley a car. He wanted to make sure that Bradley and his family could come and go as they needed to. Both he and Lorraine tried to do whatever they could to help them. I think that them having small children and of course being family, had a great deal to do with their generosity. But that generosity seemed to go unnoticed, or shall I say unappreciated. It was as if Bradley and his wife Lisa had come to expect everything. I don't even remember a simple word of gratitude being uttered.

Eventually, things had gotten out of hand and a decision needed to be made. It turns out that Bradley, had been keeping drugs in the house. He and Lisa had also started drinking almost every night and there were lots of arguments between the two of them. The environment was quickly becoming toxic. It was all just became too much. They disrespected the household and had even put their own children in danger. One of the children had gotten hold of some weed gummies and ended up having to be hospitalized. Bradley and his wife didn't even help with cleaning the house, nor did they even bother to pick up after themselves, or their children. It was all weighing heavily on both Kyle and Lorraine. They were both stressed beyond belief.

Even though it broke her heart, she knew it needed to happen this way. She and Kyle made the decision and then sat down with Bradley and Lisa to explain why they had both come to making such a difficult choice. Both Bradley and his wife were told that it wasn't working out having them and the children there in the house anymore, and that it would be better for everyone if they moved out as soon as possible. They were now beginning to bring trouble to the doorstep and we couldn't have that.

When the two of them packed up with the children and moved out, I don't remember a single thank you from either one of them. It was as if they were so angry, they had forgotten all that Kyle and Lorraine had done for them. How much help they were given. There was just no respect on their end.

Shortly after they had left, Kyle's cousin J'Von called and asked if it would be okay for him to come and stay for awhile. We were all pretty weary, given all that had recently transpired during our best efforts to help someone. Kyle and his mother talked about it, and eventually gave in.

Having J'Von around was much different than when we had Bradley and his family stay with us. J'Von was always looking to help out around the house any way he could. He was a welcome addition to our home. Kyle and I would sit up and talk with him about spirituality, the universe and all things metaphysical. That four day period that J'Von and I spent together, we became like brother and sister. He even referred to me as his little sis.

Over the period of a few weeks or so, the three of us grew closer and we all spent a great deal of time together. Time ticked by faster and faster, and next thing I know, it was time for me to leave and head back to my temporary home again. I was sad to go. We had all had so much fun together. Sharing laughs, stories and intellectual conversation. I was definitely going to miss them all. It wasn't goodbye though...just I'll see you soon. Lorraine absolutely hated anyone saying those words. She believed it brought bad luck, as it seemed so finite. Up to the point she had shared that with me, I never even bothered to look at it that way. She was right! Never say goodbye.

Kyle and I were still regularly crossing the border for visits every weekend. However, shortly after my return home, I was faced with a health issue that required surgery to remove gallstones. Kyle kindly stayed with me at my mother's for a week, ensuring that I was recovering well.

A few months later, I woke up with a numb hand, unable to grip anything. Initially, I wasn't concerned but as the days passed, I began to grow worried. We tried medication and a brace, but they didn't help at all. Further testing revealed a trapped nerve in my elbow, causing pain, numbness, and tingling. I urgently needed surgery to restore hand function, essential for my profession, and to prevent muscle wastage.

The surgery took over a year to happen, and the recovery was painful. I had to return to the hospital shortly after due to a bandage that had been wrapped too tightly and that was beginning to cut off circulation which only exacerbated the pain. I was helpless, with my arm in a sling for eight long weeks, relying on others for basic tasks like washing my hair or dressing. I also needed help bathing and showers were not permitted.

Kyle and my mother-in-law were invaluable in my recovery. I fondly remember a humorous moment when my mother in-law accidentally sprayed water on my face while washing my hair in the kitchen sink causing us all to share a good laugh. Despite my usual independence, I struggled deeply with being at the mercy of others, but I will say that their support made a world of difference.

As I struggled with the helplessness imposed by the surgery, frustration and irritability took hold. Kyle however, remained patient and full of optimism. Continually reminding me that this was only going to be a temporary setback. Yet, I couldn't shake off the feeling of being a burden, ingrained in me since childhood. We were taught to be self-sufficient and to solve our own problems, making it hard for me to accept any help.

A Journey of a Thousand Miles – A Reflections Saga

When the cast finally came off, we expected relief, but instead, my arm was frozen in place, and the pain only intensified. The immobility had taken its toll, and regaining mobility was a slow, frustrating and painful process. To our surprise, physical therapy wasn't covered, and we couldn't afford it. Kyle however, was undeterred. Together he and I found online resources and worked together to restore my range of motion.

Unfortunately, the surgery didn't completely alleviate my nerve condition, leaving me wondering if the prolonged trapping or post surgery wrapping incompetency had caused further damage. Despite the uncertainty, I chose to accept my new normal and avoid risking further surgery unless absolutely necessary. Kyle and I decided to prioritize my well-being, opting not to gamble with my health. This experience reinforced my wariness of surgery, a sentiment that had lingered for both of us long after the hysterectomy from hell.

Three months after my recovery, I finally returned to work, but my confidence had taken a hit. My mobility and sensory perception were still impaired on my dominant side, making it challenging to perform tasks with ease. Additionally, I faced issues with a new coworker who had joined the company less than a year ago. One Saturday morning, I attempted to offer him some constructive feedback on his performance and professionalism, particularly regarding patient interactions. However, he became aggressive and hostile, approaching me in the back room with clenched fists and yelling. I feared for my safety, and the incident left me shaken.

I reported the incident to my boss, who had me file a formal report — a first for me. I assumed the situation would be handled, but unfortunately, that wasn't the case. The experience was a stark reminder that my concerns weren't being taken seriously, and I began to question my personal safety in the workplace. The incident also raised concerns about the coworker's fitness for duty, given his history of mistakes and alleged drug use. The situation was far from resolved, and I felt uneasy about what might happen next.

A few days later, my boss summoned me to an early meeting, joined by the assistant manager and the contentious coworker. I was completely floored by the unfolding scenario. To my dismay, I was subjected to a performance evaluation and placed on three months' probation. I felt compelled to quit, right there on the spot, but I chose to maintain my professionalism despite the situation. The rationale behind questioning my character and allowing the man I had accused to be present during my evaluation remains unclear to this day. This experience left me walking on eggshells, transforming me from a once dedicated and enthusiastic colleague to a withdrawn and detached individual. I became a shell of my former self, merely going through the motions. In hindsight, leaving might have been the better option, but my passion for my work kept me rooted there. The fact that my coworker's unacceptable behaviour was tolerated while I faced such intense scrutiny remains a lingering astonishment.

A Journey of a Thousand Miles – A Reflections Saga

Up until that point, I had looked forward to coming to work. However, the incident with my coworker that day had changed everything. I no longer felt the same enthusiasm and camaraderie with my colleagues. They no longer seemed like family. They became strangers to me again. The only bright spot was the interactions I still had with my patients. I had decided to adopt a new approach- simply go to work, do my job and leave.

A couple of months passed, and things finally seemed to be settling down at work. Then, one day, my phone buzzed in my pocket while I was in the middle of a procedure. I couldn't answer immediately, but as soon as I had a chance, I checked the caller ID and saw Kyle's number. My heart skipped a beat. I knew that he wouldn't be calling me at work unless it was urgent.

I asked my boss if I could take an early lunch to make an important phone call. She agreed, and I made my way to the staff room, my mind racing with worst-case scenarios. As soon as I closed the door, my phone rang again. I answered, and Kyle's voice was laced with concern.

"What's wrong baby?" I asked, my hands trembling.

"It's Ma," he replied, his voice heavy with sadness.

"She had her doctor's appointment today, and they think...they're pretty sure it's lung cancer."

My world stopped in that moment, and I felt like I was being pulled into a sea of fear and uncertainty.

"Oh my God, Kyle! Are you serious? How did they confirm it's cancer?" I asked, my voice laced with disbelief and concern.

I was in shock, knowing that Lorraine had a spot on her lung that had been monitored for a year, but was told it was nothing to worry about. I had always thought she should have pushed for more answers. *We* should have!

When I read the initial report, I felt uneasy about the vague language used to describe the small mass detected in her right lung. Lorraine had struggled with COPD for years, a result of her time working in factories without proper protective equipment or safety measures. It seemed like a ticking time bomb for anyone's health.

"We'll get through this baby," I said, trying to sound reassuring. "She'll be alright. What did the doctor recommend next?" I asked, still trying to process the news.

"She needs surgery," Kyle replied. "They want to run some more tests before scheduling the procedure."

"Don't worry, they'll get it all baby," I told him, trying to sound confident in that statement. "Tell Ma I love her okay? I have to go, but I'll call you as soon as I'm done work. I love you."

"I love you too baby. Talk to you soon," Kyle replied before we hung up.

A Journey of a Thousand Miles – A Reflections Saga

Holy shit! The news caught me completely off-guard. It shook me to my core, I couldn't even think about putting any food in my stomach. I was afraid I might vomit. After Kyle and I hung up, I just remained seated there in the chair. Trying to gather my thoughts and reel in my emotions, and for the first time in a very long time, I began to pray.

Later that night, after Kyle and I had carried on a conversation regarding the days events and the latest news on Lorraine, I found myself being pulled in by some unseen force. As I drifted off to sleep after I had done a marathon healing session for Lorraine, I was suddenly jolted awake by an unblinking furry gaze. Tabitha, my mother's cat, was inches from my face, her eyes fixed on me with an unnerving intensity. I was so exhausted that I must have appeared lifeless to her curious eyes.

As I sat up with a start, Tabitha leapt backward, her tail twitching like a metronome.

"Silly cat, what's your problem?" I asked, my voice still husky with sleep.

But she just sat there, staring at me, her eyes unblinking. I turned to my left, and saw my mother still engrossed in her online poker game, completely oblivious to my presence. I remembered fragments of a dream- Kyle and I on a sun-kissed beach, our love entwined like the waves. But something had yanked me back to reality. Nature called, and I stumbled toward the bathroom, Tabitha hot on my heels.

"Can't a girl get some privacy?" I pleaded with the persistent feline.

As I flipped the light switch, it stubbornly refused to turn off.

"Mom, what's going on?" I shouted, but she remained transfixed by the screen.

I approached her, tapping her shoulder twice, but she didn't flinch. It was as if she was in a trance. That's when I saw it- the cat jumped onto the couch, and my jaw dropped in unison. Something was amiss, and I was about to uncover a mystery that would change everything.

As I turned to face the couch, my heart raced like a jackrabbit. My body still lay there, motionless. I was floating, detached and utterly bewildered.

Chapter Thirty-Three

"Holy shit!" I screamed silently. Was I dead? Had I pushed myself too far with the healing and paid the ultimate price? Panic set in like a vice, squeezing my very essence. I relived the terror of my near-death experience after the hysterectomy, and my mind reeled with fear.

A Journey of a Thousand Miles – A Reflections Saga

I sprinted back to my body, diving onto the couch with a desperation that would have been comical if it weren't so dire. The cat, startled by my sudden move, let out a blood-curdling shriek, which sent my mother jumping out of her seat.

"Jesus Christ, Tabitha! What the hell are you doing?" she exclaimed, her voice with traces of fear.

"You scared the living shit out of me. Go lay down!"

Little did she know, her cat had just witnessed a soul reentering it's physical shell. The thought sent shivers down my spine, and I lay there, gasping for breath, grateful to be back in my body. Or was I?

I experienced a sudden jolt as I attempted to get back in, but to my surprise, nothing seemed to change. It was as if my soul was refusing to reconnect. I felt like Peter Pan struggling to reattach to his shadow. Panic set in as I tried repeatedly, failing to fully inhabit my body. It wasn't until I approached the process again, this time with calmness and intention, lying down, closing my eyes and visualizing myself reconnecting, that I was finally able to successfully reintegrate. The relief I felt upon returning to my body was indescribable.

Once I had managed to settle back in and got nice and cozy again, I opened my eyes. There was Tabitha staring at me, her furry face mere inches from mine. This time she began to lick my hand. I gave her a gentle pet and then proceeded toward the bathroom to switch off the light I had failed to earlier. I wondered if my mother would take notice this time, whether she would be alerted to my presence. I was really attempting to see if I had in fact rejoined the land of the living once again.

She wasn't able to see me before when I had been out of body, but surely she would see me this time around. Oh she noticed me alright, she nearly went through the ceiling.

"Jesus Christ Ava, you scared me!" she shouted, her voice sounded a bit irritated.

"I'm sorry mom. I was just going to the bathroom. I didn't mean to scare you." I told her, leaning over for a hug.

"It's okay," she laughed. "I just wasn't expecting you to get up. You were out like a light!"

"Yeah, I had to use the bathroom." I explained.

"What the hell is that?" she asked curiously, point to the back of my shirt.

"What is what? I replied.

"There's...There's something all over the back of your shirt."

She was right. I walked over to turn on the light to get a better look.

"Hmmm now this is strange." I thought.

The entire back of my t-shirt was covered in some type of grainy residue. I rubbed some of it off and into my palm then held it under the light. It was sand! It was white sand just like in the dream I had been having not too long before I was startled awake by Tabitha. How the heck?

A Journey of a Thousand Miles – A Reflections Saga

I knew I had to share the bizarre incident with Kyle -it was too incredible to keep to myself. My mother's jaw-dropping reaction was a sight to behold! I was still trying to wrap my head around it all, and the thought of potentially bringing more dream entities into reality was both thrilling and unsettling. Kyle was captivated by the story and saw potential for a future writing inspiration. We laughed about the absurdity of it all and eagerly looked forward to exchanging more stories of unusual experiences during our next visit.

As our connection grew stronger, the distance between us became increasingly unbearable. We both felt an intense longing, like amputees experiencing phantom limb syndrome. Our souls had traversed lifetimes searching for each other; it was time to unite our families in Canada. We decided to hire an immigration lawyer to navigate the complex process, determined to overcome any obstacles and make our dream a reality.

The weekend flew by in a whirlwind of joy and happiness, as we savoured every moment spent together. With Lorraine's surgery looming, we dedicated ourselves to surrounding her with love and support. Kyle, Jaide, and I spent quality time with her, sensing her apprehension and showering her with reassurance. We filled her days with laughter and warmth, watching movies, playing games, and even belting out some karaoke tunes. The highlight was a delicious seafood feast, lovingly prepared by Kyle and I, designed to nourish the body and feed the soul. It was a weekend of togetherness, a celebration of love and connection that would sustain us all through the challenges ahead.

The day of my departure finally arrived, but I was met with an unexpected dilemma – Canada no longer felt like home. My heart belonged to Kyle, Jaide, Lorraine and the boys. Leaving was agonizing, especially since it seemed like we had just rediscovered each other. I lingered, savouring every moment, and spent what felt like an eternity kissing Kyle goodbye. Christine, waiting patiently in the driveway, eventually had to come in and get me. As she stood there in the kitchen, I begged her for just one more moment, needing to visit Lorraine, my mother-in-law first. Her radiant smile and shining eyes welcomed me into her bedroom. She beckoned me closer, and as I leaned in, she enveloped me in a warm embrace, whispering "I'm scared." in my ear. I offered words of comfort, trying to reassure her that everything would be okay.

"I love you Ma. I'll see you soon," I promised, trying to sound convincing.

The goodbye was bittersweet, but I knew our love would bridge the distance. As I made my way toward the door, I turned back to Lorraine, smiled, and then headed toward the kitchen.

"Ready now, chick?" Christine asked with a giggle.

I laughed.

"Yes, let's go! Get me out of here before I change my mind!"

A Journey of a Thousand Miles – A Reflections Saga

Kyle joined us to bid one final farewell, and I wrapped my arms around him, sharing one last kiss.

"You two need to get a room!" Christine teased.

"We have one, but you're taking her away from me again." Kyle chuckled.

He gave me one final peck on the lips.

"Leave now, or I'll keep you." he said teasingly.

As tempting as that was, I had to return to my boys.

"Tell Jaide I love her, and I'll see her next week. I love you baby." I said, before following Christine out the door.

In the car, Christine smiled at me.

"What's that look for?" I asked, feigning minor annoyance.

"You two are just adorable together," she replied. "I love seeing you happy Ava. Kyle is an amazing man, and you're so lucky to have him. His love for you is beautiful." Christine smiled and started the car.

"I'll see you soon my love." I whispered to myself, already missing Kyle and our family in Michigan.

It had been a few days since I left Kyle and our family there in Michigan, and I was eager for updates During my lunch break, I called Kyle to ask about Lorraine's surgery. He reassured me that everything had gone smoothly, and she was recovering well. Though he wasn't allowed to see her yet, I knew he was anxious to be by her side. I have always been impressed by the compassionate nurses in the recovery room. They are truly angel in disguise, providing their patients with care, kindness, and empathy. Their dedication to their work is eviden in all they do. As soon as I heard that Lorraine was in good hands, I felt a sense of relief. I wished I could have been there to support Kyle and Jaide, but I was grateful for the update. I imagined Kyle pacing anxiously waiting for news about his mother's surgery. It was his way of coping with stress, and I had grown to understand and accept it. Our conversation was brief, but reassuring.

"I'm glad everything went well baby. I wish I could have been there, but I'm glad she's okay. I have to go now, but I'll call you when I get home from work. I love you." I said.

"Okay baby. I love you too. We'll talk soon." he replied, and we hung up. Our love and support for each other palpable even over the distance.

I struggled to focus at work, my mind constantly drifting to Kyle, Lorraine and Jaide. It was distracting but I couldn't help but feel drawn to them. At one point, I even imagined myself there beside Kyle in the waiting room, holding his hand. My boss had to snap me out of my daydream, asking if I was okay. I explained that m mother-in-law had just had surgery and I was just worried. My boss was understanding and offered support, telling me to take a break if I needed to.

As I worked in the back room, preparing samples for transfer, I found some peace in my solitude. I enjoyed the quiet, the music, and the familiarity of my tasks. Sometimes I'd get lost in the music and sing my heart out. Patients and coworkers alike had complimented my voice, which was once a hidden talent. Krista had helped me overcome my fear of singing in front of others long ago, and Kyle was blown away by my voice when he first heard me sing. I was grateful to have found someone who supported me and helped me through anything. We brought out the best in each other, and I was thankful for that.

Just when I was finishing up packing samples and loaded the centrifuge, my boss informed me of a phone call on the business line. I asked her to hold the caller for a minute, washed my hands, and then took the phone from her. My heart raced as I saw ten missed calls from Kyle on my cell phone. I answered the call, trying to hide my concern.

"Hello?"

Kyle's anxious voice was on the other end.

"Baby. I'm sorry to call you at work, but it's an emergency. It's Ma. She's not waking up."

My mind raced as he explained the situation- the doctors had to put the breathing tube back down her throat, and she was being moved to the ICU due to complications from the surgery. I felt a chill run down my spine, my legs numb, and my body shaking. I struggled to compose myself, knowing Kyle needed me.

I felt an overwhelming urge to be with Kyle, just as he had been there for me in my time of need. The distance between us seemed insurmountable, but I knew I had to be by his side. After our call, I pulled myself together and requested time off from my boss, explaining the dire situation with Lorraine. She understood and encouraged me to go to Kyle, knowing he needed me. I arranged for Christine to take me to get some essentials and drive me to Kyle's the next afternoon. Though I couldn't get to him immediately, I used the time to make necessary calls and prepare a care package with his favourite items, including chocolates, cigarettes, cologne, a card, and his preferred liquor. I also included some lingerie for a future moment of solace. I wanted to surprise Kyle and bring some comfort to him during this difficult time. I knew he wouldn't expect me to drop everything and show up unexpectedly, but I was determined to be there for him, no matter what.

I called Kyle, as Christine and I crossed the border and engaged in a casual conversation to avoid raising his suspicions. I mentioned finishing work early and heading to the mall with Christine for lunch. I continued chatting with him until we pulled into his driveway. When he heard the car arrive, he asked me to hold on, and I had to mute my phone to stifle my giggles. As I stepped out of the car with bags in hand, Kyle's eyes welled up with tears. I embraced him tightly and whispered,

"I'm here baby. I'll always be here for you. Did you think I'd let you go through this alone?"

He kissed me again, his eyes locked on mine, and whispered,

"Thank you baby."

I handed him the gift bag, and his face lit up with gratitude.

"You didn't need to do that." he said, clearly touched by my thoughtful gestures.

I reassured him that I was there to stay for as long and he, Lorraine and Jaide needed, and he seemed both thrilled and surprised by my support.

After settling in and grabbing a bite to eat, we headed to the hospital to visit Lorraine, bringing along some of her favourite items to aid her in her healing. I brought my cherished crystals, which had helped me through my own traumas and hoped they would do the same for her. Nothing could have prepared us for the sight that greeted us when we entered her room. Hooked up to tubes, wires and a ventilator, she looked utterly fragile. Kyle and I stood there in silence, holding each other, taking in the solemn scene. We eventually made our way to her bedside, each holding a hand, and I placed a rose quartz in her palm, closing her hand around it. I closed my eyes and spoke to her telepathically, willing her to heal and return to us. Just then, her nurse entered with an update on her condition: poor kidney function, low input/output levels, and difficulty breathing on her own. Despite the grim situation, we refused to give up hope.

Kyle and I visited daily, praying for her recovery, but each day brought more disconcerting news. I knew the inevitable question was looming: Would we let her go peacefully or continue invasive procedures? I knew Lorraine's resilience and fighting spirit; she just needed time and someone to believe in her.

Late one evening, I decided to take matters into my own hands. A bold step. If Lorraine wasn't going to come of her own accord, I was going in there to get her and bring her back. Enough was enough. It had been three very long weeks of waiting, praying and wishing, for all of us. I took a deep breath and stepped into the astral realm, driven by a desperate hope. I had to reach her, to bring her back from that coma that had claimed her for far too long. The blue and grey house materialized before me, and I followed the sound of laughter that echoed through its walls. Lorraine's distinctive laugh, the one that had always been able to lift my spirits, grew louder with each step. My heart raced as I entered the dining room, where she sat surrounded by two women who seemed to be her family. The grandmother figure I had met before was among them, her eyes filled with deep understanding.

"Lorraine, please!" I begged, my voice shaking with emotion. "You have to come back to us. Your body is failing, and Kyle and Jaide are beside themselves with worry. We all need you."

A Journey of a Thousand Miles – A Reflections Saga

Her response was calm and reassuring, but it did little to ease my anxiety. "I'm okay baby. I'm just spending some time with family. We're sharing stories and laughter. I promise I'll be back soon."

The other women at the table gazed at me with a mix of compassion and understanding, their eyes filled with a deep wisdom. The grandmother figure spoke up, her voice soothing but firm.

"Don't worry child. She'll be back when da time is right. We're just finishing up a game."

Lorraine's smile was warm and comforting, but I knew the gravity of the situation. I couldn't bear the thought of losing her, of witnessing the devastation that would consume our lives if she didn't return.

"You have to come back." I pleaded once more. "You have to. Otherwise I'm coming back and dragging your butt out of here."

With that, I was met with a chorus of laughter, reassuring smiles and nods, but I knew that the outcome was far from certain. I could only hope that her promise would be fulfilled, and that she would return to us before it was too late.

The phone rang early, shattering the silence. Kyle and I exchanged a nervous glance as he answered. The hospital was on the line, urging Kyle to make a decision regarding Lorraine's care. Despite their best efforts to wean her off the ventilator, her trachea had become swollen, and the medical team feared causing further damage. They proposed a tracheotomy, a procedure that would create a new airway by inserting a tube through her throat by way of a hole they would need to surgically make into her windpipe. We weighed the risks and benefits, our hearts heavy with the gravity of the decision. After a tense discussion, Kyle gave the go-ahead, and we anxiously awaited the outcome.

The next day, we arrived at the hospital, only to find Lorraine's room empty. Panic set in as we frantically searched for answers. A nurse finally appeared, apologizing profusely for the confusion. Our minds raced with worst-case scenarios until she revealed the astonishing truth: Lorraine had been transferred to a rehabilitation facility. Our confusion turned into disbelief as the nurse explained that the tracheotomy had sparked a miraculous turnaround- Lorraine was awake, attempting to speak, and even eating. We exhaled a sigh of relief, our fears replaced by hope and joy. With trembling voices, we asked to see her, and the nurse smiled, giving us the directions to the rehabilitation facility where our loved one was fighting her way back to life. Kyle and I thanked her for her assistance and made our way out the door to the unit.

Kyle and I sat in the car, overwhelmed with emotion, as we processed the miraculous turn of events. We were grateful for her return and wondered if she'd recall our presence in her dreams. But in that moment, none of that mattered- we just wanted to be with her.

A Journey of a Thousand Miles – A Reflections Saga

At her hospital room door, we stood frozen, overcome with joy and gratitude. It was a truly surreal experience, going from preparing for the worst to witnessing her resilience and strength. When she saw us, she tried desperately to speak, but the tube in her throat hindered her ability. She gestured for a pen and paper, eager to communicate. I rummaged through my purse for a pen and handed it to her. She had a lot to say, starting with expressions of love. Seeing her smile again was a poignant reminder of the little things we often take for granted. The rehab staff were wonderful, making us feel like part of the team working together towards her healing. It was as if we'd all been given a second chance at life, and we were determined to make the most of it.

With each passing day, her personality shone brighter, and every small triumph was a milestone- from her first words to her first steps- was a cause for celebration. We never missed a single day of visiting her, and witnessing her transformation from a coma-like state to walking the halls with assistance. It was nothing short of miraculous. But our joy was short-lived.

One day, she seemed off, and we knew something was wrong. She asked for a pen and paper and wrote us a heart-wrenching letter detailing the subpar treatment she'd received- neglect, abandonment in her feces for hours, and no proper hygiene care. As a healthcare professional, I was appalled, and Kyle was livid. We were horrified to learn that she hadn't even had a sponge bath in over a month.

We took matters into our own hands, bringing her fresh clothes and toiletries and giving her a makeshift sponge bath and hair wash using wet wipes provided by the hospital. That evening, we were still fuming about the neglect she'd suffered. Kyle called the patient advocate to file a complaint and was directed to the head nurse, whom he confronted with a fierce determination I'd never seen before. I was glad he took charge, as I was ready to do the same the next day. The experience taught me that even in the US, hospitals can fall short, and it's up to families to advocate for their loved ones. The only difference between our healthcare system and theirs was the cost- theirs required payment, while ours was free. After speaking with the head nurse, Kyle and I began searching for alternative facilities to transfer Lorraine to, as we believed she would receive better care elsewhere. The next day, we visited Lorraine and were met with a drastic change in attitude from the staff. We were greeted with smiles and warm welcomes as we made our way to her room.

The nurse even remarked, "Good morning, Mr and Mrs Reed. Your mother is doing wonderfully today. just finished getting her ready for you, so she's fresh and clean."

A Journey of a Thousand Miles – A Reflections Saga

The treatment we received that day was almost comically excessive, as if we were some kind of royalty. When we entered Lorraine's room, she burst out laughing and wrote on a dry erase board they had recently given her.

"What the hell did you two do? They're treating me like royalty up in here."

We all erupted into laughter, and after composing ourselves, we smiled and told her,

"Oh yes! We took care of it Ma."

She smiled broadly, squeezed our hands, and mouthed "Thank you."

From that day on, we knew Lorraine would receive proper care and respect.

A week later, we brought Jaide to visit, and she was overjoyed to see her grandmother, having been deeply worried about her during those incredibly shaky moments where her recovery was left up to the universe. It had been a heavy burden on us all, but thankfully, those days were now behind us. The nurse entered with a warm smile, bearing encouraging news- Lorraine was progressing remarkably well, and her discharge was anticipated within a few weeks. This astonishing update left us all in awe. The nurse shared that Lorraine had begun breathing independently, allowing them to reduce her ventilator support. The possibility of reversing her tracheotomy was even discussed. Initially, the plan was to transfer her to a nursing home, but Kyle and I had other ideas. We decided to bring her home and I would take on her care, ensuring she could reunite with her loved ones. To make this possible, I would have to receive comprehensive training from the hospital nurses on managing her tracheotomy and using suction tools to maintain her airway. With this knowledge, we would finally be able to bring Lorraine home, surrounded by the love and support she craved.

As we eagerly awaited Lorraine's homecoming, we thoroughly cleaned and prepared the house to ensure her comfort and safety. We even looked into acquiring a hospital bed for her to ensure her utmost comfort and ease. Having been in the US for nearly two months, I longed to see my boys, but I was committed to staying and caring for Lorraine as long as necessary. I made arrangements with their fathers for regular visits and sleepovers, so they could spend quality time with me despite the distance. With everything in place, we were excited to share the news of her impending discharge with Lorraine. I also arranged for Christine to take me home for a couple of weeks, allowing me to spend time with the boys before returning to care for Lorraine. I scheduled my return for two weeks later, eager to reunite with my family. While I had initially felt obligated to support Kyle and Jaide during the challenging times, I now felt confident leaving them for a short period, knowing they could manage. Caring for Lorraine would be a significant responsibility, but I was wholeheartedly ready to embrace it. I just needed a brief time to mentally prepare myself for the task ahead.

A Journey of a Thousand Miles – A Reflections Saga

Kyle, Jaide and I headed to the hospital, eager to share the exciting news with Lorraine. As we arrived at her room, we couldn't wait to tell her that she would be coming home soon. When we finally shared the news, her face lit up with joy. She expressed heartfelt gratitude for my willingness to care for her, acknowledging the significant ask. We all shared the desire to have her home with us as soon as possible, surrounded by loved ones rather than strangers. During our visit, her respiratory therapy team arrived, inviting her on a short walk down the hall. Eager to demonstrate her progress, she enthusiastically agreed. As we waited for her return, her determination and resolve became palpable to everyone. When she emerged, beaming with pride, the therapist was absolutely thrilled.

"She's making remarkable progress! She walked the entire hallway with minimal assistance, a testament to her strength and resolve." he exclaimed.

Her unwavering determination inspired us all, and we couldn't help but feel a sense of immense pride and awe. After her walk, she appeared tired, and we all decided to let her rest. As we bid her farewell, Kyle, Jaide, and I leaned in, kissing her cheeks and expressing our love for her. We promised to return the next day, eager to support her continued progress.

The day of my departure had finally arrived, and Kyle and I struggled to sleep the night before, our minds and bodies entwined in a loving embrace. We knew it would be a week or two before I returned, and we wanted to cherish every moment we had left together. Earlier that day, we had received concerning news about Lorraine's health- fluid buildup on her lung and a potential infection. Although the doctor downplayed our concerns, I couldn't shake off my unease, knowing that complications like these were common in ventilated patients. I prayed for a compassionate doctor who would care for her like a loved one of their own.

The next morning, the phone rang, piercing the silence once again. Kyle groggily answered, and our hearts sank as we saw the caller ID- a new doctor, Dr. Alet, was requesting a family meeting. We gathered at the hospital, riddled with anxiety and fear. As we waited in the conference room, memories of a similar meeting about Aaron came flooding back to me. I clutched Kyle's hand, my heart racing. The minute the door closed, the room erupted with chatter. Everyone was carrying on conversations among themselves, trying to determine the reason we had all been called to the meeting. I tried my hardest to drown out the noise. I looked at Kyle and mouthed the words, *"I love you."* The room suddenly fell silent as Dr. Alet entered, her expression solemn. We braced ourselves for the news, our love and support for each other our only solace.

Dr. Alet began, "Hello everyone, thank you for gathering here today. I'm Dr. Alet, the physician now in charge of Lorraine's care."

A Journey of a Thousand Miles – A Reflections Saga

She suggested we go around the room and have everyone introduce themselves, but before she could continue, Kyle's uncle, Anthony stood up and took charge of the introductions, presenting everyone in the room-except me. I was taken aback, feeling overlooked and undervalued. Even Lorraine's friend was acknowledged, but I, her daughter-in-law, was not. I bit my tongue, squeezing Kyle's hand in frustration. It was especially galling given the effort Kyle had put into keeping everyone informed, even having to correct Bradley, his nephew, who had wrongly removed Kyle's contact information from the whiteboard in Lorraine's room during a previous visit, and listed himself as the emergency contact. Kyle had ensured the nurses knew he and I were the primary contacts regarding Lorraine's care. Once Anthony had finished, Dr. Alet commenced discussing Lorraine's situation, explaining the fluid buildup on her lung, and the unexpected discovery of a foreign object, likely a piece of chest tube, revealed by the morning's X-ray. She proposed monitoring the situation instead of immediate surgical intervention, citing Lorraine's progress and the potential risks of another procedure. The doctor sought our collective decision on the matter and requested we discuss it with Lorraine to ensure everyone was on the same page. As she concluded, she invited questions from the room. Once everyone had their turn to ask questions, Kyle and I stood up together and asked one of our own.

"Can we speak to you alone for a moment, Dr Alet?" Kyle and I asked in unison.

"Of course!" she smiled, nodding. "Please, have a seat." she gestured to the chairs across from her. "Everyone else, if you could please leave the room for a moment?"

Once alone, she leaned forward, her eyes locked on ours.

"What's on your minds?"

I took a deep breath. "I was wondering if congestive heart failure could be a possibility given the fluid buildup in her lungs?" I asked, drawing on my healthcare knowledge.

Dr. Alet nodded thoughtfully. "Yes, that's a valid concern. I'll order the necessary tests to rule it out."

Kyle and I exchanged a relieved glance.

"Mr. Reed," Dr. Alet continued. "I want to assure you that you are the primary decision-maker regarding your mother's care. Besides her of course. I've included the family to keep everyone informed, but ultimately, the decisions rest with you, your wife, and Lorraine herself."

"Thank you, Doctor." Kyle replied. "We appreciate your honesty. We've already made the decision and we've decided that surgery isn't the best option right now. We don't want to put any additional stress on her or cause her to have any setbacks."

Dr. Alet nodded in agreement. "I understand. That's a wise decision. I'll make sure to keep a close eye on her."

As we stood to leave, she asked, "May I have a few minutes to speak with Lorraine before you go in?"

A Journey of a Thousand Miles – A Reflections Saga

We nodded, and Kyle visited his mother first while I waited in the conference room with Lorraine's friend Diana.

Diana, whom I was meeting for the very first time, began lecturing me on what Kyle and I should be doing for his mother.

"You should be here every day, spending the whole day with her. You're being neglectful." she said, her tone condescending.

My temperature rose, and I felt my blood boiling.

"Excuse me, but who are you to tell me what I should be doing? You have no idea what we've been through or what we're doing for her! How dare you!"

Just as I was about to continue, Kyle appeared in the doorway, a look of concern on his face. Diana quickly excused herself, leaving us alone.

"What's wrong baby?" Kyle asked, studying me. "You look upset."

"That bitch!" I shouted. "She had the nerve to tell me we're not doing enough for your mother!"

Kyle's expression darkened.

"I'm sorry baby. I'll talk to her about it later."

"No. Please don't do it here," I urged. "We don't want to upset Ma. You can talk to her another time But before we go into that room, there's something else that pissed me off before all of that happened with Diana," I continued. "Your uncle Anthony. He didn't even bother to introduce me to the doctor. It's like I wasn't even sitting here. Like I was suddenly invisible. He introduced Diana though, like she was the queen of fucking Denmark. Why Kyle? Why would he do something like that?" I asked, a deep sadness in my tone.

"Oh baby, I'm so sorry. I didn't even realize he did that. That's not right. I'm gonna talk to him right now." Kyle assured me.

"Okay baby, but do me a favour? Don't mention any of this bullshit around Ma. Please?" I pleaded.

"I promise I won't baby, but this needs to be addressed right now. I'm going to find him in a minute Let's go sit with Ma for a few minutes, and then you can stay with her while I go talk to him." Kyle said.

I nodded in agreement, and Kyle helped me up from the table.

When he returned, he had his uncle Anthony with him.

"Hey, I wanted to apologize for not introducing you to the doctor earlier," Anthony said. "I got caught up in what was happening with my sister, and I honestly didn't see you sitting there."

I raised an eyebrow, skeptical.

"You didn't see me sitting right next to your nephew, who you introduced as Lorraine's son?"

Anthony shifted uncomfortably.

A Journey of a Thousand Miles – A Reflections Saga

"I know it sounds ridiculous, but I just didn't see you. I apologize."

I decided I'd accept his halfhearted apology, not wanting to cause tension.

"It's water under the bridge, Anthony. Let's just move forward."

An hour or so later, Anthony left, leaving Kyle and I sitting with Lorraine, watching her favourite TV show. When it was time for her needle aspiration procedure on her lung, we left to grab a bite to eat.

After our meal, we returned to the floor of the hospital Lorraine had been staying on. The nurse stopped us in the hallway and informed us that everything had gone smoothly, but Lorraine would be sore for a couple of days. We sat with her again, asking how she was doing. She wrote on her board that it wasn't fun at all, and the procedure had pinched a lot despite the numbing medicine they gave her. At least the worst was over now, and we would have answers soon enough. Together, we sat and watched Family Feud as we waited for her dinner to arrive. Kyle and I assisted her with her tray and helped her to eat.

Once she'd finished, the respiratory therapy team arrived once again, as per the daily routine for her evening walk. Kyle and I sat there in her room, waiting for her return. As the two of us sat in front of the TV, we overheard a heated argument in the hallway between Lorraine's doctor and her previous care physician.

"I don't care!" one of them shouted. "I want her gone!"

They continued to argue for several minutes before Lorraine and her team returned to the room. Once she was settled back in bed, she reached for her writing board and wrote:

"Did you two hear that?"

We confirmed that we had, and asked if she knew what the argument was about. She wrote in big capital letters, "ME!"

We were confused, and Kyle asked,

"What do you mean Ma?"

Lorraine explained that this wasn't the first argument she had overheard that day, and that the doctor wanted her discharged and was upset that the surgery wasn't happening because he wanted her "GONE!"

Kyle and I exchanged worried glances, wondering why this doctor was so eager to have Lorraine released for the hospital. She was always kind and considerate, rarely ringing her call bell unless absolutely necessary. What could be driving this doctor's odd behaviour? It's not every day that you get to hear two professionals just having it out right there for everyone to hear. I think it was clear to everyone that they were engaged in a heated debate. Kyle and I were definitely thanking our lucky stars that this quack had been taken off of Lorraine's case. I mean can you even imagine how much he would've set her back in her recovery?

A Journey of a Thousand Miles – A Reflections Saga

A few days later, Kyle and I received another phone call from Dr. Alet. She was sure to let us know that there was nothing urgent about the phone call, but that she wanted to set up another meeting to speak with us at our earliest convenience. We arranged to meet within an hour or so, after we had a chance to get ourselves ready for the day.

We arrived at the hospital a short time later. Dr. Alet had been expecting us and was waiting at the nurse's station. We exchanged pleasantries, and followed her back to the same conference room as we had met in once before. She closed the door behind us and motioned for Kyle and I to be seated at the table. Once again, I noticed that she had a file in her hand. She took a seat at the table across from us and flipped open the file in front of her.

"Thank you for meeting with me again Mr. And Mrs. Reed." she began. "I have a bit of news to share with the two of you regarding your mother's latest X-ray findings from this morning. It appears that whatever the foreign object was that was discovered in her lung, has miraculously disappeared!" she looked pleased as she gave us the news.

Kyle and I exchanged glances between one another. We were both in shock. How could this even be possible. We sat there for a moment, as if we were communicating telepathically and then we turned to look back at her.

"Mrs. Reed, as I promised you before, I have done the testing on your mother-in-law and I wanted to tell you that your previous suspicions have been confirmed. Lorraine does in fact have congestive heart failure, but this can be treated with proper medications. I'm glad that we were able to catch it when we did though. Now that we know what we are dealing with, we can do something about it. As for the latest finding though, I am really quite puzzled. I just don't understand how it was there one day and then just a few days later it has vanished. But we'll take the win!" she exclaimed. "Now, as for the fluid in her lung. I wanted to test to determine the cause. Unfortunately, there was a mistake in the lab and they failed to do the tests I had ordered." she continued shaking her head in disbelief at her own words. "There is also one other slight problem. My colleague, who was in charge of Lorraine's care, seems pretty insistent that she leave this facility and that she be moved to a nursing home temporarily. It's just until the two of you are ready to bring her home and until you have both had all of the training that is required to make that a possibility. I'm sorry Mr. And Mrs. Reed, but it's really out of my hands at this point. Here is a list of great facilities with exceptional care. Please have a look and choose one by the beginning of next week." she raised from her chair and extended her hand out to both of us, before quietly leaving the room.

"That fucking bastard!" Kyle shouted angrily. "Why couldn't he just mind his goddamn business?"

"I know baby. That pissed me off too, but maybe it's better this way. Think of it this way my love. Ma is one step closer to coming home...with us....where she belongs!" I smiled, squeezing his hand and leaning in for kiss. "Everything is going in the right direction baby. I mean, look at it this way. She's going to be discharged much sooner than any of us expected. Let's go sit with her for awhile and then we can go home and look at the options." I suggested.

"Okay baby. You're right! Let's get this done. Ma might be a bit upset, but we will just keep reminding her that it means she is one step closer to home. I love you. Thank you baby." he pulled me close to him and leaned in for one last kiss.

Kyle and I spent the next few days looking through all of the options for the nursing homes. We were always mindful of not only location, but also insurance coverage. When we had discussed it all with Lorraine, she had initially been upset, as we expected, but she quickly cheered up when Kyle and I explained that it was only going to be for a week and then she would be coming home. Kyle had done his best to entice her with promises of cheesecake the next time we visited. I can only imagine how sick of that hospital food she had been. There was no doubt, she was looking forward to having real food again.

The following day, I awoke with a sore throat. It was so bad, I could barely speak, and the pain...was unbearable.

"Probably strep throat." I told Kyle disappointed. "There is no way I'm gonna be able to come with you today baby. I don't want to get Ma sick. Especially when she is coming home soon. We don't want any setbacks for her."

Kyle agreed, but before leaving the house to head to the hospital, he made me a tea and gave me some medicine. I adored how loving and attentive he was. That was his way. He was extremely thoughtful too. He seemed a bit hesitant to leave me at first, but after much insistence on my part, he happily agreed.

"Just go and see Ma baby. You know she looks forward to our visits. Give her a kiss for me and tell her I love her."

"Okay baby, I will. I love you." he said, lovingly planting a kiss on the center of my forehead.

Then he leaned over, encouraged me to get comfortable and proceeded to tuck me in. It wasn't long after he left that I drifted off into a deep sleep.

My cellphone vibrated on the shelf behind my head, jarring me awake. Rubbing my eyes and stretching groggily, I reached to answer it.

"Hello?" I said sleepily.

"Hey baby. I'm sorry. Did I wake you up?" Kyle asked.

"Yeah, you did baby, but it's okay. What's up?" I inquired.

A Journey of a Thousand Miles – A Reflections Saga

"Oh baby. A LOT happened here. I'm going to tell you all about it when I get home. I'm on my way now. Let's just say, Bradley and I got into a fight at the hospital." he told me.

"What?! What do you mean you guys got into a fight? Baby, what the hell happened?" I asked, my voice filled with surprise.

"I'll explain everything when I get home baby. I'll see you soon! I love you."

My mind was spinning with all kinds of thoughts. Kyle and his nephew had always been close. He; Kyle had even helped to raise him. The two of them grew up together, side by side. I never in my wildest dreams, expected what Kyle was about to share with me. Not in a million years!

Mere minutes passed by, but they felt like hours. Kyle had arrived home and immediately began to tell me about the days crazy events. I sat there, anxious for him to get to the meat of it all, but if you know Kyle, then you would know that my husband tends to go off on these tangents, with many detours involved along the way before he finally gets to the point. Apparently, he and Bradley had not only argued, but they fought physically. Right there, in Lorraine's hospital room. Things got so heated between them that security was called and they had to throw Bradley out of the hospital. From that moment on, Bradley was told he could no longer visit. By the sounds of it, Bradley had shown up either high or intoxicated. He started ranting to Kyle about how he was always kept in the dark about Lorraine and then he had worked up the courage to try and take a swing at Kyle. Maybe it was that liquid courage.

Whatever it was, turned out to be a very big mistake. Kyle wound up having to restrain him at one point and then had to hit him to let him know that he wasn't playing around. Shortly after the fight ensued, Bradley was escorted off of hospital grounds by the security personnel. Kyle apologized to the hospital staff profusely and assured them that there would be no further incidents. The staff accepted the apology but went on to explain to him that should there be any further conflict, neither he or Bradley would be permitted to enter the hospital. Violence or aggression of any kind would not be tolerated. I was grateful for two things, the first being that wasn't there to witness the altercation, and the second was that the hospital staff had not banned Kyle from visiting Lorraine. She would've been absolutely distraught had that been the case.

The following day, Kyle and I awoke with a mission in mind. We decided to reach out to the patient advocate and explain the situation regarding Lorraine being forced out. We mentioned to her that Dr. Alet had

A Journey of a Thousand Miles – A Reflections Saga

stated that she didn't feel that Lorraine was quite ready to be transferred out just yet. The advocate seemed appalled with the information we had shared, and assured Kyle and I that it would be taken care of immediately. Lorraine had continued to battle fluid buildup in her lung, which required yet another aspiration procedure to alleviate her symptoms. She was also still currently battling an infection. We notified the advocate that we were making phone calls and were coming close to a decision on the facility she would be transferred to. We explained that we needed another week or so, but assured her that we were taking care of all of the arrangements. At this point, we had managed to narrow our selection down to three places. We couldn't believe that Lorraine's old doctor was still calling all the shots, despite having stepped away from her case. The whole thing was completely absurd. Before we hung up with the patient advocate, we arranged a meeting with Dr. Alet as well as the board director of the hospital that following Monday.

Kyle and I had been up to see Lorraine over the weekend. We mentioned our upcoming meeting regarding her care. It was set for that following Monday at 2:00PM. She seemed to be content with those arrangements and expressed her gratitude to both of us for advocating for her. Kyle and I were anxious to resolve the situation and to get Lorraine home as soon possible, but not before she was ready to leave the hospital. We had all been through so much with her. It had been quite stressful for all of us. We were certain that everything would be resolved once they had a chance to examine her for themselves. Lorraine was eager to get home. She kept talking about how much she missed Kyle's cooking and requested that on our next visit, we bring her a plate of food. Kyle and I chuckled at the request, but told her we would be more than happy to oblige her.

Monday came rather quickly and Kyle and I were anticipating our meeting later that afternoon. We had not gotten the chance to see Lorraine since the weekend. We missed seeing her smiling face and were eager to get up to the hospital for a quick visit beforehand. I had been pulled out of a deep sleep for some reason. I rolled over, glanced at the clock and noted the time...6:30 am. Too early to be up. I laid my head back down on the pillow and snuggled up to Kyle who was snoring softly. As I lay there, in the stillness of the morning light peeking through a silver curtain, I couldn't help but gaze at his peaceful form. His chest rising and falling with each gentle breath, his eyelids fluttering slightly as he chased dreams. I felt my heart swell with adoration, my love for him so intense it almost hurt. I began to trace the curves of his face with my eyes, memorizing every detail. His strong jawline, the subtle curve to the top of his nose from a childhood accident, his eyelashes that brushed against his cheek like silk. Every feature would remain forever etched in my mind like a work of art. Kyle Reed was an absolute masterpiece. His broad shoulders and that perfectly chiselled body that brought back fond memories of when they were last pressed up against me.

I felt grateful for this time, where it was just the two of us, lying there in perfect contentment. I ached for his gentle touch, for him to reach over, grab my waist and pull me into his arms where I could live forever and be safe. He always made it so easy to fall asleep. He radiated body heat like he was some kind of personal furnace, but his warmth was always comforting and soothing to me. I was head over heels for this man, and it didn't matter what it was about him, I was completely consumed by it all. Every breath he took, every word he spoke, his smile, the sound of his laughter, the way he made me laugh, how he always knew the perfect things to say to offer comfort, reassurance and encouragement. I especially loved the way he would get giggly whenever he became overtired. Here I was, caught up in the wonderment of Mr. Kyle Reed. Just when I thought I had reached the peak of my endless love for him, he would do or say something that only made me fall more in love. Lying there beside him, and watching him sleep so peacefully, I knew in that moment that I would never love anyone else. Need anyone else. He truly was my everything. My forever home.

I gently began to trace the edge of his ear with my finger, feeling his warmth and the softness of his skin as I grazed it ever so gently. My heart overflowing with emotion. I felt the tears prick up in the corner of my eyes. I was and would always be....eternally grateful for this man. For his love, for his kindness and his unwavering support.

As I continued to watch him sleep, I felt like I was witnessing a real life miracle. The beautiful, strong and gentle soul who had been through so much, but was still here despite everything he had endured and he was still mine. I felt a surge of protectiveness, a desire to shield him from all harm, to keep him safe forever. My gaze drifted to his lips, slightly parted as he slept, and I was drawn back to the moment we had shared our first kiss. The way my heart skipped a beat. The way the world around us faded into the background, leaving only the two of us in that sweet and tender moment. As if he could feel my eyes fixed on him, Kyle turned to face me, still sound asleep. I turned myself toward the wall, my back facing him, then I slid my way across the mattress, lifting his arm to wrap it around my waist. Ah...there we go. Now this, was as close to heaven as I would be permitted to get...for now. The feeling of his soft skin nestled against mine, his heart beating softly against my upper back, was enough to comfort me and draw me back into a deep sleep again.

The phone's shrill ring pierced the silence, jolting both of us awake. We both groggily reached for the phone, our hands colliding as we attempted to answer it simultaneously. Kyle finally managed to grasp the receiver, his voice husky with sleep.

"Hello?"

I snuggled in closer to him, trying to listen in on the conversation. Kyle's expression quickly turned from one of being hazy with sleep to being wide awake and shocked, his eyes locked onto mine.

"What?! When? How did this happen?" He asked, his voice raised in disbelief.

My heart began to race as I sat up, my own mind still foggy. What was going on? Who was on the phone? And what were they saying that had Kyle's gorgeous face twisted into an expression of anger and concern? I nuzzled myself into his chest and began to stroke it with my fingertips, attempting to calm the blazing fire that was quickly rising within him. His voice was tight with anger as he spoke.

"How could they do that without our permission? We were supposed to be having a meeting today to discuss your care!" he listened for a moment, his expression darkening. "No Ma, this is NOT okay. I'm calling the hospital because this right here....is bullshit! I want you moved back to the rehab place immediately."

When I realized who he was speaking to, I felt a surge of indignation and worry. My mind racing with questions. How could they do something like that without our consent? What if she's not getting the care she needs at this new place? All of the what ifs began sweeping through my mind. Kyle's eyes met mine, and I saw my own fear, concern and anger reflected back at me. We were in this together. United in our outrage and our determination to get Lorraine the care she deserved. As Kyle continued to voice his displeasure to Lorraine, I threw off the covers and got out of bed, my heart pounding in my chest. It felt like we were living in some kind of nightmare, like everything was suddenly spiralling out of control. But if there was one thing I knew for certain- we would fight for her! For her care and for our rights as her family. Kyle and I were not going to let this stand.

Chapter Thirty-Four

We had made several phone calls, spoke to several people and were stonewalled at every turn. It was downright inexplicable how all of us were being treated. Lorraine's insurance had run out and the rehab facility wasn't willing to make any exceptions under any circumstances, so unfortunately Lorraine would be forced to remain in the nursing home for the next week until we were able to finally bring her home. It was all so incredibly frustrating but we managed to support one another through it all. The nursing home was temporary, and together we were all counting down the days until she was finally back with us.

Lorraine continued to phone nightly. Kyle, Jaide, and I took turns speaking with her. She told us how much she was actually enjoying her new surroundings, and told us that she was managing to get around better here too. She was happy there. At least for the time being anyway. Unfortunately though, there had been a flu outbreak there, and as a result, visitors were not permitted at the time. We would have to wait for her to be discharged before any of us would be able to see her again.

A Journey of a Thousand Miles – A Reflections Saga

A few nights later, Lorraine was speaking with Kyle on the phone. The two of them discussed the long awaited move to Canada. She told him how happy she was that he had met me and how she knew that I was the best match for him long ago. That day, four years ago as I stood in the kitchen. It was obvious to her that Kyle and I were soulmates. She could see how deeply we loved each other and she knew in her heart that I was the one she had been praying for him to find. She also adored how close my relationship with Jaide had become. How close we had all become.

She told Kyle about how she would joke with the chef there from time to time and tell her just how good Kyle's food was and that she didn't think there was anyone who could top him. Knowing Lorraine, she was probably telling the chef that she needed lessons. The thought of that alone makes me giggle. Lorraine was sweet and caring but she was also honest, and sometimes...that honesty, could be brutal. Those who knew her understood that it was never said out of malice though. She had just always been that way. Open and honest about how she felt about something or someone. She never left you guessing. I appreciated that. It especially made me chuckle when it came to some of the nurses in the rehab facility she had been in not too long ago. She and her roommate liked to have fun with everyone, and though they may have been bedridden at the time, they were definitely still feisty women.

Speaking of her roommate, Kyle had told me about the day that he and Bradley had gotten into it. Lorraine's roommate had been absolutely floored by Bradley's behaviour. She couldn't believe the disrespect he had shown, not only towards Kyle, but to her and Lorraine as well. Thank God nothing had gotten too serious between he and Kyle. Kyle was always mindful of where they were and never lost sight of the fact that they were two fragile women in the room who were at their mercy. Both of the women were hooked up to tubes and wires galore. One wrong move and Bradley could've gone flying in the direction of either of them and something drastic may have occurred.

As I heard Kyle preparing to end the call, I was quickly drawn back to the present.

"Okay Ma, I love you too. I will. Okay we love you and we'll see you soon." he said just before hanging up.

"How did she sound baby? I asked with a smile.

"Good. She sounded real good. We were just talking about when we are finally going to make that move to Canada. She told me what she wants for dinner her first night home and she mentioned that we have a bunch of things to take care of once she's well enough to come off of the ventilator." he replied.

"Oh really? Like what baby?" I inquired further.

A Journey of a Thousand Miles – A Reflections Saga

"Well, she just wants to get everything in order. For when it comes time to sell the house and all of that. She wants to get everything finished before the big move next year. She mentioned that she wants to put my name on the deed for the house. Apparently she still has Charles on it with her." he sounded a bit shocked by the gravity of his own words.

"Oh, I thought you already were."

"Yeah, me too. I guess she just hadn't gotten around to it before she got sick. But that's okay. One thing at a time right? Let's go lay down baby. I'm beat!" he got up from the couch beside me and extended his hand, reaching for mine.

As tired as Kyle had claimed to be, he sure didn't get a chance to do much sleeping that night. He and I had stayed up for hours, talking about our excitement for the future. Time felt like it had frozen there in that moment, as I lay with my head on his chest, him running his fingers through my long and silky hair. I have always loved the way he loved me. So gentle, so attentive, so passionately. He seemed to be just as wrapped up in me as I was in him. The two of us simply couldn't get enough of one another. Even after all of these years, nothing had changed between us. If anything, it only intensified our connection. We still craved for one another. We both still felt the butterflies every time we came in proximity to each other. I think up to that point, neither one of us even knew of such possibilities.

That night, after our intense conversation, we made love again, completely immersed in the depths of our love for each other. It was the most passionate experience for either one of us to date. Our connection was boundless. Afterwards, we lay there in each other's arms. Just the two of us, breathless, hearts pounding in sync with one another, and basking in the glow of the sacred bond we shared. And then slowly, we began to pull one another in, into the deepest slumber.

I was jolted awake by the sound of someone knocking at the door incessantly, followed by the ringing of the doorbell. It took me a minute to realize what was really happening, because at first it felt like I was still asleep. I rolled over and kissed Kyle on the lips, gently trying to wake him. He barely stirred. But still, the knocking continued. It was probably someone trying to sell something. Was no one able to hear it but me? Surely I was dreaming. Jaide had been asleep in Lorraine's room which was right beside our own. Ever since Lorraine had gone in for surgery, Jaide had slept in her bed. I assume it was so that she could be close to her grandmother. The thought of that was precious to me. She and Lorraine had always been so close. Lorraine may have been her grandmother, but she was more so a mother figure to her. She had stepped in to help Kyle with raising her, when her own mother had left both her and Kyle in her moment of reckless abandonment.

A Journey of a Thousand Miles – A Reflections Saga

The knocking finally ceased, and I lay back down on the pillow, closing my eyes and willing sleep to return for me. After a moment or so, my eyes flung open and I nearly went through the ceiling as the shrilling ring of the phone reverberated off of the shelf behind us. Kyle was so deep in slumber, he didn't even begin to stir at the intrusion. Had someone drugged the two of us last night?

The knocking started up again, as did the incessant ringing of the doorbell. What the hell was going on? I sat up quickly and gently began to nudge Kyle to wake him. He rolled over and began to stretch, yawning and smiling as his eyes greeted mine.

"Kyle, baby. Someone is at the door." I told him softly, my voice still husky from sleep.

Just then, the two of us heard the sound of Jaide's footsteps as she ran across the carpet in the dining room to answer the door. The two of us just lay there for a moment, listening to the muffled sounds of a conversation being had by Jaide and another female. Then we heard a sound I will not soon forget. It was the sound of Jaide's blood curdling scream. Her scream pierced the air, a haunting wail that sent chills down our spines. Kyle and I exchanged glances, both terrified, our hearts racing in unison with the uncertainty of it all. And then, out of sheer instinct, we both jumped up and threw the covers off. Kyle went rushing for the door first I quickly cleared my throat to get his attention, reminding him of the fact that we were both in the nude. Kyle quickly grabbed his jogging pants and tank top, threw them on like the house was on fire and went rushing for the bedroom door and then for Jaide. I scrambled to find my own clothing, which had been scattered about the floor. I threw on whatever I could find that was decent and ran out after him.

Jaide was a sight that I won't soon clear from my mind. The image of her forever engraved there. She was sitting there at the dining room table, her eyes pleading for comfort. Kyle's sister was standing beside her rubbing her back to console her, her own face twisted in solemnity. Kyle turned his gaze of concern from Jaide and locked onto mine. Somehow, he and I both knew. We knew that our perfect little world was about to shatter. We both knew in that moment that nothing would be the same again.

With a sense of dread, Kyle reached out and took Jaide's hand pulling her up from the chair so he could hold her. I stood there, my heart foreboding. Bracing myself to hold the energy in the room, and to hear the words that would change our lives forever. It was the same feeling I had felt all those years ago, when somehow knew that my father had left this place.

"Ma passed away last night. She's gone!" his sister began.

As soon as those words left her lips, Kyle's legs gave out beneath him. He crumpled to the ground, his body crashing to the floor like a fallen tree. His face contorted in sheer agony and disbelief. He let out a wail that seemed to rip from the depths of his soul. Just as Jaide had moments before. I felt like I was moving in slow

A Journey of a Thousand Miles – A Reflections Saga

motion, my eyes fixed on his crumbling form, my brain struggling to process what was happening. I was in a state of shock. Jaide's scream echoed through the room, a haunting memory of Kyle's own anguished cries. His sister reached for him. Tried desperately to hold him, but she was met with resistance at every attempt. Kyle pushed her away, his fists clenched in despair.

"No! No! She can't be. She can't be gone!" he screamed, his voice echoing off of the walls. "Oh my God. Oh my God. Why?!" he pounded the floor with his fists, his body shaking uncontrollably with each sob. I knew in that moment that he needed me now more than ever before.

I rushed to his side, my heart shattering, my arms wrapping around him, trying to hold him together as he shattered into a million pieces. I held onto him as he cried out his grief. I motioned for Jaide to join us so I could hold onto them both. There we were, just the three of us, our tears flowing freely, as we formed a tragic triangle of deep sorrow. In that moment, nothing nor anyone else existed. The room seemed to dissolve around us, leaving only the three of us, lost in that sea of despair. The tidal wave of grief had struck, sweeping us all away in its relentless tide. I felt like I was drowning, suffocating under the weight of all of our pain. But I held on, holding him and Jaide as the world around us came crashing down. It was like nothing I had ever felt before and it was quickly becoming unbearable, but still I continued to hold on, to him and to Jaide as the three of us rode out the storm together. We cried, we screamed, we wailed. Our voices blending in a chorus of sorrow. In that moment I came to realize two things. The first was that our lives would never be the same again, that WE would never be the same. The second was that I finally knew who it was. I knew who I saw that day when I was helping Kyle's grandmother prepare for a loved ones arrival. The one we had made the bed for, who we had made the soothing tea for and the one who was standing there when I turned around. It was her. It was always her. The loved one we had been waiting for was Kyle's mother, Lorraine.

As the three of us lay there together on the floor, surrounded by the shattered remnants of our world, the reality of the situation slowly began to sink in. Lorraine was gone. The vibrant, fiery and loving woman who I had considered as my own mother, the centerpiece of our lives, was no longer with us on this earthly plane.

The days that followed were a blur of tears, anguish and sheer disbelief. We planned a funeral/cremation ceremony, received numerous condolences, and struggled to come to terms with the void that she had left behind. Kyle and I had even started day drinking...no...it was more like all day drinking. Each of us trying to numb the pain as we attempted to drown our sorrows in the bottle.

Kyle's cousin, J'Von who had still been staying at the house with us, remained a constant presence in all f our grief, while Jaide clung to us like a lifeline. Her own pain and loss evident in the river of her endless tears.

A Journey of a Thousand Miles – A Reflections Saga

We all went through the motions, numb and mechanical, trying to make sense of a world that no longer made sense to any of us. We found comfort in each other, in our shared grief, and in the memories of Lorraine that we cherished.

But even as we struggled to come to terms with our great loss, we knew that we had to find a way to move forward, to honour her memory and keep her spirit alive within our hearts. And so, with heavy hearts and tear-stained faces, we began the long journey of healing, of finding a sense of normalcy again in the world. The world that would never be the same again. We struggled for a long time, trying to find the rhythm in our new reality. Kyle struggled with sleep at first, haunted by the memories of his mother's final days. Jaide's grades began to slip, her focus clouded by grief. And I felt like I was drowning, trying to keep everyone afloat while struggling to keep my own head above water. And yet, even in the midst of all that pain, we began to find moments of beauty. We shared stories of Lorraine's life, her infectious laughter, her smile made of sunshine and even her wisdom. We looked at old photographs, remembering the way she made us feel. We even cooked her favourite meals, savouring the taste of the memories.

After some time had passed and we had shed every tear we possibly could, we began to laugh again, and to find joy in the little things. We realized that Lorraine's legacy was not just in our memories, but in the love we shared with each other. We realized that she had taught us how to love, how to cherish each and every moment and she taught us how to find beauty in everything.

We still missed her, every day, every hour, every minute. But we knew that she was no longer in pain, no longer suffering. We knew that she'd want us to keep living, to keep loving, and to keep her memory alive in our hearts. We vowed to honour her memory always and most of all, we vowed to rediscover the things that once brought us joy.

Kyle started playing his guitar again, the melodies flowing through the house like a warm embrace. Jaid started painting, her brushstrokes bold and colourful, a reflection of the resilience she had inherited from her grandmother. And I started writing, the words flowing out of me like a river, a testament to the power of love and loss. We all still had our moments of sorrow of course. The grief still lingered, a constant reminder of what we had lost. But somehow, we learned to embrace it, to acknowledge its presence without letting it define us.

After six months of navigating the ups and downs of life after her passing, Kyle and I realized that we badly needed a change of pace. We decided together that we would take a break from all of the chaos and to find a tranquil escape back in Canada.

Navigating the muddy waters had really taken a toll on both of us. A getaway was exactly what we both needed so desperately. It wasn't long until we stumbled upon the perfect place by the water. A serene haven that

Kimberley Hall

beckoned us to relax, unwind and recharge. We hadn't set any intentions to find a new place to call home just yet. We both just wanted a temporary moment of peace. Yet it seemed fate had other plans.

From the moment we first arrived at the cozy retreat, we both felt an inexplicable sense of belonging. Something that neither of us could explain. The breathtaking view, the soothing sound of the waves, and the warm sunlight streaming through the windows all seemed to whisper to us.

"Stay awhile. Stay forever. Make this your home together."

Oh how I had missed the familiarity of my own country. The comfort of familiar faces and the solace of a place that felt like a warm embrace. This was a place where we could make new memories. Jaide had chosen to stay behind with J'Von back in the US for the time being. She wanted us to have some time alone together. We both found ourselves missing her deeply. We wanted nothing more than for her to be with us in that place.

As Kyle and I explored the house further, we began to uncover a series of synchronicities that left us awestruck. The owner's name was Lorraine. The garden in the front yard was filled with Hostas, which just so happened to be his mother's favourite flowers. The kitchen had a unique counter-top, identical to the one we had dreamed of installing in our future home, and the view from the front porch was a precise replica of the painting we had envisioned hanging in our dream home.

Each new discovery, felt like a whispered message from the universe, confirming that this house was meant for us. We felt like we had stumbled upon a hidden treasure, a sanctuary that had been waiting for us. The synchronicities were too striking to ignore, and we knew in our hearts that this house was going to be our home.

We spent our days there lounging on the porch, watching the boats glide across the water. We were greeted each evening by some of the most beautiful sunsets we had ever seen. Our nights, were spent snuggled up by the fireplace, sharing stories and dreams. It was as if the universe had conspired to bring us this perfect haven, a sanctuary by the water's edge.

Everything finally seemed to be coming together. Kyle and I couldn't fathom ever leaving that place. Strangely enough, both of the owners felt the same way about us and that house. They felt that it was meant for us. After just a few weeks of us staying there, they offered us to stay and rent it from them. This would be the beginning of the life we would build together in Canada. This house also happened to have just the right amount of space for us and all of the kids. The energy there was like nothing I had ever felt before. Both Kyle and I believed in our hearts that Lorraine had been the one to lead us there. When she was alive, she wanted nothing more than to see us happy and together in one place.

A Journey of a Thousand Miles – A Reflections Saga

Although Kyle and I were thrilled about things beginning to move in the right direction for once, we couldn't help but think of her and how much we wished that she had been able to join us. Somehow, I think she had been there with us all along though. The signs of her presence surrounded us. Everything about this house was complete perfection. It even had positive affirmations written on plaques that adorned the walls. There were many references to Egypt. There were Hostas blooming beautifully in the front yard, a fireplace in the master bedroom, even the location was absolutely perfect. It was situated mere steps from the water, a place I could use to recharge. The relationship between the owners even closely resembled our own. The husband both a writer and an artist. His wife loved to throw down in the kitchen. They were also an interracial couple who seemed to share a profound and deep connection with each other. For Kyle and I, it was as if we were staring into our own future.

Eventually though, time passed and before we knew it, our perfect little getaway had come to a close. Kyle was forced to return to the US. It felt so strange to be there in that house without him. I felt as if I had just lost my best friend. The house that was once filled with warmth, was now barren and desolate. It had grown cold without him. Sleep evaded me. I didn't even have much of an appetite without him there by my side, but I knew I had no choice but to force myself to eat. He and I had grown so used to being together, that it felt strange when our fantasy we had been living for so long was abruptly torn from us once again.

Even though we both knew that the situation was only temporary, it had left a deep void within both of our souls. Yet we always managed to make it work. Being together in one place was always just beyond our grasp. We were so close now, we could feel it. And yet, it was going to be another year before we would be able to begin the process of he and Jaide moving to Canada for good.

Little did we know that the road ahead was paved with the most daunting trials we had endured up to this point. It was a road that was definitely not for the faint of heart. A road that would test us, that would challenge us and bring us to the very brink of insanity. A roller-coaster ride with so many ups and downs, it could manage to turn even the strongest stomach weak. Now don't get me wrong, I love roller-coasters and all, but this was one that would be sure to test the very fortitude of both Kyle and I equally. Up to this point, we both had been through so much. We had managed to overcome the most daunting of obstacles. Obstacles that most relationships would've never been able to withstand. We should've known better though. We were warned very early on just have difficult this ride would be for the both of us. My brother-in-law had looked into both of our charts and saw that they were both filled with struggles that we would face together. He warned that we would face many trials and tribulations. It was as if the universe wanted to test the strength of our bond. He told us that there would be immense struggle, but he went on to explain that everything we were about to go through, was

A Journey of a Thousand Miles – A Reflections Saga

for a purpose and that we would emerge stronger than ever. We were told that everything we would endure in our journey together, would only solidify the foundation of our relationship. It was supposedly to ensure that neither one of us would ever take what we shared for granted, as some couples often do. I guess the universe failed to read the memo. Kyle Reed and I had been through plenty of trials throughout our own individual journeys. We definitely had proven ourselves and the warriors that we are. Further trials were not necessary.

Kyle and I had always been vividly aware of what we shared together. After the way our last lifetime together had ended so abruptly, one would think that perhaps the universe would cut us a break. Allow us to breathe. I often found myself wondering why things had to be such a struggle for Kyle and I. Why did it seem that we were repeatedly being hit in the face with life? It angered me and often brought me back to the people who would say things like, *"God only gives you what he thinks you can handle"* and those who would say, *"Those who came to change the world often choose the most difficult path."* Just one question though....did the universe want those of us enduring such trials and tribulations to burn the world down or something. I mean, when you stop to think about it, doesn't it seem downright sadistic to you at times?

I must have made this soul contract long before birth. Having the self awareness that I do now, I can honestly say I understand why I was given such an arduous journey. I've always been the "go big or go home" type of person. A warrior to the core of my being. And man let me tell you, I've been through one hell of a battle.

I know they say that God is all seeing, all powerful and all knowing, but I had turned my back on all of that long ago. Yet here I was, still on some type of world peace mission...when all I had ever wanted was to find my own.

The long awaited year seemed to go by at a snail's pace. Why couldn't time do that whenever Kyle and I were together? Eventually, we both received many answers to our questions regarding the difficulties we faced together. Just a few months after Kyle's last visit, we reached out to a mutual friend and had an Akashic records reading done. Immediately we were told that we were twin flames, or at least that's what many people referred to it as. We had shared countless lifetimes together. Kyle and I had felt that from the very beginning because of how quickly our souls came together. We were also told that we had been separated over and over again. Lifetime after lifetime, and yet despite all of that, Kyle and I always seemed to find our way back to each other. We were also given some information that resonated deeply. We were a pair of twin flames that were known as anchors. It was our way to serve humanity and the power of our love would be used to create the foundation for newer timelines and energies to come through and anchor into our reality. Because of the power our unity held, there were forces who sought to keep us apart. These forces knew that individually Kyle and I were powerful, but together...we would become a force. A power couple in every way. We were to become unstoppable.

Chapter Thirty-Five

Shortly after we received our reading, Lorraine's ex husband had come back into the picture. It had been more than twenty years and yet, he was suing Kyle for Lorraine's estate. He was coming for the house and anything else he could get his hands on. Someone must have told him about her passing and tipped him off to the situation. All he probably wanted was to sell it and pocket the money. He had no other use for it. That home held so many memories within its walls. It was meaningless to him though. To us, it was everything. It was the home that Jaide grew up in. We later found out the truth behind why he had really sued, and it was quite the mind fuck to say the least. I was absolutely shocked that after all these years of being absent, this man still had a say as to Lorraine's affairs, but it turned out that because his name was still on the deed, he did in fact have power. More power than any of us could imagine. Again Kyle was notified too late in the process for the court hearing to be able to obtain any legal council. To make matters worse, they had cancelled the hearing twice and we were given notice that it was not definitive as to when it might resume. Kyle, J'Von and Jaide were still residing in that house. It was unimaginable that someone could be so cruel.

After a few months of back and forth with the courts, and Kyle missing the hearing completely, through no fault of his own, the decision was made. Due to Kyle missing the court hearing, which they claimed to have sent a letter which he never received, Lorraine's ex husband, Charles was awarded her estate. Kyle was ordered to vacate the premises within sixty days!

Now remember when I told you that we had later come to learn the truth about who was behind the whole thing? Well, as it turns out, it was Kyle's sister. She and Kyle had fought awhile back over a car that Lorraine had purchased, making it perfectly clear that it was to become Jaide's as soon as she was of age. After that argument between her and Kyle, she had decided to reach out to Lorraine's ex husband and had managed to convince him to sue for the estate. Didn't I warn you it was a real mind fuck? The sister claimed that Lorraine had not listed her intentions for the vehicle in her will, and therefore it meant that it was fair game. As for the house, it was always assumed that it would be left to both Kyle and Jaide, but apparently his sister wanted the house for her son Bradley and his family to live in.

If you think that is bad enough, then stay tuned because it's about to get a whole lot worse. After Lorraine had been cremated, Kyle and I went to the crematorium to pick up her remains, but it turns out that someone had actually beaten us to them and took them to keep for herself. Kyle never got a single speck of his own mother's ashes. The two of us were heartbroken. I couldn't believe that the people we once called family, could be so ruthless, so evil to do something that heartless to a man who had nearly lost himself when his mother passed. Hadn't he been through enough? For them, it was all about money and vengeance it seemed. Maybe his sister had gotten mad over Kyle and Lorraine kicking Bradley and his family out of the house. It wasn't as if they had put them out on the street though. Or maybe she was mad about the fight that Bradley and Kyle had gotten into that day at the hospital. I guess this was just her way of thanking Kyle and his mother for all they had done to help them. We should've known better. I think that was the hardest part about it all. We had dropped our guard. Never again.

I still remember how odd everything seemed after Lorraine's passing. Her body had yet to be cremated, and the sister and her girlfriend came over to the house. They immediately started rummaging through all of her things. Looking for things they wanted to either keep for themselves or sell. Lorraine had left all of her jewellery to Jaide in her will, and yet, they tried taking those from her too. At first, when they came over, they claimed it was about finding an outfit to put on Lorraine for the service. Looking back at how it all went down now, it was just an excuse. Why is that? All too often after someone passes away, people become blinded by their greed. It's like they somehow forgot that at one point they called each other family. That there was once love between them.

I didn't understand the sense of entitlement that some people felt. A person who had rarely even been around. So little in fact that during the entire course of mine and Kyle's relationship, I had only ever seen her maybe a handful of times at the most. Yet now somehow, here she was, feeling like she deserved everything she could possibly get her hands on. I have seen it happen time and time again. Families being torn apart after the death of a loved one. Consumed by their greed, rather than choosing to come together to support one another through a difficult time. I never wanted that for Kyle, yet somehow, I feel like I had made that prediction long ago. The signs and red flags were practically in my face, but still I chose to ignore them. I had actually dropped my guard, and gave everyone a chance to get to know me. A regret I will most likely maintain for an eternity.

The day we decided to take the plunge and start the immigration process, was one that was filled with hope and anticipation. Nearly five years worth. Little did we know, it was to be the beginning of a grueling journey for both of us and that it would test our limits in every way.

The process was like navigating a never-ending labyrinth, with twists and turns that led us to dead ends and disappointments. Setbacks and rejection became the norm for us, and Kyle's inability to work due to his immigration status, left me as the sole breadwinner.

A Journey of a Thousand Miles – A Reflections Saga

Just when we thought that things couldn't possibly be much worse, Kyle and Jaide were now faced with the terrifying prospect of homelessness, lingering just beyond the horizon. Adding yet another area of stress to our already overwhelming situation. The weight of responsibility fell heavily on my shoulders, and the pressure mounted with each passing day. I was struggling to keep up with the demands of working three jobs, dealing with what seemed like an endless stream of bills that needed to be paid, paperwork for the immigration application as well as being a wife and a mother of six. To top it all off, we had recently moved to a new home. I tried my best to keep it together, but eventually I cracked under the strain of it all.

Depression crept in like a thief in the night, stealing my joy, my energy and my willingness to stay in the fight. Medication helped, but it just wasn't enough to counter the unrelenting stress I was dealing with. My body had begun to betray me, with a serious illness that forced me to take time off of work again and again. With no income and safety net to fall back on, we teetered on the brink of homelessness and starvation. The fear of losing everything we had worked so hard for, was suffocating. Yet even through some of my darkest moments, our love and determination kept us clinging to hope.

We fought, we cried, we persevered, and slowly, incrementally we began to rebuild.

The immigration process remained a constant battle, but we faced it together, hand in hand, drawing strength from each other's resilience. It seemed that through it all, Lorraine had always been right there with us cheering us on.

After all of the drama had calmed down, photos of certain family members began to just fall off of the wall with no explanation. One of the frames had been completely smashed. I believe if memory serves me correctly, it was the photograph of Bradley. As if that wasn't odd, the day that Kyle left to come and visit me in Canada with no intention to stay for good, the basement flooded out of nowhere. The house had become completely destroyed. I'd like to think that it was Lorraine with one last "Fuck you" to all of those who tried to take what never belonged to them in the first place.

Nearly two year into the immigration process, with me in the hospital for the third time and trying not to succumb to the illness that had been trying to overtake me for the past three months, Kyle and I were both feeling broken and defeated. Then we got the news that we had been waiting desperately to hear. Kyle's permanent residency had finally been approved. I could honestly write another whole book on what that process alone was like for all of us. It had most certainly been an arduous journey for everyone. As Kyle and I sat there

A Journey of a Thousand Miles – A Reflections Saga

reading the letter that felt like we had been waiting lifetimes for, tears of joy streamed down my face. Kyle grabbed my hand, his eyes shining with happiness.

"We did it baby! Oh my God...We did it! It's finally over!" he shouted excitedly.

In that moment, all of the struggles, all of the setbacks, and all of the hardships suddenly seemed worth it for the both of us. We had made it through the storm, and our love emerged stronger than ever on the other side of it all. It had been a long and winding journey, one that tested us both beyond measure, but through it all...our love remained a guiding light through the darkest parts of the storm. And just when we felt that there was nothing left to hold onto, we held onto each other. When it felt like the world might just tear us apart, in the end, it was our love that saw us through. It had been a testament to the power of true devotion and the unbreakable bonds that united us. In the end, our love and determination triumphed over all of the odds, and we emerged stronger, wiser, and more grateful for each and every moment we shared with one another.

As I looked into Kyle's eyes, I knew that we had finally found our haven, our sanctuary, our home. The journey was treacherous, but we remained steadfast and allowed our love to light the way, to guide us through the darkness. With Kyle's permanent residency in hand, we felt like we could finally, after all of this time, exhale. We could finally start building the life we had always dreamed of having. We knew that there would be challenges ahead, but we were ready to face them together, hand in hand.

As I lay there in my hospital bed, surrounded by the beeping of machines, the sterile smell of antiseptic, I finally felt that sense of peace I had been searching my entire lifetime for. I knew then, that I was exactly where I was always meant to be- with the man I loved and in the country we had chosen to call home, surrounded by more love than I think either of us had ever imagined. We were finally...a family!

Our love story was one of resilience, of determination, and of the human spirit's capacity to overcome even the most daunting of obstacles. It was a reminder that home was not just a physical place, but a sense of belonging, of safety, and most of all love. The home I had searched lifetimes to find, to remember and to simply just be. It had always been here, waiting for me. Home was right there in Kyle's arms, surrounded by our beautiful children.

Kyle was right there by my side, all while I recovered from my illness, nursing me back to health with a love and care that only grew stronger with each passing day. And when I finally felt well enough to walk outside again, he took my hand and we stepped out into the sunshine, feeling the warmth on our faces, and the gentle breeze as it softly caressed our skin. We looked up to the sky, and I knew that my heart was full. Kyle Reed is and will forever be my soulmate. In that moment I knew that we would face whatever life threw our way, hand in hand, heart to heart and soul to soul. Our love had been tested to no bounds and we had weathered that storm together. I guess I can now confirm, beyond a shadow of any doubt, that love truly does conquer all. The road to get here, to meeting Kyle, Jaide, Lorraine and all of the people I had come to love, had been a long one, but I know now that every detour, big or small was always leading me somewhere. Though at the time it felt like I had taken three steps back, it was only ever to realign me on my path to finding him again. Every struggle, every heartache, every trial and tribulation. They weren't failures or setbacks. They were always leading me to him. I love you Kyle Reed. Now, forever and always, in *ALL* ways.

Epilogue

Sitting here now, I have the opportunity to reflect on where I've been and where I am now. It's been a hell of a journey. I could say, it's been a journey of a thousand miles. You can imagine, my feet are tired. My soul has been tested. But I can say now, I'm unbreakable. I know what strength is. I proudly stand in it. I know who I am. It wasn't without its trials. Here again, I say, I stand strong in who I am – and it wasn't without the help of others. When I thought I was alone, I didn't know ... no ... I couldn't foresee that all the love and support I would ever need was just within reach once I'd surrendered to it. I can't imagine where I would be now without those who have come to be by my side. My safe havens. I love you all so dearly. In saying so, I think it's important to reflect. The best I can do for this moment is immortalize it on paper. As I think fondly on my life, and yes, even the traumatic aspects of it, I am brought to the influences that have positively shaped me.

To Lorraine, Kyle's father and my dear father,

Where words fail, love speaks. And today, our hearts are overflowing with gratitude and love for all of you. Your unwavering support, guidance, and love have been the pillars that have held us together through the storm.

Your selflessness, generosity, and compassion have been a constant source of strength for us. You have shown us that love knows no borders, no boundaries, and no obstacles. Your steadfast belief in our love has been the beacon that has guided us home.

Today, as we stand united, hand in hand, heart to heart, and soul to soul, we honour you all as the architects of our happiness. Your love, wisdom, and support have helped to build a foundation that will last a lifetime.

A Journey of a Thousand Miles – A Reflections Saga

Thank you, Lorraine, for being a mother-in-law who has become a mother to me in every way. Your kindness, empathy, and understanding have truly been a gift from the heavens. Though you are no longer with us, your love and legacy live on in our hearts. We are forever grateful for the blessing of you.

Thank you, Kyle's father, for being a rock, a mentor, and a father figure who has shown us that love can conquer all.

And thank you, Dad, for being my confidant, and my guiding light. Your unrelenting support and love have been the very foundation on which I have built my life.

Kyle and I are forever grateful to all of you for the sacrifices you have made, the tears you have dried, and the dreams you have helped us realize. You have shown us that family is not just about blood ties but about the love that binds us together.

As we begin this new chapter in our lives, we honour you all as the pillars that will forever hold our family together. We promise to make you all proud, to build a life that is filled with love, laughter, and adventure. We will always cherish the love that you all have instilled in us.

Thank you for uniting us as one. We love you more than words can express.

And last but certainly not least...

To the loves of my life,

My dear husband, Kyle, you are the sunshine that brightens every page of my story. Your unwavering support, unconditional love, and unrelenting encouragement inspire me every day to write our tale. You are my rock, my soulmate and my forever home.

To our precious children, Jaide, Jaxson, Aaron, Christopher, Jason and Mathew, you are the ink that fills my heart with colour, the rhythm that makes my soul sing, and the joy that makes this journey worthwhile. Your laughter is the music that fills our home, your smiles are the light that guides us, and your love is the foundation that holds us strong.

A Journey of a Thousand Miles – A Reflections Saga

This book is a testament to the love we share, a love that is the stuff of dreams, the substance of hope, and the foundation of our family. I am forever grateful for the gift of our life together.

With all my heart, now and forever.

About the Author

Kimberley Lynn Marie Hall was born July 13th on a Friday in 1984 in Windsor Ontario, Canada. Like the storm that hosted her into this world, she has been an unstoppable force overcoming the obstacles that have come in her path.

A loving mother of 5 boys and a girl, she has set herself on a path to be the example that no matter the hardship, dreams do come true. With hard work and patience, Kimberley found her way into the medical field and into the arms of her loving husband with whom she shares a life and partnership with.

Now, Kimberley wants to take her stories and spirituality to not only inspire her children, but all others who may feel voiceless in the depths of despair. She lays it all bare to share her healing journey through fiction in her work so that others may begin to shed their plights.

A Journey of a Thousand Miles – A Reflections Saga